THE
SECRET
TWINS
OF PARIS

BOOKS BY SUZANNE KELMAN

THE PARIS SISTERS SERIES

The Paris Orphans

The Last Day in Paris

The Bookseller of Paris

The Paris Promise

STANDALONE NOVELS

A View Across the Rooftops

When We Were Brave

Under a Sky on Fire

When the Nightingale Sings

Garden of Secrets

We Fly Beneath the Stars

THE
SECRET
TWINS
OF PARIS

SUZANNE KELMAN

Bookouture

Published by Bookouture in 2026

An imprint of Storyfire Ltd.
Carmelite House
50 Victoria Embankment
London EC4Y 0DZ

www.bookouture.com

The authorised representative in the EEA is Hachette Ireland
8 Castlecourt Centre
Dublin 15 D15 XTP3
Ireland
(email: info@hbgi.ie)

ISBN: 978-1-83790-534-8
eBook ISBN: 978-1-83790-533-1

Dedicated to those who danced, sang and stitched courage into the shadows when the world was at its darkest. You showed us that performance is not only a mirror; it mends what is broken, restores what was stolen, and calls us home to who we truly are. And with deepest gratitude to the memory of Josephine Baker, who inspired the character of Joséphine Duval; her performances defied fear, her courage saved lives and her legacy continues to remind each of us that, whatever our personal 'stage' in life, we carry the power to make a difference.

PROLOGUE

PARIS, JANUARY 1943

The train whistle pierced the fog, its shrill urgency pulling the platform taut. Gigi set her hands on the twins' slender shoulders, small bones under wool coats, bird-fragile and warm. The engine spat steam that came rolling towards them as two young faces tipped up to her, identical chins quivering, their wide-eyed gazes searching for an answer she couldn't give.

Her stomach clenched. *Am I doing the right thing, sending these children away?* The question rolled through her like an ache. But these girls had no one now. Their father was gone, and their mother had made a heart-wrenching decision to keep them safe by keeping her identity secret.

Gigi tried to offer a smile that didn't tremble. She tightened the scarf at Rebecca's throat, and adjusted the beret over her twin Rachel's brow. 'Remember,' she whispered, gripping each word to keep it from wavering, 'do everything Charlotte tells you, and you will be safe.'

She wished she felt as certain as the words. The truth was hard; the road ahead would be long, and when they returned, *if* they returned, who would be waiting for them?

Gigi's sister Charlotte called through the mist, gathering the other children she was taking to safety. Gigi knelt so her eyes met the little girls'. Fear and bewilderment mingled as their breath came in short, sharp bursts of frigid air. They were doing their best to keep it together.

'You are so brave,' she breathed. 'So strong. My beautiful ballerinas.' She brushed back hair from their temples and kissed each forehead. 'No matter what happens. Take care of each other.'

She guided them hand in hand toward the carriage.

At the door, Rebecca turned and raised her hand to wave a final goodbye, and Rachel followed, two small, fragile gestures that made Gigi realise just how young and vulnerable they were at only ten, in a world where their only crime was being Jewish.

Now, they were gone from her, gone maybe forever.

For a long beat, Gigi stood with her hand still in the air, as if their fingers might come back to fill it. The platform widened around her. The fog pressed in. Something inside her slipped its hold, and the sound that tore out of her wasn't a breath and wasn't a word.

It was a sob.

1

PROVINS, SUMMER 2011

Lily

With its sterile walls and relentless machines, the cold, antiseptic-scented stillness of a hospital room in Provins felt a world away from Lily Tremaine's life in Paris. In the room where her mother lay, time appeared suspended, marked only by the hum of existence and the scent of wilting carnations on the windowsill.

Lily walked to the window, where drizzle whispered against the glass. Below, the medieval buildings of her childhood stood silhouetted in the blue dawn, their weathered stones anchoring her once again.

In the glass, she caught a glimpse of herself, pale and drawn, her blonde hair unravelling from her ponytail into damp strands. Exhaustion dulled her grey eyes, revealing her sleepless night and unspoken fears. Her face without make-up was stripped to its raw self, caught between her past and present, life and death.

Her sister's late-night call still echoed: '*Maman has suffered a stroke. Come immediately.*' Lily had jumped in her car, leaving a note for Marcus, desperate to comfort her sister and their vibrant mother. But she had been too late. Now the woman in the bed seemed a stranger, too quiet, too still.

Her mother had once seemed invincible, a ballerina who had survived loss and war. Now Rebecca lay motionless, her delicate features pale, her chest rising only to the monitors' steady beep.

The door opened with a soft creak and Lily's sister, Clare, entered, bringing in a draught of cooler air.

She was a softer echo of Lily, with the same stormy grey eyes but lighter hair that curled in waves down her shoulders and a rounder face, etched with a kindness she was known for.

Her sister wore jeans and a Breton-striped sweater with rain-darkened boots. Clare was practical, no-nonsense and always in motion.

'I brought coffee,' she said softly, extending a paper cup toward her.

Lily managed the ghost of a smile, and took the cup, but didn't drink. 'She hasn't moved,' she murmured, looking at their mother. Clare stood at her side, silent for a moment. Then she spoke, her voice lowered.

'She's holding steady. The neurologist says she has even odds.' Her words faltered, but she recovered quickly, as she always did.

Seeming to remember something, Clare set her coffee aside and dug into her bag. 'When Maman first fell ill, she refused the ambulance. She clung to me, insisting I bring you this first.'

Clare pressed a brass key into her sister's palm, as Lily's eyes widened in surprise.

'She was adamant I give it to you, saying, "She needs to go to my bank in Paris. All the answers are there."'

'What answers?' Lily whispered.

Clare shrugged. 'Maybe it's her will or important documents, I never even knew she had a safe deposit box.'

'Nor did I.'

As they paused to absorb this, the monitor continued to beep steadily beside their mother's bed, a faint reminder of the fragile tether still holding her to this world.

'You should go home. The doctor said she could be like this for days,' Clare insisted.

'I don't want to leave you alone,' Lily responded, the words hollowed by guilt. 'And what if she wakes up?'

'If she wakes up, I'll call you immediately. I *swear*. But you should go home to Marcus, to your job. There is no point in two of us sitting here. My kids are old enough now to care for themselves, and I can be here more easily. Your life is in Paris.'

Lily hesitated, fingers curling around the key with a heavy heart. Finally, she relented, the weight of weariness pulling at her bones as she decided. Clare's logic was sound, even if it felt like Lily was abandoning her mother. Her sister was right. She could be back here in just over an hour if the traffic were light.

Lily departed from the hospital after she had kissed her mother softly on the forehead and hugged her sister goodbye. Outside, the chilly morning struck her like a wall, sharp and immediate, forcing her to pull her coat tighter around herself.

She thought about the key in her bag. Why did her mother have a safe deposit box? And what could be so important that she had needed to make sure Lily had it before she lost consciousness?

Lily slid into the driver's seat, breath fogging the windscreen momentarily before the defroster kicked in.

She didn't move, hands gripping the wheel, eyes on the misty horizon. She glanced over at her phone, checking for messages. There were none, not even from her husband, Marcus, which was disappointing.

She started her car and pulled out of the hospital car park

and back onto the winding road that led back to Paris. She tried not to think about how pale her mother looked under hospital lights.

When she arrived home, the sky over Paris was still pale, a bleary grey when Lily stepped into her building's courtyard, her shoulders stiff with fatigue from the long drive.

Inside the apartment, the air was warm and still, filled with the faint scent of espresso and Marcus's cologne.

Her husband looked up from the kitchen counter as she stepped through the door, blinking in surprise. He was already dressed, charcoal slacks and a white shirt unbuttoned at the collar.

He placed his cup down and greeted her. 'You're back. How is she?'

Lily slipped off her coat, fighting to suppress the swell of emotion.

'She's stable. Still unconscious. The doctors don't yet know the extent of the damage. She asked for me before they took her in. Clare said she kept repeating strange things, fragments, names that didn't make sense...'

Marcus nodded, but gave no reply.

'And she gave me this.' Lily held up the brass key.

Marcus frowned at it. 'What's it for?'

'A safe deposit box, from when she and my father lived here in Paris.'

His brow lifted. 'Interesting.'

'I'll go this morning and see what it is, before work. But first I need a bath.'

Marcus rinsed his cup in the sink. 'Coffee before I leave?'

She shook her head. 'I've already had plenty.'

The silence lingered as he reached for his coat. Lily almost brought up the distance between them, the way his casualness stung when her mother lay so ill, but she let it pass.

She was too tired, too raw. She forced a smile when he

brushed her lips with a dry kiss, and they wished each other a good day.

As she slipped into the steaming bathtub, she closed her eyes, and her mind returned to the key in her purse. Whatever was in that deposit box had mattered enough for her mother to cling to consciousness until Lily had it. Her will? Somehow, that didn't sound like something her mother would insist on her retrieving; she had never cared about her estate details or legal affairs.

What else could it be? And why had her mother never spoken about it before?

'*All the answers are there,*' her mother had said.

But what answers? And to what questions?

The thought left Lily not just puzzled but profoundly uneasy. An inexplicable sense of dread crept over her, a creeping anxiety about what she might uncover.

2

PARIS, JUNE 1940

Gigi

'Gigi, why do you torment me? Why won't you marry me?' Pierre's voice rang up from the street below, rich with mock despair, as Paris stretched awake beneath a soft wash of morning light.

Already in her leotard, Gigi Valette leaned over the glossy black railing of her shared balcony, her red hair tumbling in loose waves beneath her chin, catching the early sun like burnished copper.

She smiled as she spotted Pierre on the cobblestones below, his arms overflowing with roses so vivid they seemed to defy the world's growing gloom. His untamed dark curls, lopsided grin and dirt-smudged sleeves made him look every bit the rakish romantic. She didn't take his daily proposals seriously, but he never missed one.

'Pierre, you ask me every morning,' she called down. 'Don't you ever tire of rejection?'

'Tire of you?' he scoffed. 'Never.'

She tossed a crumb from her croissant to the scruffy stray

cat perched on the edge of her wrought-iron table. 'We went to school together. You're like a brother to me.'

'One day, you'll say yes!' Pierre called, brandishing a rose. 'And I'll be the happiest man in Paris.'

From the adjacent apartment, Claudette Mercier stepped onto her balcony, her presence as polished as her neatly pressed blouse and skirt.

Silky blonde hair was pinned into an elegant twist and her cream-toned skin glowing with a natural radiance that made her look effortlessly composed.

She carried a porcelain teacup brimming with dark coffee, and lifted it to her lips and glanced downward sharply.

'Gigi, don't encourage him,' she chided. 'Pierre, must you propose before we've even had our coffee?'

Pierre declared grandly that love waits for no man as he blew Gigi a kiss and then departed with dramatic flair.

'Honestly,' Claudette muttered with a smirk. 'Does he ever sell any flowers?'

From the third apartment Eloise Morel appeared, carrying an indigo fabric roll across her hip. Sunlight created a speckled pattern amidst her balcony's dense arrangement of ivy and plants. Her dark curls framed her thoughtful face, her features softer and more reserved than those of the other girls. Her voice carried a familiar edge of dry humour.

'With all the talk of war,' she said softly, 'it's nice to hear someone reminding us that a little goodness still exists somewhere in the world.'

Malina Laurent-Masson approached from the last of the four apartments with her signature air of quiet urgency. Her dark, oversized sweater hung loosely over her frame, stylish yet practical, while her cropped black hair was as wild as ever. A newspaper was clutched under her arm.

She leaned across and slapped it onto Gigi's small table, scattering crumbs and sending the cat fleeing. Bold headlines screamed at them: FRENCH ARMY RETREATS, GERMANS ADVANCE ON PARIS.

'They've said that before,' Gigi managed, but her voice came thin, betraying the tremor in her chest. 'It's just fear-mongering.'

Malina didn't smile. 'Not this time. The army's crumbling, Gigi. It's as if they opened the gates and invited the Germans in.'

Claudette set down her cup and scanned the front page. 'If this is true, things will change fast. We need to be ready.'

Eloise turned from her lavender pot, her gaze low. 'Paris has always endured. Maybe it won't be as bad as we think.'

Malina rounded on her. 'Endure *what*? Watching neighbours vanish in the night? I'm not waiting to find out.'

'She's right,' Claudette said quietly. 'Better to act than react.'

Eloise gave a slight nod, though the tension in her shoulders didn't ease. 'It just feels... distant. Like it's happening to someone else.'

A chill ran through Gigi. She thought of her sisters scattered across the city, of her parents, who had already lived through one war. Would they be safe if the Germans marched into Paris? Her breath caught, and before she could stop herself the question tumbled out.

'Do you think the Nazis would shut down the theatre?' she asked suddenly.

Claudette answered first. 'Tyrants always go after the arts, Gigi. We should prepare for anything.'

'Oh!' Gigi pressed a hand to her chest, her eyes wide. 'I almost forgot, I have something to tell you,' she said, bright with excitement. 'I've been asked to audition for Serge Lifar's new show. They want me to try for principal dancer. At the Palais Garnier.'

Claudette looked up from the theatre script she'd been marking up.

Eloise gasped and leapt to her feet. 'Gigi, that's *incredible!* I can't believe you could be a principal dancer at only eighteen years old.' She threw her arms around her friend. 'We'll be working in the same place every day!'

Malina glanced up from her spot by the railing, ink-stained fingers resting on the letter she'd been writing to the newspaper. 'Took them long enough. You were born for a lead role.'

Claudette, always composed, raised her cup. 'To Gigi, our rising star, until we find something stronger to toast with later.'

'Ah, ah!' Gigi grinned, wagging a finger. 'Let's not jinx it just yet. But thank you.'

Eloise returned to her blanket, smoothing out the indigo fabric. 'Something by Lifar, of all things! He's the director everyone's talking about. If you get it, which you will, I'll be sewing your costumes.'

'Which means,' Gigi said, eyes gleaming, 'we're celebrating tonight. Le Chat Noir. No excuses.'

Eloise hesitated. 'But I have so much to do—'

'You can sew by day and sip champagne by night,' Gigi cut in, triumphant.

Eloise laughed. 'You're impossible when you're happy.'

'Fine,' Claudette added, closing her notebook. 'But I'm not staying out until dawn. I've got cue notes to finalise.'

Malina stood, tucking her letter into her satchel. 'I need to post this, but I'll meet you there. Tonight, we toast to Gigi.'

The familiar hum of le Chat Noir wrapped around them like an old friend. Smoky air, dim lights and the sway of a jazz band filled the space with a heady mix of escape and rhythm. Laughter rose and fell; troubles were momentarily drowned beneath the music.

The four women took a table near the back, its scarred wooden surface worn from years of use. A bottle of champagne arrived, compliments of the owner, who had once seen Gigi dance and now offered his congratulations with a grin.

'To Gigi,' Eloise toasted, lifting her glass. 'Good luck at your audition! They would be crazy not to hire you.'

'To Gigi!' the others echoed, laughter tumbling over the rims of their glasses.

For a while, joy carried them, champagne bubbles rising and fizzing, heels tapping beneath the table. But when the band moved into a slower tune, Malina rose and quietly slipped away.

Gigi watched her move toward the bar. 'What's she up to now?'

Claudette shrugged, sipping her wine. 'It's Malina. Who knows?'

Nearly an hour passed before Malina returned, and settled back into her seat with a different air, quieter, tenser. Her gaze scanned the room, checking for listening ears, before she leaned in.

'I've been talking to someone,' she said, her voice low and deliberate. 'A... *contact*.'

Eloise stiffened. 'What kind of contact?'

Malina hesitated, then met their eyes. 'Someone from the Resistance.'

The word struck like flint, sparking tension across the table.

Claudette's lips pressed into a tight line. Eloise gripped her glass. Gigi blinked, caught between disbelief and fascination.

'You're serious?' she whispered.

Malina nodded. 'They're looking for people who can move unseen, artists, performers. People who blend in.'

'You're thinking about joining them?' Eloise asked, her voice cracking.

'I already have,' Malina responded. 'And I'm asking you all to think about it too.'

Silence fell, thick and unmoving, as her words landed.

'We've all heard the stories,' she continued. 'Arrests. Disappearances. Cities gutted by fear. If they reach Paris, and they will, it won't matter if we stay quiet or not. It'll be too late.'

Claudette set her glass down, her fingers tightening. 'Do you realise how dangerous this is?'

Gigi caught the edge in her voice; it was fear, not just caution.

Malina leaned closer, her voice rising. 'And you think doing nothing is safer? You think if we stay silent, they'll spare us?'

No one answered.

'My uncle lived in Germany,' Malina said quietly. 'He thought silence would protect him. He spoke out once, and they took him. One night, he was there, and the next, he wasn't.'

The confession stunned them. Malina rarely spoke of her family.

'I'm sorry,' Claudette said, her voice faltering. 'But I couldn't live like that.'

'It's not that I don't care,' Gigi added. 'But what if this *is* just another scare?'

'And what if it's *not*?' Malina shot back.

The question hung there.

'I still think we should wait and see,' Gigi murmured, though the words felt flimsy even as she said them. She glanced at Claudette, hoping for agreement, but she had already folded her arms, and her face was set like stone.

Eloise said nothing, but Gigi noticed that her hands trembled slightly against the table.

Malina's breath came fast. 'You're all waiting for someone else to act. But we don't have that luxury. We have to save ourselves, save Paris.'

The band struck up a brighter tune, the saxophone rising with forced cheer, but none of them moved.

Around them, the club laughed, glasses clinked, a couple

danced drunkenly by the bar. The world spun on, oblivious. Yet at their table, the air seemed to still, pressed down by the weight of Malina's words.

Resistance.

The word had changed everything. It had crept into the room and now lingered, sharp, inescapable.

Malina pushed her chair back. The scrape against the floor made Gigi flinch.

'Enjoy the rest of your evening,' Malina said. Then she walked into the smoky dark, and was swallowed whole by the music and the crowd.

Gigi watched her go, her chest tight. For the first time that night, le Chat Noir no longer felt like a refuge; shadows were too deep, laughter too brittle, the brassy music desperate against the silence gnawing at her thoughts.

She glanced at her friends. Claudette's lips were pressed into a thin, unyielding line. Eloise's hands trembled as though she might shatter the glass in her grip. None of them spoke. None of them dared.

And though the band played on, bright and brash, the champagne had gone flat. The laughter around them sounded hollow. All Gigi could hear was the echo of Malina's voice and the question she had left behind.

What if she was right?

3

PARIS, SUMMER 2011

Lily

Lily stepped onto the quiet street as the morning light brushed the Paris rooftops in soft, pale gold. Summer had settled over the city, the air already warm and carrying the sweet, heady scent of jasmine from a nearby courtyard.

She wrapped her jacket closer to her body and slipped on her sunglasses, creating a barrier against both the external world and her troubled thoughts.

Traffic was light, the city still stretching itself awake. She moved through it like a ghost, the usual buzz of Parisian life muted by the pulse in her ears. She wasn't sure if it was exhaustion, adrenaline or the tug of the unknown, nestled in the key tucked securely in her coat pocket.

Its metal felt heavy and symbolic.

Inside, the hush of the hall was immediate and enveloping. Sunlight filtered through tall windows, pooling on black-and-white tiled floors. The air smelled faintly of polished wood and quiet wealth.

A sleek blank clerk in a tailored blue blazer looked up as Lily approached the desk.

'*Bonjour, Mademoiselle.*'

'I'm here to access a safe deposit box,' Lily said, offering the key. 'It belongs to my mother, Rebecca Tremaine.'

After taking the key, the clerk took a quick look at it before directing her attention to the monitor. 'One moment, please.'

Despite her quickening pulse, Lily maintained her composure as she waited. The woman pressed several keys while her eyes scanned the screen rapidly.

'I'll need to confirm who you are. May I see some identification?'

Lily slid her bank card across the desk. The woman examined it, typed something and then nodded, her expression shifting subtly.

'Your name is listed on the account. Madame Tremaine added it several years ago.'

Lily blinked. 'She did?'

'Yes,' the woman said, tone professional and with a gentle smile.

Lily nodded slowly, absorbing this unexpected detail. Her mother had planned this, quietly, deliberately. Why hadn't she ever said anything?

'If you'll follow me?' the woman continued.

The clerk led her down a hushed corridor, its marble floors gleaming beneath soft pools of light. Brass sconces lit their path, and the silence between them was filled only with the click of heels.

They reached a discreet, windowless room.

The woman produced a second key from a chain around her neck, and unlocked the narrow brushed-steel door. Inside, she slipped the key Lily had given her and a master key into a box. After pulling it out carefully, she placed it on a table before stepping away, saying, 'Take all the time you need. If you wish to take some items with you, there are boxes and envelopes on the desk.'

The safe deposit box creaked softly as Lily opened it. Inside, layers of delicately folded tissue paper obscured whatever lay beneath. Lily reached in, gently pulling the papers aside, her fingers grazing the objects wrapped inside.

On the top was a pair of ballet shoes.

Soft, pale pink, their satin ribbons faded and fraying, the soles darkened from long-ago performances. They were small – they had clearly belonged to someone with tiny feet – and worn enough to have danced hundreds of hours.

Her throat tightened as she lifted them. Her mother had never spoken much about her childhood. Had these been hers? Or someone else's?

Beneath the shoes was an envelope, addressed in her mother's flowing, looping hand:

To my daughters, Lily and Clare.

But Lily couldn't open it yet. Her fingers trembled just holding it.

She set it aside, and reached deeper. Next, a stack of yellowing letters bundled with twine caught her eye. The top envelope bore a faint red stamp: RETURNED TO SENDER. She untied them with care, her eyes scanning the aged paper.

Each was addressed in the same handwriting, her mother's, care of addresses across Europe. The dates spanned decades: 1953, 1961, 1979, 1986.

All were addressed to the same person, someone called Rachel Durand.

Lily froze.

Durand was her mother's maiden name. But she'd never heard of Rachel.

She picked up one envelope and opened it slowly, her heart beginning to pound.

Dear Rachel,

I know this may never reach you. I don't even know if you're still alive. But I have to keep trying.

Lily blinked hard. Rachel. Alive? Her mother had been looking for someone, someone named Rachel. But who was she? Another letter revealed only a single line:

I want to believe you are still alive. I have to believe it. Please find your way back to me.

Confusion swelled in Lily's chest. She reached further into the box and uncovered a photograph wrapped in soft velvet.

A man stood with two young girls, side by side, identical. Dressed in matching ballet costumes, their hair pulled into tight buns, they smiled with the unselfconscious joy of youth. Their arms were wrapped tightly around each other.

She flipped it over. Faint handwriting across the back read: *Uncle Jacques, Rebecca and Rachel*

Lily's breath caught in her throat.

Rebecca.

Rachel.

Her mother... and someone who looked exactly like her.

She stared back at the image, her heart thudding wildly. How was this possible? Her mother had never once mentioned a sister, let alone a twin.

She drew in a long slow breath, letting it tease out the well of emotions rising within her. Struggling to come to terms with all that this box revealed. She felt as if she was opening a door to a different life.

She sifted through the remaining items. A newspaper clipping, folded and fragile, about war orphans, listing organisations helping locate children lost during the war.

She finally opened the letter addressed to her and her sister. Her mother's handwriting spilled across the page.

My beautiful girls,

If you're reading this, I may no longer be able to tell you the truth in person. There are things I never shared out of fear, shame and the weight of never knowing for sure. But the time has come to tell you what I can.

You had an aunt, my twin. Her name was Rachel. We were separated during the war, during a raid in Saint-Antoine-sur-Mer, I wasn't sure what happened to her but something inside of me believed she was still out there. When you were both young, I became obsessed with the idea. Not one day has gone by that I haven't thought about her.

I know you are thinking, 'Why didn't you tell us about her?' That's easy. When you girls were young, I was possessed with trying to find her, so much so that I missed everything about your childhood. One day, your father found me sobbing in the garden. Clare had pulled a pan of hot water from the stove, and it missed her by an inch. I had been distracted by my search. He gently asked me to let go so I could live, and I agreed. But I didn't want to get rid of anything I had already discovered. So I rented this box and never told your father. Then, when I felt a pang of missing her, I would return to looking for her, but now it was in secret.

When your father died a few years ago, I had planned to tell you, but somehow, I could never find the right words or the right time. So, this is my attempt at a confession. I have looked in vain, realised I am too old to continue, and have given up hope of seeing her again. But maybe you will locate her and tell her of my life and how I never gave up looking for her and loving her. Not one day has gone by that I haven't thought about her. If she is still alive as I believe, find her and tell her I love her.

With love always

Maman x

Lily's eyes filled with tears as she sat in stunned silence, the letter trembling in her hands. She folded it with care, her hands numb. The weight of truth pressed down on her chest, but even heavier was the ache of what had been left unsaid for decades.

She reached for her coat, her mother's words still echoing: *Find her and tell her I love her.*

She carefully put everything she had found in a box.

When she left the building, the wind had picked up, tugging at her coat and whipping a lock of hair across her cheek. But she barely felt it.

Her fingers tightened around the box in her hands. Her thoughts were spinning – the photograph, the ballet shoes, the letters, the name Rachel, a twin, a part of her mother's life she had never known existed.

After depositing the box at home, she went to the gallery where she worked.

Galerie Lumière was nestled on rue de Furstemberg, tucked between a bakery and an antique bookshop. She had been a part of this gallery for years, ever since the owner, Madame Eléadora La Rue, whom everyone called Effy, had taken Lily under her wing straight out of school. Now, as the vibrant older woman gracefully aged, it felt as though their roles were slowly reversing.

As Lily stepped through the gallery's door, the scent of aged canvas and fresh paint greeted her.

Effy, as always, commanded the room, today wearing a deep plum silk kimono embellished with intricate embroidery and secured with a wide sash of sapphire blue. As she moved, the fabric billowed, and the colours caught the light to create the illusion of a living masterpiece. Her silver hair, always styled with intention, had been pinned into an elaborate twist, reminiscent of a grand opera star from the 1920s.

Effy looked up as she walked in, her expression shifting from joy to immediate concern.

'Darling, you look so pale.'

Lily dropped her bag onto the counter and ran a hand through her hair, pacing once, before speaking. 'Effy, I need a cup of tea. A strong one. And then I need to tell you something so strange and huge that I'm not even sure I believe it yet.'

To her credit, Effy said nothing. She simply turned toward the tiny kitchen tucked at the back of the gallery and returned with a steaming cup, which she pushed gently into Lily's hands.

As Lily sat at the worktable by the back window, she told her everything about her mother's stroke, the safe deposit box, the photo, the letters and the name Rachel.

Effy leaned back in her chair after she'd finished her story, her expression incredulous. 'I'm so sorry about your mother. But she had a twin sister? That's... unbelievable.'

'Yes,' Lily whispered. 'And she never told us. I just don't understand.'

'Your mother is from a different time, when husbands knew best.' The older woman shook her head as she continued with philosophical insight. 'We all carry our secrets.'

Lily took her phone from her pocket, called her sister, telling her everything she had found.

'Are you *serious*?' Clare asked.

'I'm holding a picture of them. Identical. Mum has been searching for her since the war.'

Clare let out a breath. 'I can't believe it.'

Lily smiled faintly. 'I know.'

'What now?' Clare asked.

'I need to find her. Our... aunt.'

The words felt strange in her mouth, a person she never knew existed. Lily stared down at the photograph, her thumb brushing the timeworn edge like it might somehow reveal more. Somewhere out there, the truth about Rachel waited in silence, buried beneath decades of secrets.

'I have to do this for Maman,' Lily continued. 'Before it is too late.'

4

Gigi

Against the dim evening sky, the Palais Garnier rose, its grand facade appearing softer under the fading light. Gigi paused. It was the day of her audition. Her eyes followed the line of towering columns and the intricately carved figures flanking the doors.

Memories flooded her: the first time she'd entered as a child, her hand clutching her mother's, the red carpet underfoot, the pre-show buzz, and crystal chandeliers casting shimmering reflections across the marble staircases. She had believed then, with all the faith of a child, that magic lived within these walls.

With a jolt, she realised that today she was auditioning to create that same magic for others. A flutter of nerves stirred in her, and she slipped quickly through the stage door, its creak familiar and comforting.

Monsieur Léon, the elderly doorman, wrapped in the layers of brown wool he wore year-round, looked up from his post. She had known him for years; he was not only a friend of her father's, but also someone she encountered whenever she visited Eloise or Claudette here. His white moustache twitched as he squinted at her. 'Mademoiselle Gigi,' his voice rumbled like gravel underfoot. 'Audition day, no?'

'Yes,' Gigi replied, her voice tight.

'You will do fine.' He chuckled, sensing her nerves. 'Your father always told me you dance with fire in your soul.' He winked, the lines on his face crinkling with warmth.

Gigi offered Monsieur Léon a grateful smile as she scooted past him and backstage.

She took a moment to absorb the familiar sights and sounds of the theatre. It always felt like coming home after a long journey. The air carried the unmistakable tang of dust and painted scenery drying in the wings. From the rehearsal studio, the soft strains of a piano echoed, accompanied by the muffled rhythm of a dancer's steps tapping across the stage, punctuated by occasional bursts of instruction from a distant voice.

Nearby, a group of dancers lined up against the wall, waiting for their chance to audition. Some stretched their legs or traced invisible movements with their arms, while others sat cross-legged on the floor, adjusting the ribbons on their pointe shoes. Nervous laughter flickered through their whispers, peppered with the quiet hum of anticipation.

She went straight to the call sheet to see what time she was to audition and was disheartened to see her name was near the bottom; she would have to deal with her nerves for over an hour.

She glanced at the throng of dancers swirling in the cramped space, then sauntered past them to the labyrinth of stairs and dim hallways that took her high into the building. The heat near the top was a sharp contrast to the coolness of the lower floors. She stopped outside the door marked 'Costumes' and knocked expectantly.

After a muffled, 'Come in,' Gigi entered.

The costume department was everything you would expect from a prestigious theatre. Racks of elaborate costumes lined the walls, each piece a work of art in itself. The air was heavy with the scent of fabric and starch, and Gigi felt a sense of reverence wash over her. Eloise was seated at her worktable, bent over a piece of sparkly fabric with her usual focus. The hum of her sewing machine filled the room with its comforting whir.

'All alone?' Gigi enquired, with a smile.

Eloise welcomed her enthusiastically. 'I thought you would be auditioning?'

'I'm near the bottom of the list so I didn't wait downstairs – I couldn't handle the tension.'

'You can stay here if you want; Madame Fleurette is in a costume design meeting,' Eloise explained about the main wardrobe mistress and Eloise's mentor. 'I will make us a coffee, and you can keep me company until you have to go.'

Gigi took a seat in the small kitchenette while her friend started brewing coffee. The strong scent engulfed the tiny space and surrounded them with warmth. The gentle sounds of background music from a radio on a shelf cluttered with fabric created a cosy atmosphere, which helped soothe Gigi's nerves.

Gigi stretched out, pulled a white floppy hat with an enormous white peacock feather from its stand and tried it on. 'I hope this is not for the production I'm auditioning for,' she enquired, as the brim was so large it dropped below her nose.

Her friend giggled. 'No, that's actually for an upcoming production of *The Three Musketeers*. Madame Fleurette wanted to add a touch of whimsy to the costumes this time. Quite a departure from her usual elegant designs.'

The girls continued to chat until, suddenly, the big band number they were listening to on the radio stopped abruptly, and the voice of a spokesman with a serious air filled the airwaves.

'We interrupt this programme to bring you an important news bulletin.' His voice was grave and urgent. Gigi and Eloise exchanged a glance, a flicker of concern passing between them as they sipped their coffee.

The broadcaster announced that German troops had penetrated their final defence line and entered the outskirts of Paris. They would most likely reach the centre by tomorrow morning. He called on every citizen to remain indoors, and stay calm.

The radio broadcast droned on in an ominous tone, each word striking heavier than the last. Eloise's hands stilled on the coffee pot, her knuckles whitening as the announcement settled in the room.

'I can't believe it's real,' Gigi whispered. She tugged the flamboyant hat from her head and clutched it against her chest. The room seemed to tilt around her, the air suddenly thin. Her eyes flicked to Eloise, desperate for reassurance, but she found none, only the same fear mirrored back.

'God help us,' Eloise muttered.

Eloise set down the coffee pot just as Madame Fleurette swept through the door, breathless, strands of silver hair escaping from her pins.

Her willowy frame, softened by slightly rounded shoulders from years spent bent over sewing machines, was wrapped in a dove-grey dress with lace-trimmed cuffs and a belt cinched at the waist. Her reading glasses swayed on a faux-pearl chain, and she clasped her favourite fabric swatch book in her hand.

'Did you hear?' Madame Fleurette's urgency mirrored the tension in the air.

Gigi and Eloise exchanged a quick glance before nodding.

'We are doomed; we will all die,' she proclaimed with a certainty that stilled the air. 'I should have left with my sister when she went south, but this show...'

'Have a cup of coffee, it will help,' Eloise offered, sensing the mistress's rising distress. She poured a fresh cup and handed it to Madame Fleurette, who accepted it with a shaky hand.

'I should probably get to my audition,' Gigi mumbled, rising to leave the room. As she did, Madame Fleurette grabbed her with a claw-like grip.

'Gigi, I'm sorry you must audition under such difficult circumstances. Try not to let it affect you. I genuinely hope you land this role. Though who knows if there will even be a show when the Nazis goose-step in, demanding we produce distasteful performances filled with sordid German drinking songs for their Führer.'

Gigi's heart sank at Madame Fleurette's words, the weight of the impending danger threatening to crush her hopes and dreams.

As Gigi returned downstairs, her thoughts were filled with her family. Her father, Bernard, had fought through World War One and spent the rest of his life avoiding conflict and violence; he did not want his daughters to face the same horrors. One of her older sisters, Isabelle, worked at the Louvre, and they had been moving art out of the city for months. Another sister, Antoinette, was married to a Jewish man, and Madeline, her oldest sister, was still grieving the loss of her own husband. None of them needed this war.

Gigi pushed open the heavy doors and stepped back into the dimly lit hallway. The once-familiar surroundings now felt tinged with an undercurrent of fear and uncertainty.

As she headed to the rehearsal studio, she realised nobody in there knew yet what she had just learned. The theatre's protective cocoon shielded the group of dancers from the harsh reality just beyond its walls.

She looked at the innocent scene before her, and her heart ached with the weight of the knowledge she carried.

When her name was called, she was barely nervous as she made her way to the stage, now in shock at what she had learned.

Serge Lifar's voice called out from the darkened auditorium, 'In your own time, Miss Valette.'

She closed her eyes briefly, inhaling the scent of dust settled on the heated wiring from the bright lights, mingling with the rich smell of aged velvet from the seats, willing herself to believe that magic still lingered here.

At a slight nod to the pianist, the music began. The signature piece from her favourite ballet, *Giselle*.

The opening chords were soft and tentative. She raised her arms, tension coiled in her muscles, and surrendered to the dance. The role demanded vulnerability and grace, but today she danced not for the part, but to keep the dread at bay.

Each leap, each pirouette, cast off another layer of fear. The world outside the Palais Garnier vanished, replaced by the story she wore like a second skin: a peasant girl in love, betrayed, broken and ultimately transcendent. Her movements flowed, tears clouding her vision.

But she didn't stop. The movements weren't for Giselle. They belonged to her friends and family and the city that stood on the brink of invasion. For a future slipping through her fingers.

When the final note sounded, the silence was deafening. Her chest rose and fell as she fought for breath and, for a moment, the world held still. Then, applause rippled gently from the shadows where the director sat.

'*Merci*, Mademoiselle Valette,' came his voice, polished but detached. 'Wait in the wings with the others for consideration.'

Gigi curtseyed, her face hot with emotion. As she straightened, she glimpsed Lifar leaning toward his assistant, whispering something, and her pulse quickened. Had she done enough? Had they seen the fire that Monsieur Léon had reminded her of just an hour earlier?

She left the stage and made her way to the wings to wait

with the others, her body trembling from the exertion. But her mind refused to rest.

The wait was merciless as two more dancers took to the stage. The collective anxiety beside her was palpable as the others paced and fidgeted.

Finally, the director called them all back to the stage.

Gigi's heart raced as she joined the other dancers. She clasped her hands tightly in front of her, her feet positioned in first. She had wanted to work with this director for as long as she could remember.

'Thank you all for your hard work and dedication today. The decision was not an easy one, but after much consideration...' The director paused, his eyes lingering on each dancer, before speaking again. 'For this production, I am pleased to announce that the role of the lead ballerina will be entrusted to Mademoiselle Gigi Valette.'

A wave of emotions surged through Gigi. Her face flushed, and her body began to shake. Was it true? Had she heard correctly? She had imagined these words so many times that she couldn't trust her ears now.

Gigi let herself believe it when the surrounding dancers exploded into applause and their excitement filled the atmosphere. Tears threatened to spill from her eyes while she attempted to maintain her composure, because her heart soared between relief and elation.

Her voice trembled as she stepped forward to accept the honour.

'Thank you, thank you so much, Monsieur. I will not disappoint you,' she managed to say, barely above a whisper.

After she floated off the stage, she raced up the stairs to tell Eloise the good news. She rushed into the costume department and threw her arms around Eloise, who was still seated at her sewing machine, unable to contain her excitement any longer.

'I got the part!' she exclaimed, her voice filled with disbelief and joy.

Eloise leapt up from her machine, her eyes shining with pride and relief, and pulled Gigi into another embrace.

'I never doubted you for a moment,' she exclaimed.

Madame Fleurette approached quietly, her red-rimmed eyes a reminder of the news Gigi had temporarily forgotten. A hand rested gently on Gigi's shoulder. 'I'm proud of you, *mon enfant*,' she whispered, her voice tight with emotion. The warmth in Madame Fleurette's words reminded Gigi of the war she'd briefly escaped in her triumph, and her joy faltered.

Outside, muffled sounds filtered through the thick theatre walls – a child's wail, followed by the sharp clang of a suitcase being dropped on the street below. Madame Fleurette turned her head sharply toward the window and strode toward it, Eloise and Gigi in tow. Madame Fleurette's hand shook as she gripped the windowsill, her knuckles turning white under the strain.

The street was transformed from its Parisian leisurely pace into a chaotic scene. Suitcases scraped along the cobblestones as families moved quickly. A woman stumbled, clutching a child to her chest as she struggled to keep up with her husband, who carried a crate of possessions balanced precariously in his arms. An older man sat slumped on the kerb, motionless, as others rushed past him without looking back.

Horse-drawn carts, overstuffed with belongings, rattled by, and the honk of car horns created a cacophony that drowned out the cries of children and the desperate shouts of parents calling to one another.

Gigi's stomach twisted, the weight of the scene pressing down on her.

'Fleeing before tomorrow comes,' Eloise murmured, her breath ghosting against the window.

The air inside the theatre felt suddenly stifling, suffocating, as though the building itself were mourning the loss of the world outside. Madame Fleurette pressed her hand against her mouth, her shoulders shaking as she tried to hold back a sob.

'They will be here soon,' she whispered.

Gigi stared out of the window with a growing fear. She had wanted this opportunity her entire life, had fought for it, dreamed of it, but now, standing on the precipice of her most significant achievement, it felt like a cruel joke.

'I should go home,' she whispered, her voice fragile as glass. 'My family has waited a long time for this news.'

She turned away from the window, her breath still shaky as she hugged her friend.

'I will see you later at the apartment.'

As Gigi stepped out into the evening streets, the lights of Paris flickered like dying stars. For the first time, her dream felt painfully frivolous against the weight of what so many were facing.

Fear clawed at her insides. Would the life she had fought so hard to claim vanish before she could ever touch it again?

Yet even as the dread pressed in, something fiercer rose to meet it. She could not let the Nazis take everything, her family, her city, the fire inside her.

If dreams could not be protected by chance, then she would protect them by choice.

Whatever it cost, she would find a way to fight back.

5

PARIS, SUMMER 2011

Lily

Lily balanced her yogurt bowl in one hand while reaching for the honey with the other. She had been on the phone with Clare checking in about her mother, with whom there had been no change, and was now rushing, trying to eat before she left for work.

Across the kitchen, Marcus sat at the small dining table, coffee in one hand, a croissant torn into even pieces on his plate. His tie was knotted, his crisp white shirt unwrinkled. He was a man who had taken his time this morning. He was quiet and thoughtful. The silence between them stretched, held together only by the occasional rustle of the newspaper as he flicked through its pages.

She broke through the quiet, licking honey from her little finger.

'So, you're working late tonight?'

Marcus barely looked up, his eyes scanning an article, absorbed. 'Hmm?'

She set her spoon down, forcing patience. 'You mentioned something about a dinner?'

'Oh, yeah.' He turned a page. 'Just a work thing. Might run late.'

She tried to ignore the prickle of unease. He wasn't just preoccupied, he was elsewhere, even when he was right in front of her.

'You never said which client.' She reached for her tea, keeping her voice casual.

Marcus finally lowered the paper just enough to meet her gaze for the first time that morning. 'It's not a client meeting,' he admitted. 'Just a few of us from the office. You know how it is.'

Lily nodded, though she wasn't sure she did. Something in his tone was too light, too practised, and it made her skin prickle. It was just a faint unease, nothing she could name. Was he lying to her? She dismissed the thought.

Marcus checked his watch. It was earlier than he usually left, yet he was already standing, brushing invisible crumbs from his shirt and dropping his half-finished coffee cup into the sink.

Lily frowned. 'You're leaving already?'

'Mm, I've got a lot on today,' he muttered as he lifted his briefcase from the chair.

Then he turned toward the door without kissing her goodbye.

Lily froze, standing in the middle of the kitchen, yogurt forgotten in her hands.

Before she could stop herself, she blurted, 'Hey... did you forget something?'

Marcus, already at the door, paused. Something like hesitation crossed his face for a moment, just a flicker. Then, chuckling, he turned back, walked toward her and pressed a quick, absent-minded kiss to her cheek.

'Have a good day,' he murmured, offering the smallest of smiles, before heading out.

Lily stood there, rooted to the spot, listening to the sound of the door clicking shut behind him.

She exhaled, long and slow, before moving to the table.

There might be some truth to the rumours about the seven-year itch. They had celebrated that anniversary just the previous month. That had to be it, she tried to reassure herself.

Marcus had left his newspaper behind, folded neatly in half. She reached for it, intending to clear it away, but a headline in the culture section caught her eye.

A LOST PARIS: THE FORGOTTEN PHOTOGRAPHS OF VICTOR RENAUD, AN EXCLUSIVE EXHIBITION AT THE MUSÉE DE LA PHOTOGRAPHIE

With her yogurt and steaming cup of tea in hand, she settled into a chair at the kitchen table, the morning light filtering softly through the window. As she skimmed the article, her fingers lightly traced the headline.

Could this be the same Victor Renaud? Her boss Effy had often spoken of him with such admiration.

According to the article, Renaud's grandson had recently taken over his grandfather's old camera shop, a place steeped in history and nostalgia. While sorting through dusty, time-worn boxes, he stumbled upon one of his grandfather's vintage cameras. The camera was a relic, but the true discovery was inside: a roll of undeveloped film from the war years in Paris.

She skipped to the end of the article. Julien Renaud had painstakingly restored the images and was showcasing them to the public for the first time, offering a rare glimpse into 1940s Paris.

Lily sat back, her mind racing.

She was still preoccupied with thoughts of the exhibition as she hurried to the art gallery.

'Lily, you're just in time,' Effy purred as she entered. She gestured toward a large painting leaning against the wall, waiting to be hung. 'Could you please help me?'

Lily studied the piece, a riot of colour, each brushstroke exuding a kind of wild energy as if the artist had painted not just with their hand but with their soul. She carefully lifted the frame, feeling the weight of its passion and chaos.

Effy, watching her closely, folded her arms. 'How is your mother doing?'

Lily filled her friend in on her mother's progress, but Effy's sharp, deep-set eyes, the colour of old cognac, missed nothing.

She took Lily's hand. 'She will pull through. Rebecca is the toughest person I know.'

Lily nodded, swallowing down her tears.

Later, she told Effy about the exhibition she was planning to attend.

Effy clasped her hands together, eyes twinkling. 'It sounds *fascinating*. We shall go together.'

The Musée de la Photographie was nestled in the heart of the Marais, its facade an elegant blend of old stone and modern glass. Vaulted ceilings soared above carefully curated exhibits, and the museum's hush lent the space an air of quiet reverence.

Lily moved through the crowd, Effy striding beside her. Over her silk kimono, the older woman wore a dramatic embroidered shawl of deep emerald green, its fringed edges swaying with each graceful step. A single antique brooch, an ornate Art Nouveau piece in gold and jade, fastened the fabric at her shoulder, glinting under the museum lights.

Lily mused on how she often felt very underdressed in Effy's presence.

They navigated through groups of people who studied the black-and-white pictures on the walls, whispering to each other.

The photographs haunted Lily. Each image pulled her deeper into the past – faces frozen in moments that no longer existed, a city she knew transformed by occupation and fear.

One photo showed German soldiers lined up outside a charming bakery while their rifles hung carelessly over their shoulders. The baker handed them bread with a strained, too-polite smile, a moment of uneasy civility in an occupied city.

Another showed a young woman in a threadbare coat, her eyes shadowed and distant, standing by the banks of the Seine, watching the water flow past with a mixture of resignation and hope.

And then there was a ballerina, caught mid-leap on a grand stage, her grace almost defiant against the war-torn world beyond the gilded theatre walls.

Effy exhaled softly, shaking her head as she whispered. 'Even in war, the world still made room for beauty.'

Lily's gaze flicked toward the front of the room, where a makeshift stage had been set up. A projector screen cast flickering images, illuminating the figure of the man standing before it.

Julien Renaud.

As they moved closer, Lily's pulse quickened with anticipation.

He was younger than she had expected, in his early thirties, with unruly dark curls that softened the sharp angles of his face. There was something effortless about him, an air of quiet confidence rather than arrogance, as though he understood the weight of the history he was presenting. His tailored suit was slightly rumpled, as if he had been too preoccupied with his work to care about appearances.

She found herself watching him longer than she meant to.

The room settled into expectant silence as Julien began to speak.

As he presented each photograph, Lily found herself drawn deeper into the world he was revealing. She could feel the weight of history in every image, the fear and resilience of a city under occupation.

His dedication to historical preservation was evident in his enthusiasm.

Julien's voice carried through the hall, steady but edged with emotion. 'When I found my grandfather's camera, it had been forgotten for nearly seven decades. The film inside was fragile, barely salvageable. But when I developed the images, I realised that my grandfather had left behind something extraordinary, a window into a world that no longer exists.'

He stepped aside, allowing the next photograph to appear on the screen.

It showed a bridge covered in mist. German officers stood at one end, a silent blockade, while Parisians trudged toward them, their heads bowed as if carrying the weight of the war itself. The light in the image was eerie, beautiful but haunting.

Julien's voice softened. 'My grandfather worked in secret,' he continued. 'He used his camera not just to document, but to warn. To bear witness. To record the truth for those who might never get the chance to speak it.'

Lily felt a tightness in her chest, an ache she hadn't expected. The weight of history pressed in, its presence tangible, undeniable.

Then, the next photograph appeared.

And Lily stopped breathing.

A train station.

Children.

There was a group of them, small figures standing on the platform, their faces turned toward the camera. Some were smiling, others confused or afraid.

And at the centre...

Two identical girls, their hands clasped tightly together.

Lily's pulse thundered in her ears.

She *knew* those faces.

Beside her, Effy noticed her shift immediately. She reached out and gave Lily's hand a gentle but firm squeeze.

'Lily, *ma chérie*, are you all right?' Her voice was soft but carried weight, a thread of concern running through it.

Lily tore her gaze from the photograph and turned to Effy with wide, stunned eyes.

'The twins in this photograph... I think they're my mother and her sister.'

Julien, still speaking, seemed to sense the shift in atmosphere too. His gaze flickered toward her, curiosity stirring beneath his professional poise.

'Are you certain?' Effy asked softly, her gaze narrowing as she studied Lily's reaction. Lily could barely speak. She nodded.

Julien's voice filtered through the haze of her thoughts.

'This was taken at the Gare de Lyon in 1943,' he said. 'The children you see here seem to be part of a group, and I've always wondered, were they being evacuated?'

Evacuated.

Lily's thoughts raced, colliding with the memories her mother had shared. Was this the moment they were taken away for safety? Or had this been something else entirely?

The presentation ended, and before she could second-guess herself Lily weaved through the dispersing crowd until she reached the edge of the stage. Her pulse quickened as she drew a breath.

'Excuse me, Julien?'

He turned at the sound of her voice. His dark eyes, curious and warm, found hers, and for a moment she felt pinned by the quiet gravity of his attention. Up close, his presence was both intense and strangely familiar.

'Yes?' His voice was low, inviting, and it unsettled her more than she cared to admit.

Heat prickled her skin. For a heartbeat, caught in the way the light glanced off his dark curls and the way his expression softened as he looked at her, she forgot why she had come.

She steadied her voice, though it still came out more hushed than intended.

'The photograph of the children at the train station,' she said, gesturing toward the now-empty screen. 'The twins in the centre, do you know who they are?'

Julien tilted his head, studying her. 'No, I don't. My grand-father's notes were incomplete. Many identities were left unrecorded, perhaps for safety reasons.'

Lily's hands curled against her handbag. 'I think they're my mother and her sister.'

Surprise flickered across his face. He stepped closer, his gaze intent, as though searching her features for some trace of the girls in the photo. 'Your mother?' His voice was quieter now, almost intimate.

'Her name is Rebecca and her twin sister was Rachel.'

For a beat, neither moved. His eyes lingered on her, sharp and thoughtful in a way that made her stomach tighten.

'Do you have any more photos of them? Anything else from that collection?' she asked, her voice a little too urgent.

Julien nodded slowly. 'I can't be certain... but I have more images from that roll. They're grainy, but you would be welcome to stop by my shop and take a look.'

Her breath caught at the offer. 'Thank you,' she said, and the words felt smaller than the moment.

She found Effy waiting by the doorway, watching her with a curious expression.

'I'm going to visit his shop,' Lily told her, a thread of antici-pation woven through her tone.

Effy arched a brow, sharp as always. 'Of course you are.'

Lily frowned. 'It's just about the photos, Effy.'

Effy's gaze flicked past her. Julien was across the room, speaking to someone else, but his attention wandered back to Lily, just for a second.

A knowing smile curved Effy's lips. 'Life has an interesting way of bringing us what we need, when we need it.'

Lily caught the implication instantly. Her face heated, and a nervous laugh escaped her.

'Oh, Effy,' she murmured, shaking her head. 'Did you forget I'm married?'

Effy's shrug was slow, deliberate, almost mischievous. 'No, *ma chérie*. I hadn't forgotten.'

As they turned to leave, Lily risked one last glance over her shoulder. Julien was still watching her, his gaze steady and impossible to ignore. Their eyes met for a heartbeat too long, and something inside her shifted, intense and undeniable, before she finally forced herself to walk away.

6

———

PARIS, JUNE 1940

Gigi

Gigi moved swiftly through the streets of Paris, feeling the weight of the day's conflicting emotions.

The cobblestones beneath her step were warm from the June sun, though the air carried a tension that had settled over the city like an unspoken warning. The news of the German advance still rang in her ears as she stepped aside to let a handcart piled with blankets and cases pass her. She noticed a solemn-looking gendarme pasting a curfew notice to a lamppost. Gigi forced her eyes away from it. If she let herself think too long about what might come, about what might happen to her family, about the fall of her beloved city, she would drown. Instead, she clung to the one piece of light she carried: the dream she had chased for years was, at last, within reach.

As she neared the familiar streets of Montmartre, the city's grand boulevards gave way to winding alleyways, their charm untouched by the creeping fear of war.

Her mother's garden gave the small family cottage its

unique character, with colourful flowers that stood out against the gloomy atmosphere of the city.

At the gate, Gigi stopped and ran her hand gently over a full-blooming pink rose, its soft petals yielding to her small hand.

Taking a deep breath, she stepped through the tiny gate, and its hinges groaned in greeting as she scurried up the brick pathway. At the door, her sister Charlotte greeted her. Her hair was tied up in a messy bun, loose strands framing her face, and flour speckles dotted her cheeks like freckles. She wore her favourite apron, a lively fabric covered in cheerful designs. Gigi stopped for a moment, observing her sister's look of worry. Charlotte tended to bake when she was anxious.

Charlotte wiped her hands on the apron before pulling Gigi into a tight embrace. 'It's a terrible time, to be sure,' Charlotte murmured, her voice a soothing balm. Gigi leaned into the embrace, finding solace in her sister's arms.

'Are Mama and Papa here?' Gigi asked.

Charlotte nodded. 'Papa is glued to his radio in his study, and Mama is furiously writing letters to everybody she knows.'

Gigi sucked in a breath and paused for just a second before saying, 'I got the part, Charlotte. I'm going to dance for Serge Lifar.'

Charlotte's eyes widened with astonishment as she swept her sister up into a hug. 'That's incredible and perfect! Mama and Papa need some good news today.'

Charlotte disappeared down the narrow hallway as she called out, 'Gigi is home, and she has something *wonderful* to tell you!'

Delphine immediately appeared at the kitchen door. She had an uncanny way of intimately knowing all her daughters' lives, and guessed before her youngest daughter could speak.

'You got the part you wanted in Lifar's ballet?'

Gigi nodded, tears welling up in her eyes.

Delphine rushed forward, enveloping her daughter in a tight hug as she called out to her husband. But the door remained closed, and the radio continued to crackle with the latest news of the advancing German troops. Delphine encouraged her youngest daughter towards the study.

Gigi hesitated for only a moment before pushing open the heavy wooden door. The familiar scent of pipe smoke and old books filled the dimly lit room. Bernard sat hunched over his radio, fingers drumming against the desk, his face drawn with concern. The broadcast sputtered between clear reports and bursts of static, but the words were unmistakable.

'*Citizens are reminded that blackout curtains must be drawn after dusk,*' the announcer was saying, '*and to expect long delays on the southern roads due to columns of refugees and military convoys. Government offices are relocating further south to ensure continuity of operations.*'

Bernard turned his head sharply as Gigi entered. His dark eyes, so often filled with warmth, were now heavy with concern. He switched off the radio with a decisive click as if silencing the news could hold back the war itself.

'Gigi, *mon trésor.*' His voice carried both relief and exhaustion. 'What are you doing at home this evening?'

'I got the part, Papa.' The words spilled from her lips, hopeful yet tentative.

For a moment, the weight in Bernard's eyes lifted. He rose and crossed the room to grasp Gigi's shoulders. 'Lifar's ballet?'

She nodded.

A proud smile ghosted his lips. 'My little dancer.' He kissed the top of her head. 'You have worked so hard for this. But...' His expression dimmed again, a shadow passing over his face. 'The war, Gigi... I don't know how long we will have ballet, theatre, or anything that makes life beautiful.'

A pang of fear twisted in her chest. 'You think the performances will be cancelled?'

Bernard exhaled, rubbing a hand over his weary face. 'The world is changing faster than we can keep up. We will just have to see.'

A soft knock at the door broke the moment.

Another of Gigi's older sisters, Isabelle, peeked inside, her wide blue eyes sparkling with curiosity. 'Did I hear correctly? Lifar's new ballet?'

Gigi turned, a grin breaking through the tension. 'Yes! It's called *Entre deux rondes*, it's about a nightwatchman at the Louvre. In the ballet, the paintings come to life!'

Isabelle's hands flew to her mouth. She stepped forward eagerly. 'Tell me *everything*. Which paintings come alive?'

Gigi laughed, for a moment swept away by her sister's excitement about the ballet inspired by Isabelle's place of work. 'I don't know yet! Rehearsals start next week. But isn't it marvellous?'

For a moment, the house was alight with warmth and wonder.

Then the air shifted.

A loud, rhythmic pounding at the front door sent a jolt through them all. Bernard's head snapped toward the sound, and Delphine's smile faded.

Bernard moved first, striding toward the door. He paused only long enough to glance at his wife as Delphine gave the slightest nod, pressing a hand to her chest.

As he pulled the door open, the warm glow of home met the cold, encroaching shadow of war.

And just like that, the fragile spell of normality shattered.

On their doorstep stood one of their neighbours. His face was pale and twisted in fear. His words spilled out in a rush, barely coherent.

'Bernard, Delphine, we are leaving. We just got word from my sister that they have a place for us in the south. We leave in an hour. Marion wanted to let you know you are welcome to any food in our garden.'

Delphine stepped forward, a sense of urgency in her movements. 'Thank you for letting us know, Mathieu. We'll watch over your home and tend to your garden as our own.'

Bernard seized his neighbour's shoulder with his hand, silently promising solidarity in the face of terror: 'Safe trip, my friend. We will keep you in our prayers.'

Mathieu nodded hastily, his eyes darting around as if expecting shadows to leap out at him. 'You take care as well.' With that, he turned on his heel and hurried back towards his own house, disappearing into the gathering dusk.

The Valette family stood in the doorway, watching Mathieu's retreating figure until he vanished.

Unexpressed fears filled the air, uncertainty hanging heavy like an unmistakable presence.

Bernard closed the door, shutting out the outside world.

'Are we making the right decision by staying?' Delphine whispered to her husband, her voice steady despite the worry beneath it.

'We've made our choice,' Bernard confirmed.

'*You* could leave, Mama. But leaving the Louvre is unthinkable for me,' Isabelle insisted. 'The art needs to be protected. The thought of something happening to it breaks my heart.'

'And I might never get another chance to dance with Lifar,' Gigi added, her eyes shining with determination.

'Antoinette's son is so young, leaving would be difficult,' Charlotte added, referring to their middle sister.

The family fell into a heavy silence, each facing their own difficult decision to remain amid growing threats. Delphine's gaze swept over her loved ones. She took hold of Gigi and Isabelle's hands and together, through their united determination, they formed an unspoken alliance.

The girls' mother announced in a steadfast voice, 'This is

our home, our life. Fear will not force us to abandon all that we treasure.'

Bernard solemnly nodded toward his wife, his eyes revealing a faint glimmer of pride.

But even as their voices fell silent, the air tightened around the family, heavy with things unspoken. Outside, the city waited.

And although no one dared say it aloud, a question pressed at the edges of their resolve, sharp as a blade.

What will it cost us to stay?

7

PARIS, SUMMER 2011

Lily

On the shelves of Renaud Photography, where faded photographs were displayed next to dusty albums, the soft lighting made the vintage cameras gleam. The air of the shop was heavy with the pungent aroma of developing chemicals and printed paper.

At first, the shop seemed empty. Then from behind the counter came a loud thud, followed by a rapid, muffled curse. A figure emerged abruptly from beneath it.

Julien, sleeves pushed to his elbows, his dark curls even more dishevelled than before, clutched a box in one ink-stained hand while rubbing his wrist with the other.

It struck Lily how his boyish charm, even in this unguarded moment, only seemed to heighten how striking he was. She found herself staring, caught off guard by the sudden realisation of just how gorgeous he was, even when he wasn't trying.

She stifled a laugh, quickly pressing her lips together, hoping it disguised the flush rising in her cheeks.

When Julien finally looked up and saw her standing there,

his expression shifted from frustration to surprise. Then his eyes widened slightly, before a crooked, sheepish smile pulled at his lips.

'I swear, the box started it,' he said. 'Normally, I'm much cooler,' he added, his face reddening slightly.

She doubted that somehow, and couldn't help but chuckle. There was something endearing about Julien's slightly embarrassed demeanour. He set down the box and grabbed a cloth, making a show of wiping ink from his hands.

His hair fell in disarray over his forehead, and his dark eyes were as warm and intense as she had remembered from the night before. A stark contrast to her husband's ever-precise, carefully curated exterior.

'There, presentable enough,' he said, flashing her a grin as he tossed the cloth aside, though the last traces of ink still lingered on the backs of his hands.

'Barely,' she replied, happily returning his smile.

'Let me show you what I found before I ruin my entire reputation,' Julien added.

Lily followed him past cluttered shelves and old camera displays. The door to the darkroom clicked shut behind them, enclosing them in a world of soft red light. The scent of developer solution and old film wrapped around Lily as her eyes adjusted to the dim glow.

Photographs dangled from thin wires clipped carefully in place, ghostly fragments of the past captured in sepia tones and soft greys. The air was thick with stillness, punctuated only by the occasional drip of water into the rinse basin.

Julien flicked on the lightbox, and a soft glow illuminated the small table. He sifted through a neat stack of developed prints. Lily leaned in, her sleeve brushing his. The faint spice of his aftershave drifted up, clean and warm, and something inside her jolted, unexpected, electric. Her breath caught, the photograph blurring for a heartbeat. She was more aware of him standing beside her than of the image in her hands.

Julien seemed unaware as he began to speak. 'My grandfather had a knack for capturing people without them noticing.'

She forced herself to focus on the photograph. The picture was of Paris in 1940. Patrons filled the café, huddled around small tables, their expressions ranging from shock to dismay.

In the foreground, a man in a tailored suit gripped a newspaper, his knuckles white. The bold headline across the front page declared the fall of France.

'You can feel it, can't you?' Julien murmured, his voice lower now, as if they were intruding on the stillness of the past. 'The exact moment people realised everything was about to change.'

Lily nodded. The tension in the image was palpable: cigarettes burned down to their filters, untouched drinks sat abandoned on tabletops, forgotten in the wake of fear, disbelief and resignation.

Lily felt Julien shift closer, the heat of his body just behind her, his breath ghosting over her neck as he leaned in to study the photograph's details. His gaze lingered a heartbeat too long, not on the picture but on her. Then he looked away, quickly, as if afraid she might notice.

The air between them crackled, tightening the space until it felt charged with a weight neither of them was prepared to acknowledge.

Julien passed her more photographs, his fingertips grazing her palm. She felt the contact like a spark against her skin that carried a thrill that sent her pulse racing.

'This next one... I didn't even notice the background until I enlarged it.'

He slid the new photograph beneath the glass.

A ballet class.

Taken from the back of a grand studio, the image focused on a row of young dancers stretching at the barre, their delicate forms outlined against the tall, light-filled windows. Frozen in time, their movements were a study of discipline and grace, a stark contrast to the war creeping into every other corner of their city.

Lily stared, momentarily lost in the beauty of the scene.

Julien pointed to a faint reflection in the studio mirrors of a man holding a camera.

'That's my grandfather,' he said, tapping the shadowy figure just off-centre. 'He worked tirelessly with the Resistance during the war.'

Lily followed his gaze and then gasped.

Standing next to the photographer was another man, laughing, caught mid-conversation, completely unaware that he had been immortalised in the reflection of the studio's wide mirrors.

Julien turned to her, concern flickering in his dark eyes. 'Lily?'

She barely heard him as she gripped the edge of the lightbox and leaned in, staring.

'That man,' she finally said, 'I have a picture of him; his name is Jacques. He was my mother's uncle.'

A flicker of astonishment crossed Julien's face. He scanned the reflection, as if seeing it for the first time.

'How extraordinary. They must have known each other. If he knew my grandfather well, they could have been in the Resistance together,' he concluded.

Lily's mind raced with the implications. Had her mother, the woman who had spent a lifetime cloaked in elegance and reserve, even as a little girl, once fought against the Nazis?

She felt the weight of how intertwined their pasts were; two men standing side by side in a moment of quiet camaraderie.

'Does your mother remember anything about that time?' Julien enquired.

Lily sighed heavily. 'My mother was adopted as a baby; her

adoptive parents died during the war. This man, Uncle Jacques, is my first connection with any real family member on my mother's side. I'm trying to find my aunt for my mother; she has been missing since the war.'

Julien nodded, his gaze dropping to the photograph as though steadying himself, before he spoke. 'Maybe we can work together and solve both our family mysteries? These men obviously knew each other; there are bound to be clues in their stories.' His voice carried a note of quiet hope, as if he wasn't only suggesting research but something more, maybe a reason to keep seeing her.

Lily felt something stir deep within her, a thrill at the idea of working with Julien, of unravelling secrets together. She told herself it was the mystery, the chase, the chance to finally uncover the truth. But as her gaze lingered on him, she knew it was also Julien himself. He met her gaze, his eyes the darkest shade of onyx in the dim light, the unspoken connection threading between them. It was dangerous, this pull, and yet impossible to ignore.

'There's a lot to go through,' he said, all business, but she noticed a tightness in his throat. 'We should go over the notes I have from my grandfather and see if they mention Jacques anywhere.'

Lily nodded. 'That would be great.'

He hesitated for a beat, then added casually, 'If you're free later, we could grab dinner and go through them?'

Her stomach tightened.

Dinner.

She almost said yes. Almost.

Her hand twitched toward her bare ring finger before she caught herself, the reminder striking harder for its absence. *Marcus.*

'Oh,' she said quickly, tucking a stray strand of hair behind her ear, willing the warmth creeping up her neck to settle. 'I... can't tonight. I have plans with my husband.'

There. It wasn't forced. It wasn't an announcement, just a simple fact.

Julien blinked, taken aback for half a second, before something flashed across his features. Disappointment? But it was gone as quickly as it had come, replaced by a slight nod.

'Of course.' He smiled, though it didn't quite reach his eyes as they drifted to the place where her wedding ring should sit, if it hadn't been sitting in jewellery-cleaning fluid at home.

'Another time, then?'

The air between them shifted. Something had subtly changed.

Lily felt it.

She gripped the strap of her bag a little tighter. 'I should go. I want to check in with Effy at the gallery before I go home.'

Julien nodded, his gaze lingering on her momentarily, before he looked away.

As they moved back into the shop, she turned to him.

'Thank you,' she said, her voice filled with sincerity. 'For offering to help. I truly appreciate it.'

His eyes met hers, something warm passing between them before he continued.

'It's important to both of us.'

Lily made her way outside. She hesitated briefly, glancing back to see him watching her intently, and her stomach clenched with a mixture of apprehension and longing.

A light drizzle had begun to fall, the cool droplets landing softly on her skin as she stepped onto the wet pavement. Her mind reeled with everything that had just happened.

As she crossed the street toward the gallery, it wasn't just the prospect of uncovering her past that made her heart race, it was the unspoken connection she felt with Julien.

Lily quickened her pace as if the damp air might wash away the warmth curling through her.

She was married, she reminded herself, yet the flicker of attraction had caught her off guard. She pressed her lips together, willing herself to focus.

This wasn't about Julien. It was about her mother and the answers she was chasing.

But as she stepped through the gallery door, she couldn't shake the quiet truth settling in her chest. Somewhere in the tangled threads of history and fate, she was beginning to feel undone, not only by the secrets her mother had carried all these years, but also by the disarming presence of Julien. The way he seemed to see her more clearly than Marcus ever had.

It left her unsteady, caught between past and present, loyalty and desire.

8

PARIS, JULY 1940

Gigi

The rehearsal studio at the Palais Garnier buzzed and pulsed with life, the soaring strains of the piano filling the vaulted space as dancers moved in perfect harmony.

Beneath the stark rehearsal lights, Gigi was in mid-flow. All around her, limbs unfurled, feet whispered across polished boards and ragged breaths thickened the air. From the open windows above, the far-off whine of a German staff car reminded her that the world outside these walls was no longer their own.

The work consumed Gigi as she moved instinctively through familiar steps, the discipline of years shaping each movement. She leapt, arms extended, the sensation momentarily lifting her beyond the reality of war and curfews.

'Again,' came Serge Lifar's voice, measured yet edged with an intensity that demanded nothing short of perfection. He stood at the front of the studio, arms folded, his dark eyes drinking in every detail. 'And this time, Mademoiselle Valette, feel the weight of the moment. This is not just a step. It is longing. It is despair. Dance as though you feel that despair.'

Gigi nodded, lungs searing, a sharp stitch throbbing at her side. She had barely pivoted back into position to begin again when the doors at the far end of the room slammed open.

A ripple of unease swept through the company, dancers faltering mid-movement and the pianist's fingers crashing on the keys with a discordant clang.

Boots.

Their sound, rhythmic, deliberate, filled the space, a metronome of impending doom. The figures that strode inside were unmistakable: black uniforms and red armbands emblazoned with the hated insignia.

A hush fell over the hall as four men entered, their presence turning the ornate rehearsal room into something foreign and tainted. The lead officer, a man with a sculpted face and ice-chip eyes, surveyed the room with the slow precision of a collector inspecting rare artefacts. He clasped his hands behind his back, exuding the self-assurance of a man accustomed to bending the world to his will.

Serge Lifar took a measured step forward, his face carefully composed. 'Messieurs,' he greeted them, voice controlled. 'Can I help you?'

The officer's thin lips curled into something that might have been a smile had it not been so devoid of warmth.

'Who is in charge here?'

Serge cleared his throat. 'I am the director. How can I assist you, Monsieur?'

The Nazi handed written orders to Lifar.

'This is for you and your company. We are inspecting all cultural institutions in Paris. You will cooperate fully and provide any information or assistance required. Failure to do so will result in severe consequences,' he spat out, his accent slicing through the words like a blade. 'As of today, all artistic institutions in Paris will comply with Reich regulations. Theatres. Concert halls. Ballets. You are now under our jurisdiction.'

A murmur rippled through the dancers. A few gasped audibly, hands flying to their mouths as Lifar skimmed the decree. His expression remained impassive as he scanned the words, though the tightening of his jaw did not go unnoticed.

'What sort of regulations?' he asked, his tone even but edged with steel.

The officer stiffened. 'For one,' he began, 'all Jewish artists, musicians and staff are to be removed from the company immediately.'

The silence that followed was suffocating. Gigi's chest tightened, her pulse hammering beneath her ribcage. Across the room, she saw Eloise stiffen. As the company dresser on morning call, she had been mending a torn hem when the announcement was read.

Gigi's gaze flicked to the others, the Jewish dancers among them, their eyes wide, their faces pale with a fear they could not disguise. Her heart splintered. She knew what this meant for them. Their very existence in the company was a risk. For all their grace, for all their talent, none of it would protect them from what the enemy could decide.

'This is very harsh,' Lifar said, his voice eerily calm. 'There are exceptional Jewish dancers here. Their religion has nothing to do with their art.'

The officer barely spared him a glance. 'It is not a *request*.'

A sob broke the silence. Miriam, one of the young chorus dancers, trembling where she stood. Her face had gone pale, her wide brown eyes filled with something like disbelief. She had spent years perfecting her craft, devoting herself to the stage. And now, with the stroke of a pen, she was erased.

The company raised a hum of protest at this injustice, but Lifar lifted a hand, a subtle warning.

The officer continued, his voice carrying the weight of inevitability. 'Furthermore, performances must reflect the cultural values of the Reich. There will be no more decadent French compositions. The theatre will incorporate German works into the repertoire.'

Gigi inhaled sharply. It was a blow almost as devastating as the first.

'The Palais Garnier,' the officer went on, 'will also accommodate our officers. They are to be given preferential seating, and all performances will conclude before curfew.'

Gigi clenched her fists at her sides, her nails biting into her palms. The very idea of these men, these invaders, lounging in the gilded seats of the Palais Garnier, watching their art as if they owned it, made her stomach turn.

A sickening silence followed as Serge Lifar exhaled slowly. 'And if we refuse?'

The officer's smile was reptilian. 'Then you will find yourselves without a theatre. Without a career. Or worse.'

The weight of the words hung heavy in the air.

With a brisk nod, the officer turned on his heel, and his men followed. Their boots echoed against the wooden floors. The doors slammed shut behind them; a breathless, stunned quiet filled the hall.

A ragged sob escaped Miriam; she dropped to her knees as another dancer hurried to her side.

The others stood frozen in place, staring at the now-empty doorway as though expecting the shadows of the Nazis to remain imprinted on the floor.

Claudette sat beside Lifar, clipboard held tight against her ribs, a tremor in her shoulders. She met Gigi's gaze, and understanding passed between them.

Lifar stepped forward, at last, his expression serious.

'We may need to comply with their orders for now,' he announced, his voice heavy with resignation but his eyes burning with fierce resolve. 'But I promise I will find a way to protect those at risk. We will not abandon our own.' His gaze settled on Miriam, and his words were a balm to the raw nerves of the company, a declaration of defiance in the face of this tyranny. 'Let's take a break so I can speak to the show's producers.'

The dancers dispersed, the weight of the Nazi decree heavy upon their shoulders. Gigi moved toward Claudette and Eloise as they made their way to a secluded corner of the now-tainted rehearsal hall.

Eloise was shaking, her face pale.

'Let's get you back to the costume department,' Claudette suggested.

Gigi placed an arm around their friend and led her up the stairs to the warmth of the attic room.

Inside, Madame Fleurette was pinning the fabric of an elaborate, half-finished gown to a tailor's dummy, the rich blue silk draped over her arm.

The elderly seamstress looked up, and her eyes widened at Eloise's distress.

'What's the matter?' she asked, taking off her glasses and hurrying over to Eloise, who had collapsed into a chair in the kitchenette. Gigi recounted the entire story, and the costume mistress let out a '*Mon Dieu*' every time she drew in a breath.

As Gigi spoke, Claudette made coffee, wordless but efficient, the scent filling the space.

Madame Fleurette looked out the window as she stirred her coffee, and Gigi finished. 'This means the theatre won't just be a place for art any more. It will be a tool for them.'

Eloise's eyes fixed on the steaming cup while her knuckles turned white against the porcelain handle.

'What do we do?' Claudette finally asked, her voice barely above a whisper.

'We stay united,' Gigi declared, her calm but resolute tone

filling the room. 'We look after each other, no matter the circumstances.' She gently rested her hand on Eloise's shaking arm as Malina's words drifted back to her. '*You're all waiting for someone else to act. But we don't have that luxury. We have to save ourselves, save Paris.*'

Silence stretched between them until Eloise, who had not spoken, suddenly let out a shuddering breath. And then, a quiet sob.

Madame Fleurette reached out with a tender touch, concern deeply etched into the weathered lines of her face. 'Eloise, *mon cœur*, what is it?' she asked.

At first, Eloise shook her head, unable to form words as tears flowed silently down her cheeks.

'Eloise,' Gigi urged softly, 'you can trust us.'

Eloise finally lifted her gaze. Her eyes were pools of fear, raw and unhidden. When it came, her voice was barely a whisper.

'I've kept something from all of you,' Eloise said, her eyes drifting to the floor. She inhaled sharply, her fingers twisting together before she spoke, 'The truth is, like Miriam, I'm also Jewish.'

9

PARIS, SUMMER 2011

Lily

Lily stood at her counter, the rhythmic sound of the knife against the cutting board grounding her as she chopped fresh herbs for the lamb she had been marinating since the morning.

The rich aroma of garlic and rosemary filled the apartment, mingling with the buttery scent of potatoes roasting in the oven. It was a ritual; every Friday, she cooked something special meant to mark the end of the work week, a small act of love and normality in their marriage.

She poured a glass of wine and took a slow sip, exhaling as she glanced at the clock. Marcus should be home by now.

She tried not to dwell on it, or let the creeping unease settle over her. Instead, she set the table with care, arranging the linen napkins and adjusting the flickering candles, determined to hold on to the evening she had envisioned.

An hour passed. Then another.

The meal was ready, plated and cooling. The apartment was quiet save for the soft hum of music. She called his office, but no one picked up. By the time she heard the jingle of his keys in the lock, the unease had solidified into something heavier.

Marcus stepped inside, smelling faintly of wine. His tie was loosened, his shirt slightly wrinkled.

'Did you forget it was Friday? You're late,' she said, keeping her voice even.

He sighed, running a hand through his hair as he set his briefcase down. 'I had a lot going on. I told you I might be delayed.'

'I didn't expect that to be two hours.'

He looked at the beautifully set table, the untouched plates of food. 'Lily...' he began, but his voice trailed off.

She took a deep breath, unwilling to start a fight but unable to ignore the disappointment tightening in her chest. 'Have you eaten?'

Marcus hesitated, just for a fraction of a second. 'Not really.'

The lie, or maybe the omission, hung between them.

She swallowed hard, then gestured to the dining table. 'Well, it shouldn't go to waste.'

For a brief moment, something shifted. He exhaled, his posture easing as he pulled out a chair and sat down. 'I'm so sorry, truly, I forgot it was Friday.'

Relief flickered through her. He had just forgotten. She tried to convince herself it didn't mean anything as she reheated the food.

They ate in tentative silence at first, but then Marcus commented on the lamb, how she always managed to get the seasoning just right. That led to a warm recollection, of their honeymoon in Provence, when they had stumbled upon a small countryside restaurant with the best roast lamb they had ever tasted. Lily laughed, recalling how he had tried to charm the elderly chef into revealing his secret.

'He never did tell us, did he?' Marcus said, with a soft chuckle.

'No,' she said, shaking her head.

For a brief moment, life felt normal again.

She poured them both coffee and brought out his favourite dessert, a pear tart with almond cream. As they ate, she told him about the photograph, about her grandfather and Julien.

Marcus listened but with detachment, nodding but not really engaging.

'That's... interesting,' he said vaguely, stirring his coffee.

She casually mentioned the trip to Provence they always talked about. 'I was thinking... maybe we should finally book it. I think a getaway is just what we need. It would be nice.'

Marcus shifted in his chair. 'I don't know. Work is... a lot right now.'

'But you love the South of France,' she pressed, fighting to keep her tone light. 'You always said we should go back every year.'

'I just don't think it's the right time.'

Lily sat back, something settling deep in her stomach. It wasn't just about the trip. It was the reluctance to commit to anything beyond the immediate future.

Her gaze dropped to her hands, but in the silence that followed another image rose unbidden: Julien's steady eyes, the way he listened, how his presence seemed to quiet the noise inside her. The thought brought a flicker of warmth, immediately followed by guilt. She pushed it down, but it lingered all the same, a reminder of what was missing here.

She realised then that she hadn't been overreacting. She had been right all along that there was a growing distance between her and her husband.

She just didn't know how to bridge it.

· · ·

Later, as they climbed into bed, the weight of the evening lingering between them, Lily turned to Marcus, searching his face.

'What's wrong?' she asked, her voice quiet but firm. 'You've been distant from me for the last few weeks.'

Marcus let out a slow breath, rubbing his forehead. 'Lily, please. The last thing I need right now is pressure from you. Work is enough as it is.'

Her heart clenched. 'I'm not trying to pressure you. I just don't want us to drift apart.'

There was a flicker of something in his expression – guilt, maybe? Then he sighed. '*Lily.*'

She reached for him then, pressing her lips to his, desperate for connection. He kissed her back for a moment, and she felt the ghost of something familiar, something she thought they had lost.

But then he pulled away.

'I'm exhausted,' he murmured, stroking her cheek, before turning onto his side.

And just like that, the moment was gone.

Lily lay awake long after his breathing had evened out, staring at the ceiling, her mind restless. Finally, she slipped out of bed and padded into the living room and, wrapping a blanket around herself, she settled onto the couch.

Lily reached for the stack of photographs Julien had given her, her fingers tracing the image of war-torn Paris. The past felt closer than ever, as if whispering to her, urging her to listen.

Her eyes landed on the bistro scene, the moment Parisians had learned of the Nazi invasion. Patrons frozen in time, their lives split into before and after. A man clutched his newspaper, his grip tight, his expression tense. Denial? Resignation? A woman sat across from him, stirring a drink she had long since forgotten. Her gaze cast downward as if trying to will the world to stay the same for just a moment longer.

Lily exhaled slowly.

That moment before everything changes.

She felt the same moment occurring in her own life.

She ran a fingertip over the faces in the photo, their quiet dread mirroring the unease coiling inside her. Did they know? Did they sense it the way she sensed it now? The unravelling of something they thought was unshakeable?

Her mind drifted back over her day.

She had returned to the gallery that afternoon, still reeling from everything she had uncovered at Julien's shop: the photograph of her great-uncle, the unexpected connection between their families, and... Julien himself.

Effy had taken one look at her, the sharp edge of her gaze missing nothing, waiting for Lily to say more. But she hadn't. Not about the way her pulse had quickened when Julien's hand had brushed against hers.

Not about the warmth that had lingered in her chest when he had smiled at her.

'It's not just about the photographs, is it?' Effy had said, her voice gentle but knowing.

Lily had opened her mouth to deny it, to argue, but something had stopped her.

And then, Effy had given her that look that always made Lily feel as if she were being studied like a painting, as if the older woman were peeling back the layers of her carefully curated life.

'Be open to what life is offering you, *ma chérie*. We all deserve to be loved.'

Lily had tried to laugh it off, shocked by the astuteness of her old friend's observation. She had waved a hand as if shooing away the weight of those words.

'What are you talking about? I am loved; I'm married.'

Effy had smiled then, but it had been a sad sort of smile, the kind that hinted at past regrets.

'I thought that too, once.'

Lily stiffened, remembering Effy's story; the quiet, painful account of the fact that she had spent years in a marriage that had drained her instead of filling her. Effy had convinced herself love was supposed to be hard, that if she just waited long enough things would change.

But they hadn't.

'Don't stay where you're only half-loved,' her friend had said.

Lily had bristled, and defended Marcus without thinking.

'It's not like that, Marcus and I are just going through a dry patch. We have had many happy years,' she had said, too quickly.

Effy hadn't argued. She had given her that look again before going to serve a customer, as if planting the thought in Lily's mind and waiting for it to take root.

Now, as she sat alone in the quiet dark of their apartment, the wine glasses still half-full on the table, the meal she had so carefully prepared a distant memory, she finally allowed herself to wonder.

Was Effy right?

Had she already been half-loved for longer than she cared to admit?

10

PARIS, AUGUST 1940

Gigi

Jean-Paul, her dance partner for the new ballet, slipped through the heavy stage door with her, giving a quick nod to Monsieur Léon, leaving behind the morning's grim headlines.

Inside, the Palais Garnier enveloped them in its hallowed silence, a world apart from the occupied city beyond its walls. The rehearsal studio hummed with the quiet discipline of craft. Dancers moved in blurred arcs of light and shadow across the mirrored wall at one end of the vast space. The pianist at the corner coaxed out runs of music, notes spilling into the cavernous room with delicate urgency.

Jean-Paul, tall and lean, ran a hand through his damp curls, his grin sharp-edged, almost defiant. His hazel eyes flicked toward Gigi as he spoke while she took off her coat, already dressed in her rehearsal clothing.

'Even the café had nothing but ration bread and chicory,' he muttered as he shrugged out of his jacket, the gesture brisk, restless. 'No butter. No sugar. This war steals everything, even coffee.'

Gigi set her cardigan neatly on the bench and straightening her skirt over her leotard. 'At least it hasn't stolen *this*,' she whispered, glancing at the studio, the mirrors, the music.

Jean-Paul's jaw eased, just a little. 'Not yet,' he responded as he stretched his arms, the muscles rippling beneath his T-shirt. 'But the day is young.'

The dancers were called to the centre of the room and the rehearsal began, the music swelling through the space as their bodies fell into perfect synchronicity. Gigi felt herself disappear into the movement, the piano's tempo becoming a second heartbeat. The way Jean-Paul guided her, the precision of his grip at her waist as he lifted her into the air, felt instinctive, effortless. She trusted him completely. The feeling of suspension, the cool air against her skin mid-leap and the powerful steadiness of his hands, as he held her aloft, were a kind of magic.

Halfway through their dance, in the middle of a grand lift, Jean-Paul's grip faltered slightly. Gigi gasped as he caught her just in time, and their laughter mingled in the air.

Before she could comment, a loud commotion in the hallway brought the rehearsal to an abrupt stop. Monsieur Léon seemed to be arguing with someone outside their rehearsal room. He could clearly be heard saying, 'You can't just barge in like this, there is a rehearsal taking place!'

A ripple of shock spread through the room as, ignoring his pleas, a group of Nazis forced their way inside. The lead officer moved forward and stood with his leather-gloved hands behind his back.

Serge signalled to the pianist to stop playing as the dancers froze, eyes darting to one another, the doors and the officers who now commanded the space.

'*Vos papiers!*' The sharp order to line up and present their papers snapped through the studio like a whip.

Gigi felt Jean-Paul's hands tighten briefly at her waist as everyone rummaged through their belongings frantically, searching for their identification papers. Her mouth was dry as she reached into her dance bag, fingers fumbling for her documents. Her mind raced with the fear of anything being amiss.

Back in the line, Jean-Paul stiffened beside her, his papers clenched in his hand. His face, usually full of mischief, had drained of colour, and his expression was haunted.

Her gaze flicked upward toward the staircase leading to the costume department. There, just for a second, she caught a glimpse of Eloise disappearing into the shadows, hurrying away from where she had been working. Gigi's heart clenched.

The soldiers moved methodically down the line, scrutinising each set of papers with an almost leisurely menace. When one dancer hesitated for a second too long, an officer yanked the documents from her grasp and studied them before tossing them back with a sneer.

Then they reached Gigi. She forced herself to remain still, lifting her chin slightly as she handed over her papers.

The officer flicked his eyes over them, then his gaze pierced hers. Her skin prickled, but she kept her expression neutral. The seconds stretched unbearably. Then, with a sneer, he threw her papers back at her.

She exhaled quietly as they moved on to Jean-Paul.

He swallowed hard, his fingers gripping the edge of his papers tightly as he handed them over. The officer scrutinised them, turning the pages toward the light. Then his lips curled into a smirk.

'Where did you get these, Monsieur?'

'The same place as everyone else. It's all in order, I promise,' he managed, his eyes flickering toward Gigi briefly, seeking reassurance in her unwavering gaze.

'Do you have something to hide?'

'No!' he shot back defensively, too fast for it to sound genuine.

'I think you do. These are forged,' the officer said flatly.

Gigi's stomach dropped.

'That's not possible,' Jean-Paul said, his voice barely above a whisper.

The officer gave a slow nod, waving another soldier forward. 'See? This is very sloppy. You should have chosen a better forger, Monsieur.'

Jean-Paul's breath came in shallow gasps. 'Please,' he tried again. 'I don't know what you're talking about. I am just a dancer, I have nothing against you.'

The officer smirked. 'Dancing means nothing to the Reich.'

Two soldiers seized him, yanking his arms behind his back.

'This is a mistake!' Jean-Paul struggled, his voice rising.

Gigi jumped in front of him protectively as cries erupted from the other dancers. One of the younger girls sobbed into her hands.

'*Don't!*' Gigi begged, her voice breaking as she raised her hands. She clung to Jean-Paul's arm, holding tight as though she could anchor him there by sheer force of will. 'Please, this is a mistake! Don't hurt him, he's my partner, I'm begging you!' Her eyes darted from face to face, searching for any flicker of compassion, any hint that someone might relent.

The officer regarded her with an icy gaze, his expression unmoved by her plea. 'You would do well to know your place, Mademoiselle,' he spat out, his tone laced with contempt. 'Unless you want to accompany him to our headquarters for further questioning.'

Serge Lifar stepped forward, his face pale but composed. 'Monsieur, surely there has been an error. Jean-Paul is an invaluable member of this company.'

The officer turned his cold smile on Lifar. 'An invaluable member? A criminal, you mean. The man obviously has something to hide, and forged papers carry a heavy penalty.'

He moved nearer to Serge, lowering his voice but maintaining enough volume that everyone could hear him. 'You have a beautiful theatre here. It would be a shame if it were to close.'

A hush fell over the dancers. The weight of the unspoken threat tightened like a noose.

Serge's hands curled into fists, but he forced himself to remain still.

The soldiers began to drag Jean-Paul away, his eyes wide with terror.

'Gigi, help me!' he shouted desperately as their eyes locked one last time, before the soldiers pulled him out of the studio and his pleas were cut off by the slamming of the doors.

'*No!*' Gigi screamed, the sound tearing from her throat raw and primal. Around her, some of the dancers flinched. Some sobbing openly, others frozen in horror.

The silence that followed roared in her ears, her heart splintering with one unbearable thought that echoed with each pulse.

What if that was the last time she ever saw him?

11

PARIS, SUMMER 2011

Lily

Lily woke before her alarm, the quiet hum of the city filtering through the windows as she lay still for a moment. She stared at the ceiling, the unease between her and Marcus from the night before pressing down on her.

She slipped out of bed, walked barefoot into the living room and curled up on the sofa, her usual blanket around her shoulders. The box containing the documents from the safe deposit box sat on the coffee table where she'd left it. Something compelled her forward now. Maybe she hoped that, by untangling her mother's past, she could somehow make sense of her own life, that feeling that everything she had built was slipping away.

Or maybe it was just the need to hold on to something tangible that still mattered.

She reached for the first bundle, flipped through old letters and records, and found within the letters her mother's handwritten notes of all she had remembered. She must have missed them the first time she searched the box. They were like journal entries but not bound; they were loose pages that looked as if they had been pulled from a notebook.

Lily swallowed, turning the fragile papers with care. It didn't take long to find what she was looking for. A strange comfort settled over her as she recognised her mother's slanted handwriting, unravelling the story of a girl caught in the chaos of the Second World War. She had written it after the war to help get all her memories in one place. Maybe while she had been searching when Lily was young. Each word etched on the yellowed pages painted a vivid picture of struggle and resilience, and, finally, the reference Lily had been searching for.

The last time I saw Rachel, we were hiding in a cottage in southern France.

A tiny village called Saint-Antoine-sur-Mer.

Though I didn't remember his name, the man who sheltered us, a Resistance fighter, was careful. He always watched the roads and told us to be ready to run. But in the end it wasn't enough.

The night they came, it was chaos. Screaming. Gunfire. Rachel had twisted her ankle, but pushed me toward the back door. 'Run,' she said. 'Now.'

I ran. I didn't see what happened after that. But I heard the shots.

And know more than one life was taken that night. It was the last time I ever saw my sister.

Her breath hitched as she read the last words, her mother's pain etched into the page.

Lily's fingers trembled as she flipped to another page, but the words blurred through her tears. She wished she could talk to her mother.

She pulled out the photo of the twins again, and found her heart aching for the aunt she never knew.

Marcus appeared for breakfast, in a tailored suit that sharpened the angles of his lean frame. The deep navy hue made the blue of his eyes more piercing, a contrast that still made her heart flutter. The crisp lines of his shirt, the perfectly knotted tie, every detail was immaculate, effortless.

As he moved past her the scent of his cologne lingered, a heady blend of bergamot and sandalwood, understated yet commanding. It was a scent designed to leave an impression, to exude quiet luxury, and it did, just like everything else about him. It hinted at the exorbitant price he had paid for it, but, more than that, it reminded Lily of how carefully curated Marcus was and how every part of him fitted into the life he had built. Or at least, the life she had thought they were building together.

He glanced up as she set his breakfast and coffee in front of him, but whatever tension had lingered between them the night before had been neatly tucked away beneath his usual composed demeanour.

Lily poured herself a cup of tea, her heart thudding, as she sat across from him. She wasn't going to overthink this. She just had to say it.

'I found something,' she started, her voice steady but breathless with the weight of discovery. She quickly laid out everything she had read in her mother's notes: the village, the Resistance fighter, the night of the raid.

Marcus listened, stirring his coffee absent-mindedly.

'I need to go to Saint-Antoine-sur-Mer,' she finished. 'To find out more.'

Marcus barely reacted. He looked at her over the rim of his coffee cup. 'When?'

'This weekend.'

He gave a small shrug. 'That's quite a way, four or five hours from here?' His tone was casual, as though the distance mattered more to him than why she needed to go.

'I know,' she admitted, 'but I can't ignore this.'

She stopped herself from adding, *My mother might be dying, and this is her last wish, so I'm not going to wait around.*

Instead, she steadied her voice and forced a small smile. 'I thought maybe we could make a weekend of it.'

He exhaled, leaning back in his chair. 'Lily...'

She already knew what was coming. The same excuses, the same reluctance.

'Please, don't just say no straight away; think about it. It would be fun, just the two of us getting away from it all.'

He exhaled, glancing at the clock as if suddenly pressed for time. 'I'll think about it.'

Then he planted a kiss on her cheek, leaving just a hint of his expensive cologne on her skin, and was gone.

Alone in their quiet apartment, Lily's heart ached with disappointment. She had to face it: something was seriously wrong with her marriage. Tears streamed down her face as she prepared for work.

She had no idea how to fix this.

When Lily arrived at the gallery it was already buzzing, the scent of fresh coffee and Effy's infectious laughter filling the space. As the older woman escorted a favoured customer to the door, she turned to Lily, her sharp gaze sweeping over her face.

'Well, *ma chérie*,' she declared, frowning slightly. 'You have the look of someone who's been thinking too much. You don't want to do that, it will cause a little line right here.' She tapped the space between her eyebrows.

Lily managed a small laugh. 'I'm already a lost cause.'

Around lunchtime, while sorting through frames in the back of the shop, Effy called out to her.

'Lily, someone's here to see you!' she announced with amusement.

Lily brushed her damp fringe away from her forehead with the heel of her hand in an effort to look presentable. But she stopped short as she entered the front of the shop, her stomach flip-flopping unexpectedly.

Julien stood near the counter, a small envelope in his hand, a broad smile spreading across his face.

He looked as handsome as ever, his dark curls tousled in a way that made him seem effortlessly put together. His chestnut-brown eyes were warm and expectant, and he radiated his usual quiet confidence.

Lily felt a rush of heat creep up her neck at the sight of him, unexpected but not unwelcome. Her pulse skipped. For an instant, before she could gather herself, she wondered if he could see it in her face, if he might notice how her breath had caught.

She forced a smile. 'Julien, what a surprise.'

'I hope you don't mind me stopping by,' he said, his voice carrying an easy charm, though beneath it was the faintest flicker of nervousness. He handed her the envelope. 'I came across these, and thought you might be interested.'

Lily took it, her curiosity piqued. 'What is it?'

'More photographs from my grandfather's time during the war,' Julien explained, his eyes searching hers as if trying to gauge her reaction. 'I've been going through them, and I thought you might...' He petered out, his cheeks reddening slightly.

Effy, who had been watching the exchange from behind the counter, smirked knowingly as the silence between them stretched a little too long.

'Perfect timing,' she interjected, breaking the moment with her signature confidence. 'Lily was just about to go on her lunch break.'

Lily blinked, her brow furrowing. 'But I haven't finished sorting the frames in the back...' she protested weakly.

Effy waved a hand dismissively. 'Frames can wait. Your mother's story can't.'

Lily hesitated, torn between the curiosity tugging at her and the sense of duty pulling her back to work. Julien's presence had stirred something within her, a mix of excitement and apprehension that she couldn't quite define.

She glanced at her boss. 'Are you sure?'

Without answering, Effy sauntered to the door and opened it for them.

Julien beamed. 'I know the perfect place. A new restaurant that just opened down the street. It's quiet, and the food is great.'

As they strolled into the warm embrace of the afternoon sunshine, their conversation flowed more effortlessly. The unease she had woken up with that morning began to melt away.

The restaurant Julien had suggested was a classic Parisian bistro tucked into a quiet side street. Its terrace, framed by lush greenery, had an unhurried elegance, wrought-iron chairs, crisp white linen-covered tables and terracotta planters overflowing with fresh lavender and rosemary. Sunlight glinted off polished silverware as servers moved with practised grace, refilling glasses of chilled white wine and delivering delicate plates of food.

Julien gestured toward an empty table beneath the striped awning, and they settled in. The gentle wind brought floral scents from a nearby planter, combined with the kitchen's welcoming aromas.

Julien declared it was a perfect day, and revealed his summer-tanned forearms as he rolled up his white sleeves.

Lily nodded, letting the tension in her shoulders ease as she glanced at the menu. Something light, something that wouldn't sit too heavily in her stomach when her thoughts were already tangled.

When the waiter arrived, they both opted for fresh, seasonal dishes. Lily ordered a niçoise salad. The vibrant heirloom tomatoes, crisp haricots verts and delicate slices of seared tuna drizzled in a bright lemon vinaigrette were perfect. Julien went for a *tarte fine aux légumes*, a thin, flaky pastry topped with roasted courgette, peppers and a touch of goat cheese. The dish arrived golden and crisp, glistening under the sunlight.

They sipped on chilled rosé, its light, fruity notes complementing the lazy warmth of the afternoon.

As they ate, Lily shared the insights she had gathered that morning: the diary entry, her mother's account of Rachel's disappearance, and the tiny village in the South of France where it had all happened.

Julien leaned back in his chair, watching her with quiet intensity. 'So you are going to the south?'

Lily swirled her fork through her salad, hesitating momentarily, before nodding. 'I think so, maybe this weekend.'

Julien set his fork down, exhaling. 'I have a trip planned there for the end of this month. I could bring it forward and come with you to help.' He paused, studying her reaction.

Lily glanced up. The easy comfort of their lunch suddenly shifted into something more weighted. The sun caught in his dark eyes, and she held his gaze for a second too long.

She took a sip of wine, choosing her words carefully. 'I'll probably be going with my husband.'

'Of course,' he said lightly, though there was a note of disappointment in his voice. 'It'll be a lovely trip for you both. This time of year, the countryside is stunning.'

Lily smiled, but something in her stomach swirled a little with her own disappointment.

Julien moved quickly to a new topic by showing her the photographs he had found. Though she appeared to pay attention by nodding at the details he pointed out, Lily's mind was filled with conflicting emotions.

The rational part of her knew she should focus on the images in front of her, on the historical weight they carried, but another part, one she was trying hard to suppress, was thrilled that he wanted to spend time with her.

The turmoil still hadn't settled when Lily arrived home that evening. She was surprised to hear the shower running. Marcus was home early.

She slipped off her shoes, and crossed the threshold of their bedroom. A pile of his clothes lay discarded on the floor. She bent to gather them and her fingers brushed against something stiff and crinkled in his trouser pocket.

A receipt.

She flattened it out, and her heart thudded as she scanned the print.

A meal for two.

At her favourite restaurant.

Today's date.

Her stomach twisted. That place wasn't for clients or casual meetings; it was the kind of intimate setting reserved for anniversaries and quiet, romantic celebrations. A place she hadn't stepped into in over a year.

The bathroom door creaked open. Marcus emerged, rubbing a towel through his hair, another slung around his hips. The scent of his shampoo, sea salt and citrus, hit her. She used to love it, but now it made her throat tighten.

'Hey,' he said, stepping toward her, lips brushing hers. 'You're home early.'

She didn't return the kiss. Instead, she held up the receipt between two fingers. 'What's this?'

He blinked, glanced at it, and shrugged with a small laugh. 'Oh, that. It was just lunch with a client.'

'*La Chambre Bleue?*' Her voice cracked with disbelief. 'That's not exactly your usual business lunch spot.'

Marcus tossed the towel onto a chair. 'Come on, Lily. Don't make this into a thing.'

'I'm not making it into anything,' she said tightly. 'I just want to know why you were at *our* restaurant. Today, with someone else.'

He sighed and brushed past her toward the dresser. 'It was a big meeting. An important client. She's...' He paused. 'High-value. I needed the setting to be... persuasive.'

'*She?*' Lily echoed.

He turned, annoyed now. 'Yes, *she*. Are we really doing this?'

Lily stared at him, the paper trembling slightly in her hand. 'I think we already were.'

'You're overreacting.' His tone was clipped now. 'It's part of my job to entertain clients. You know that.'

'At the same place you took me for our anniversary?' Her voice was quiet but steady. 'You didn't think I'd find out?'

'I didn't think it mattered.'

The words hung there between them. Cold. Dismissive.

She stepped back, her arms folding over her chest like armour. 'I thought that place was special to us, so yes, it matters to me.'

Marcus ran a hand through his hair, exasperated. 'Lily, I'm exhausted. Can we not do this right now?'

But it was already done.

Dinner was a blur. She moved through the motions, chopping, stirring, plating, barely registering what she was doing. The food in front of her stayed untouched. Her stomach, knotted with unease, refused to settle.

Marcus poured the wine and made small talk as if nothing

had happened. 'So,' he said, settling back in his chair, 'how was your day?'

She mentioned Julien's surprise visit, the trip he had offered to accompany her on.

Marcus perked up instantly. 'That sounds great,' he said, too eagerly. 'You should go. It'll be good for you.'

She studied him, searching for hesitation, for even a flicker of jealousy that might mean he still cared. 'You're okay with me travelling with another man?'

'Of course.' He smiled, raising his glass. 'I trust you.' His tone implied that she should trust him too. Something inside her cracked at his easy smile, the way he offered her up without a second thought. She wanted him to protest, to fight, to claim her as his. Instead, his detachment hollowed her.

She didn't smile back.

That night, once again sleep evaded her. She lay stiff beside him, watching the ceiling and listening to the slow, even rhythm of his breath. Lack of sleep was becoming a habit she was not enjoying.

Outside, the city glowed, indifferent, silent.

Effy's voice echoed: *'Don't stay where you're only half-loved.'*

Her throat tightened. Her mother had endured war, betrayal and impossible choices, yet she had kept fighting for something better.

Lily's tears came without warning. She wasn't ready to make serious decisions about her marriage, not yet. But tomorrow, she would call Julien.

A weekend away might bring the clarity she needed.

12

PARIS, OCTOBER 1940

Gigi

The crisp October air clung to Paris that evening, the kind of cool that crept beneath a coat collar and seeped into your limbs.

The Palais Garnier still glowed from the success of Gigi's recent opening night, a performance met with rapturous applause, despite the shadow of occupation. For a brief moment, she had felt the war retreat to the far edges of the city, replaced by music, light and the steady rhythm of a life in the theatre.

Yet even in her triumph, Jean-Paul's absence pierced her. He should have been there beside her, their steps in perfect unison, but instead he was gone. The memory of his laughter, of the way he lifted her effortlessly in rehearsal, haunted her now. Without him the applause sounded hollow, a reminder of all that had already been stolen.

When they received a call to gather on the stage before a performance one evening, nobody, not even Claudette, knew why.

'I was simply informed that the company needed to gather on the stage before the audience arrived,' she explained to Gigi.

The grand stage of the Palais Garnier was bathed in the glow of the footlights, the golden proscenium arch framing the scene like a painting come to life. Dozens of dancers arrived in their costumes, adjusting ribbons and skirts nervously.

Gigi finished placing the pearl headpiece in her red curls and arranging the delicate chiffon of her opening costume. The white bodice fitted snugly against her ribs and the layered tulle skirt brushed against her thighs as she stretched absently.

Serge Lifar strode onto the stage. There was no mistaking the tension in his jaw, the way his hands clenched at his sides before he forced them to relax.

'The Germans have invited us to a soirée. They have visiting dignitaries in Paris who want to meet you.'

A ripple of unease moved through the company.

Gigi caught Claudette and Eloise's eyes. There was a silent exchange of disgust between them.

'And before you all give me reasons why you couldn't possibly come,' he continued, eyes scanning the group, 'I have been informed that attendance is mandatory. It will be held in the grand foyer tomorrow night after the performance.'

The company groaned.

From behind the thick red velvet, the murmur of the audience swelled, excited voices, the rustle of silk gowns. The house was open. The orchestra began playing the overture in the pit, and Serge stepped back into the wings.

'I will see you all tomorrow. Positions!' he called out as he departed. A low ripple of voices stirred through the dancers, a murmur of resentment laced with fear.

As Gigi forced herself to move, a chill ran down her spine at the thought of being forced to socialise with Nazis.

. . .

The following evening, the dressing room was a flurry of movement, the scent of talcum powder and make-up remover thick in the air.

Costumes from the evening's performance lay discarded across chairs, silk tutus and beaded bodices shimmering in the mirrored light. The space was small, shared by too many dancers, yet it pulsed with energy, half exhaustion, half nerves.

Girls clustered around the mirrors at the long vanity, dabbing rouge onto their cheeks and powdering away the last traces of sweat. Someone swore as their stocking snagged against a chair, and another immediately reached for a tiny bottle of nail polish.

'Hold still,' she muttered, bending down to paint a clear line just above the tear, halting the run before it could spread.

'Maybe I should just go without,' the dancer grumbled, balancing on one foot. 'If we're supposed to be entertaining Nazis, who cares.'

Gigi smirked as she tugged a brush through her hair, watching the girls' easy camaraderie. Their laughter was light, but there was an edge beneath it, a weariness, an unspoken understanding that none of them wanted to be here.

Across the room, Eloise was fastening tiny pearl buttons on another dancer's gown. Already dressed in a long blue dress, her dark curls pinned back, she worked in silence.

Gigi pulled her own dress over her head, a crimson gown borrowed from Claudette. The beading caught the soft glow of the vanity lights. She turned to the mirror and adjusted the delicate straps, and adjusting the silk at her waist.

Just then the door swung open and Claudette arrived, with a bottle of champagne lifted in the air.

'I liberated some champagne from a Nazi,' she announced, grinning mischievously. 'We may as well be a little drunk before we face the enemy.'

A small cheer went up in the dressing room as Claudette

passed the bottle around, and each girl filled up whatever they had, from paper cups to coffee mugs.

But as the fizz stung her tongue, Gigi's eye caught Eloise's, and she remembered her friend was Jewish. Her thoughts drifted to Jean-Paul.

He should be drinking champagne with them too.

Gigi stepped inside the Palais Garnier's Foyer de la Danse with Claudette and Eloise. The foyer glittered, displaying painted figures in graceful poses. Golden chandeliers bathed the vast hall in warm light, their soft glow reflecting off the massive mirrors that lined the walls. The scents of expensive perfume and champagne clung to the air, mingling with the quiet hum of conversation.

Dancers in silk and chiffon moved like figures in a painting; their laughter was forced, their smiles practised. The officers in attendance, stiff in their pristine uniforms, watched with predatory amusement, sipping champagne from crystal flutes.

Gigi took one from a passing tray, the glass cool in her fingers. She could feel Eloise tense beside her.

'I *hate* this,' Eloise muttered under her breath, her dark eyes darting across the room. 'I have costumes to wash and repair. I should be doing that instead.'

Members of the orchestra were playing music, and some of the officers began asking the girls to dance.

One officer had been watching Gigi since she arrived, his eyes trailing her from across the room, lingering in a way that made her skin crawl. Now he strode toward her with a confident swagger, his uniform impeccable and his dark hair slicked back.

Gigi forced a polite smile as he approached, her grip on the champagne flute tightening imperceptibly.

'Mademoiselle Valette, isn't it?' The officer's voice was

silken, but there was a hardness in his eyes that set Gigi shivering.

'Yes, that's correct,' she replied evenly.

'I couldn't help but notice your performance earlier. You truly are a vision on stage,' he said, his gaze lingering on her.

Gigi's heart raced, but she kept her expression neutral. 'Thank you, Monsieur.'

He extended a gloved hand. 'I insist on a dance.'

It was not a request.

Claudette shot Gigi a warning look, but Gigi smiled, setting down her glass. She could play the game.

The officer pulled her close as the orchestra launched into a waltz. His grip was too tight, his palm heavy against her back. Gigi kept her face neutral, gliding effortlessly across the floor, though every muscle in her body ached to push away.

'You are very talented,' the officer murmured, his breath warm against her ear. 'Perhaps one night you will dance just for me.'

Gigi's steps faltered. Anger flared in her chest.

'How dare you,' she seethed, her voice rising in anger.

The officer's grip tightened on her waist, his smile turning cold. 'Watch your tongue, Mademoiselle, remember who I am,' he hissed.

Gigi was about to deliver a sharp lesson in manners when a new voice, silken, laced with mischief, cut through the tension.

'There you are, darling,' the man said lightly. 'I hope she hasn't been making a nuisance of herself, Officer.'

Gigi barely had time to register the warm hand that slid around her waist before she was spun neatly out of the German's grip.

The officer blinked in surprise, momentarily caught off guard.

Before he could find words, Gigi was already being swept

across the floor, the stranger's hold firm yet effortless, guiding her away with practised ease.

Her heart raced as she took in his face: a strong jawline, sandy blond hair and eyes that danced with trouble. He was smirking as if he'd done this a thousand times before.

'And you are?' Gigi asked.

'Saving you. No need to thank me,' he responded nonchalantly. 'You were about to make a terrible mistake.'

Gigi narrowed her eyes. 'I had it handled.'

His smirk widened. 'Of course you did. But I rather think you will dance better without broken legs.'

Once safely away from her predator, the man pulled her into his arms and began to dance with her.

'How do I know I just didn't get plucked from the frying pan to be thrown into the fire?' Gigi asked, turning to face him head-on for the first time.

What a handsome face it was.

'You don't.' He smiled. 'Isn't that the fun of living dangerously?'

'Well, I'm not so sure of that,' she responded.

As they twirled around the dance floor, Gigi found herself studying the man with a mix of curiosity and caution. His touch was confident yet gentle, guiding her with a skill that spoke of experience. She noticed the subtle way his eyes scanned the room, as if he was assessing every detail.

'You never answered my question,' she remarked, her voice low.

'I didn't, did I?' he responded cryptically.

'So you're not going to tell me who you are?'

He chuckled, a low, melodious sound that sent a shiver down Gigi's spine.

'Who I am is not important. What matters is that you are safe now,' he replied.

The music stopped, and he released her from his arms.

'Thank you for the dance. Enjoy the rest of your evening, Mademoiselle Valette,' he said with a playful glance, and she realised that he knew her name.

And then he was gone, disappearing into the crowd as quickly as he had appeared.

Gigi stared after him, breathless, pulse still racing. She could feel the press of his warm hand at her back, the way his presence had steadied her even as it unsettled her.

Across the room, Eloise was watching with raised eyebrows, her expression somewhere between disbelief and knowing amusement. Gigi quickly looked away, unwilling to admit, even to herself, how her heart fluttered at the memory of his touch.

13

PARIS, SUMMER 2011

Lily

Lily adjusted the strap of her overnight bag, her fingers tightening around the handle as she glanced at the departure board. The train was listed as being on time, and she bought a ticket at the kiosk. Had she made the right decision to come away with Julien instead of her husband? She wasn't sure, but it was too late to change her mind now.

She exhaled slowly, trying to steady herself.

The morning chill clung to the air despite the press of bodies moving around her. She shoved her hands into her coat pockets, rubbing her thumb and finger together in absent distraction.

Would Marcus message her before he went to work?

She had left quietly that morning, slipping out before he woke up. He hadn't said anything about her leaving, hadn't asked for the details. '*I trust you,*' he had said the night before when she had raised the fact that she was going with Julien. But his detachment had hollowed her out, leaving only unease.

'No proper journey begins without good coffee and terrible station croissants.'

Julien's voice broke through the fog of her thoughts, warm and easy.

She turned as he strode toward her, his ever-present camera slung over his shoulder, a bag of pastries in one hand, two paper cups of coffee balanced in the other. He was dressed simply, a navy sweater beneath a well-worn jacket, jeans, boots scuffed from travel. A look that made him seem as though he belonged anywhere.

He leaned in to kiss her cheeks in greeting, his smooth skin brushing her face, his aftershave warm and clean. For a fleeting second, she almost turned, just slightly, imagining what it would feel like if his lips found hers instead. The thought jolted through her and she forced herself back, and accepted a paper cup with a smile that wavered at the edges.

'I hope you're not telling me you actually bought the croissants from the station bakery,' she said, her voice tight.

Julien smirked, handing her the paper bag. 'I'd never insult you like that. I got them from the terrible place around the corner.' He tapped his temple. 'I'm learning.'

Lily smiled.

A whistle blew in the distance and Julien nudged his bag higher on his shoulder.

'Ready?'

Lily hesitated.

On instinct, her fingers reached for her phone and she unlocked the screen.

Nothing from Marcus.

A hollow ache opened inside her chest.

Without a word, Julien shifted his grip on his coffee, reached for her overnight bag and took it from her shoulder.

'What are you doing? I can manage that,' she said, startled.

He flashed a grin. 'Carrying your bag like the gentleman my

mother told me to be. Also, you look like you're about to change your mind, and I'd rather not have to explain to Effy why I let you ditch me at the last second.'

She huffed a small laugh, rolling her eyes. 'Fine, lead the way.'

They strode side by side toward the waiting train, their footsteps merging with the station's pulse.

As Lily stepped onto the platform she turned one last time, scanning the station as if Marcus might have decided to come after all.

He wasn't there.

As the train doors slid shut behind them, she told herself it didn't matter.

The rhythmic clatter of the train over the tracks had a soothing quality, lulling the other passengers into a gentle hush. The soft hum of conversation, the occasional rustle of a newspaper and the quiet clink of cutlery from the dining car all blended into a steady background noise, a world in motion. At the same time, Lily's thoughts remained fixed.

She watched the countryside blur past the window, the Parisian suburbs giving way to rolling fields and distant clusters of stone farmhouses, their shutters thrown open to the morning sun.

It should have felt freeing, an escape, however temporary. But as she cradled her cup of coffee, she found her mind drifting back to the receipt she had found.

Marcus had gone there with someone, probably sat at their usual table. Ordered a bottle of wine, shared a quiet conversation over candlelight.

Lily swallowed hard, her fingers tightening slightly around the cup.

Who was she? A colleague, a friend? Or something worse?

What was he doing right now?

Was he at work? Would he notice she was gone? Would he care—?

'Lily?'

Julien's voice pulled her back to the present. She turned to find him watching her over his own coffee, his expression curious.

'You seem a million miles away.'

She forced a small smile. 'Just thinking.'

He raised an eyebrow. 'Dangerous habit.'

She let out a small breath of amusement. 'So I've been told.'

Julien glanced at the gold band, newly cleaned, on her left hand. 'And your husband is okay with you taking off for the weekend with a strange man?'

Lily hesitated. She should say yes. She should reassure him, reassure herself, that her husband had wished her well, had kissed her goodbye that morning, had wanted her to go.

Instead, she found herself answering honestly. 'He didn't say much about it.'

Julien studied her for a beat longer before nodding slowly.

She changed the subject before he could press further. 'Tell me more about your grandfather,' she said, setting her cup down. 'You said he was part of the Resistance.'

A flicker of something crossed Julien's expression, pride, but also something heavier, something he held back. 'Yes, but he never talked about it much. Not to my father, not even to me. Most of what I know comes from the photographs he left behind.'

Lily leaned in slightly, drawn by his voice and the reverence with which he spoke.

'I believe he risked everything,' Julien continued. 'He used his camera the way some used weapons, documenting, record-ing, keeping proof of what was happening when so many were trying to erase it.'

Lily felt a chill despite the warmth of the sun filtering

through the window. Thinking of what kind of world it had been under occupation.

The conversation drifted, the silences between them comfortable rather than awkward.

Later they went to the dining car and lingered over plates of fresh fruit, the light sweetness of strawberries and ripe peaches complementing the dark richness of the coffee.

Everything felt... easy. A stark contrast to eating with Marcus, which had become more about a heavy silence than conversation, more about routine than connection.

She hated that she was even making the comparison.

When they had finished, they stepped into the narrow corridor to return to their seats. The space between them was smaller and more confined here.

The train gave a sudden, lurching jolt.

Lily stumbled, her hand shooting out instinctively to brace herself against the wall. Before she could catch her balance, Julien's arm was around her waist, steadying her.

His warmth was immediate, the press of his hand on her hip firm and his body close to hers.

She felt the brush of his dark curls against her cheek, his cedarwood aftershave lingering on skin.

Her breath hitched.

For a moment, neither of them moved.

She wasn't sure if she was frozen by its unexpectedness, or something else entirely.

Then, as quickly as it had happened, she straightened and stepped back as the train steadied itself.

Julien's arm dropped to his side. He looked at her, something intense flickering in his expression. Then, with a slow, teasing smile, he said, 'I'd forgotten what it feels like to have someone fall for me.'

Heat rushed into Lily's cheeks before she could stop it. She opened her mouth to answer, but no words came. Julien glanced away and, though his smile lingered, the faint flush along his cheekbones betrayed him.

The train slowed as it pulled into Saint-Antoine-sur-Mer, its rhythmic hum fading into the soft screech of brakes. Lily took in the sight of the small station as it came into view – a single platform, edged by sun-warmed stone buildings with terracotta roofs, their shutters painted in soft blues and greens. A few travellers disembarked, and were greeted by waiting relatives or wandered toward the narrow street that led into the heart of the village.

She hadn't been sure what to expect. Saint-Antoine was barely a pinprick on the map, and yet, as she stepped off the train and onto the platform, a strange feeling settled over her: this had been the last place the twins had been together.

Julien was beside her, slinging his bag over his shoulder as he surveyed their surroundings. 'Quaint,' he murmured.

Lily took a slow breath, adjusting the strap of her own bag. The scent of salt hung in the air, carried by a gentle breeze from the nearby coast. Somewhere beyond the station, she could hear the distant cry of seagulls.

They walked toward the village, its cobbled and winding streets flanked by whitewashed buildings with ivy climbing up their facades. Flower pots overflowed with bursts of colour, poppies, wild lavender, clusters of pale pink roses. The scent of pastries drifted from a boulangerie, where a few locals stood chatting outside, wicker baskets looped over their arms.

Julien turned to her. 'Feels like a different world, doesn't it?'

Lily nodded. It did. Slower, simpler. But beneath the charm of it, there was something else: a weight, a history.

This is the last place my mother saw Rachel.

The thought made her chest tighten. She reached into her bag, pulled out her mother's notes and flipped through the delicate pages until she found the familiar passage about their time here.

They passed a small café, its name painted in elegant cursive on the window: CAFÉ DES AMIS. An older woman, her silver hair twisted into a loose chignon, was wiping down a table outside.

They approached and the woman looked up, her deep-set eyes sharp despite her years.

'Excuse me,' Lily said. 'I am researching my family history, and I was wondering if you might know anything about the raid that happened here during the war, including a group of children who may have sheltered here. There was a Resistance fighter who helped people hide.'

The woman's brow furrowed. For a moment, Lily thought she might dismiss them outright. But then she exhaled, setting the cloth down.

'My grandmother told me many stories about the war when I was a girl,' she said. 'But no details. Only that soldiers came, and that blood was spilled.'

Disappointment settled in Lily's chest, but she forced a grateful smile. 'Thank you,' she said, her voice quiet.

Julien nodded to the woman before gently steering Lily back toward the street.

'Well,' he said, 'at least we know the story still lingers here. That means there's something to find.'

Lily looked down at the notes again, flipping the pages as the two of them walked. The words glaring off in the sunlight, but then a detail caught her eye.

'My mother wrote about a place in town,' she murmured, stopping short.

She read aloud. '*There was an old fountain, covered in moss. We were allowed to play near it, and I always thought it looked magical, like something out of a fairy tale.*'

She looked up. 'She also mentions that it was close to where they hid.'

They walked for a while looking for the fountain, and

nearly gave up hope. Julien had just suggested they go and get a drink at a local bar when she spotted it.

It was nestled between two weathered old houses, its basin now dry and silent. The edges were thickly draped in vibrant green moss.

'This,' Lily whispered, her voice tinged with awe and breathlessness, 'this could be where the children came.'

She moved closer, her fingers gently skimming the worn pages again.

We would drink from the fountain, and then walk across the road to go home, and we used to pick the little white flowers that grew near the cottage. Rachel liked them best.

Her head snapped up, her eyes scanning the landscape with renewed purpose. A vibrant array of wildflowers edged the side of the road in bursts of colour.

Nearby, an older woman was tending to her garden, pulling weeds with steady hands. Lily approached her, asking if she knew anything about the house her mother had described in her journal pages.

The woman spoke with a voice heavy with deep, reverent fear, and gestured towards an abandoned house a little way off. 'That house is evil. No one lives there. People died there.'

Lily's heart pounded faster. Was Rachel one of the 'people' the woman referred to?

She pressed her for details, but the woman dismissed her questions with a shrug, as if speaking of it might somehow bring a curse upon her.

Lily felt it – an undeniable pull. Something about the house the woman had mentioned called to her, drawing her inexorably forward.

She stepped carefully down the overgrown path and pushed open the half-rotten wooden gate. The air inside was cooler, the scent of musty damp stones and dust filling her nose.

They stepped into what had once been a living space, now filled only with silence and remnants of a past life.

A jolt of recognition went through her as her eyes landed on the fireplace.

It was identical to the one her mother had described, the stonework uneven, the wooden mantel dark with age.

She could almost hear children's laughter, the whispered warnings of their Resistance guardian.

Then, just as they were about to leave, a shadow fell across the doorway.

A voice, rough with age, but steady.

'The woman at the café told me you were here. Are you looking for the little girl who went missing?'

Lily whirled around.

An older man stood in the doorway, his lined face expectant.

Lily felt the air leave her lungs.

The little girl who went missing.

Was he talking about Rachel? Her heart leapt with anticipation.

'Do you know something about the children who were here during the war?' she asked, her pulse pounding in her ears, the words catching in her throat.

The man studied them, his gaze sharp despite his age. Then, after a long pause, he murmured, 'My name is Gus. Come to my house in the morning. There's something very important you need to see.'

He shoved a piece of crumpled paper with a scribbled address on it towards them.

And with that, he turned and disappeared down the road.

14

PARIS, OCTOBER 1940

Claudette

The morning light filtered through the sheer ivory drapes of Claudette Mercier's apartment, casting an amber glow across the polished parquet floor.

Claudette sat at the dining table, her stage notes abandoned, stirring her ration of coffee with slow, deliberate movements, though she had yet to take a sip. Today, it brought no comfort. Her mind was elsewhere, back at the theatre, where the memory of the raid during rehearsals still felt raw and jagged.

The image of Jean-Paul's terrified face as they dragged him past her haunted her. She had watched, frozen, as everyone fell into stunned silence. She knew that Jean-Paul and Gigi were good friends, and she doubted they would ever see each other again.

She clenched her jaw, pressing a hand against her forehead. She knew it wasn't as important, but something bigger gnawed at her inside, something much closer to home. That thought twisted in her gut, bringing with it a marrow-deep fear. If Lifar resisted, if anyone at the theatre did, if they refused to bend to the Germans, they would shut the theatre down. And if that happened...

A chill ran through her body.

She had spent too many years fighting to get where she was. She had clawed her way from nothing to a career as a stage manager, a life she loved. She would not let anyone take it from her.

A memory surfaced, unbidden and unwelcome.

The scent of damp stone and mildew, the cramped, darkened room where she and Philippe had huddled as children. Their mother's worn hands sorting scraps of cloth, trying to stitch together something she could sell for a few centimes. The sharp pangs of hunger that had gnawed at Claudette's insides so often they had become a part of her.

She had sworn, long ago, that she would never be poor again.

Just then, a loud knock at the door shattered the quiet. She exhaled sharply, pushing the thoughts away.

The knock came again, precise. Impatient.

Her heart thumped heavily against her ribs as she stood, smoothing the silk of her dressing gown against her form and drawing it close against the autumn chill. She crossed the room with measured grace, but inside her mind raced.

She unlocked the door and pulled it open.

Her brother Philippe stood in the doorway in his French policeman's uniform. Her stomach twisted. She couldn't believe she had just been thinking about him and their childhood. It had been years since she had last seen him.

The navy fabric was crisp but worn, reflecting long days in occupied Paris. Brass buttons lined his high-collared tunic, and a leather belt with a holstered gun cinched his waist. His kepi, marked with the police insignia, sat firmly on his head, its visor casting a shadow over his brow.

In a state of shock, she stared at him, noticing that the rich brown of his eyes had lost the warmth they once shared. Instead, they carried a hardened, distant gaze, a testament to the divergent paths they had taken in response to their upbringing. While she had been driven to overachieve, striving for success and recognition as a way to rise above their past, he had been propelled toward a simmering desire for revenge, a relentless pursuit to settle the scores of the injustice he had endured.

'Philippe, this is very unexpected.'

His face broke into a rakish grin as he moved past her without waiting for an invitation, observing her apartment with cool indifference, eyeing her belongings as if assessing her worth.

'Did you miss me?' he challenged, lifting a vase to check underneath, as if gauging its value.

Philippe never made casual visits, and his sudden reappearance had triggered a deep fear in the pit of her stomach.

'What are you doing here?' she asked; her voice held a mixture of irritation and caution as she watched him closely.

Ignoring her, he continued. 'You've done well for yourself, haven't you, *ma sœur?*'

'I've worked hard for what I have,' she replied, her voice measured, but laced with an edge.

He chuckled, slow and deliberate, as he removed his cap and made himself comfortable in one of her chairs.

'Is that what you tell yourself?' He turned, his gaze locking onto hers, sharp as a knife.

She didn't like what he was insinuating. But before she could respond, he spoke again.

'Not even an offer of a cup of coffee for your only brother after all these years?'

Claudette's jaw tensed as she poured him a cup, the task giving her a moment to collect her thoughts. She placed the steaming cup in front of him, her expression guarded.

'What do you want, Philippe?' Her voice was firm, demanding an answer without pretence.

He blew on the liquid, taking his time while she waited.

'You always like to get straight to the point. I like that about you,' he finally said. He took a sip, then continued. 'The authorities sent me back to work in this area of Paris.'

Claudette's eyes narrowed with suspicion. Philippe never made casual visits, and his sudden reappearance had triggered a deep fear in the pit of her stomach.

'I will be working alongside Obersturmführer Gerhard Neumann, the new German officer in charge of enforcing curfews and overseeing security in this sector.'

'And what does that have to do with me, Philippe?' Claudette's voice was steady, a veil of steel coating her words as she stared at her brother.

'The Palais Garnier comes under that jurisdiction. And I'm looking to score points, I'm due a promotion.'

Her stomach tightened at the mention of the beloved theatre she worked at. She glared at him. 'So?'

He took another large gulp of his coffee before speaking again. 'I want someone on the inside. Someone I can trust.'

'Ah,' she scoffed, the penny finally dropping. 'And you think *I'm* that person? A person who will spy on my colleagues, my friends?'

Philippe chuckled, darkly, as he leaned back in the chair and placed his cup on her polished side table, where it was certain to leave a mark.

He plucked an apple from the bowl without asking, taking his time to reply as he casually polished it on his sleeve before biting into it.

'I was wondering how the members of the board at the Palais Garnier would feel if they knew some of the sordid things you have done in the past, including falsifying your papers to get the job?'

Claudette's stomach twisted, but she kept her face composed. 'I earned my place.'

'You *cheated* for your place.' His voice was mild, but the weight of the words landed heavy between them.

She clenched her jaw. 'I did what I had to do. No one was going to hand me an opportunity, not someone from where we came from. You know that. I've changed since then, and I've worked hard to become who I am today.'

'Then perhaps the board at the theatre would be more interested in your other little secret.'

Her pulse slammed. 'You wouldn't.'

He sat back, almost leisurely. 'Why not? A stage manager getting pregnant with her own stepfather. Imagine the scandal.'

'I did not sleep with him.' Claudette's voice broke. 'He *raped* me. You know that.'

Philippe's shrug was merciless. 'That is your side of the story. Others might prefer a different version. Rich people care about appearances, and appearances,' he said with a smirk, 'can ruin you.'

Her whole body went cold. The pregnancy had nearly destroyed her once already. If he revealed it now, every scrap of respect she had earned would crumble.

A noise outside on the balcony made Philippe pause. He stood, sauntered to the window and pulled back Claudette's heavy, expensive drapes.

'Ahh, your *friends*, no doubt,' he said, watching them closely as he continued to eat his apple.

Claudette's mind reeled as she tried to comprehend all he was saying. She absently followed his gaze, watching the morning rituals of her fellow tenants play out.

Gigi leaned against the railing, her cardigan pulled tight against the cold, her red curls catching the sunlight as, below, the voice of Pierre the flower vendor echoed up. 'Eternally yours, Gigi!' he declared with the same theatrical devotion as he did every morning.

A few feet away, Eloise knelt by her collection of potted herbs, her hands deep in the dark soil as she repotted a sprig of lavender, fingerless gloves protecting her hands from the chill. The wind stirred the loose strands of her dark curls, and she looked entirely at peace, focused on her work.

And then there was Malina, seated cross-legged on a cushion on the floor, one foot tapping idly against the iron balcony rail as she read aloud from the newspaper.

'Interesting girls,' Philippe continued, his tone calculating.

Malina's voice could be heard from outside.

'They're rounding up more people in the Marais,' she announced, her expression dark with frustration. 'Families. Children. Vanishing overnight.' Her hands clenched around the newspaper. 'They call it "relocation".' She scoffed bitterly. 'But we know what it really is.' She tapped a headline about the new anti-Jewish statutes that had posted the month before.

Philippe watched her with interest. 'She has opinions, doesn't she, that Malina?'

Claudette balked. *How does he know her name?*

He continued, as if reading her mind. 'Malina Laurent-Masson, born 1912 in Lyon, cradled in wealth from her first breath, though you would never know it to look at her.' He recoiled with disdain. 'She works as an artist, if you can call her angry pictures art. She has a reputation for being quite vocal about her dislike for the current political climate. Quite the firebrand, I'd say. Not like Eloise over there – she is more of a mystery just waiting to be unravelled.'

Claudette forced herself to breathe evenly, remembering Eloise's confession of being Jewish. She thought again of Jean-Paul being dragged away and desperately wanted to protect her friend. Philippe had come prepared. He was telling her what would happen if she didn't comply: he would go after the people she most cared about, and she could never let that happen. As if hearing her thoughts, he continued.

'It pays to know the value of the people around you, doesn't it, Claudette?' Philippe's voice was oily, almost taunting as he turned from the window and fixed her with a predatory gleam.

'What information do you want from me, Philippe?' she asked through gritted teeth, her voice tight with suppressed anger.

A slow smile spread across his face, devoid of any warmth. 'Anything out of the ordinary, people or situations that might be of concern for the current ruling forces. Nothing too difficult for a clever woman like you.'

Claudette felt the weight of his words pressing down on her, suffocating her with their implications. Her mind raced, trying to find a way out of this dangerous dance he was leading her into. She glanced at the women outside, each engrossed in their own activities, unaware of the storm brewing inside her home.

With a deep breath to steady herself, Claudette fixed Philippe with a steely gaze. 'I won't betray my friends. Not for you, not for *anyone*,' she declared, her voice firm and unwavering.

'No one is asking you to betray anyone. Just keep your ears open, Claudette. It's a simple request, really,' Philippe replied, his tone calculated and persuasive as he threw the apple core down onto her cream tablecloth and picked up his hat.

'It's been nice seeing you again, *ma petite sœur*,' he sneered, his voice dripping with condescension, as he strode confidently toward the door.

The door slammed behind him, leaving a silence that seemed to swallow the room whole.

15

PARIS, OCTOBER 1940

Gigi

The wardrobe department of the Palais Garnier was a world of fabric, silks and velvets that swayed like ghosts from overstuffed racks as Madame Fleurette worked at her station, her needle darting with ruthless precision.

Gigi stood on a wooden platform in the centre of the room, arms outstretched, as Eloise knelt before her, pinning a fresh length of trim to the hem of her gown. 'You're fidgeting,' Eloise muttered, biting off a thread. 'Do you want me to stab you?'

'I can't help it.' Gigi sighed dramatically. 'I have a lot on my mind.'

'Ah, let me guess.' Eloise smirked as she secured another pin. 'Your gallant rescuer?'

Gigi rolled her eyes, but the heat creeping up her neck betrayed her. 'He wasn't my rescuer.'

'No? Because from where I was standing, he swept you away from that Nazi like a hero in a novel.' Eloise sat back on her heels, grinning. 'And *mon Dieu*, he was handsome.'

Madame Fleurette let out a scoffing noise from her worktable. 'Men were always chivalrous in my day,' she muttered, threading her needle with an exaggerated sigh. 'You should have seen the gentlemen who courted me when I was younger.'

Eloise arched a brow. 'Oh? And were *you* ever saved by a mysterious stranger?'

A knowing smile tugged at the corner of Madame Fleurette's lips as she focused on her stitching. 'Many times,' she said wistfully.

Both girls leaned in, intrigued.

'And did you fall madly in love?' Gigi asked.

Madame Fleurette lifted her gaze, her dark eyes twinkling with mischief. 'Many times,' she repeated, her voice tinged with something wistful. 'I never forgot all my loves.'

For a moment, the room was silent except for the quiet snip of scissors and the rustling of fabric. Then Madame Fleurette shook her head and returned to her work. 'Men were different back then, more romantic.'

Eloise turned back to Gigi, raising her brows suggestively. 'I don't know... this was pretty romantic.'

Gigi huffed. 'It was one dance, Eloise.'

'Yes, one dance with a man who pulled you out of the hands of a Nazi.'

Gigi ignored the warmth blooming in her chest. 'I just want to know who he is, that's all.'

Madame Fleurette let out a noise of approval. 'Describe him.'

Gigi's description spilled out: 'Tall, sandy-coloured hair, thick, unruly, like he's always running his hands through it. Sharp cheekbones, and his eyes so blue but also...' She frowned, trying to put it into words. 'There was something about them. Mischievous, maybe? But like there was something... *deeper* underneath.'

Madame Fleurette's hand stilled mid-stitch.

For a moment, she didn't say anything. Then, she exhaled

and shook her head. 'I think you might be talking about Olivier Moreau. I saw him there at the party.'

Gigi's stomach flipped. 'You know him?'

Madame Fleurette nodded slowly. 'I knew his mother.'

The room seemed to tighten around them.

Gigi glanced at Eloise, whose expression mirrored her own curiosity. 'Tell us more, we want to know everything!'

Madame Fleurette sighed, setting down her needle and finally looking up. 'He's had a difficult life, that one.'

Eloise perked up. 'What happened?'

Madame Fleurette picked up her work again, her eyes sharp beneath her spectacles. 'If it was him, you'll know soon enough. Olivier isn't someone to remain in the shadows.'

Gigi didn't have long to wait. The next morning, she arrived early at the theatre for some extra rehearsal time before the rest of the dancers flooded in. She had been struggling with part of the routine and wanted time to practise alone.

Haunting melody drifted through the corridors of the Palais Garnier, curling around the stone arches and slipping through the air. The notes were soft, yet commanding, melancholic and full of longing. Gigi paused outside the rehearsal room, drawn in by the sound, like a thread pulling her forward.

Through the crack in the doorway, she spotted him.

The man who had saved her sat at the grand piano, his fingers gliding effortlessly over the keys. He was completely lost in the music, his sandy hair flopping over his eyes, caught in a world of his own making. The dim rehearsal light cast golden shadows across his face, accentuating the sharp angles of his jaw.

Gigi leaned against the doorway, watching.

It was rare to see someone so unguarded. So consumed.

The moment she stepped inside, his hands slowed.

'You didn't introduce yourself the other night,' she said, folding her arms.

His smile curved, faint but knowing. Without looking up, his fingers traced a languid chord across the keys, coaxing out a melody that sent shivers up her spine.

'Didn't I?'

Her brow furrowed. 'No. You didn't.'

He glanced up. His eyes, of the deepest blue, made her stomach tighten a little as he stared at her with amusement. 'Then tell me, who would you like me to be? It might be far more interesting than who I really am.'

She arched an eyebrow. 'I'd prefer the truth.'

A soft laugh escaped him, low and unhurried. 'The truth? The truth is my reputation is nothing compared to yours, Gigi Valette.'

Her name on his lips sent a shiver through her. 'You know who I am, then?'

'Who in Paris doesn't?' His gaze lingered, deliberate. 'The way you command a stage, every movement so precise and so beautiful, capable of undoing a man. When you danced last night, you left me wondering whether it was choreography or sorcery that made me forget to breathe.'

Colour warmed her cheeks despite herself. She tried for composure. 'You're very practised at compliments.'

His smile deepened. 'Compliments are cheap. You asked for the truth.'

The words hung between them, heavier now, charged with something more dangerous than flattery.

A slow smile spread across his face as his fingers stilled on the keys. He leaned back slightly, plucked the waiting cigarette from the ashtray perched on the piano, and took a deliberate drag. Smoke curled upward, veiling his expression.

The air crackled with tension as Gigi stood beside him, close enough to feel the heat of his body.

She studied him, taking in the way his eyes held a depth she couldn't quite decipher. There was a flicker of vulnerability there, hidden beneath layers of confidence.

'Olivier Moreau,' he said easily, inclining his head as he held out his hand. 'Composer. And occasional ballroom saviour, nice to meet you.'

His hand was warm and soft, fingers entwining with hers in a gesture that felt strangely intimate.

She gasped with surprise; Madame Fleurette had been right. 'And what exactly are you composing?'

Olivier's smirk deepened. 'The Germans have hired me to score their new ballets.'

Gigi stiffened. Her arms folded tighter across her chest. 'So, you're working for them?'

He lifted a shoulder in an effortless shrug. 'A man has to survive.'

The words hung in the air, ambiguous.

Gigi's instincts screamed that there was more to him than he was letting on. His expression was too carefully composed, his body too relaxed for someone whose livelihood depended on pleasing the occupiers.

But she had learned long ago that secrets were currency in Paris these days. And Olivier Moreau seemed rich in them.

'You didn't ask what the piece was called,' he noted.

She raised her eyebrows, questioningly.

His hands ghosted over the keys once more, coaxing the final notes with reverence. Then his gaze met hers, something flickering behind his dark eyes.

'It's called "The Dancer in the Shadows".' His voice was softer now, almost solemn. 'I wrote it last night, after I left you.'

The weight of the words pressed against her ribs as their eyes met, and he broke into a rakish smile that undercut the gravity, leaving her unsteady.

All at once, a harsh voice cut through the dim hush of the room.

'*Giselle!*'

Only one person in the world called her by her full name like that.

She stopped and turned toward the voice, her spine straightening. Jacques Leclerc, her ballet teacher, stood in the doorway.

'I need to speak to you,' he continued in a commanding way.

When she entered the corridor, he pulled her aside, his arms folded, his gaze sharp beneath his thick brows.

'You need to be careful,' he said, his voice low. 'I saw you with him at the party, too.'

Gigi lifted her chin, feigning innocence. 'I hardly know him, we just met. Why do I have to be careful?'

Jacques's mouth pressed into a firm line. 'Whatever you think he is, he isn't.'

Gigi narrowed her eyes. 'And what do you think he is?'

She expected Jacques to give her an answer, to confirm or deny the concern curling in her stomach.

But he didn't.

Instead, his expression darkened, his jaw tightening as he shook his head. 'Just know that some doors shouldn't be opened, Gigi.'

With that, he turned and disappeared down the hall, his footsteps heavy against the wooden floors.

Gigi felt full of fear at Jacques's stern warning; he had never cared who her friends were before. When she turned to look back into the studio, Olivier had already left via the side door. Her pulse was thrumming in her throat.

Why did everybody speak so mysteriously about him?

. . .

After the final curtain call that evening, and with the roar of the audience still thrumming through her veins, Gigi made her way back to the dressing room, her mind still racing with her memories of Olivier from earlier that day.

The adrenaline of the performance clung to her skin, mixing with her stage make-up and perspiration. The Palais Garnier was alive with the excitement of a good performance. The raised voices of other dancers in the corridors, the distant hum of the musicians congratulating one another in the orchestra pit, and the audience talking animatedly about all they had experienced, made it a world that lived and breathed beyond the stage.

She unpinned her headdress, fingers deftly working through her curls. Then something caught her eye.

A small envelope, tucked neatly into the corner of her mirror.

Gigi's breath hitched.

Her name was written on the front in a elegant, confident hand.

She glanced over her shoulder, heart pounding, but the corridor outside was empty save for a few tired stagehands, yawning as they reset the stage.

Turning back, she slid her finger beneath the seal and pulled out a folded sheet of paper.

But it wasn't paper.

It was sheet music.

Her eyes traced the notes and she instantly recognised them. 'The Dancer in the Shadows'. The same melody Olivier had played that morning in the rehearsal room.

At the bottom, in small, careful script, was a single line.

Meet me on the rooftop of the opera house at midnight tomorrow.

This was way past curfew. Being caught on the roof after midnight could be dangerous.

Gigi's pulse fluttered.

The Palais Garnier's rooftop.

An unusual meeting place. Dangerous, even.

But a thrill laced through her nerves, uncoiling something inside her.

She felt like Olivier Moreau was playing a game with her.

And against all reason, she found herself wanting to play.

16

PARIS, SUMMER 2011

Lily

Under the moonlight, the sea outside Lily's window churned restlessly. The words of the older man rolled around in her mind. What little girl had he been talking about?

The waves crashing on the cliffs seem to amplify her inner turmoil as she stared at the ceiling. Sleep refused to come.

After dinner, she and Julien had lingered on the terrace, the warmth of the evening wrapping around them as they talked, truly talked, for the first time since they had arrived. Under the soft glow of lantern light, he had opened up, sharing stories of his past, his voice low and thoughtful.

'I was in love once,' he admitted, tracing the rim of his glass with a fingertip. 'A few years ago. We talked about a future together, about forever. But love isn't always enough, is it?'

Lily studied him. 'What happened?'

Julien gave a small, almost self-deprecating laugh. 'She left. Said she needed to find herself before she settled down.'

Lily's heart twisted. 'I'm sorry.'

'It was a long time ago,' he said with a shrug, but something in his eyes told her the wound had never fully healed. 'But enough about my failed romance. What about you and Marcus? You said he was always busy with work – is everything okay with you both?'

The question settled heavily between them.

Lily hesitated, swirling the last of her wine. 'I don't know any more,' she admitted softly. 'He used to tell me everything, but now it feels like there's a wall between us. And the more I try to get close, the more he pulls away.'

She had looked out over the sea then, feeling the weight of her own words. Julien had only nodded, not pushing her further, just letting her sit with her thoughts.

Now, alone in her room, Lily picked up her phone and dialled Marcus's number. It rang once. Then straight to voicemail.

She squeezed her eyes shut as she listened to the automated message.

'*You've reached Marcus. Leave a message, and I'll get back to you.*'

The familiar beep echoed in her ears. She hesitated, then pressed end call.

Tears pricked at the edges of her vision.

The next morning, she met Julien for breakfast and they made their way to the older man's house.

The salty breeze carried the scent of the sea as Lily and Julien navigated the narrow stone path leading to Gus's small cottage. It sat perched on a gentle slope overlooking the water, the kind of place built to withstand time itself, its shutters weathered but sturdy, its garden neatly tended. Beyond the garden wall the Mediterranean stretched out in endless blue, waves shimmering beneath the morning sun.

Gus greeted them and gestured for them to follow him with

the slow, measured steps of a man who had seen too much, and carried the weight of memories that refused to fade. He pointed toward a set of wicker chairs on the patio, which was shaded by a wooden pergola heavy with climbing vines.

'Sit,' he said, his voice rough but not unkind. 'If you've come looking for ghosts, you might as well be comfortable while I tell you about them.'

Julien pulled out a chair for Lily before settling into one beside her. The warmth of the stone underfoot radiated the heat of the morning, and a jug of water with slices of lemon and sprigs of fresh mint rested on the table between them. Gus poured them each a glass, then sat back, eyes drifting toward the sea, as if searching for something only he could see.

Lily's heart raced. The past had never felt so near.

'You said you had something to share,' she prompted gently.

Gus exhaled deeply, running a hand over his stubbled chin. 'I knew the children who came here during the war. I remember them arriving and the shocking way they left.'

Lily drew in and held her breath as he continued.

'I remember the raid. That was a bad night,' he murmured. 'The war had taken so much from us already, but that night... it stole something different.'

He took a slow sip of water before continuing.

'There were children in that house. I remember them well. We all did. Always creeping through the square, playing near the fountain. There was a boy, maybe six or seven, fair-haired and full of mischief. Another boy, older, with a sour face, always complaining about something. There was a dark-haired girl, maybe nine, never without a battered teddy bear tucked under her arm. And then there were the twins,' Gus said, his gaze shifting toward her. 'Dark hair, dark eyes. Maybe ten years old. They were inseparable, always whispering to each other, picking wildflowers near the water's edge. They were careful, though. Always watching, as if they were waiting for something terrible to happen.'

A shiver passed through Lily, despite the warmth of the day.

'The night the Germans came,' Gus continued, his voice heavier now, 'we woke to the sound of screams. And then... gunfire.'

A hush fell over the patio, the weight of his words pressing into the space between them.

'We were afraid,' he admitted. 'No one dared go near that house until morning. When we did, the place was ruined. Blood on the floor. Bullet holes in the walls. And the children...' His voice dropped to almost a whisper. 'Gone.'

Lily swallowed hard. 'All of them?'

Gus nodded slowly. 'All except one.'

The wind stirred through the vines above them, sending dappled shadows across the stone.

'We found her in the wreckage,' he said. 'One of the twins. She was alive, but barely. She wouldn't speak, wouldn't eat at first. Just sat curled up in the corner, waiting for someone to come back for her.'

Lily's hands tightened in her lap.

'My wife and I took her in, nursed her back to health,' Gus said. 'We had no children of our own. We told ourselves we'd care for her until her family found her.'

'But they never did,' Lily murmured.

Gus shook his head. 'She told us she had no family left in this world. She missed her sister, but believed she must too be dead. Rachel believed she was alone in the world.'

Lily's breath caught. The name rang in her chest. Her mother's twin. To hear it now, alive in someone else's mouth, made her real somehow.

His voice softened. 'As days turned into weeks, we thought we'd raise her as our own. And then one day... she was gone.'

'Gone?' Julien asked, frowning. 'What do you mean?'

'Vanished,' Gus said simply. 'We searched everywhere, asked everyone. But no one saw her leave, no one knew where she went.'

With careful fingers, he pulled out a small, yellowed image from a folded envelope and placed it on the table. The photograph was worn soft at the corners, the paper thinned from decades of handling. Julien leaned closer, but Lily hesitated.

The girl in the picture was standing just outside Gus's house. A rough wooden shutter hung crooked behind her. Lily stared at the image, trying to focus through the haze of emotion. The girl had dark, intelligent eyes and thick hair that curled slightly at the edges, so much like her mother's. She wore a worn wool cardigan that looked too big for her, sleeves pushed up to the elbows, and her expression was part defiance, part fear.

Julien leaned in, frowning. He turned to Gus. 'Do you have a magnifying glass?'

Gus nodded and shuffled off to another room, where he could be heard rummaging in a drawer.

Lily whispered to Julien as they waited. 'It proves nothing. He's old. Memories blur. That could just be a picture of my mother while she was here for all we know.'

Gus produced an ancient magnifying glass with a scratched brass rim.

Julien held it over the picture and went very still.

'Lily,' he said quietly, 'did your mother ever injure her hand? Do something that left a scar?'

She blinked, confused. 'No...'

Wordlessly, Julien shifted the photograph so she could see it under the magnifier.

There it was. Just visible, a pale crescent-shaped scar on the girl's right hand, cutting through the skin between thumb and forefinger.

Lily's breath caught in her throat.

This was not her mother.

She leaned back in her seat, her hand trembling as she pressed her palm to her chest.

It was Rachel with a small scar on her right hand. A scar her mother didn't have.

A wave of emotion crashed over her, stealing her breath.

Here was a photo of the sister her mother had never stopped believing was alive.

Julien's hand rested lightly on her forearm, grounding her.

'I think it is her,' she said softly.

Julien nodded, unable to speak.

A silence stretched between them, filled only by the distant cries of gulls overhead.

Finally, Lily turned to Gus. Her voice came out steadier than she expected. 'Thank you,' she said. 'For everything you did for her.'

Rachel hadn't been killed that night. She had survived.

Lily's throat tightened. 'Did you ever hear from her again?'

Gus sighed and shook his head, his weathered hands folding together.

Lily gripped the photo like a lifeline.

As they left Gus's cottage, the afternoon sky had begun to shift to gold, and the light casting long shadows over the village. Lily and Julien walked in silence toward the cliffs overlooking the sea, the discovery settling between them like something too fragile to touch.

Lily wrapped her arms around herself. Julien walked beside her, hands tucked into his pockets, eyes fixed on the endless horizon. Lily inhaled, the salt air filling her lungs.

Julien broke the silence. 'It's strange, isn't it? How a single photograph can change everything we thought we knew about the past.'

Lily nodded, her mind racing with questions and possibilities.

'I don't know where this will lead,' she admitted, her voice barely above a whisper. 'But I have to follow.'

Julien smiled softly, a quiet reassurance in his expression. 'Good, because I'm not letting you do this alone.'

Something about the certainty in his voice made her throat tighten. For a fleeting moment, she wanted to reach for his hand, to steady herself against the emotions threatening to pull her under. But instead, she hugged her cardigan tighter, grounding herself in the past, in Rachel.

Julien exhaled and turned back toward the sea. 'What do you want to do next?'

'Once I get back to Paris, I will continue researching.' They exchanged a look that communicated that neither of them were in a rush to leave this place, to let go of the tether that had brought them together.

'I have to go and see that client tomorrow,' he said with a hint of hesitation, 'so if you are okay to wait, I can travel with you to Paris in the afternoon?'

Lily nodded, but the assurance felt hollow. A strange, unexpected emptiness settled in her chest. The idea of leaving this place, of being without him back in Paris, was pulling something loose inside her. Then, her phone rang.

Marcus.

She stiffened, her fingers tightening around the device as she gestured to Julien that she needed to take the call. As she stepped away, a rush of emotions churned beneath her ribs: guilt, confusion, something dangerously close to longing. And for the first time in their marriage, she felt a pull towards someone other than her husband.

A yearning that left her deeply unsettled.

17

PARIS, OCTOBER 1940

Claudette

L'Asphodèle café was dingy and reeked of old smoke and bitter coffee. Claudette sat in the corner, an untouched mug before her, every nerve braced for Philippe. She shouldn't have come, but his note had made it clear she had no choice.

He arrived late, uniform immaculate, expression cool. He slid into the seat opposite, and set his gloves on the table with deliberate precision.

'You've had a week,' he said without greeting her. 'What have you learned?'

Claudette forced her voice to stay steady. 'Jean-Luc spoke of his daughter's birthday. Jacques visits a bakery during his breaks.'

Philippe's eyes narrowed. 'Trifles.'

'They're all I have. The theatre runs on discipline, people keep their heads down.'

He leaned in, voice soft, dangerous. 'I need more than scraps, Claudette. Do not mistake me. This isn't a request.'

She clenched her hands beneath the table. She had

promised herself she would give him only the safest fragments, meaningless details that betrayed no one. But even as she thought it, fear curdled in her stomach. He could destroy her with a word.

'Perhaps I was mistaken to expect more from you,' he said coldly, sliding a file across the table. A photograph slipped free: it was of a stagehand, Jean-Luc, caught mid-step outside a bookshop.

Claudette's throat closed. Jean-Luc, with his quiet smile and his little girls who adored the magic of backstage.

Philippe's gaze sharpened. 'This man is part of something larger. You will find out what. Or the theatre board may discover what you would prefer they never hear.' He rose, gathering his gloves. 'You will meet me here next week. Bring me something real.'

As he left, Claudette sat frozen, the weight of the photo burning her hands. She reminded herself: *Scraps only. Nothing more.*

But she wasn't sure how long she could keep him satisfied with just trifles.

18

PARIS, OCTOBER 1940

Gigi

The next night, the theatre emptied, and its marble halls echoing only with the faded hush of footsteps and the lingering scents of powder and rosin, Gigi slipped through a backstage passage, clutching her jacket, and climbed the narrow stairwell toward the roof.

At the final door she paused, drew a ragged breath and pushed it open.

The Palais Garnier's rooftop stretched before her, cloaked in shadow, slate tiles glowing under the moon. Paris shimmered below, endless and unknowable.

And then she saw him.

Olivier stood near the balustrade, jacket slung over one shoulder, the wind teasing his sandy curls. Her breath caught; something about the way he seemed to belong to the night sky sent heat rushing through her. She knew seeing him here was dangerous, in more ways than one.

He turned, a slow smile spreading. 'I was beginning to think you wouldn't come.' His low voice curled around her like an invitation.

'I wasn't sure I should,' she admitted, breathless, not from the climb but from the sight of him.

'I'm glad you did.'

For a moment they stood in silence, the city humming beneath them. Then he tipped his head toward the skyline. 'Listen.'

From across the boulevard, faint piano notes drifted from a glowing window. A nocturne, tender and aching, carried through the night.

'He plays when he can't sleep,' Olivier murmured. 'Sometimes I come up here just to listen. It's the only time Paris feels still.'

'It's beautiful,' Gigi whispered. 'Like he's searching for something.'

'Aren't we all?'

He turned to her, eyes catching the moonlight. 'Dance with me. Close your eyes, let the music guide you. I want to know how you move when no one's watching.'

Without thinking, she placed her hand in his.

He drew her toward the rooftop's centre. His hand at her back was not formal or practised but intimate, steady, warm. They began to move, no steps, no choreography, just trust. Their bodies brushed close, her pulse stumbling at the nearness of his cheek, the scent of brandy and citrus in his hair.

'You move like the music is inside you,' he whispered.

She couldn't answer. No one had ever seen her so unguarded.

When the last notes faded, they still didn't let go. Not at once. When they did, it was slow, reluctant.

Shaken, Gigi wrapped her arms around herself. Olivier reached for her hand again. 'There's something I want to show you.'

Her gaze flicked to the stairwell. 'I'm not sure I should...'

'Ah,' he said lightly, 'the warning bells.'

'You have a... reputation.'

'Jacques?' he guessed, smiling without surprise.

Her silence was answer enough.

Olivier leaned on the balustrade, looking out across Paris. 'No doubt he says I'm dangerous. And perhaps I am. But not in the way they think.' His eyes found hers again, unexpectedly vulnerable. 'There are many sides to a man. The one I show the world isn't always the one I live with.'

She hesitated, caught between reason and instinct.

'I won't claim I'm safe,' he said softly. 'But I would never let harm touch you. If you don't want to come, I'll take you back down, and you'll never see me again. But there is someone I want you to meet.'

Something in his tone, honest, unpressured, pulled her forward. She followed him down into the velvet-dark streets of Paris.

They slipped past checkpoints and shuttered cafés, through narrow lanes where shadows gathered. Olivier pointed things out as they walked: the courtyard where he once slept beneath a broken statue, a bar whose cellar led to secrets deeper than wine, a laundress who hummed jazz as she washed, who had taught him the rhythm of kindness.

Finally, he stopped before a green door tucked between a boulangerie and a closed bookstore. He knocked three times, then twice more. The door opened onto a stairwell lit with amber sconces, and laughter curling up to greet them.

Inside, the club pulsed like another world, velvet curtains, smoke, a trumpet's sultry cry. Patrons snapped their fingers in place of clapping, sequins flashing in the dim.

'You know everyone,' Gigi whispered.

'I've lived many lives,' Olivier said, eyes glinting.

And then a voice rose from the shadows of the side curtain.

'Well, well, well. Look who is here. Olivier Moreau.'

The crowd parted.

Joséphine Duval, the famous nightclub singer, stepped into the light. Even out of costume she radiated magnetism, her eyes sharp, her mouth curled in something between amusement and suspicion. Her dark skin glistened with the heat.

Olivier bowed slightly. 'Mademoiselle Duval. May I introduce Gigi Valette?'

Joséphine's gaze swept over Gigi like a searchlight, assessing and appraising. Then she smiled, dazzling and fierce.

'Ah, the ballerina,' she said. 'I've heard of you.'

Gigi felt her cheeks flush. 'You have?'

'Oh darling, there's not much I don't hear.'

She offered her hand. Gigi took it, surprised at the strength of the grip.

The music shifted, slow, sultry jazz drifting through the haze of the club. A server appeared with a silver tray, delivering a trio of mismatched glasses and a bottle of something deep amber.

'Rum,' Olivier explained as he poured generously. 'The real kind. Smuggled in from Marseille.'

Joséphine raised her glass. 'To good company in low places.'

They clinked glasses, and Gigi took a cautious sip. The burn was immediate, but the warmth that followed eased some of the tension winding through her chest. Around them, the club moved like a dream, musicians tuning up for another set, couples laughing over candlelit tables, the weight of war held at bay by smoke and song.

Joséphine studied her over the rim of her glass. 'You're not like the others.'

Gigi blinked. 'What do you mean?'

'The girls on the stage. Most of them keep their heads down. Dance, smile, survive. But you...' She gestured, a lazy circle with her glass. 'You *feel* everything.'

Gigi wasn't sure how to respond. The compliment unnerved her as much as it thrilled her.

'She's braver than she knows,' Olivier said simply.

They drank and talked as the hours stretched gently forward. Joséphine told stories of the early days in Paris, the glamour, the danger, the moments of reckless beauty before the city fell under grey uniforms and black boots.

'I once danced with a prince,' she said with a grin. 'He said I was the only reason he stayed in France that winter.'

'What happened to him?' Gigi asked.

Joséphine shrugged. 'He ran. I stayed.'

Her eyes flicked to Gigi, suddenly serious. 'That's the thing about war. When things get dark, you learn who runs and who fights.'

The words settled into the quiet between them, pressing gently against the edges of Gigi's resolve.

Then Joséphine leaned in, her voice lower now, her expression steady. 'I have a question for you.'

Gigi's breath caught.

Joséphine's gaze locked with hers, unwavering. 'Do you only dance for applause? Or are you willing to dance for... something more?'

Beside her, Olivier shifted, suddenly ill at ease.

Gigi blinked, the question lingering in the smoky air between them.

'Dance for something more?' she repeated slowly, uncertain whether it was a metaphor or a test.

Joséphine leaned back, fingers drumming lightly against the base of her glass. 'Not everyone can. Not everyone should. But I have friends, girls like you, who've learned to dance in shadow. Who know how to listen for what's not being said.' Her voice softened.

Gigi's heart thudded. Malina's face flashed in her mind, the way she had leaned across the table at le Chat Noir, her voice fierce and urgent as she spoke of saving Paris. Gigi had dismissed her then, but now... now it didn't feel quite so far-fetched.

'You're... part of the Resistance?'

Joséphine paused. 'I'm part of something that says *no*. And sometimes, that comes wrapped in dance shoes and sequins.'

Olivier sat quietly beside her now. The mischief had drained from his eyes, replaced by something closer to concern.

Joséphine continued, 'We dance, we distract, we smuggle, we pass messages.'

Gigi sat frozen, caught somewhere between disbelief and something dangerously close to exhilaration.

Joséphine watched her for a beat, then smiled knowingly. 'I've seen your kind of fire before. It either gets snuffed out or turned into something unforgettable.'

But before Gigi could answer, Olivier's voice cut gently through the air.

'I don't think she would be the right fit.'

Both women turned to look at him. He didn't flinch under Joséphine's raised eyebrow.

'I mean it,' he said quietly, now looking only at Gigi. 'You're an artist. An incredible dancer. That's your strength. Let someone else play this game.'

Gigi's jaw tightened. 'You think I can't handle it?'

'No,' he said, gently. 'I think you shouldn't have to.'

The words landed more heavily than she expected. Joséphine said nothing, only watched them both with a curious glint in her eye.

Gigi forced a smile and lifted her glass. 'To the shadows, then.'

'To the dancer in them,' Olivier replied with a knowing nod toward Gigi.

Joséphine's voice was softer this time, almost an apology. 'And to not getting lost in the dark.'

Outside, the air was sharp with the scent of rain on warm stone, the city slicked with moonlight and distant jazz. Gigi and Olivier stepped into the quiet night, Gigi's heels clicking softly on the cobblestones.

They didn't speak at first. The silence between them buzzed with everything that had been said and everything that hadn't.

Gigi glanced at him. 'That was... not what I expected.'

Olivier gave a wry half-smile. 'Joséphine rarely is.'

They walked in step, Paris folding around them like a soft velvet curtain. Gigi hugged her coat tighter. Malina's voice came rushing back to her, reminding her that no one was going to save them, and if they wanted their city back they would have to save it themselves.

'Do you really think I couldn't do it?'

He looked over, eyes shaded in the glow of the moon. 'I think you already have the courage. I just don't want you to throw everything away for this war.'

She hesitated. 'You're protecting me?'

'Or maybe I just want you to keep dancing for yourself, not for some cause that doesn't deserve your soul—'

'I don't need your protection.'

'I'm sure you don't. I just know more of what's going on here, and I ask you to think hard before you agree to do anything that could jeopardise everything you have worked for. There isn't much dancing in jail.'

They reached her building. She stopped at the bottom of the steps and turned to him.

'Olivier... what do you want from me?'

He smiled faintly, but his voice was serious. 'Whatever you want to give.'

'And what do you want to give right now?' she whispered.

He stepped closer, his voice low. 'Right now?' His gaze dropped to her lips, then lifted slowly. 'I want to kiss you.'

She swallowed, her heart hammering.

He moved slowly, as if afraid to break the spell. His hand slid gently around her waist, his other brushing the side of her jaw. When his lips met hers, it was quiet, tender, like an inhale held too long, finally released. He smelled of fresh night air and citrus, and there was the faintest trace of rum on his breath. His thumb found the hollow just below her ear and her pulse leapt to meet it. He pulled her in closer and his heartbeat was steady against her palm, not hurried, simply sure.

And then it deepened.

He breathed out against her lower lip, a soft, disbelieving sigh that warmed her mouth, slow and even, a quiet yes that she felt as much as heard. He was tender, yet masterful, seeming to know what would give her the most pleasure.

She had never been kissed like this before. Heat unspooled low in her belly, and her knees went loose until the wall steadied her.

Her palm found his shoulder; the wool was warm under her fingers, and her skin came away damp with her own sweat. She felt that if he stopped now she might forget how to breathe; if he kept going she knew she would. Thoughts tried to rise, neat and sensible, and then with his gentle caress every thought fell quiet, and she let the world narrow to that steady thrum.

When they parted, she was breathless, her skin flushed. Her fingers were shaking, not from fear, but from the shock of being wanted like this.

He rested his forehead to hers for a beat, his breath a pale cloud between them, and a low, helpless yes caught in his throat, the kind that comes when one has a desire for much more. He drew a steady breath, let the heat soften, then he gently pulled back and the old mischief returned to his eyes; and he offered a crooked, easy smile.

'Goodnight, Gigi,' he murmured. 'I'm going to be gone for a while, to Germany, but I know we will meet again.' His thumb brushed her lower lip once more, and then he turned away and vanished into the shadows.

Gigi stood motionless.

She leaned back against the wall, pressing her fingertips to her mouth. There was something untamed about Olivier Moreau, something that frightened her. But what scared her more was how much of herself she saw reflected in that wildness.

And how much she wanted to follow it.

19

FRANCE, SUMMER 2011

Lily

The train carriage seemed to exist outside of time, a pause between everything she had learned and whatever lay ahead in Paris.

Julien sat across from her, his satchel balanced on his knees, his fingers tracing the strap absently. The air between them carried the warmth of familiarity and a current of tension, as if both were waiting for the other to cross an invisible line. His gaze flicked to hers, then away, the barest hesitation that made her pulse quicken.

Lily, desperate to displace the charged air between them, asked a question. 'Tell me more about your grandfather.'

His voice dropped lower, and Lily felt the intimacy of it settle over her like a blanket.

'He always said the war stole his chance to build a normal life. A home. More children. Sometimes I wonder if I've been doing the same, hiding behind my work.'

Her breath caught. The raw honesty in his tone pierced something in her chest. Lily's heart went out to him, aching at the thought of this man carrying both his grandfather's regrets and his own solitude.

'Do you want a family of your own?' she asked softly.

Julien looked down for a moment, thumb grazing the edge of his satchel as if bracing himself. When his gaze lifted again, it was steady, but softer than she had ever seen it.

'Yes,' he said simply. 'One day, I'd like a family. A home that feels alive, not just a place I pass through on my way to the shop. And a wife who wants the same.'

The unspoken words pressed between them, thick with possibility. Marcus didn't want children and Lily's chest tightened with longing because, for a fleeting moment, she wanted to be that for Julien.

Their shared vulnerabilities hung in the air between them, unspoken but understood. The train began to slow, the outskirts of Paris coming into view. As they gathered their things and prepared to disembark, Lily lingered by the window, reluctant to leave the warmth and safety of his presence. Julien stood beside her, adjusting the strap on his shoulder.

He glanced sideways at her. 'When I get back, I'm going to start going through the boxes at the back of the shop. He kept everything: photos, letters and even film canisters. If there's anything else connecting him to Jacques, or anyone else in your family, I'll find it.'

Lily's heart swelled with gratitude.

'Thank you,' she said quietly.

The train hissed to a stop at Gare de Lyon, brakes squealing against steel. Lily stepped down onto the platform with Julien beside her, the photograph of Rachel still heavy in her bag, her mother's face flickering in her mind.

The crowd pressed around them in a blur of suit jackets, rolling cases and hurried voices.

Julien looked down at her, his dark eyes searching hers in that way that had become familiar over their journey. The golden afternoon light caught in his dark curls as he shifted his bag to his other shoulder. Lily felt a pang of reluctance at the thought of saying goodbye to their easy conversations and his genuine interest in her mother's story.

As if plucking the thought from her mind, he gestured toward the station's ornate archway. 'Perhaps a coffee before we return to real life, at the bakery I told you about? Best cakes in Paris. It's tucked away; hardly anyone knows about it.'

She agreed to go. Marcus's phone call the day before had informed her that he would be very late home that evening, so she had nothing to rush back for. They weaved through the sea of travellers heading through Paris until he led her down a side street she had never been down before.

But when they arrived Lily froze mid-step, the air hitched in her lungs in a sharp spike of shock.

Marcus.

He stood outside the bakery, coffee in hand, head tipped back in laughter. Beside him was a woman in a scarlet scarf. She stood close, her hand brushing his arm, the connection between them so natural it was unmistakable. His companion leaned in, whispering something that sent him into easy, unrestrained laughter. His eyes lit with the spark Lily hadn't seen since their first years of marriage, the kind of warmth that used to be hers alone.

Her stomach twisted hard at the obvious intimacy between them.

Julien stopped beside her and followed her gaze. His brow furrowed. 'Are you all right?'

Her voice broke as she said. 'That's... my husband.'

Julien turned fully toward her, surprise flashing across his face. 'Marcus?'

Before she could answer, the woman at Marcus's side leaned closer, long glossy blonde hair catching the afternoon light. She had the kind of elegance Marcus admired and endlessly strove for himself: a silk blouse cut to flatter, white trousers that spoke of money in their impracticality, a designer handbag hooked carelessly over one arm. Her lips brushed near his ear and Marcus laughed again, louder this time, his whole body leaning toward her with easy familiarity.

Lily's throat closed, and it felt like the ground had shifted beneath her.

Julien's expression darkened. He didn't ask more. Quietly, firmly, he placed a steadying hand at her back. Not claiming, not crowding, just anchoring, as if saying, *I'm here.*

Marcus looked up and saw Lily. The laughter died on his lips. His body stiffened, the colour draining from his face as his eyes locked on her. The polished calm she knew so well was gone. He muttered something to the woman, and she took her paper cup of coffee and disappeared down the street. Marcus half-ran across the road as if speed could undo what she'd already seen.

'Lily,' he blurted breathlessly, his tie askew. 'I was just about to call you.'

The lie quivered in the air, thin and breakable.

Julien's hand remained at her back, a warm anchor, as she drew a steadying breath and squared her shoulders.

'You must be the person Lily mentioned,' Marcus said, thrusting his hand toward Julien with forced cordiality, his tone overly bright, the motion too eager, too obvious.

'Julien Renaud,' Julien answered, his voice cool as they exchanged a brief, stiff handshake. 'I've been assisting Lily with her family research.'

Marcus's gaze flicked to Julien's hand on Lily's back, his jaw tightening. 'I'll take my wife home now,' he said possessively, emphasising the word 'wife'. Lily remained mute. The image of him laughing burned into her brain on a continuous loop.

Julien's goodbye was a blur of motion at the edge of her vision as Lily's footsteps fell mechanically beside Marcus through streets that seemed suddenly colourless. Her throat tightened with each swallow. She looked at the pavement, staring at cracks, feeling humiliated. Her wedding ring felt suddenly heavy, almost foreign against her skin. Lily's stomach was clenched so hard it hurt. Tears pricked at her eyes. The growing distance in their marriage had been a dull ache for months, but this, this was a wound torn open without warning, leaving her hollow and gut-punched.

Once inside their home, Lily couldn't contain the storm raging inside her any longer. With a sharp, guttural cry of frustration, she flung her bag across the room, and the sound of its impact echoed off the walls. Tears pricked her eyes, blurring her vision as she tried to make sense of the turmoil rising inside her.

Marcus watched her outburst with a mixture of shock and apprehension, his facade of calm cracking under the weight of her raw emotions.

'Who is she, Marcus?' she spat out.

He dragged a hand through his hair, forcing a short, dismissive laugh. 'She's no one, Lily, a client. We happened to leave a meeting at the same time, stopped for coffee. That's it.'

Her eyes burned. 'You don't look at a client like that. You don't let them touch you like that.'

His jaw clenched. 'You're reading into it.'

'I *saw* you!' she snapped, her voice breaking. 'I saw everything.'

Lily narrowed her gaze, her body trembling as the picture of them laughing together burned a hole in her stomach.

'Is this the woman you were with at our restaurant?'

Marcus froze but remained mute.

'I could make a call,' Lily pressed, her voice sharp now. 'The maître d' knows us well. He knows who you were with. Should I ask him?'

The silence stretched, thick as tar. Marcus's jaw worked, his composure fraying.

Finally, he exhaled, voice breaking.

'All right! She's a client who's been after me for months. Yes, we've met. Yes, we've talked. But I swear, Lily, I swear on my life, it never went beyond that.' He added, 'She means nothing to me, I'll cut her off right now.'

'Or maybe we should end this so you can go and be with her?' she spat back, her pain raw and unfettered.

He stepped toward her and tried to take her hands, his desperation now evident. Lily jerked her own away as if his touch burned, the weight of his words heavy in the air between them. She stared at him, searching his face for any sign of deception. He appeared desperate.

'Please,' he said, his voice thick with emotion, 'don't do this. We love each other, Lily, I'll cut her off.' Marcus whispered, 'I want to be with you. Please, believe me.'

She stared at her husband, her chest aching with the urge to believe him, yet every instinct screamed to run.

In the terrible silence that followed, Lily realised she no longer knew which betrayal would destroy her more: trusting him, or walking away.

2O

PARIS, NOVEMBER 1940

Claudette

Claudette sat at the stage manager's desk in the Palais Garnier, her clipboard balanced on one knee as the company prepared for their dress rehearsal.

The main stage of the theatre was a world unto itself, a world apart from the war, apart from the city with its checkpoints, rations and watchful eyes. The theatre buzzed with the usual clamour, dancers were stretching, stagehands hammering, musicians tuning their instruments but her stomach churned with unease.

Her mind was elsewhere. She couldn't stop thinking of that grimy café with its smoke-stained walls and bitter stench of burnt food, where she and her brother had been meeting regularly. Philippe's words, *'I see I will have to take matters into my own hands,'* loomed larger than the stage itself.

She pushed all thoughts of him from her mind as she immersed herself in the work she loved.

They were rehearsing with new dancers; as people left Paris for a variety of desperate reasons, the war was stripping them of talent. The backdrop, a vast, painted canvas depicting the interior of the Louvre, stood glistening, its bold brushstrokes hinting at their resilience, at something undefeated.

Claudette moved between the crew, clipboard in hand, noting adjustments to be made to the set, pieces to be repaired.

All at once, the doors at the back of the house were flung open and French police officers barged in.

Voices fell silent. The laughter evaporated. People were clearly remembering Jean-Paul's arrest.

Her breath hitched as she recognised the face of her brother. Claudette felt it like a physical blow to the chest. What was he doing here?

Philippe strolled in with deliberate ease. Behind him, two uniformed officers followed, their expressions impassive.

Philippe's voice carried effortlessly through the vast space.

'Sergeant Mercier, of the French police.'

The name echoed through the vast expanse of the theatre, and, though the workers continued their tasks, she saw the way they tensed: a collective tightening, as if the room itself had drawn breath and refused to release it.

Jean-Luc turned from his work. His face was carefully neutral, but the flicker of fear in his eyes betrayed him. Eloise stiffened, her fingers gripping the fabric she had been adjusting so tightly that her knuckles turned white.

Philippe's slow, deliberate steps across the polished stage filled the silence. He was enjoying this moment, savouring the power he held over them.

'I have come to ensure compliance.' His voice was silken, deliberate. He let the phrase settle, let it seep into the bones of everyone in the room before continuing. 'We've been reviewing artistic content in France.'

He gestured lazily toward the backdrop behind him, his fingers barely moving, as though even the effort of acknowledging their work was beneath him.

'Certain themes, those that undermine the Reich, are no longer permitted.'

Serge Lifar stepped forward quickly, swallowing hard. 'We comply with all regulations, Officer,' he said.

Philippe's smile was small, knowing, entirely without warmth. 'I'm pleased to hear it.' His tone suggested otherwise. He let the moment stretch, a snake coiled, waiting to strike.

Then, with a flick of his wrist, he gestured toward the set behind him.

'This will need to be removed,' Philippe declared, his voice deceptively casual. 'The current authorities in Paris believe the performance could just as easily be staged in Germany.'

A murmur swept through the company, disbelief tangled with fear.

The director stepped forward, his hands twitching slightly, his breath uneven. 'But this ballet is already open, and it is set at the Louvre, right here in Paris. How can we accommodate that request?'

Philippe turned his head slowly, his gaze landing on the man as if he were a bug to be crushed. The silence stretched, thick and suffocating.

'Don't you think they have impressive galleries in Germany where you could stage your ballet? Or are you unwilling to acknowledge Germany's cultural abilities?'

The shift was subtle, but the meaning was unmistakable.

A warning.

The director opened his mouth, then closed it again. Beads of sweat formed at his temple.

'This reeks of anti-German sentiment,' Philippe continued.

A ripple of unease spread through the cast and crew. Whispers rose and fell, a desperate, hushed attempt to make sense of what was happening.

Claudette clenched her fists, her nails digging into her palms.

He was punishing her.

For her resistance. For her defiance, for not falling in line.

She forced herself to step forward, though every instinct screamed at her to stay still. To stay silent.

'Surely, Sergeant, there is a compromise we can reach?' she said, keeping her voice even, steady, though it took every ounce of control. 'Another way, perhaps? The set is finished, and the show is open.'

She hated the way she sounded, like she was pleading.

'Yes,' Lifar echoed quickly, grasping at the lifeline she offered.

Philippe's gaze flickered toward her, and for the briefest moment she saw it – the satisfaction. He had been waiting for her to speak. Waiting for her to acknowledge, publicly, the power he held over her.

He turned toward her fully, and stepped close, too close, until the space between them felt suffocating. His gaze dragged over her, assessing, calculating, drinking in her discomfort like fine wine.

'We need to know you are committed to doing what we need.'

The mockery in his tone wasn't just for her. It was for everyone in the room to hear.

She knew what he was saying. He was reminding her that this wasn't about the Nazis; it wasn't about artistic regulations or political compliance.

This was his game. His power. His control. And if she didn't fall in line, he would tighten the grip until she choked.

'Maybe we can find another way to honour Germany?' she suggested, hating the words she was saying.

'There is always a way to get things done if you put your mind to it,' he said with a knowing smirk. The double meaning was obvious. His eyes glittered with cruel satisfaction. 'I think the visiting forces would like to see their flag more prominently in this establishment. It would be more welcoming.'

'We can talk about this further, Sergeant Mercier,' Lifar suggested, the relief evident in his voice. 'Please, accompany me to my office.'

As she watched them walk away, dread settled in her chest.

Later that evening, the air on the connected balconies was pleasantly warm as all four girls sat together, each cradling a glass of wine. The night sky was a tapestry of shimmering stars, twinkling like diamonds scattered across a velvet canvas. It would have been perfect if Claudette hadn't felt frozen inside.

Gigi turned to her. 'Strange day, wasn't it?'

Claudette sipped her wine. 'How so?'

'The police officer,' Gigi said, stretching. 'Mercier. Same name as yours.'

The words sent a chill down her spine, and she averted her gaze.

'He isn't a relative, is he?'

'No, no relation,' Claudette replied, her voice tight as she forced a casual smile.

'What happened?' Malina asked, her Resistance instincts alerted.

Gigi relayed the whole story as Claudette's insides twisted with discomfort.

Malina swore. 'What right do they have? Those Nazi puppets are a disgrace to their French uniform.'

'What makes them think they can waltz in and dictate what we can do, what we can create? Don't worry, I'm making a note of his name. I will do all I can to find out everything about him and expose any weaknesses we can exploit,' Malina declared; her eyes blazed with determination.

Claudette's breath stuttered. What if Malina found out Philippe was her brother?

That night, as she lay in her bed, Claudette couldn't shake the chilling thoughts that plagued her mind. She tossed and turned as childhood memories resurfaced. Their life of poverty, the unbreakable bond they had once shared.

She recalled her brother's infectious laughter, his playful teasing, his fierce protectiveness. How could he have transformed into this monstrous figure, a puppet of the Nazi regime, a ruthless wielder of fear and control?

And how deep into his abyss would he drag her with him?

21

PARIS, MARCH 1941

Gigi

The invitation arrived on a damp, grey afternoon. Gigi pulled the elegant envelope from her mailbox. Her name was written in deep blue ink, in swirling script that looked too fancy for wartime Paris.

Inside, the thick, cream-coloured paper was embossed in silver:

Miss Gigi Valette,

You are warmly invited to spend an evening at le Lys Noir. There will be dancing, singing and music. Feel free to bring along friends.

It was signed by Joséphine Duval, with the name of the club and an address scrawled at the bottom.

Her heart gave a small flutter as she thought of Olivier. Months had passed since she had last seen him.

Le Lys Noir wasn't just any jazz club; it was one of the

city's most bohemian establishments, hidden deep in shadowy back streets, frequented by artists, creatives and people who didn't quite belong anywhere else.

She ran up to her apartment, her heels clicking excitedly against the worn staircase.

On the shared balcony, Eloise was tending to her row of tiny potted herbs, Malina was painting Resistance symbols on a banner that she quickly covered with a rag when Gigi appeared, and Claudette was lounging in the sun with a book.

'Girls, look what just arrived!' Gigi held the invitation aloft like a prize. 'We're going to le Lys Noir!'

They all scrambled over. Eloise reached out first. 'Let me see! I can't believe Miss Duval has invited us!'

Claudette raised an eyebrow. 'It's very upmarket. A good place to be seen.'

Malina muttered, 'It just seems frivolous, dancing and singing while people are starving and being taken from the city.'

'Malina,' Gigi said, her tone teasing, 'frivolity is all that's holding Paris together right now, let us have this moment.'

That evening, they prepared in their own apartments, but the shared balcony connected them. Doors were flung open, and voices called across the space between them.

'Has anyone seen my pearl clip?'

'Your black heels are under my bed!'

'If you want my blue scarf, you'd better let me borrow your earrings!'

By the time they stepped out into the night, they were a vision of Parisian elegance. Gigi wore an emerald-green gown that caught the light when she moved. Eloise's sleek black dress clung to her gracefully, and Claudette's cream dress shimmered subtly beneath her borrowed scarf. Even Malina, though dressed more simply, held a certain quiet beauty.

The club was tucked into a nondescript alley, its entrance marked only by a small, flickering neon sign. Inside, the atmosphere hit them like heat: smoke, jazz, perfume and something electric.

A woman in a tower of jewellery met them inside. It was Madame Leroux, who also worked the box office at the Palais Garnier.

Gigi stopped short. 'Madame Leroux? You're here.'

The older woman laughed. 'Darlings!' she cried, kissing them all on both cheeks. 'I see the right people always find the right places. Come, let me get you settled.'

They settled into a booth near the back. The jazz band played a sultry set on a raised stage beneath a chandelier that threw fractured light across the room.

Gigi studied the crowd, and that was when she saw him.

Olivier.

He stood near the bar, his sandy-coloured curls tousled, half in shadow as he spoke in hushed tones to two men in overcoats. They looked out of place here, serious, tense. Not like the rest of the crowd of artists and theatre people.

One of the men passed something small into Olivier's palm. He slipped it into his coat pocket without a word.

Gigi's breath caught.

She hadn't seen him since the rooftop. But now he was here, and the effect he had on her was immediate and demanding.

He looked older somehow. Worn and bruised. One cheekbone was discoloured, as though healing from a blow. And though he hadn't seen her yet, something about his posture was guarded and made her pulse quicken.

'What is it?' Eloise asked, following her gaze.

'Nothing,' Gigi said quickly. 'Just... someone I didn't expect to see.'

She turned her attention back to the stage as Joséphine Duval appeared, commanding the room with her voice and presence. For the next hour, Joséphine held the audience captive. But even as the crowd swayed and applauded, Gigi couldn't shake the image of Olivier and those men, the quiet intensity of the exchange.

What had happened to him?

Why hadn't he come back to see her, as he had promised?

And what exactly was he mixed up in?

Even the music, sweet and sultry, couldn't drown out the hum of questions in her head.

The last note from Joséphine's trumpet player lingered in the smoky air as the crowd erupted into applause, but Gigi barely registered it.

Her eyes were fixed on Olivier. He hadn't looked her way once.

When Joséphine disappeared behind the velvet curtain, Gigi slid out of the booth with a murmur to her friends and began to weave her way through the room, her heart drumming, her knees trembling beneath her skirt of her own gown. She wasn't even sure what she was going to say, only that she had to say something.

She found him at the edge of the bar, alone, nursing a short glass of something amber, his face half-turned to the shadows. Up close, the bruising beneath his cheekbone was more visible. Faint but unmistakable.

'Olivier.'

He turned slowly. For a heartbeat, concern flickered across his face, then something softer.

'Gigi.'

'You've been avoiding me.'

'Not intentionally,' he said, swirling his glass. 'Though I've been... elsewhere.'

'Where?'

'Around.' His smirk didn't reach his eyes.

'You've been gone for months.'

'Have I?' He looked at his drink, then back at her. 'I hadn't noticed.'

The words stung. She folded her arms. 'You look like hell.'

'Thank you. Lovely to see you too.'

She wanted to say *I missed you*, but instead asked, 'Who were those men you were talking to?'

His eyes darkened. 'You're very good at asking the wrong questions.'

'And you're very good at not answering them.'

Silence hung between them, the club's noise fading to a hum.

'Why not just tell me the truth?' she asked.

'Because I don't know what truth you're ready to hear.'

Her throat tightened. 'You vanished. After the last time we met, I thought...'

'I know,' he said gently. 'I wanted to come back. But things got complicated.'

Her gaze caught the bruise on his cheek. 'I can see that.'

He gave a dry laugh. 'A disagreement with a so-called patriot. Nothing worth worrying about.'

She swallowed. 'I told myself none of it mattered.'

'And now?'

'I don't know,' she admitted. 'Seeing you again makes me forget what I told myself.'

'Then maybe don't forget,' he murmured. 'Remember it differently.'

Before she could respond, Claudette called across the room. 'Gigi! We're leaving. The curfew!'

Olivier's eyes lingered on her.

She had taken only a few steps away from him when an arm slid firmly around her waist. Her breath caught. She turned and found herself inches from him, his breath warm against her skin, his chest brushing hers as he steered her onto the dance floor.

'Don't leave me alone,' he whispered.

She meant to protest, to say something sharp about him leaving *her,* but the words dissolved as his hand spread across the small of her back, anchoring her.

'Just one dance,' he murmured, voice low and coaxing. 'I know I haven't earned it, but I need to feel you in my arms, if only to believe you're real.'

Lights glowed above, golden halos drifting across smoke-thick air. His body moved against hers, guiding her into the rhythm of the music, their steps slow, deliberate, intimate. Every shift brought them closer, the brush of his thigh, the warmth of his palm, the steady thrum of his heartbeat against her chest.

'I forgot how beautiful you are,' he said, conviction raw in his voice.

Her lips parted on a trembling breath. His nearness made her head spin. The sheer attraction between them was intoxicating. She almost tipped her face upward, imagining how easy it would be to close the distance, to feel his mouth on hers.

Instead she whispered, 'I need you to know, I'm not looking for love.'

'No one ever is,' he replied. His fingers pressed more firmly at her waist. 'Sometimes we don't get a choice. That's when it matters most.'

He drew back just enough to look into her eyes, the space between them taut, electric, almost unbearable. 'I'm sorry for the lies. Can we meet again soon?'

The question hung there, pulsing between them like the beat of the music. Gigi's heart raced as she gave the smallest nod, before she could talk herself out of it.

And then he smiled, that same mischievous, knowing smile, let her go and disappeared into the crowd once more.

Under the veil of the darkened sky, Gigi walked home beside her friends, though her mind was elsewhere. Even Claudette's chatter and Eloise's thoughtful silence felt distant.

Back at the apartment, Gigi slipped out onto her balcony, to watch the light of the moon shimmer on the Seine. Her thoughts raced: Olivier's closeness, his words, the way he had looked at her like she wasn't just another girl, but someone who could change things.

She didn't know whether to be frightened or flattered. Maybe both.

And yet... the look in his eyes had been real. Honest and vulnerable.

That night, sleep evaded her.

She sat at her desk, and wrote in her journal.

I want to know more about him. He intrigues me. It looked casual in ink, but inside, she was restless. He felt dangerous, not in a way that warned her off, but in a way that pulled her in. He slipped past her defences too easily, intruding without apology. She knew he was hiding something; she could feel the weight of it. And yet, with her, he was unguarded, almost disarmingly so.

Already, something had shifted inside her. She was opening up in a way she had never known before, as if some locked part of herself had stirred at his touch.

And once awakened, it refused to go back to sleep.

22

PARIS, SUMMER 2011

Lily

The gallery was quiet in the early morning, warmed by the golden shafts of sunlight. Lily busied herself tidying frames, though her hands shook with the memory of the day before.

Outside the bakery, Marcus was laughing. A woman in a scarlet scarf was leaning close, her hand brushing his arm. There was a warmth in his eyes, a spark Lily hadn't seen in years.

Her stomach twisted at the thought of it, and then Marcus's face when he saw her, shock, colour draining, words tumbling out in a guilty jumble.

She set a frame back too sharply, and the glass rattled. She couldn't afford to splinter, not now. Her mother needed her. The mystery of her family was something she could cling to, something solid, something true.

A kettle hissed somewhere behind the counter.

'How are you getting on?' Effy asked, sweeping in. She looked as if she'd floated out of a painting. She wore a flowing saffron-yellow kaftan patterned with enormous teal cranes, a string of amber beads that clattered at her throat, and on her feet a pair of bejewelled sandals that jingled with every step. Her wild curls were pulled back with a velvet ribbon dyed deep indigo.

Lily sighed. 'I've been diving into every corner of the internet, but it's like searching for a needle in a haystack. If only Maman were awake she could tell me something about Rachel. Clare remembered the ballet school where this photo was taken, but it's long gone.'

Effy took the photo to the back of the gallery, waving Lily to follow. 'Come on, it's time we did this properly.'

She unearthed a corkboard, pinned up the two photos they had, then scrawled *Find Rachel* beneath the photo of the twins. 'There. Our anchor. From here, we build.'

Lily smiled faintly, loving her friend's enthusiasm.

Effy grabbed a roll of string, scissors and paper from a cracked drawer labelled BITS, BOBS AND BUTTONS.

'We're going to need categories,' she said, pulling a piece of paper toward her. 'Okay, timeline, confirmed facts, maybes and big mysterious blanks.'

'I think that last one's going to fill up fast,' Lily said.

'Oh ye of little faith. If Miss Marple can do it so can we,' Effy replied with a grin, as she pinned up a page labelled KEY QUESTIONS in bold black letters.

Who is Lily's biological grandmother?
What happened to Rachel?
How were the twins separated?
What happened to Uncle Jacques?

Before Lily could respond, the bell above the door chimed and Julien stepped inside. His eyes went straight to Lily, checking her face with concern. He crossed the gallery toward them.

'Perfect timing!' Effy declared, already pressing a marker into his hand. 'You can help us fill in the blanks. I'll fetch you a cup of tea.'

She swept away, humming, leaving them alone.

Julien turned back to Lily, his voice quiet. 'How are you? After yesterday?'

Her throat tightened. 'He swore it was nothing...'

'Do you believe him?'

She shrugged, and Julien's jaw shifted, as if he wanted to say more, to offer comfort. For a moment his hand lifted slightly, as though he might take her in his arms, but he stopped. Instead, he rested his palm gently against her arm, giving it the lightest squeeze. 'What are you going to do?'

His eyes met hers and held, a silent question passing between them. Lily felt a shiver run down her spine at the intensity in his gaze.

'I don't know,' she admitted softly. 'I feel like I'm standing on the edge of a cliff, unsure if I should step back or leap into the unknown. Right now it seems easier to give him the benefit of the doubt, rather than stare into the ruins of my marriage.'

Julien nodded, his expression mirroring her turmoil. 'You don't have to go through this alone, Lily. I'm here for you, whatever you need.'

As she looked into his earnest eyes, a part of her longed to lean into his support, to find solace in his arms. But the weight of her marriage pressed down on her.

'I appreciate your friendship, Julien,' she murmured as the gallery around them seemed to fade away, leaving only the two of them standing in a bubble of shared understanding.

Effy bustled back in with a cup of tea. 'Here we are, darlings. Fortification for our new detectives.' They stepped quickly away from each other, but not before Effy's observant gaze flickered between them.

'I've just remembered some gallery business that simply

can't wait,' she announced with deliberate casualness, the beads at her throat clacking as she retreated. 'You two keep building the board,' she instructed them as her kaftan billowed behind her.

Lily cleared her throat, breaking the heavy silence that had settled between them. 'We should focus on the task at hand,' she suggested gently, gesturing towards the corkboard, and Julien nodded, though his gaze lingered a moment longer before he turned to the board.

Together, they stood before the pinned photo of the twins and their uncle, and the one taken of Rachel in the south.

'We don't have much,' Lily murmured.

Julien uncapped the marker Effy had left him. 'It's a beginning,' he said. His voice was steady, practical, yet there was a quiet fire beneath it that made Lily's chest ache.

Under the words *Find Rachel* he drew two lines branching out. 'One for other family members. One for your aunt. Let's see where they take us.'

Lily leaned against the table, watching him work. The way his brow furrowed in concentration, the neatness of his letters, the sure line of his shoulders. For a fleeting second, she imagined Marcus beside her like this, invested, determined, working toward something that mattered to them both. But that picture dissolved before it could fully form, leaving only the hollow reminder of yesterday.

Julien glanced over, catching her gaze before she could look away. 'Tell me everything you know. Even the smallest details.'

She drew a breath, steadying herself, and told every little breadcrumb she remembered from her mother's childhood, but there wasn't much. She finished with, 'Clare remembered the whereabouts and name of the ballet school. That's where this photo was taken. But it's gone now, replaced by a supermarket.'

Julien pulled a card from his pocket and jotted down the name of the ballet school. 'Someone will remember it,' he said confidently. 'Places don't just vanish without leaving traces. There will certainly be memories.'

His certainty warmed her, cut through the fog of doubt that had wrapped itself around her since yesterday.

Effy poked her head around the partition to see how they were getting on.

Her sharp eyes caught the card with the ballet school's name scribbled across it.

'Ah,' she said, her bangles clinking as she pointed. 'That might be something I can help with. You two carry on here.'

She disappeared into the back office and returned a moment later with her beloved address book, a fat, dog-eared volume with an embroidered cover of exotic birds. She held it aloft like a talisman.

'This has served me faithfully for forty years,' she announced. 'No internet required.'

Lily smiled. She'd long since given up trying to convince Effy to digitise her contacts. Effy would only pat the book fondly and say, 'If it isn't broken, why fix it?'

Setting herself up at the counter, Effy began making calls in her sing-song voice. Snippets drifted through the open door: 'Hello, darling, it's me, Effy La Rue. I wonder if you can assist me with a real-life mystery.'

While she worked, Lily and Julien settled into a rhythm at the corkboard. He pencilled names and dates in his careful hand; she pinned them up where they might fit. Occasionally, their shoulders brushed, and each time Lily felt the faintest pull of awareness. They compared timelines, debated gaps and added to their growing column of unanswered questions until the board began to resemble a map of tangled lives.

Time slipped by; then, from the back room, Effy's jubilant cry broke the spell.

'Aha! Got you!'

A rustle of paper followed, then the triumphant tear of a

page being pulled from her notebook. Effy burst into the back of the gallery, her cheeks flushed with victory, the book clutched to her chest.

Lily looked up to see Effy practically glowing with excitement, her amber beads jingling as she waved a scrap of paper in front of her nose.

'I found someone!' Effy declared. 'A woman who might remember the ballet school. She was younger than your *maman*, but she was there during the war and after. She claims she remembers everything.'

Lily raised a brow. 'Do you think she would see us?'

'I've already invited her,' Effy said with satisfaction. 'Her name is Lucille. She'll be here later this afternoon.'

Julien, who had been standing near the corkboard studying the pinned photo of the twins, turned at that. 'That's quick,' he said, a small smile tugging at the corner of his mouth. 'Remind me never to underestimate Effy La Rue.'

Effy winked at him. 'Very wise, Monsieur.'

Effy's flat above the gallery was the sort of place that refused to be tamed. Strings of fairy lights were woven through bookshelves, patterned throws draped across mismatched chairs, and the scent of citrus and herbs hung in the air. Lily curled into a deep armchair beneath a beaded lamp that cast golden rings on the walls, while Julien leaned forward on the edge of a faded velvet sofa, elbows resting on his knees, his keen eyes flicking between the photo in Lily's lap and the notes Effy had scattered across the table.

Effy moved about the kitchen with her usual grace, humming as she arranged a teapot, delicate china cups and a plate of lemon shortbread on a floral tray. At precisely four o'clock, there was a knock on the door.

Effy swept it open to reveal a petite silver-haired woman with bright eyes and a soft pink scarf tucked into her coat.

'Lucille!' Effy exclaimed warmly. 'Come in, come in. These are my friends Lily and Julien.'

Lucille smiled as she stepped inside. Though her posture was a little stooped, her gaze was remarkably steady, sharpened rather than dulled by time.

'Thank you for having me,' she said, lowering herself carefully into a chair. 'It's been years since anyone asked about the old ballet school. Most people have forgotten it existed.'

Effy poured tea and passed around the cups before gently prompting, 'Lily's researching something very close to her family. We thought you might be able to help.'

Lucille turned to Lily with kind curiosity.

'I'm trying to find my aunt,' Lily explained. 'My mother's name was Rebecca Durand. She had a twin sister, Rachel.'

Lucille's brow furrowed. She shook her head slowly. 'I don't recall dancing with any twins. I was very young, and the older girls kept to themselves.'

Julien leaned forward. 'Would you mind looking at a photo?' he asked, his tone respectful but insistent. Lily handed over the picture of the twins with their uncle and Lucille gasped softly.

'You recognise them?' Lily asked, her heart leaping.

'I'm sorry, no,' Lucille replied. 'But this man, he was the ballet teacher who owned the school. It's been years since I've seen him. I think he passed away during the war. The school continued for a while, run by one of his students. But...' She trailed off with a sigh, then frowned as she turned the photo over. 'Uncle Jacques? That's strange.'

Julien's brows knitted together. 'Strange in what way?'

Lucille glanced between them. 'My mother knew the family. He was an only child.'

'Perhaps it was a term of endearment?' Lily suggested hopefully.

Lucille gave a small, dismissive huff. 'You clearly didn't know Jacques. He was very stern. A hard taskmaster, not the "uncle" type at all.'

Julien pressed gently, 'Do you have any idea what his relationship to these girls might have been?'

Lucille's gaze went distant. 'No. But... I do remember overhearing him once, speaking about twins. I was waiting before class. He sounded angry, upset. He said something like, "The twins' mother lives above the studio. And she doesn't know about the girls, and I want to keep it that way." I remember because I'd always dreamed of being a twin myself, it seemed so marvellous.'

Lily's breath caught. 'Did he mention who the twins' mother was?'

Lucille shook her head. 'I never heard a name. But how many sets of twins could there have been at the school? These may well be the ones your great-uncle meant.'

'Do you remember who lived above the dance school?' Julien asked quietly, leaning in.

'Yes,' Lucille said, brightening at the memory. 'There were a few young women, dancers, theatre girls. Always laughing, always together. We called them "the girls upstairs".'

Effy leaned forward, teacup halfway to her lips. 'Do you remember their names?'

Lucille smiled. 'One very clearly, Gigi Valette. She was kind to the little ones. I looked up to her. I'm not sure what became of her, but her sister, Madeline, is still in Paris, or was. She owned a bookshop. After the war, I told her I'd been a student at the ballet school, and she said her sister Gigi had lived above it. So yes, I believe it's the same person. It would be too much of a coincidence otherwise.'

'Do you remember the name of the bookshop?' Julien asked.

Lucille shook her head again, but Effy chimed in at once. 'I do. I've met Madeline. It's a charming shop on the corner of rue de la Pompe and avenue Foch.'

Lucille finished her tea with a glance at the clock. 'Oh, look at the time. My husband is a stickler for routine, and dinner must be ready. Do you need anything else from me?'

Lily's voice was soft. 'No, you've given us more than you know.'

Lucille smiled gently and reached for a piece of shortbread as she rose. 'I'm glad someone's asking questions. Too many stories get buried.'

When the door had closed behind her, Lily went back down into the back room and updated the board with swift, bold strokes: *If he's not their uncle, then how was he connected to the girls?* Underneath, she added, *The twins' mother might have lived above the studio. Gigi Valette was one of the girls upstairs.*

Effy stepped back, hands on her hips, admiring the growing web of clues. 'Well, my dears,' she said with delight, 'Agatha Christie would be proud of us. The next step,' she declared, 'is obvious. You two must go to Madeline's bookshop.'

Julien glanced at Lily, his brows lifting. 'Tomorrow?'

Lily felt warmth rising to her cheeks but managed a quiet, 'Yes, tomorrow.'

Effy gave a satisfied nod and swept off, already humming to herself.

Julien lingered near the corkboard, tracing a finger lightly along the edge of the pinned photograph of the twins. 'Well, you're closer than you were yesterday,' he said, his voice low but certain.

Lily studied him, the quiet strength in his profile, the steadiness that seemed to radiate from him. She wondered not for the first time what it would be like to lean into that steadiness fully, without hesitation.

When he turned back to her, there was a softness in his eyes that made her breath catch. He reached for his bag, hesitated, then stepped close.

'Until tomorrow,' he murmured. He bent and brushed a kiss against her cheek, then the other. Yet he lingered just a fraction too long for a polite goodbye, close enough that Lily caught the faint scent of cedarwood.

Her pulse stumbled. By the time he stepped back, her heart was racing.

'Have a good evening, Lily,' Julien said, his voice low, almost intimate.

She could only nod, the echo of his touch warming her skin as he left.

23

PARIS, MAY 1941

Claudette

The afternoon light slanted through the high windows of the Palais Garnier, while sawdust, fresh paint and ageing velvet filled the air and blended with the distant sounds of the orchestra rehearsing from another part of the building.

Claudette moved briskly through the maze of half-finished set pieces and props, clipboard in hand, ticking off last-minute adjustments for the show.

The chaos of theatre work had, for a few blessed hours, allowed her to push aside thoughts of Philippe, their ongoing meetings at the café, of his visit and threat at the theatre and of the impossible position he had forced her into.

A sharp bump as a stagehand knocked against her elbow sent a tin of red paint toppling over. It spilled in a thick, garish pool across the floor, and a few spots landed on her blouse.

'Sorry!' the young stagehand stammered. She nodded, accepting his apology, but swore under her breath, jerking back as the liquid seeped into the fabric of her sleeves.

'Turpentine,' she muttered to herself and headed towards the paint shop.

She rushed to Marcel's space. He was one of the stagehands and always kept a stash of supplies, too many supplies, if you asked her. He was away for a few days, which meant his little corner of the backstage chaos was unoccupied. Moving quickly, she pushed through the door to his cluttered workroom and stepped past half-finished wooden props and discarded costume sketches.

Her fingers were trailing over the shelves, searching for the familiar tin, when something else caught her eye.

A package wrapped in plain brown paper, tucked between wooden crates, nearly hidden.

Her brow furrowed. Marcel wasn't careless with his own property. For all his faults, he guarded his things like a dragon hoarding treasure.

She extended her hand and felt the coarse texture of the paper under her fingers. The twine holding it together seemed to have been tied in a rushed manner. She flipped it over, and it fell apart in her hands. If there was something illegal inside, she needed to know. The theatre had strict policies about drugs. But instead there were food items that were almost impossible to obtain.

She wasn't surprised to see proof of what Marcel was probably mixed up in.

Marcel, who praised the Germans and boasted of a France thriving under Reich rule, was known to sympathise with the Nazis. Having him dismissed from the theatre wouldn't be a hard decision. He was hated among the stagehands.

A bitter taste settled in her mouth.

Her grip tightened around the parcel, the weight of it grounding her. It wasn't her place to judge, but this?

For once, she wasn't hesitant.

After she had tended to the paint splatter, she tucked the

parcel under her arm and headed towards the stage door. As she approached, Monsieur Léon rose from his comfortable chair at his post.

'There was a police checkpoint here again earlier,' the doorman muttered as he stepped towards her. 'They searched everyone as they left, but they are gone now.'

She rolled her shoulders back and loosened her grip on the parcel.

Later that day, inside the police station, the air was thick with authority and fear, a stark contrast to the chaotic warmth of the theatre. Claudette's breath was shallow and her grip tightened around the package as she approached the front desk.

The walls were plastered with propaganda posters, calls for loyalty, for silence, for vigilance. A long line of civilians sat rigidly on wooden benches, their faces drawn, their eyes carefully downcast.

Some were here to plead for missing loved ones. Others to answer questions they did not want to be asked.

Claudette forced herself to breathe evenly, to keep her posture straight.

She leaned toward the clerk behind the desk, her voice barely above a whisper.

'I need to speak with Sergeant Mercier,' she murmured. 'I have information for him.'

The clerk, a thin man with hollow cheeks, barely spared her a glance as he pushed back from his chair and disappeared through the door behind him.

The silence in the waiting room seeped into her bones. The scrape of a chair. The occasional cough. The tension that thickened the air.

The clerk returned quickly.

'Sergeant Mercier will see you now,' he announced loudly,

his words cutting through the hush like a blade. 'You may go into his office.'

Claudette felt the air shift as every pair of eyes in the room lifted.

Furtive glances. Stiffened shoulders. The flicker of recognition, of judgement.

The word 'traitor' wasn't spoken, but she felt it press into her skin like a brand.

She gripped the parcel tighter and hurried past the stares, hating who she had become.

She told herself this wasn't about self-preservation. It was about Jean-Luc and his girls, about Eloise, about the fragile circle of people still clinging to some semblance of safety inside the theatre. She had seen what happened to those who got in his way, who said no.

If she handed this over, maybe, just maybe, it would be enough to satisfy him. A small betrayal, yes. But a controlled one. Calculated. One she could live with, if it kept him from looking deeper, from lashing out at someone more vulnerable.

She hadn't slept, not properly, not since this had all begun. And even though everything about this felt wrong, even though it scraped against the grain of who she believed herself to be, she had to protect the people who couldn't protect themselves.

She could carry the weight of this choice, if it meant they didn't have to.

She barely registered the clerk holding open the door, hardly noticed the dark hallway stretching before her, her only focus on escaping the weight of their gaze.

When the door to Philippe's office clicked shut behind her, she finally let herself breathe.

Philippe sat at his desk, his polished boots crossed neatly at the ankles, his expression as calm and composed as ever. But he was not alone.

Seated across from him was a man in full SS uniform, his

blond hair neatly slicked back, his sharp blue eyes piercing as he regarded her with vague amusement.

Her blood ran cold.

Philippe gestured toward the seat across from him.

'Claudette,' he said lightly, as though this were a social call. 'Come in.'

She hesitated, but he nodded toward the chair, his smile barely shifting. Her eyes darted to the man in the dreaded German uniform.

'You may speak freely,' he assured her. 'My old friend Obersturmführer Neumann is more than trustworthy.'

Neumann's thin lips curved, a smile that did not reach his eyes.

'I have heard so much about you, Mademoiselle Mercier,' he said, his voice cool and precise. 'Your brother speaks highly of your commitment to our cause.'

Claudette's stomach twisted.

Her brother couldn't have planned her visit better.

The next day, the morning air was crisp and bright, carrying a faint promise of spring, though winter still clung stubbornly to the city. Claudette walked arm in arm with Gigi and Eloise, their voices light, their laughter threading through the streets as they made their way toward the theatre.

'When this war is over,' Gigi declared, adjusting the worn cuffs of her coat, 'I'm buying the most ridiculous, extravagant gown imaginable, yards of silk, layers of lace, something completely impractical.'

Eloise scoffed. 'And where exactly are you going to wear this gown of excess?'

'Everywhere,' Gigi said with a dramatic sigh. 'To the market, to rehearsals, hell, to bed, if I can.'

Claudette chuckled. 'I'll settle for new shoes that aren't held together by sheer willpower.'

'And butter,' Eloise added. 'Real butter, dripping off a warm baguette. No more thin slivers, no more stretching a single pat for a week.'

Gigi groaned longingly. 'And perfume. The expensive kind, not the weak stuff you can barely smell. A single drop behind my ears and' – she gestured airily – 'I'll be irresistible.'

Claudette smirked. 'You say that as if you aren't already.'

They laughed, allowing themselves to slip into a future where ration books and curfews were memories, where silk and perfume and butter weren't luxuries but normal again.

They turned the final corner, and the golden facade of the Palais Garnier rose before them, its opulence a stark contrast to the grey city.

Monsieur Léon was away from his chair; now he stood at the entrance, his usual easy manner absent, his face drawn with tension.

His voice was low, urgent as they approached. 'Girls, go straight upstairs to the costume department.'

Their laughter died instantly.

Claudette's stomach tightened. 'What's happened?'

Monsieur Léon's gaze flickered toward the doors before settling back on them. 'The police are inside searching everywhere, again.'

Eloise's breath hitched. 'For what?'

'That's the question, isn't it?' Monsieur Léon muttered, lowering his voice. 'They arrived half an hour ago, going through props, set pieces, dressing rooms. Madame Fleurette told me to send you straight to her the second you arrived.'

Claudette felt cold.

She exchanged glances with Gigi and Eloise, then, without another word, they hurried inside, their footsteps echoing against the wooden floors as they climbed the staircase.

The moment they stepped into the cramped, fabric-strewn haven of the costume department, they were met with a hushed, tense atmosphere.

Near the sewing table, Jean-Luc Boucher's two daughters sat cross-legged on the floor, their small hands rummaging through a pile of fabric scraps Madame Fleurette had given them to play with. Claudette had never seen them up here before.

The older girl, perhaps seven or eight, folded a swatch of deep blue satin into careful squares, her movements slow, methodical. The younger child, barely five, clutched a piece of gold fringe between her fingers, running it over her hands absent-mindedly, her big brown eyes glassy as she stared at nothing.

Claudette's heart twisted painfully.

Gigi cleared her throat. 'What's going on?'

Madame Fleurette stood nearby, her expression tight, her hands wringing at her apron. When she saw the three women enter, she motioned them further inside.

'Come,' she whispered. 'Not here.'

Madame Fleurette poured four cups of coffee, adding a generous splash of brandy into each, before pushing one into Claudette's hands.

'What happened?' Gigi demanded, perching on the edge of the wooden table.

Madame glanced toward the children, still playing quietly. Then, lowering her voice, she began.

'It's Marguerite,' she whispered. 'Jean-Luc's wife. They've arrested her.'

Eloise inhaled sharply. Gigi muttered a curse. Claudette could barely breathe.

'The police tracked her through the food parcels she was hiding,' Madame continued. 'She was buying black market food to help a Jewish family whose ration cards had been revoked. She used her own money. She risked everything.'

Claudette's stomach lurched as the ground beneath her feet seemed to shift.

'How did they find out about her?' Eloise whispered.

Madame's eyes darkened. 'Because of a package she left at the theatre.'

'She was here?' she managed.

Madame nodded gravely. 'She came to collect extra sewing work from me, just like she always does. She had the package with her that day. But when she saw the police at the stage door, she panicked. She didn't want to be searched. So she left the parcel in Marcel's space, intending to have Jean-Luc collect it later.'

Claudette's pulse thundered in her ears.

'But when Jean-Luc went back for it...' Madame Fleurette hesitated, exhaling a heavy sigh.

'It was already gone.'

Claudette's world narrowed. It had been her fault. Assuming it belonged to Marcel.

'The police must have found something inside the parcel that led them back to her,' Madame Fleurette added.

'What?' Gigi asked.

'Jean-Luc thinks she realised, too late, that she had left her own ration card with it.'

'And Jean-Luc?' Eloise's voice was tight.

'Trying to get her released,' Madame Fleurette said softly. 'But in the meantime, he needed somewhere safe for the girls.'

Claudette felt sick.

'The poor things,' Eloise murmured, glancing back toward the little girls. 'What will they do?'

'We will look after them,' Madame Fleurette said firmly. 'They will not be alone.'

But Claudette was barely listening. Her guilt felt unbearable. She had done this. She had thought she was catching Marcel, a Nazi sympathiser. Instead, she had led the police straight to Marguerite.

She set her cup down, her hands trembling.

'These people are despicable,' Gigi muttered darkly.

Claudette's stomach continued to twist.

She couldn't tell them. Couldn't explain.

And then.

'*Maman?*'

The soft, uncertain voice cut through the room. They all turned.

The younger child had abandoned her scraps of fabric, and was gazing at them with wide, hopeful eyes.

'When will she come to get us?'

The silence was absolute. No one spoke.

'Soon,' Madame Fleurette said, trying to appease her.

And then, the little girl's lip trembled. Before anyone could stop it, she burst into tears. A wretched, broken sound. She threw herself against Madame Fleurette's skirts, sobbing, her tiny fingers grasping at the fabric as if clinging to something solid, something safe.

Madame bent, gathering her up, murmuring soft reassurances. But the child kept crying.

Claudette couldn't move. The weight was too much.

Eloise turned away, her fingers pressed to her lips, as if holding in some terrible fear of her own.

Gigi exhaled sharply.

Claudette was drowning in it all. Her betrayal. The truth that she had done this.

The truth that no amount of justification, no amount of reasoning, could ever make it right.

24

PARIS, MAY 1941

Gigi

Two days later, in the early hours, Olivier led Gigi uphill through Montmartre, the city slick with the previous day's drizzle.

Gigi's breath puffed in small clouds in front of her, her heels clicking softly against cobblestones damp with fog. They passed shuttered cafés and faded posters peeling from the walls, shows long cancelled, war bonds urgently advertised. A German patrol truck growled somewhere in the distance before fading into the quiet.

They had been seeing one another sporadically since March; he appeared without warning, late at night or at dawn, always when she least expected him.

She tugged her lightweight coat tighter, heart racing not from the climb but from the intimacy of walking beside him, his hand occasionally brushing hers. He had woken her from a dead sleep at dawn and told her to get dressed. They were going on an adventure. It had sounded exciting at the time.

'Are you planning to kidnap me?' she whispered as they

continued their climb, with a small smile, half teasing, half breathless.

'If I were, I'd choose a less uphill route,' he huffed back, glancing sideways at her. 'We're almost there.'

They crested the last hill, and there it was.

The old carousel stood quiet in the square, its paint long faded to a ghostly pastel. White horses, chipped and noble, stared ahead with a glassy gaze. Ribbons hung limp from the iron frame. A few tattered paper lanterns still swayed in the breeze. The music box at its centre had been silent for years.

Gigi stepped closer. 'It's beautiful,' she murmured. 'And sad.'

Olivier's voice softened. 'I used to work here. When I was a boy.'

She turned toward him in surprise.

'I'd polish the brass poles, sweep up, keep the coin drawer from sticking,' he continued. 'In exchange, the owner, paid me enough to cover my music lessons. It was the only way I could afford them.'

'You worked here?' Gigi looked around again, seeing it now with new eyes.

He nodded. 'I learned the rhythm here.' He walked to the carousel and placed a hand on one of the poles. 'Most people think it's broken. It's just forgotten. The man who owned it, Monsieur Lefèvre, died two winters ago. Pneumonia.' Olivier brushed a layer of dust from the wooden railing. 'He took care of this carousel like it was a living thing. He taught me how to work the crank, how to wind the gears so it turned evenly. Let me ride for free in the summers if I helped out.'

He stepped around to the back and crouched near a faded panel.

'What are you doing?' Gigi asked, the smallest smile on her lips.

'Resurrecting it.'

He opened the side compartment, which gave a low creak, and flipped a rusted switch. The generator coughed once, then whirred to life. Somewhere inside, unseen mechanics stirred, dust shook loose from gears, and then...

Light.

Small bulbs, dulled with age, flickered on one by one around the rim. The chipped gold trim glowed warm against the mirrored walls.

Gigi's lips parted. *'You kept it alive.'*

She gazed up at him for a moment, caught in the romance. He stepped forward and held out his hand. 'May I escort you aboard?'

She hesitated, then gave a small curtsey. 'Of course, Monsieur.'

He helped her up onto one of the chipped white horses. Its once-gilded mane was dulled, but it was still noble. She arranged her skirt over the saddle, laughing under her breath.

'Does it still turn?'

'Only one way to find out.'

He circled to the rear, knelt at the same faded panel, and flipped a second switch.

Then a crackling strain of calliope music broke the silence, a little warped, a little slow, but still sweet. Still whole. With a groan and a wobble, the platform began to spin.

Slowly, magically.

The horses glided up and down in a dance of their own. He didn't ride. He simply stood beside her, his hands in his pockets, watching her with a look that made her throat tighten. The kind of look you get to keep. The kind you remember for the rest of your life.

Then, quietly, he said, 'Monsieur Lefèvre used to say the heart of its magic was the music, that it lives inside the carousel, just like it does in you and me. We just have to remember how to listen for it... in each other.'

The words stirred something deep inside her.

They stayed in that moment until the music ended, and, as the carousel slowed to a gentle stop, he stepped forward and offered both hands to help her down. She took them, steady and warm, and let herself slide off the saddle, landing just inches from him.

'I wish you could've seen yourself just now,' he said softly. 'For a moment... it was like watching you as a girl. You let go. And it was beautiful.'

She blinked, caught off guard by the gentleness in his voice. *As a girl.*

The words struck something in her chest, something buried. Her childhood hadn't been carefree; it had been measured in metronomes and muscle strain, in perfect posture and pointed toes. She hadn't known how to play, only how to perform. But just now, gliding to the music, she had let go. And he'd seen it.

Before she could stop herself, she opened up to him, with a small, almost disbelieving laugh.

'I didn't give myself much of a childhood,' she said, eyes dropping to the ground. 'There was always another barre to hold, another routine to master. I don't think I ever knew how to just... *be.*'

He leaned closer, voice low. 'Then maybe it's time you found out. Not as the girl you were, but as the woman you are now. You deserve that. And lucky for you, I happen to be an expert in knowing how to play. First lesson: no routines, no rules. Just joy.'

She smiled as she studied his face, his blue eyes alight with a sense of mischief. They were still holding hands and his breath was warm in the space between them. The flickering carousel lights cast shadows around them. Her fingers tightened around his. And for a moment, the world stilled.

He looked as if he was about to kiss her, his breath brushing on her chilled lips.

But just as they drew closer together, a distant sound shattered the moment.

A German patrol. Loud, distant. But enough.

They stepped apart.

Olivier gazed at her. The spell was broken. 'We have to go,' he said gently. 'I have a lot more to show you.'

They walked through morning streets. Most shops were shuttered; the city felt half-asleep, bruised by too many headlines and too many men in boots.

Olivier moved with quiet purpose, one hand deep in his coat pocket, the other resting gently in hers, his fingers wrapped around her own with a quiet certainty that made her chest thrum.

Gigi didn't speak. She didn't need to.

They turned down a narrow alley and stopped before a door painted a striking rose gold with a brass opera mask hung above it. There was no sign, just a brass doorknob shaped like a lion's head.

He knocked three times, then twice more.

A long pause.

The door creaked open, revealing a slender striking woman in her seventies, her silver hair swept into a dramatic chignon and a silk scarf wrapped twice around her neck. A brooch of the comedy and tragedy masks glittered at her breast, and through the open door drifted the strains of opera from a gramophone.

Her eyes widened. '*Mon Dieu*, if it isn't Olivier Moreau!'

'Madame Mireille,' he responded warmly. 'And this is Gigi Valette.'

'*Bienvenue*, Mademoiselle,' the woman said with a nod.

Looking back at Olivier, she took him in with a sweep of her gaze and a slow, knowing smile.

'I suppose you will be wanting some breakfast,' she decided as she ushered them in.

Inside, the house was a time capsule of old Paris, if Paris

had once lived backstage at one of the theatres. Gilt-framed mirrors lined the walls, each one reflecting soft candlelight. Red velvet curtains were swagged around arched windows, and an enormous chandelier hung slightly askew from the ceiling. An intimate space for entertaining guests. On one side, a wall was entirely covered in autographed opera playbills, each one signed with names like Caruso, Nellie Melba and Mary Garden.

From a back room, the gentle crackle of a record player spun a delicate soprano aria; the voice wavered with the thin, warbled edges of an old, well-loved record.

'Is that... Claudia Muzio?' Gigi whispered as she caught sight of another one of the signed pictures.

The woman nodded, wistful. 'She sang me to sleep once, in Venice.'

'You knew her?'

'I knew them all,' the woman said breezily, waving one jewelled hand. 'I shared a dressing room with Emma Calvé. Spilled vermouth on Chaliapin. Fell in love with Titta Ruffo for precisely seventeen hours.'

She parted the bead curtain. 'Sit, you must be hungry,' she called over her shoulder, then slipped from view.

They sat at a table with an antique piano bench and velvet cushions for chairs.

'She used to be a great soprano,' Olivier informed her. 'Once headlined in Berlin, Milan, Vienna... then ten years ago, she vanished from the public eye.'

'She didn't vanish,' Madame Mireille called from behind the curtain. 'I reinvented.'

She reappeared a moment later, holding a tray with two steaming cups of coffee and the most exquisite breakfast pastry Gigi had ever seen, a delicate *galette à la crème d'amande*, dusted with sugar and speckled with sliced orange peel.

'I couldn't live without creativity,' Madame Mireille said, setting down the tray. 'So I began to bake. At least dough behaves when you sing to it. Just don't ask me where I get my ingredients from during this dark time.' She winked. 'I have learned to be very resourceful, because nothing quiets a soul like butter and aria.'

The coffee was strong, floral with hints of cardamom. The pastry melted into a dream of almond and vanilla on Gigi's tongue. She closed her eyes for a moment, as the flavours curled through her like memory.

'I didn't realise how hungry I was,' she whispered.

'That's because you haven't been fed properly,' Madame Mireille replied with a sly smile. 'By the look of you I'm guessing you are a dancer, no?'

Gigi's cheeks flushed. 'Yes, ballet.'

'I always know. Like I knew about Olivier. Do you know how I met this man?' she asked, her voice quieter now, touched by something raw and remembered.

Gigi shook her head as she looked up, mid-sip of coffee.

'He was ten when I first met him, skinny and trouble. I gave him lessons once a week, right here in the back room. But then came the affair,' she said simply, brushing a crumb from the tablecloth. 'I fell in love with a tenor from Milan. When my lover left, I thought the music left with him.' Her voice dropped. 'I stayed in bed. Let the dust gather. Olivier came anyway.'

She looked at him again, something reverent in her gaze. 'And do you know what he did when I told him there would be no more lessons?'

Gigi shook her head.

'He boiled water. Made toast,' she said with a crooked smile. 'Then sat at that piano and played every song he remembered I loved. *Awfully*. But he kept coming. Day after day. Until one morning, I was so furious with his butchering of *Pelléas et Mélisande*, I got out of bed and marched down here to correct his left hand.'

He rubbed the back of his neck, sheepish. 'In my defence, the left hand survived.'

She laughed, the sound low and warm. 'And that's when I realised I hadn't thought about the tenor in three days.'

A pause. Then, softly she continued. 'He didn't just rescue me with kindness. He rescued me with persistence. With music. I believe that any shattered heart can be healed, one note at a time.'

She reached for Olivier's hand across the table, and gave it a quick, elegant squeeze.

'I know he has a reputation for being a rogue and I've heard all the stories,' she said to Gigi, her voice a mix of concern and nostalgia. 'But remember, deep inside, there's still a kind little boy who once saved my life.'

They stayed a little longer before chairs scraped back; cups clinked. 'Come again,' Madame Mireille called as she drew the bead curtain aside.

The rain had started while they were still laughing over the last spoonfuls of crème and stories of long-lost composers. Gigi pulled her scarf tighter as they stepped out onto the damp cobbles, the sky draped in the kind of grey that softened everything except the cold.

Olivier took her hand again, easily now, as if it belonged there, and they began to walk without speaking, the echo of Madame Mireille's aria still floating between them.

After a few streets, Gigi glanced sideways at him.

'Why do people speak of you as a rogue?'

He didn't answer.

They rounded a corner into a narrower street, the cobblestones slick. 'I'd like to know the truth.'

He exhaled slowly with the weight of the question. He stopped beneath the awning of a shuttered gallery and turned to her, sheltering her from rivulets of rain that had begun to cascade.

'I've done things in my past I'm not proud of,' he said quietly.

'Much is blown out of proportion. Like my reputation...' He turned away, his eyes shadowed with something between mischief and melancholy. 'It sounds far more thrilling than I really am.'

Gigi raised an eyebrow. 'So, you're not a seducer of dancers?'

He chuckled, the sound low and unexpected. 'Alas I am not that gallant. I'm mostly a man with terrible timing and an incurable weakness for the wrong things.'

'Would that include me?'

Gigi's question hung in the air.

'You?' he began, his voice tinged with a vulnerability that caught her off guard. 'You are the exception, Gigi Valette. A light in the darkness that has clouded my past.'

He reached out to tuck a loose strand of her hair behind her ear, his touch feather-light yet charged with a depth of feeling that left her a little breathless.

'I may be haunted by my mistakes,' Olivier continued, his words a whisper in the rain-soaked air, 'but when I look at you, I see the possibility of redemption. You remind me of the goodness I once believed was in this world.'

She narrowed her eyes, so wanting to believe him but also unable to ignore the shadows of doubt that lingered in her mind.

He smiled wistfully and continued walking.

The rain began to pick up, soft and steady. He held tighter to her hand.

'Come on,' he said. 'I want to show you where I go when the world feels too loud.'

They ducked into another alley, one she didn't know, and the city shifted again.

They turned the corner, and he stopped beneath a faded

awning with scalloped edges and a small, hand-painted sign barely visible in the drizzle: LA LIBRAIRIE DU TEMPS PERDU.

'This is it,' he said softly. 'My sanctuary.'

He pushed the door open and a golden warmth spilled out, tinged with the scent of old paper and pipe smoke. The bell above gave a gentle chime.

Inside, the bookshop was a cocoon of stillness. Narrow aisles twisted between tall shelves crowded with novels, books of poetry and forgotten atlases. A drowsy tabby cat slept curled in a box marked FIRST EDITIONS – HALF PRICE. The velvet sofa near the fireplace sagged in the middle but looked inviting.

'My sister Madeline owns a bookshop,' Gigi murmured. 'She would love this place.'

He smiled. 'We'll bring her here someday.'

They didn't speak much after that. They each found a book, hers a slim volume of Colette, his an old copy of *Les Fleurs du Mal*, and they curled up together on the worn sofa. The cat eventually decided to join them.

Gigi replaced her Colette on the shelf, her fingers lingering on the other worn spines. When she returned she realised Olivier had left the sofa and maybe drifted deeper into the maze of aisles. She ambled through the stacks to locate him.

A flicker of movement in the corner of her eye drew her to the front window. Through the fogged glass she glimpsed two figures just beyond the awning, speaking German in low voices. One stood rigid, his posture unmistakable even before the glint of silver insignia caught the dim light. The other leaned in, his easy stance with a long-limbed build so like Olivier's.

Her breath stilled.

She wove quickly through the shelves, her shoes whispering over the warped floorboards, but when she slipped the door open to peer outside, the German officer was already striding away, boots striking a clipped rhythm against the wet cobblestones.

Alone now, his silhouette cut sharp and menacing against the pale drizzle.

'Gigi?'

She startled. Olivier's voice came from just behind her. He carried *Les Fleurs du Mal* in one hand, his expression casual, almost amused.

'What are you doing out here?' he asked lightly.

Gigi blinked, her pulse racing. 'I thought I saw...' She trailed off, uncertain how much to confess. Perhaps it was nothing. Perhaps the rain and fog had played tricks.

He smiled, untroubled, and guided her gently back inside. 'We should get you home,' he said, his voice warm but brooking no argument.

But as she let him lead her in, she couldn't shake the image of that officer's insignia, gleaming cold in the drizzle.

When the rain faded into silence, they slipped back out with their treasures tucked under one arm, and, with the last of their ration coupons, stopped to buy a wedge of cheese, a pear and two crusty rolls wrapped in paper.

Back at Gigi's apartment, the windows were fogged with heat from the radiators and they spread the food on the floor atop a vintage embroidered tablecloth. Gigi sat cross-legged, her back to the bookshelf, while Olivier lay beside her, head propped in one hand. The cheese tasted of earthy richness, and the pear was juicy and sweet.

She told him about summer nights dancing barefoot in the garden of her childhood home, about the sound of crickets and the smell of warm stone. He told her about his younger brother, Jean, who had gone to the front the year before at nineteen and never come back.

Olivier turned his palm up, catching hers gently. 'I never knew home could feel like a person,' he murmured. 'Until you.'

She smiled faintly, taking his hand and squeezing it in a silent reassurance.

They stayed there like that for a long while, silence pulsing like a heartbeat between them. As dusk softened into twilight, he brushed a curl from her forehead, and she leaned into the touch without thinking.

When he kissed her, she felt a profound sense of completeness, as if they were two halves of a whole, seamlessly intertwined. Woven together in an infinite loop, with no discernible beginning or end.

And when he gently lifted her into his arms and carried her into the bedroom, it was not the start of something reckless; it was the moment they finally let go of pretending.

Outside, the city continued to smoulder beneath the weight of war. But in that room, for a few hours at least, there was only warmth.

When he finally made love to her with a deliberate tenderness, each movement slow and meticulous, she sought to commend every fleeting moment into her memory, preserving it against the encroaching darkness outside. And when at last their bodies were spent, they lay intertwined in a tangle of limbs and shared breaths, the rhythm of their hearts slowing to match the quiet cadence of the rain against the windowpanes.

Gigi could feel the rise and fall of Olivier's chest beneath her cheek, a steady anchor in a world that seemed to spin out of control.

As sleep began to blur the edges of the room, two voices echoed in her mind: Jacques's warning to stay away, and the old woman's quiet certainty, '*deep inside, there's still a kind little boy who once saved my life*'.

She didn't know yet who Olivier truly was.

But she knew she was falling for him. And something deep inside warned her that loving him might be the most dangerous thing she had ever done. And that terrified her.

25

PARIS, SUMMER 2011

Lily

L'Élégance de l'Encre was a charming, small bookstore tucked away in a cobblestoned side street, with a hand-painted wooden sign above the arched entrance proclaiming that it had been serving the discerning readers of Paris for more than sixty years.

The tall windows were misted by the sultry heat of late afternoon, creating pockets of light around the antique volumes displayed behind them. A tarnished brass bell jingled melodically overhead as Lily moved inside, Julien hovering just a step behind, close enough that Lily could sense his steady presence and catch the faint scent of his cedarwood cologne.

It was the kind of shop that didn't try to impress but succeeded effortlessly: labyrinthine narrow aisles, towering mahogany shelves that reached the elegant ceiling, and leather-bound books stacked in gentle, tilting towers. A small brass reading lamp with a green glass shade glowed near the back, casting a pool of honeyed light where a young woman was serving a white-haired customer. Beside her, an elderly woman with white hair twisted into an elegant chignon sat, silver-rimmed pen in her weathered hand, meticulously correcting something in a journal.

She looked up as they approached, her brown eyes sharp despite her years.

'Excuse me, Madame – are you Madeline?' Lily asked, her voice gentle against the hushed atmosphere of the shop.

The woman nodded, folding her tortoiseshell glasses deliberately and setting them down on the journal. 'I am. Can I help you?'

Julien gave a quick, encouraging glance toward Lily.

'My name is Lily Tremaine,' Lily said, her voice steady despite the nerves pulsing beneath. 'I believe you're the sister of a woman named Gigi Valette. My mother may have known her. We're researching the ballet school Gigi was a member of during the war.'

Something flickered in Madeline's eyes. Surprise, yes, but something else too.

'Gigi lives in Portugal now, near the coast. She hasn't been well. But she has a quiet life. Books, her garden. Why don't you join me upstairs for a cup of tea? And I will see if I can help you.'

Madeline stood, and moved carefully as they followed her up the stairs to her little apartment.

The soothing aroma of lavender and the rich scent of aged leather drifted out to greet them and Lily and Julien sank into a burgundy velvet sofa with fraying tassels, its cushions moulded to the shape of years of visitors. First-edition novels with gilt-edged pages stood in precarious towers beside sepia photographs in ornate frames, each object placed with the deliberate care of a curator preserving moments of a life fully lived.

As they told Madeline their story, the young woman from behind the counter went to make tea. Madeline hummed to herself as she rifled through a drawer, and then pulled out a bundle in a small box.

'Gigi was a beautiful dancer,' she mused, voice low and warm, as she placed a small pile of prints into Lily's outstretched hand.

Lily and Julien examined the black-and-white images one by one: Gigi in a grand jeté, her slender silhouette arching above gleaming stage lights; in another, balanced en pointe in a diaphanous tutu. Each photograph captured a moment of effortless grace, a fleeting testament to a career that had carried her to the stages of Paris.

Lily paused, clearing her throat, then asked, 'Do you know anything about the people who lived with her above the dance school?'

Madeline's eyes softened. 'My parents worried when she moved out at eighteen,' she recalled, gently lifting a slightly curled image. 'But Gigi wouldn't be deterred. She rented a tiny apartment right above the ballet school. There were three other young women there. They all lived in apartments that shared a narrow balcony. I believe I have a group shot here...'

With careful hands, she produced a photograph marked simply *Gigi* in looping script. The black-and-white image showed four girls standing side by side on a wrought-iron balcony, arms draped around one another's shoulders. Suitcases stood at their feet, silent witnesses to new beginnings. Though the photo's edges were frayed and the contrast had faded, their bright laughter seemed almost audible.

She turned it over. On the back, scrawled in a delicate hand, was a short dedication: *First day. Let's never forget who we are. – Gigi, Malina, Claudette & Eloise.*

'They were inseparable, all worked in theatre or the arts. Eloise was a seamstress, Malina a painter and Claudette worked behind the curtain at the theatre for years. She practically lived there.' Madeline offered the photo to Lily. 'This was the day they moved into their apartments. So young, so full of dreams.'

Julien lifted his camera and photographed the print.

'Do you know if one of them had twins in 1932?' Lily asked, voice hushed.

Madeline's brow creased. She shook her head slowly. 'They kept each other's confidences. But it wasn't my own sister, she would have been too young at the time.'

'Would it be possible to talk to Gigi, do you think? Maybe one of the other girls talked about twins?'

Madeline's face clouded. 'She has only just recovered from a serious illness. I'll write to her, but don't pin your hopes on it. Her memory comes and goes.'

Lily left the card for the gallery and they both thanked Madeline before leaving.

'Coffee?' Julien asked quietly, gesturing toward a small café at the corner.

Lily only hesitated for a moment, a flicker of guilt about Marcus, then nodded. They sat at a little table under the awning, the air scented with roasted beans and rain-washed pavement.

Julien stirred his cup slowly as Lily's mind buzzed with the unanswered questions.

'I will download the photo and bring it over to the gallery if you want and we can add it to the board. And tomorrow we'll pick up where we left off,' he said. 'We'll follow this thread of Madeline's sister.'

Lily sighed and asked softly, 'Julien... what about your business? All this time you're spending with me, it must be pulling you away from the shop.'

He leaned back, surprise flickering across his face, before giving a quiet laugh. 'The shop will survive. And this' – he gestured to the folder of notes she carried – 'this *matters*. Your mother is ill, time is of the utmost importance.'

Something in his tone silenced her. He wasn't here out of obligation; he wanted to be. That realisation both steadied and unsettled her as she wondered why her husband didn't see it that way.

'Have you found out anything more about your grandfather? About what he did during the war?' she asked.

His expression shifted, the usual steadiness shadowed by something heavier. He drew a quiet breath. 'I continued to unpack his belongings. I came across a letter. Hidden away in an old wallet. It was in his handwriting, addressed to my grandmother, but never sent.'

Lily's chest tightened. 'What did it say?'

Julien's gaze dropped to the table. 'I think my grandmother was having an affair. It was a plea. He asked her to give him another chance. He wrote that the other man would never love her the way he did, never give her the life he had tried to. His words...' He trailed off, searching. 'They were raw. Heartbreaking. And he must have written them when he was about my age.'

The ache in his voice made Lily's stomach twist. She thought of Marcus, of the woman in the scarlet scarf, of the laughter she had overheard.

She swallowed. 'Do you know who the other man was?'

Julien shook his head. 'No. I'll never know if she truly betrayed him, or if it was just suspicion eating him alive. But finding something that personal, that wounded, decades later...' His hand tightened briefly on the handle of his cup. 'It made him human to me in a way he never was before.'

Lily studied him, her throat tight. She imagined Julien's grandfather at their age, desperate, begging for another chance, to be chosen. The parallel pressed too close for comfort.

The rain drummed softly against the awning, a steady rhythm that only made the silence between them more charged. For a moment, she had the irrational urge to reach across the table and take his hand, to let him know she understood. But she curled her fingers into her lap instead, terrified of what that gesture might suggest.

'It blindsided me,' he said finally, his voice low. 'You build this image of your grandparents as these pillars, especially during wartime. Finding out they were just as broken as the rest of us...'

'When did you discover the letter?' she asked.

'After we returned to Paris.'

The question of why he'd kept this from her rose to her lips, then died there. Of course – he'd seen the fractures in her marriage, had been careful not to press against those tender spots with his own family's history of betrayal.

At last he looked up, his gaze steady. 'I didn't mean to burden you with this.'

'You didn't burden me,' Lily said quickly. 'If anything, it helps. To know you understand what it feels like to live with... uncertainty.'

Julien gave a faint nod, the corners of his mouth tightening.

Lily glanced down at her watch and felt her stomach dip. *Friday.* She had promised herself she would keep some semblance of normality, and that meant dinner, the ritual Marcus still expected, no matter the state of their marriage.

'I should go,' she said reluctantly, pushing her chair back. 'It's Friday, and I...' She forced a small, brittle smile. 'Well, I ought to make dinner.'

Julien stood with her, his hand brushing hers, the touch light but steady. 'Of course. I'll walk you to the corner.'

They stepped out from beneath the awning. The street was sweet and slick with rain, the air tinged with the earthy scent of wet foliage. For a moment neither moved, reluctant to break whatever fragile thread had bound them through the conversation.

Julien turned to her at last. 'Rest tonight,' he said softly. 'Tomorrow we'll begin again. Together.'

Something in his tone made Lily's throat ache.

Then, without hesitation, he reached for her hand. His hand closed firmly around hers. The steady pressure of his fingers wrapped around her palm spoke of certainty, of someone unwilling to let her drift. He held on a moment longer than courtesy required, and something warm and electric moved through her veins, impossible to dismiss.

She wanted to hold on, to keep him standing there with her, but he released her gently.

Lily stood rooted as he walked away, his stride unhurried, shoulders broad and straight beneath his jacket. The early evening light touched the edges of his dark curls, damp from the rain, and the strong line of his jaw as he turned briefly to glance back. There was an ease to the way he moved, a quiet confidence that made him impossibly good-looking without seeming to try.

Lily went through the motions when she got home, moving into the rhythm of Friday night as though nothing inside her had shifted.

Later, she slipped into bed beside Marcus. His back was already turned, his breathing steady and even.

She stared at the ceiling, guilt pressing down hard. Wasn't she just as bad as him now, thinking of another man while lying here as his wife?

Yet beneath the shame a pull she couldn't deny. Julien's words, his fingers warm around hers. She had begun to need him, to measure her days by his presence.

And as she finally slipped into uneasy sleep, it wasn't Marcus she dreamed of; it was Julien.

26

———

PARIS, JUNE 1941

Gigi

The rehearsal studio held the echo of forgotten performances, dusty velvet curtains, warped mirrors and floorboards that creaked in rhythm with the ghosts. The piano in the corner, scuffed and slightly out of tune, had become their meeting ground over the past weeks. Olivier was composing a new piece and a friend had let him use the place when he needed it.

He played with his usual quiet intensity, fingers coaxing out the beginnings of a melody they'd been shaping together. Gigi danced barefoot across the floor, her movements inspired by his music.

She spun to a stop, breathless. 'If you keep playing like that,' she said, brushing a curl from her cheek, 'I might fall in love with you by accident.'

He didn't look up from the keys, but a smile tugged at the corner of his mouth. 'Only by accident?'

She smiled broadly in reply and slowed to listen, her arms falling to her sides, breath catching in her chest.

She stepped toward him as the last notes faded. 'That's the most beautiful thing I have ever heard.'

He looked up, smiling, then stopped to add notations to the paper, and she crossed the final distance between them in two strides.

Running her arms down his, she gently kissed the back of his neck.

Olivier exhaled, his arms winding around her waist as he eased her gently into his lap.

The bench groaned beneath them, but the sound faded against the rush of quiet between them. Their lips met, slowly at first, then with growing urgency as if they'd both been reaching for this moment all day without knowing it.

When she finally tore herself away, breath shallow, heart thudding, she whispered, 'I keep thinking the urge to be with you will fade. That if I stay away long enough, it'll ease, the wanting.'

He didn't smile, but something in his expression shifted, a flicker of understanding. 'Let me guess, it doesn't?' he said softly.

She shook her head. 'No,' she said. 'It only gets louder.'

His hand slid to the small of her back, grounding her even as she felt untethered.

'For me,' he said, voice rougher now, 'it's like carrying an ache I never asked for. One I never want to lose.'

Her breath hitched. There it was, that soft place in him she rarely saw.

'I could never forget you when we're apart,' he added, quieter now. 'It would be like trying not to breathe.'

She stilled, her gaze locking with his. The truth of it settled deep, unspoken but understood.

He reached up, gently brushing a strand of hair from her forehead, his touch reverent. Then, with a tenderness that unravelled her, he leaned in and pressed a kiss to the place he'd cleared, light, certain and impossibly gentle.

She closed her eyes. And in the hush that followed, she let herself believe him.

They stayed like that for a long while, wrapped in each other's arms, unable to get enough of the feeling of contentment when they were together.

'I know,' she finally said with a playful glint in her eyes, 'let's go out and dine at one of those charming bistros in the heart of town. We can show everyone we are a couple.'

He shifted awkwardly in his seat, and she felt him pull back, physically and emotionally. Something in his posture made her stomach tighten.

'I can't today, I have to be somewhere,' he said evasively, his expression clouded with tension.

Gigi struggled to conceal her disappointment.

'Tomorrow, then?' she suggested.

He didn't reply, but when the next day came around the answer was the same.

As the days passed, Gigi began to notice a pattern.

He never walked her home during the day. Never lingered in the studio after they finished. He was always off somewhere, coat half-buttoned, glancing at the clock. The excuses came readily.

I promised to meet someone, I have a rehearsal across town, tonight's not good, tomorrow, maybe...

Tomorrow never came.

Finally, one morning, she leaned on the piano and said, 'You know, you've refused everything I've suggested for weeks.'

He didn't meet her gaze.

'Chestnut crêpes. A walk along the river. The bookshop in

Montmartre. Even the puppet theatre I know you secretly love...'

He smiled faintly at that, but still he said nothing.

'And now I will not let you say no. Claudette's birthday is tomorrow night and she is a very good friend of mine,' Gigi added, folding her arms.

He looked up, sheepish.

'Gigi—'

'No.' She leaned forward, catching his hands in hers. '*Please*. I want you to spend one evening with me with people I adore, eat whatever they can scrape up during this war and drink terrible wine.'

He studied her for a long beat. Then slowly, finally, he nodded.

'I'll come.'

She threw her arms around his neck and kissed him firmly on the lips.

The café was tucked down a side street in the Marais. It was lit with strings of mismatched bulbs and gave off the scents of garlic butter and cheap wine. The windows steamed from inside, laughter bleeding into the darkening street.

The little group gathered around two pushed-together tables, artists, writers, dancers, people who lived for their art. Claudette sat at the centre, swathed in midnight-blue velvet, a paper crown Eloise had made for her tilted over one ear.

Olivier arrived late, with no trace of apology.

He swept in, hair still damp from the rain. He gave the birthday girl a beautiful bouquet of white lilies and kissed her hand with exaggerated flourish.

'To the birthday queen,' he said, bowing dramatically. 'And may her reign be long and full of wine.'

Claudette laughed, clearly delighted. 'This one I like, Gigi. He's got flair.'

Gigi flushed with quiet pride as Olivier took the empty seat beside her. His hand brushed her knee under the table. A warm, secret touch.

For a while, it was easy. He was charming and witty, effortlessly engaged in conversation. He told a story about a violinist who got so drunk he fell into the Seine with his instrument. '"Save the instrument," someone yelled, "not the man, he's a terrible player!"' and everyone roared with laughter.

They ordered cheap red wine and onion soup, and Claudette made a toast.

'To all the misfits who find each other in this chaotic world,' Claudette proclaimed, as they all raised their glasses high.

But Gigi began to notice that, while Olivier was smiling, his gaze drifted more than usual. He tensed when the door opened. How he didn't drink as much as he usually would, not enough for someone trying to appear relaxed.

She leaned in. 'Everything all right?'

'Of course,' he said, too quickly.

The door opened again.

Two men stepped in, shaking the rain from their hats. One wore the grey uniform of the SS, the eagle insignia catching the flicker of candlelight.

Gigi felt Olivier go still beside her.

The room changed. It was subtle, but palpable. A few conversations dimmed. Someone near the door left mid-bite.

Olivier stood.

'I'll be right back,' he said, brushing her hand from his arm.

She watched, heart tightening, as he crossed to the bar, where the officer stood ordering brandy. Olivier greeted him with a handshake. A quiet exchange followed, too low to hear, but not brief. The officer nodded once, gave a half-smile as he ordered a drink.

Malina leaned in across the table. Her dark brows were drawn tight. 'That's Oberstleutnant Hartmann,' she said coolly. 'Head of operations for the SS command in this quarter.'

The words made Gigi's stomach tighten. A man that high in the SS, chatting like old friends with Olivier, made the air feel suddenly thinner, every sound in the café sharper, more dangerous.

Gigi blinked. 'You're sure?'

'I never forget a uniform. This isn't good, Gigi. Why is your boyfriend talking to him?'

Her blood ran cold, dread flooding her body until she could scarcely breathe. Everything around her faded into a dull roar as her gaze locked on Olivier beside the officer. His casual posture, so at odds with the rigid Nazi at his shoulder, sent a chill through her.

Olivier returned to the table moments later, and slid back into his seat as if nothing had happened.

But the colour had drained from his face.

Gigi stared at him. 'Do you *know* him?'

'A little.' His voice was light, but something behind his eyes was shuttered. 'I met him briefly in Germany.'

He poured himself a glass of wine. His hand trembled slightly.

Malina said nothing more, but her gaze lingered on Olivier's face.

Gigi forced herself to laugh at Olivier's next joke, but the sound felt brittle in her throat. The warmth between them, so effortless moments ago, had thinned to something tense and uncertain. Every word he spoke felt slightly off-pitch, too rehearsed, too polished.

She nodded along, smiled in the right places, but her mind spun in quiet panic. Malina's warning echoed behind every syllable: *'This isn't good, Gigi.'*

She kept replaying it, the way he leaned in toward the officer, the familiarity in his stance, the too-casual smile he wore. It hadn't been fear on his face. It had been comfort, the ease of recognition.

Her fingers tightened around her wine glass. She didn't dare look at Malina again, didn't dare meet the sharp knowing in her friend's eyes.

She wanted to believe Olivier. She wanted the night to return to what it had been an hour ago, light, teasing, safe. But now everything felt touched by shadow.

He said something else, something clever, and she managed another smile. But inside, a silent, steady question took root.

Who are you really, and what are you hiding?

They left the café in silence. The laughter and candlelight faded behind them, replaced by the hush of damp cobblestones and the distant roll of thunder. Rain clung to the edges of the rooftops, the kind that hadn't yet fallen but promised it would.

Gigi walked slightly ahead, arms folded tight against the night air, her heels clicking a little too fast on the pavement. Olivier kept pace beside her, quiet. She felt him glance at her once, twice. On the third time, he reached for her hand.

She pulled it away, sharply.

The space between them widened like a crack in the ice.

He let out a quiet breath. 'Gigi... what's wrong?'

She stopped walking. The rain began, soft, steady, inevitable.

She turned to face him, her voice low but sharp as broken glass. 'Oberstleutnant Hartmann. That's what's wrong.'

He froze, his expression dark in the shifting shadows.

'I didn't lie to you. I told you I did work for them,' he said finally, voice rough.

Her throat ached; her chest was tight. 'You didn't tell me the whole truth either, did you?' The words cracked, heavy with hurt.

Olivier took a step toward her. 'You think I can?'

She shook her head, tears burning hot. 'And what happens to the people who trust you? To *me*?' Her voice wavered, half fury, half grief. 'You made me feel safe, Olivier. And now I don't know who you are.'

'Do you know what happens to people who talk?' Olivier shot back defensively.

Her jaw clenched. 'And what happens to the ones who say nothing at all? Who smile and shake hands with murderers like Hartmann? What happens to the people who just... play music and pretend?'

His mouth opened, stunned. 'Is that what you think I'm doing?'

'You tell me!' she snapped, her voice echoing off the wet stone walls. 'Because from where I stood, it looked like two old friends having a very comfortable chat.'

'I am surviving,' he said tightly. 'Navigating. Every word I say to him is a performance. Every smile is for the part I'm playing.'

She stepped toward him now, chest heaving. 'You think I don't know about *performing*? Every day, we dance for these monsters, pretending they don't see us, praying they don't pick us next.'

Her voice broke. 'But I saw you, Olivier. I saw you laughing with him, joking, having fun. If that's performing, you should be on the stage, not just playing for people on it. Watching you there... I felt something in me crack.'

He stared at her, soaked and silent, his blue eyes piercing hers, his hands curled into fists at his sides.

'I didn't want to believe it,' she whispered. 'God, I didn't. I wanted to come home tonight and pretend everything was still good. But I can't unsee that moment.'

Olivier's voice was hoarse now. 'You don't know what I am risking—'

'Because you won't tell me!' she cried. 'You keep me in the dark, and expect me to just… love you anyway.'

He stepped back, eyes flashing, then his voice dropped to a husky whisper. 'You're right, I have been selfish. Because being with you is the only real thing I have left that is unblemished. Untouched by all the darkness in my life. But I haven't been fair to you.'

Silence fell between them, stunned and raw.

Rain ran down her cheeks, indistinguishable from the tears now gathering in her eyes.

He moved toward her again, slower this time, seeming to break apart with every step. 'I'm sorry,' he said, almost a whisper. 'I wanted to protect you from this. From *me*. But I think I waited too long.'

He hesitated, then added, 'Can we talk in your apartment, somewhere we can't be heard? I promise I'll tell you everything.'

Her arms fell to her sides. She looked at him, really looked, and saw the truth unravelling behind his eyes.

The exhaustion. The terror. The loneliness.

Without saying another word, she marched to her apartment with Olivier following behind. Once the door was closed, she turned to him. Her voice came out thin. 'Tell me all of it. No more performances.'

Olivier looked at her again, gaze clearer now. 'I'm not what you think I am, Gigi.'

'Then what are you?'

'I work deep undercover for the Resistance, go where they need me to be, hear what needs hearing, pass it along to those who need to know. I wear one face for them, another for everyone else. And every day I wonder how long I have before one of them sees through me.'

'Why wouldn't you tell me that?'

'Because it is complicated. No one is supposed to know, and the less you know the safer you are.'

She crossed the room slowly, her voice trembling. 'Tonight, at the café, you looked happy, Olivier. Comfortable. With a *monster*.'

'I wasn't,' he said.

'I don't know what to believe—'

'Then believe this,' he said, stepping closer, his voice taut with emotion. 'Every word I've said to you when we're alone, that's the truth. That's the only place I get to be myself.'

She wanted to believe it. God, she wanted to. But something in her chest had begun to crack. And beneath the splintering was something harder. Colder.

Her voice came out barely above a breath. 'So, what happens now?'

He looked away. Exhaled slowly. 'I can't keep doing this. Not to you.'

The words sliced through her. 'What are you saying?'

'It's a game, Gigi. A dangerous, deadly game. And I've already made peace with how it ends for me. But you...' He shook his head, pained. 'You still have your whole life ahead of you. I won't drag you into this.'

'What are you talking about?' she asked, her voice breaking. 'You're not dragging me anywhere. I chose this. I chose you.'

He gave a hollow laugh and ran a hand through his damp, sandy hair. 'How old are you? Twenty-three? Twenty-four?'

'I'm nineteen.'

That stopped him cold.

He stared at her for a long moment, then whispered, 'Nineteen...' He looked like someone who'd just realised he'd stepped over a line he could never uncross. 'What was I thinking,' he murmured. 'I should go.'

A panic bloomed in her chest. 'Will I see you tomorrow?'

His eyes darkened. 'No, this is the last time I'll see you like this.'

Her heart plummeted, her throat closing around a thousand unsaid things.

She spoke, her voice trembling. 'The risk you're taking? I don't care. I trust you.'

His jaw tightened. His gaze locked on hers, filled with a burning intensity that made her stomach flip. 'I'm the last person you want to trust,' he said, voice low, rough and deadly quiet.

He reached for the door, his hand closing around the handle. And something inside her broke.

She crossed the space between them in a heartbeat, grabbed his coat and pulled his mouth down to hers with the full force of everything she couldn't say.

His body responded instantly, one hand tangling in her hair, the other clutching at her like a drowning man, fisting the back of her coat, pulling her against him as though he could burn the memory of her into his skin.

Gigi clung to him, fingers curled so tightly into his lapels her knuckles ached. Her breath came in short, broken gasps between kisses, her legs trembling beneath her, barely holding her upright. She pressed closer, needing the weight of him, the heat, anything to keep from splintering completely.

The kiss was desperate, bruising, a collision of want and sorrow, as if they could stop time by clinging hard enough to each other.

When he finally pulled away, she felt hollow and weightless, like the air had been torn from her lungs.

His lips hovered near her ear, his breath still uneven.

'Don't,' she whispered. 'Don't say anything that will ruin this.'

He pressed a kiss to her temple, soft and final.

'Goodbye, Gigi,' he said. 'Promise you'll keep dancing.'

Then he stepped back. And before she could ask what any

of it truly meant, before she could make sense of why it hurt so much, he was gone.

She stood frozen in the stillness he left behind and, for a long moment, she didn't move.

Then her knees gave out. She sank to the floor in silence, arms wrapped around herself, his scent still clinging to her coat.

27

PARIS, SUMMER 2011

Lily

Effy's back room smelled faintly of black tea, dried paint and a forgotten lavender candle she had lit hours ago. The corkboard loomed in the corner, holding the photograph's scraps of scribbled notes and red string that looked more sad than connected.

Lily sat cross-legged on the floor, her notebook open but untouched. Effy hovered nearby, arms crossed, one sequinned slipper tapping a rhythm against the scuffed wood floor.

'We have Gigi's full name,' Effy said, frowning up at the photo of the four women on the balcony. 'But not the other girls'. And that's the problem.'

Lily sighed and leaned back against the edge of the table. 'We know their faces. We know they lived together. But I can't access anything official, no birth records, no death notices, not even school enrolment, without surnames.'

Effy plucked a sticky note off the edge of the board and crumpled it. 'We could be staring at your grandmother and we'd have no way of knowing.'

Lily rubbed at her temple, feeling the weight of the

unknown pressing in. 'We've traced Rebecca and Rachel to the ballet school. We know the twins were taken to the South of France in 1943. But without knowing who gave birth to them we are kind of stuck...' Her voice trailed off.

Effy moved to the window and cracked it open. A gust of air swept in, stirring the pages on the worktable.

And then, just as she was about to suggest they take a break, the bell over the gallery door chimed.

Footsteps echoed briefly on the polished wood floor, followed by a familiar voice calling, 'I'm not interrupting, am I?'

Effy leaned her head around the doorframe. 'Only our spiral into archival despair.'

Julien appeared a moment later with his laptop tucked under his arm, raindrops clinging to the shoulders of his jacket. He looked sheepish and vaguely windblown in a way that made Lily's stomach flip for no good reason at all.

'I figured you might want to see something,' he said. 'I cleaned up the photo of the girls I took, adjusted the contrast and enlarged it. There's a detail I think we missed.'

Effy raised an eyebrow. 'We are in desperate need of details. Welcome to the mess.'

Julien pulled out a wooden chair, its legs scraping softly against the floor, and opened his sleek, silver laptop. The soft glow from the screen illuminated his face as he settled in. Across the table, Lily moved closer, and an almost palpable charge seemed to hum in the air between them, an invisible thread of connection that sent a shiver down her spine.

The screen flickered to life, and there was the image: four women, arms looped together, their luggage piled at their feet.

Julien zoomed in slowly, carefully, guiding their eyes to the bottom right corner of the image. There, half-shadowed beneath one of the suitcases, was a slim, rectangular tag hanging from a leather handle.

'I thought it might be a brand,' he said. 'But look.'

He adjusted the exposure slightly, and the letters became clearer. Elegant script, faint but unmistakable.

M. Laurent-Masson

Lily's breath caught. '"M" for Malina?'

Effy sat up straighter. 'Laurent-Masson?'

Julien glanced between them. 'Does that mean something?'

Effy blinked, then gave a low whistle. 'Laurent-Masson is not just any name. That's old industrialist empire money. I've seen it on restoration donor plaques, auction lists, you name it. They buy expensive art and anonymity in equal measure.'

Lily stared at the tag on the screen, her thoughts racing. 'So, Malina might have come from money?'

Julien closed the laptop gently. 'I thought you'd want to know.'

Lily smiled, something in her chest tightening, not just because he'd found the name but because he'd thought to bring it, unasked, as if he understood how much it mattered.

'Thank you,' she said softly.

Julien gave a small nod. For a moment his eyes lingered on her, and she felt the unspoken weight of it, a flicker of something that made her look away first.

'So, what's our next move?' she asked, her voice a little too light, a little too casual.

Effy was already on her feet, heading toward the dusty bookshelf near the back wall.

'Now,' she said, 'we break out the good tea and my stash of 1930s society magazines. If that girl had a last name like that, she was photographed, gossiped about and thoroughly documented. Somewhere in those pages.'

Julien raised an eyebrow. 'You collect society magazines?'

Effy grinned. 'Like most people collect regrets. Now help me find the box marked "guilty pleasures".'

After flipping the gallery sign to closed for lunch, they trekked up to Effy's flat with boxes of old magazines.

Julien spread himself across the sofa, looking both out of place and completely at home, flipping through a magazine with a woman absurdly adorned in feathers on the cover. Lily curled into an armchair, balancing a stack of issues on one knee. Effy moved between them, doling out tea in delicate mismatched china and placing a silver tray of lemon biscuits in the centre.

'This,' she declared, settling in with a flourish, 'is where the secrets live.'

The pages crackled like old parchment as they turned them, the scent of aged paper mixing with bergamot. Headlines danced with exaggerated glamour:

Winter Debutante Ball Brings Back the Charleston

Who's Courting Whom? The Riviera's Most Eligible Men

The Paris Darlings You've Never Heard Of, Yet

'Who wrote these?' Julien asked, flipping through a centre-fold of perfume ads. 'Fitzgerald with a side of gossip columnist?'

'Exactly,' Effy said, already scanning a table of contents. 'This stuff was the social media of the day. If Malina was a Laurent-Masson, she was one of these women.'

Lily suddenly sat up straight. 'This might be something.'

Effy leaned closer as Lily read aloud from a formal column titled *Naissances*: births.

'M. et Mme Édouard Laurent-Masson ont la joie d'annoncer la
naissance de leur fille, Malina Thérèse Laurent-Masson, née le
14 février 1914 à Paris.'

Malina's birth announcement. They all crowded around to read it together.

The elegant script of the magazine told them what they had been searching for. Malina had indeed been a part of the famous Laurent-Masson family and had been born on the fourteenth of February 1914.

Now, feeling as though they were on the right track, they all continued to search the magazines for more clues. After some time, Effy slapped the paper, startling everyone.

'*Springtime Soirée: Laurent-Masson Heiress Charms the Room*,' she announced, holding up the page for them all to see. Julien read aloud from the article:

'Malina Thérèse Laurent-Masson, nineteen, attended a garden
luncheon hosted by the Comtesse de Rochefort, wearing a pale
blue silk dress and pearls gifted by her father.'

The article described her as 'dark-haired, lovely and destined for high places'.

'There she is. That's her!' Lily exclaimed.

Though the picture of the woman in Madeline's photo had cropped her hair short since this article was published, it was undoubtably the same person.

Julien's brow furrowed. 'That would've been just before—'

'1932,' Lily confirmed. 'The year the twins were born.'

They turned the next few pages in silence, until Effy gave a soft gasp.

'Oh, here. This is just referencing the garden party there is more on the next pages.'

She read aloud:

'Miss Laurent-Masson, eldest daughter of Édouard and Camille, has temporarily withdrawn from society due to a mild illness. She is said to be recovering at the Fontaine-Blanche Health Retreat outside Paris, known for its discretion and luxurious approach to rest and reflection.'

Lily stared at the line, heart hammering. 'Translation?'

'Pregnant, unwed and sent away,' Effy responded with one brow arched. 'It happened a lot back then.'

Julien's expression had shifted and was softer, more focused. 'She disappeared.'

Lily sat back, the photo of Malina's smiling face with her friends flashing through her mind. 'And it sounds like she came back someone else. Let's see if we can find out more about this place she was sent,' Lily continued.

After some searching, Lily found a reference on a little-known website called *Histoire Oubliée – Archives of Hidden France.*

She clicked through to an article titled: The Other Side of Fontaine-Blanche. Originally published: 3 April 1975.

For years, the Fontaine-Blanche Health Retreat was known as a sanctuary for the elite, offering rest and recuperation for high-born women in need of privacy. But testimonies from former staff and patients suggest a different legacy.

In truth, Fontaine-Blanche functioned as a discreet maternity clinic, sheltering the unwed daughters of France's wealthiest families. These women were sent away to give birth far from the eyes of Parisian society, and were often discouraged from speaking of what happened there ever again.

Many of the babies were adopted. The mothers, their pregnancies hidden and their babies taken, returned to Paris and married, their time at the retreat quietly erased. Their respectability restored, they never spoke of what happened there.

Effy sat down slowly on the floor beside them. 'So... Malina went there to give birth.'

Julien nodded. 'She wasn't alone. This happened to many women.'

Lily stood and crossed the room to the board. She pinned a new card under Malina's name and wrote:

1932 – *Malina was at Fontaine-Blanche Health Retreat. Was she pregnant with the twins?*

'I need to go there,' she said quietly. 'To see it.'

Julien closed his laptop. 'I might be able to help with that.'

Effy turned to him. 'You are a man of many talents.'

Julien smiled, sheepish. 'I did a photo residency last year. The nonprofit I worked with is based at Fontaine-Blanche now, it's an artists' retreat. I still have a contact there.'

Effy looked impressed. 'Of course you do.'

Julien continued, 'I think I can get us access.'

Lily glanced back at the board, her voice unwavering and calm. 'Then let's go. Effy, would you like to go on a field trip?'

Effy shifted her gaze between the two of them. 'I think you two can handle this one,' she replied with a slight smile.

Lily felt warmth rise to her cheeks as Julien mumbled something in the affirmative under his breath. After finalising their plans, she watched him walk away, her heart fluttering with excitement at the thought of being alone with him again. She turned to her boss, who stood behind the counter with a knowing smile.

'Yes, this is all coming together nicely,' Effy said, a twinkle in her eye.

'I hope you mean following these clues,' Lily replied sceptically. Effy moved away with a nonchalant flick of her wrist, her bracelets jangling softly as she departed. 'That too,' she said with a teasing lilt in her voice.

Before Lily could remind Effy of her marital status again, the woman had already swept away with a knowing glance that said everything.

28

PARIS, JUNE 1941

Claudette

The midday sun slanted through the tall windows of Café Leveque, pooling in lazy golden patches across the worn tile floor. The air was thick with the scent of strong coffee, buttered bread and the faint tang of cigarette smoke curling from the lips of patrons deep in conversation.

It was a place Claudette had always loved, a pocket of normality tucked away from the tightening grip of the war. Here, the rhythms of the theatre world bled into real life, chorus girls chatting over bowls of *café au lait*, set designers sketching grand backdrops on napkins, costumers unspooling gossip as they mended loose seams.

She had come here for the illusion of an ordinary afternoon. But the moment she felt his presence beside her, that fragile illusion shattered.

A chair scraped sharply against the tile and, without invitation, Philippe slid into the seat opposite her, his crisp uniform dark against the sunlit warmth of the café.

'You shouldn't look so surprised, *sœur*.' His voice was measured, each syllable weighted with quiet authority. 'You should always expect me.'

Claudette's spine stiffened. Her fingers curled around her porcelain cup, as if the warmth might anchor her to something solid. The café was full of familiar faces, people who knew her, worked with her, trusted her. And yet, in that moment, she had never felt more alone.

'You can stop glancing around like that,' Philippe said, a flicker of amusement in his eyes. 'What is more natural than a brother and sister having lunch together?'

Claudette forced herself to keep her voice level. 'What do you want?'

'A small favour.' He reached into his coat, pulled out a cigarette case and tapped one free.

Out of the corner of her eye she saw a woman who worked on some of the theatre set designs whisper to her friend.

'You enjoy working at the Palais Garnier, don't you?'

She swallowed hard. 'I won't betray anybody else.'

Philippe smiled, a slow, patient smile, the kind that made her stomach turn. He took his time lighting his cigarette, before exhaling a thin trail of smoke into the space between them.

'Yes, you did well there.'

She felt sick as he continued.

'You misunderstand. I don't need much. Just your eyes and ears.' He leaned in, voice dropping lower. 'We have a tip-off from another loyal supporter. There's a meeting happening at the theatre's loading dock tomorrow night. Find out who is involved. That's all. If I can uncover the cell working in the theatre and what they are doing, it could be very good for me.'

His words settled in her chest like a lead weight.

Claudette shook her head before he'd even finished. 'No.'

Her defiant declaration reverberated through the café. The clinking of silverware and murmured conversations seemed to hush in the wake of her response. Philippe regarded her with a calculating gaze as he took a slow drag from his cigarette.

'Stubborn as ever, Claudette,' he said coldly. 'But you, of all people, know the cost of defiance.'

'These people are my friends. My *family*,' she replied, her voice firm despite the tremor beneath it.

She could feel the weight of his gaze, measuring, calculating. The tension between them crackled like a storm gathering in the silence.

Philippe leaned back in his chair, his eyes never leaving hers. '*I* am your family,' he growled. 'Or have you forgotten what we were to each other? You wouldn't have survived childhood without me.'

'Likewise,' she shot back, her voice edged with steel. 'You owe me too, Philippe. And the least you can do, the very least, is respect the life I've managed to build. Especially after the childhood we endured.'

'Your defiance leaves me no choice. I will have to arrest Marguerite's husband. The Nazis have more persuasive ways to get the information we need and, like his wife, he is obviously working with the Resistance.'

Claudette was horrified. 'But he has two young daughters and he is all alone since you took away their mother.'

'Most unfortunate,' Philippe responded with a cold detachment that sent a chill through Claudette's whole body as he stared at her. A sick dread coiled in her chest, her breath catching as if the walls of the room had suddenly closed in. The bustling café seemed to fade into the background, leaving only the sharp tension between the two adversaries.

Then he blew out air, and said in a nonchalant tone, 'I will do what needs to be done, I just thought you might like to spare one member of your precious *family*, cause them a little less pain.' With that, he rose from his seat to leave.

She reached out her hand and grabbed his arm.

'Wait!' she implored, her voice barely above a whisper, her fingers digging into his sleeve.

Philippe paused, his gaze flickering down to where her hand gripped his arm. He regarded Claudette for a long moment, and she felt the tension between them in the air. Slowly, he lowered himself back into his seat, his gaze never leaving hers.

Claudette took a steadying breath, her fingers releasing their tight grip on Philippe's sleeve.

'I will do it. But this is the last time.'

He gave her the details and was just about to leave when she spoke again.

'Philippe, what happened to you? What makes you so cruel?'

For a moment she saw a flicker of something soften in his eyes, a brief glimpse of the brother she used to know buried beneath the layers of duty and betrayal. But just as quickly, it vanished, replaced by a mask of indifference.

'You know what happened, Claudette,' he replied, his voice hard and bitter. 'You know what we've both endured. No one is ever going to treat me like I am worthless again. I vowed to myself that I would never be at the mercy of others. It's a lesson you should learn too.'

'Even if you are the one that is forcing me?' Claudette's voice was angry, her eyes searching for any shred of the brother she once knew.

But Philippe's gaze remained steely with a bitter resolve.

'It doesn't matter who it is. We are all pawns in this game, Claudette. Better to be the one moving the pieces than the one being taken,' he replied.

Then he stood from his seat, adjusted his uniform with practised precision and strode away.

. . .

Later that evening, in Gigi's apartment, Claudette sat curled in an armchair, nursing a lukewarm cup of chicory coffee, listening as Gigi rattled on about the latest theatre gossip.

But she wasn't really listening. Her thoughts spun, tangled, fraying at the edges. It had been years since she had felt unsafe – the world she had created had become her sanctuary; but now she was more fearful than she had been when she was begging as a small child.

There was a pause in their conversation and she felt an impulse, an overwhelming desire to confess, to pull back the curtain and let Gigi see the horror she had tangled herself in.

Instead, she found herself whispering, 'Have you ever done something that went against your principles?'

Gigi frowned, setting her cup down, obviously surprised at the sudden shift in their conversation. 'What do you mean?'

'Hypothetically... how do you know when bending the rules is justified?'

'What is going on?'

Claudette shook her head, not wanting to give her friend any details, but continued. 'I'm in that kind of position,' she admitted softly. 'A choice that could alter everything I believe in... everything I am.'

Gigi studied her, considering her words. 'Bending the rules and betraying yourself are two different things.'

Claudette felt the words land like a blow.

Gigi reached out her hand, offering a silent reassurance. 'Sometimes, the hardest choices are the ones that define us,' she said softly.

'But what if refusing to give in to the pressure means sacrificing another?'

Gigi held Claudette's gaze, her expression understanding. 'I don't know, Claudette, that sounds like a difficult choice. Only you can decide where your loyalty truly lies.' She sighed, leaning back into the worn cushions of her armchair. 'But be careful,' she added quietly, a rare seriousness creeping into her voice. 'The moment you justify one small betrayal, it becomes easier to justify the next... until you don't recognise yourself any more.'

Claudette's throat tightened. A sharp pang of guilt lanced through her, tightening like a cord around her chest.

She had told herself this wasn't a betrayal. That she had no choice. But wasn't that exactly how it started?

Gigi gave her fingers a gentle squeeze before reaching for her cup again. 'You've always known who you are, Claudette, I have always loved that about you,' she murmured. 'I hope you don't let someone take that from you.'

Claudette forced a smile, but it felt hollow. She wasn't sure she knew any more.

Gigi continued. 'Have you noticed how survival means making choices we never thought we would ever have to make?' she asked, swirling the last dregs of coffee in her cup. 'War doesn't let us stay innocent, Claudette.'

The words settled over her, heavy, suffocating, true.

'I just don't want to make the wrong choice...' Claudette murmured.

Gigi weighed her words 'Then maybe ask yourself this – who are you doing this for? And can you live with the answer?'

Claudette inhaled slowly.

For Jean-Luc's daughters. For the theatre. For myself.

That was what she would tell herself. Besides, she didn't have to share everything she overheard at the Resistance meeting.

The next night the back alleys of the Palais Garnier were draped in shadows, the towering columns of the loading dock casting long, jagged lines beneath the pale glow of the full moon.

Claudette pressed herself against a wooden crate, her breath shallow. She had come to listen, to observe, to report. But very quickly she realised this wasn't a meeting.

It was an exchange.

She clapped her hand over her mouth to stop herself from being heard as she started. She couldn't believe it. In the midst of it was Malina, one of her best friends, her coat drawn tightly around her small frame, speaking in hushed tones to the men unloading something from the theatre's prop van.

The men worked swiftly, exchanging whispered instructions with Malina. Claudette strained to catch fragments of their conversation, her heart pounding in her chest. What was Malina involved in?

And then she saw them. A group of people, bags packed, harrowed expressions. She recognised one straight away: the Jewish man who had played the cello in the orchestra. His eyes were filled with fear as he glanced around, searching for any sign of danger.

Oh my God, Malina was helping smuggle Jewish people out of the city. She saw two small figures, young children. Small, pale figures clinging to each other, their eyes wide with fear.

Claudette's stomach plummeted violently as her vision blurred.

She had come here to spy on a meeting. Instead, she had stumbled into a desperate attempt to get Jewish children out of occupied Paris.

A sudden ripple of urgency passed through the gathered figures. One of the men, wiry and sharp-eyed, stepped forward.

'We have a problem,' he whispered hoarsely.

Malina stiffened, her eyes darting to the shadows.

'What do you mean?' she asked, keeping her voice low.

Claudette strained to hear.

'Word just came in from the man we have at the police department. The sergeant was bragging about sending someone here tonight. Someone who knows the theatre.'

A wave of panic surged through the group. The refugees huddled closer together, whispering among themselves, eyes darting towards the exits.

Claudette pressed herself further into the darkness, her pulse hammering.

No, no, no. This wasn't how it was supposed to go. She took an involuntary step back, and her heel caught on something unseen.

A crate tumbled over, its contents clattering against the stone floor, and the loud crash shattered the fragile silence.

The Resistance members spun around. One stepped forward, gun half-drawn. But it was Malina who raced to the spot, her features illuminated by the sliver of moonlight breaking through the towering arches. Claudette barely had time to turn before a hand clamped around her arm, yanking her forward.

Her heart stopped as she found herself face to face with Malina.

Malina's eyes widened in shock, the realisation crashing over her like a tidal wave.

'*Claudette?*'

The single word was thick with betrayal.

Claudette opened her mouth, but no sound escaped.

Malina's grip tightened, her voice breaking, a whisper torn raw from somewhere deep inside.

'I can't believe it is you! You, of all people.'

The words struck like a blow. Claudette's stomach turned, bile rising. Her throat burned with words she could not form, explanations, apologies, anything, but nothing would come.

The others froze, the air trembling with the weight of the revelation. Claudette felt the ground tilt beneath her feet, as though the world itself had shifted.

And in Malina's eyes she saw not just anger but grief, like something precious had died between them.

29

―――

PARIS, SUMMER 2011

Lily

The kettle clicked off with a sharp snap, steam curling up past the window as Lily poured hot water into the teapot. The morning light was soft, that filtered through the gauzy curtains.

She placed the teapot and two mugs on the table, then sat across from Marcus. She hadn't felt this energised in days.

'So,' she said, reaching for the milk, 'we're heading out to Fontaine-Blanche this afternoon. It's an old retreat just outside the city. The place where Malina stayed when she was pregnant.'

Marcus looked up from his phone, forcing a smile that didn't quite reach his eyes. 'The one from the photograph?'

Lily nodded. 'We think she was sent there in 1932 It's been converted into an artists' residency. Julien managed to get us access. He's done photography work for the non-profit that runs it now.'

That got his attention. He set his phone down, slowly. 'Julien's going with you, again?'

She stirred her tea with deliberate calm. 'Yes. He knows the place, and he can help document things while I look through the archives.'

There was a pause.

'That's... convenient,' Marcus said, and, though his tone was neutral, the edge was there, as if he were observing something from a distance he didn't care to close.

Lily looked at him, searching for something: support, curiosity, even the tiniest flicker of warmth. But all she saw was the careful mask of effort, the faint strain of a man trying to hold together a performance he'd already grown tired of.

'It's a lead,' she said, trying to keep her voice steady. 'Maybe the first real one we've had.'

Marcus picked up his mug, sipped, and said nothing for a moment. Then: 'You seem really invested in all of this. Is it just about your mother's past?'

His question carried weight beyond the words themselves. The subtext was clear: he was making the effort to remain faithful; was she? Lily felt her heartbeat quicken even as she kept her voice casual. 'Of course it is.'

She gripped her plate, stood and carried it to the sink. Behind her, his chair scraped back.

'Well,' he said lightly, his voice pitched too bright, 'have a good time playing detective.' He leaned across the sink to press a kiss to her lips, too slow, too deliberate, as though physical affection might patch the cracks words could not. 'Don't forget to come home to me.'

'You too,' she added, acidly.

He froze just a beat too long, his eyebrows furrowing, as though weighing whether her words were a jab or just banter. Choosing the easier answer, he relaxed his expression back into that tired, careful calm.

When the door clicked shut behind him, Lily let out a slow

breath and leaned on the counter, staring at the quiet kitchen. The teapot was still steaming, untouched. Her stomach twisted, not just from irritation, but from something far more complicated.

She was angry at Marcus, at his half-hearted effort, the way he performed concern without ever truly feeling it. But beneath that, something colder stirred.

Guilt.

Because even as she fumed at his distance, she could feel herself slipping further into something dangerous. Something warm and careful and entirely new that took the shape of Julien's steady gaze, the way he always made room for her questions, her excitement, her grief. She hated that part of her that wanted to tell him things she no longer trusted Marcus to hear.

The truth was, she wasn't just fighting Marcus's disinterest.

She was fighting her own heart.

The drive out to Fontaine-Blanche was quiet, the kind of quiet that held a current beneath it. Mist clung to the hedgerows as Lily and Julien passed rows of trees and crooked stone walls. When the estate finally came into view, it rose like a memory, tall iron gates, ivy-covered stone, and a gravel path leading up to a sprawling manor, the kind of serenity that conceals secrets.

'It looks... *ancient*,' Lily murmured as the car rolled to a stop.

The front door opened before they could knock. A woman in her late sixties stood perfectly still on the threshold, a keyring in one hand, the other clasped across her stomach. Her grey hair was pinned in a tight, practical bun, and her expression was the same: tight, practical; she was not here for small talk.

'You must be Monsieur Renaud and Madame Tremaine.' Her voice was low and clipped, with the weight of someone used to being obeyed. 'I'm Madame Maret. The groundskeeper and general steward of Fontaine-Blanche.'

She turned without waiting for acknowledgement and led them through a high-ceilinged entryway that smelled faintly of polish and pressed linen. The place was beautiful in the way a stage set is beautiful, carefully curated, devoid of warmth.

'Thank you for allowing us access,' Julien said politely.

'I'm simply fulfilling a courtesy to the organisation,' Madame Maret said. 'We don't typically open the historical annexe, but since this is for a private heritage project we've made an exception.'

Lily quickened her step to match Madame Maret's brisk pace. 'We're researching a woman who stayed here in the early 1930s. Malina Laurent-Masson. Have you ever come across that name?'

Madame Maret didn't break stride. 'We don't keep detailed records of every guest, Madame In those days, Fontaine-Blanche was simply a spa. A retreat for ladies of refinement suffering from exhaustion or nerves. That's all.'

Julien's glance caught Lily's. This was exactly the line they'd expected.

'We read an article suggesting it may have functioned as more than a spa,' Lily pressed, her tone careful but firm. 'That it may have been a discreet maternity facility for certain families.'

Madame Maret stopped and turned to face them. Her hands were still folded neatly in front of her.

'There are always stories,' she said crisply. 'Rumours. Speculation. People enjoy turning ordinary things into secrets.' Her smile was brittle. 'The truth is far less dramatic. Fontaine-Blanche was a place of rest. Nothing more.'

Without waiting for a response, she turned sharply down a side corridor towards a heavy wooden door.

The key turned with a clean, sharp click. Madame Maret

stepped aside as the door creaked open, revealing a small, immaculate room lined with wooden filing cabinets and a single antique desk at its centre. The windows were shuttered tight, the light inside cold and clinical, flickering slightly under a too-bright bulb.

'This is our official archive,' she said, her tone even and dispassionate. 'What records we've kept are in here..'

Lily stepped inside slowly, her shoes tapping softly against the floor. The air smelled faintly of lavender polish and the scent of timeworn documents.

'Thank you. We'll give it a look,' she said politely.

Madame Maret nodded. 'Please take your time.'

The door closed behind her with a whisper of finality and her footsteps echoed down the corridor.

Lily walked to the drawers marked 1930–1935 and opened the first one. The folders inside were arranged by month, each bearing neat labels in crisp handwriting.

'This isn't authentic,' Julien murmured, scanning a guest-book ledger on the desk. 'It's too... new.'

Lily didn't reply. Her fingers flipped through the files anyway, willing something out of them, some proof, some mistake. But every document she pulled was mundane: dietary recommendations, spa bookings, invoices for sessions.

She turned to the page marked *Admissions, 1932* and scanned the names. A few were written as initials: C.D., V.L. and L.M.

She leaned in, breath catching as she looked for the date. But the corresponding entry read: *Louise Marchand. One-week stay. Nervous exhaustion.*

Not Malina.

Julien crossed to her side and lifted a slim logbook from a shelf. 'Do you think they erased her?' he asked softly.

Lily shut the drawer more firmly than she meant to. The sharp click echoed in the silence.

They worked in silence for another twenty minutes. And then nothing. No mention of a Laurent-Masson, no guest registry, no letters, no room numbers.

When Madame Maret returned, her smile was tight. 'Did you find what you were looking for?'

Lily turned to face her. 'No.'

The older woman gave a small, stiff nod. 'Sometimes there's simply nothing to find.' And with that, she turned and walked them back through the hallway, each step slow and polished.

As they stepped back outside, Lily blinked in the pale afternoon light. The stone courtyard felt colder than before. 'I think that was a performance,' she said quietly.

Julien, nodding, picked up his camera and began to take shots of the building.

They were halfway to the car, gravel crunching underfoot, when a voice called out behind them.

'Julien?'

Lily turned to see a man in his late forties crossing the courtyard from a side path. He wore a charcoal sweater pushed to the elbows and wire-framed glasses that caught the light. His expression was warm.

Julien's face brightened. '*Étienne!*'

The two men clasped hands briefly. Lily stood beside them, slightly breathless from the weight of disappointment still dragging at her chest.

'Thank you for getting me in, I didn't think you were going to be here today,' Julien said.

Étienne smiled. 'I meant to greet you, but got caught up in my latest work. How did you get on?'

'We were looking into someone who may have stayed here in 1932' Julien said. 'Malina Laurent-Masson.'

'We went through the official archive,' Lily said. 'There was nothing. It felt... curated.'

Étienne looked around the courtyard, scanning the windows. Then he stepped closer and said quietly, 'Follow me.'

He led them around the side of the estate to his painting studio. Inside the air was thick with the smell of turpentine and linseed oil. Canvases lined the walls, each one a riot of colour and emotion frozen in time. Étienne gestured for them to enter, his eyes alight with adventure.

He closed the door behind them, then knelt and pulled out a thick ledger wrapped in linen from beneath a shelf.

'This shouldn't exist,' he said without looking up. 'During the estate sale five years ago, someone boxed this with garden invoices by mistake. By the time I opened it, the rest of the collection had already been shipped or shredded.'

He set the ledger on the desk and peeled back the linen. The cover was scuffed leather, hand-bound, no title.

'I kept it,' Étienne said. 'Just in case someone came looking.'

He opened the book to a section near the middle. The entries were handwritten in fading brown ink, nothing like the clean ledgers in the curated archive. Each line was discreet, encoded, sparse.

'Here,' he said, sliding the book toward Lily. 'They kept a second record. One the official registry didn't acknowledge.'

Lily stepped closer, her eyes scanning the pages until they landed on the one she wanted to find.

Laurent-Masson, Malina Thérèse – Admitted 3 October 1932 – Private Recovery Suite.
Attending Physician: Dr Chabert
Status: Confidential – See Summary

Lily turned the page quickly. Julien stood silently beside her as her eyes and finger moved across the faded script, taking in the brief, clinical note.

She sucked in a breath of shock as she read one line. Julien's gaze followed the place she had stopped, and he let out a low whistle through his teeth.

'*Mon Dieu*,' he said softly.

She didn't look up, her voice shaky, her finger trembling on the line.

'Well, I never expected this,' she whispered.

30

PARIS, JUNE 1941

Claudette

The moment Malina's fingers clamped around her arm, Claudette knew it was over.

Malina's eyes, fierce and unrelenting, bored into hers.

'*You?*' The single word was thick with disbelief, accusation woven through every syllable.

Claudette's throat went dry.

She had known this moment would come, had known, deep down, that walking this line, playing both sides, would eventually force her into an impossible choice. But she had never expected it to come at Malina's hands.

'I...' Her voice failed her, cracking under the weight of panic.

Malina's grip tightened. 'Why are you here so late at night? You can't be working this late.'

The words rang in Claudette's ears. She could hear her friend trying to find a reason.

The other Resistance members had frozen in place, every gaze locked onto her, their expressions ranging from suspicion to outright hostility.

Murmurs rippled through the gathered crowd, uncertainty blooming like a storm cloud overhead.

Claudette tried to pull away, but Malina's grasp was unyielding. 'Malina, please...'

'Please tell me you are not the person that has been working for the Nazis?' Malina's voice was lower this time, dangerous.

Claudette grasped for an answer, for anything that might ease the weight of suspicion pressing down on her. 'I... I didn't have a choice!'

A voice spoke from behind them.

'That's a lie, I saw her.'

Claudette's heart stopped.

A woman, one of the Resistance members, stepped out of the shadows, her gaze cold. 'I saw her at the police headquarters once,' she said, her voice steady and calm, but no less brutal. 'She was taking information to *them*.'

Silence fell over the group.

The weight of their stares crushed the air from Claudette's lungs.

Malina's grip slackened, as if the words had stolen her strength. Slowly, her fingers slipped away.

Claudette opened her mouth to explain, to defend herself, to say *anything*... But before she could, hands seized her arms from both sides.

'Wait! No!'

'Get her in the van,' someone ordered.

Claudette struggled, but there was no use.

The men dragged her toward another vehicle, the metal doors yawning open like the jaws of a beast. A thick cloth was shoved over her eyes, plunging her world into darkness.

She heard the doors slam shut.

The engine roared to life.

Then they were moving.

The blindfold stayed on for the entire journey.

Claudette lost all sense of time, the rough jostling of the van making her stomach churn. She tried to count the turns, to map the route in her head, but panic had stolen her focus.

When the vehicle finally rolled to a stop, she was yanked forward, her feet barely keeping pace as they dragged her inside.

The air had changed and was no longer cold and damp, like the theatre dock, but warmer, tinged with the scent of old wood and smoke. Footsteps echoed against wooden floorboards. A door creaked open, and then she was shoved into a chair.

A moment later, the blindfold was ripped away.

Blinking hard against the sudden light, Claudette found herself in a dimly lit room, its walls lined with bookshelves and old furniture.

Malina stood before her, arms crossed, her expression serious.

The others, some of the men from the theatre dock, stood just behind, their faces a mixture of suspicion and restrained fury.

'Start talking,' Malina said.

Claudette swallowed hard. 'Please, you have to believe me!'

'Believe you?' Malina let out a short, sharp laugh. 'You were spying on us, Claudette. Taking information to the police.'

'I told you I didn't have a choice!' Claudette burst out, desperation lacing her words. 'Philippe Mercier is my brother.'

Malina's expression darkened at the mention of Philippe's name.

Claudette continued, her voice raw. 'He forced me into this, threatened me, blackmailed me, I didn't want to betray anyone, I swear it.'

Malina studied her, searching her face for any sign of deception.

Her friend scoffed. 'Convenient excuse.'

Claudette turned to him. 'Do you think I wanted any of this?' She felt the anger rise now, cutting through the fear. 'You think I don't know what he's done? I *hate* him for what he's made me do. For what I've become.'

Malina's eyes softened, just briefly.

There was a long pause. Then she let out a breath and murmured, 'If this is true, you should have come to me.'

Claudette's chest tightened.

'You could have told me,' Malina continued, shaking her head. 'I would have helped you.'

Claudette's throat burned. The realisation cut deep, deeper than she expected.

She had spent so long fighting alone, believing she had no choice but to shoulder everything herself. But what if she had been wrong? What if she had reached out before it was too late? She had always been so independent. But independence had nearly destroyed her.

Claudette's voice was barely a whisper. 'I didn't know how.'

Malina exhaled. 'Then maybe it's time you learned to trust people.'

A heavy silence followed.

Claudette looked down, shame curling through her. She had spent so much time trying to protect herself that she had shut out the one person who might have helped her.

Then, finally, Malina spoke again.

'Tell me about Philippe.'

Claudette lifted her gaze, meeting Malina's steady eyes.

And told them everything.

About her brother and his threats, his control. About the secrets she thought were buried. The rape by her stepfather that resulted in her pregnancy. All the things she had done to cover up her past and secure her future. By the time she was done, the room was silent, thick with tension.

Then Malina nodded once. 'Then let's make sure he pays.'

A plan began to take shape. And for the first time in weeks, Claudette felt something like hope.

'We have other information on Philippe. He is not just working for the Nazis,' she said. 'He's profiting off them.'

Claudette frowned. 'What do you mean?'

Malina continued. 'We know someone who tried to escape through him, a Jewish businessman. Philippe promised him papers, safe passage out of France. The man paid him everything he had. But the papers never came, and the Gestapo arrested him.'

Claudette felt her stomach turn. 'Are you saying Philippe—'

'Sold him out? Yes.'

Claudette closed her eyes.

It made sense. The money. The power. Philippe had always wanted to be untouchable. And now he had found a way to do it, at the cost of innocent lives.

'We can take him down,' Malina said, her voice low and certain. 'But we need your help.'

Claudette opened her eyes, dread still coiled in them. 'How?'

Malina leaned in, each word deliberate. 'We'll use his own greed against him.'

A shiver ran through Claudette. 'Okay... I will do anything.' The words cracked under the weight of months of blackmail, of nights spent certain that her secret would destroy her life if it ever surfaced. Even as hope flickered to life, a quiet voice inside warned her that ending this might only open the door to something worse.

They spoke in urgent whispers, weaving the plan together until every detail was locked in place. The agreement was made. Claudette would be allowed to leave.

'Malina.' Claudette's voice trembled. 'Thank you. And promise me you won't tell our friends. If they knew...' Her throat closed. 'I'd lose everything.'

Malina's usually stoic face softened. 'We've all made mistakes, Claudette. Let's put this right so no one ever needs to know your secret. It will always be safe with me.'

The words undid her. Claudette lunged forward, clutching her friend in a desperate embrace. The tears came hard and fast, tears of gratitude for Malina's loyalty, of raw relief at the chance of being freed from his grip, and of bitter regret for the choices that had led her here.

She knew she would carry that regret forever. But tonight, for the first time in months, she could breathe.

At their next planned meeting, L'Asphodèle café was as grim as ever. Philippe was already there when she arrived, seated at a corner table, his gloved fingers drumming idly against the surface.

Claudette took a steadying breath before walking toward him.

He looked up, his smirk sharp as a blade. 'Sœur,' he greeted her. 'I was beginning to think you'd stood me up.'

She slid into the seat across from him, mirroring his smirk. 'I've been busy.'

His gaze flickered with interest. 'I assume you have something for me?'

Claudette leaned forward, lowering her voice. 'I've heard whispers,' she said, careful to keep her expression neutral. 'I went to the theatre the night you told me and overheard a conversation. There's a Jewish family trying to get out. They have money. A lot of it.'

Philippe's expression didn't change, but she saw it, the slight dilation of his pupils, the way his fingers stilled.

'How much?' he asked, voice casual.

Claudette shrugged. 'Enough to make it worth someone's while.'

Philippe exhaled, leaning back in his chair. 'I'll need names.'

Claudette shook her head. 'I have to do further investigation.' She let the silence stretch, watched as his frustration flickered, then disappeared beneath well-practised amusement.

'Fine, but I'll need your contact to meet me in person. Me *only*, understand?'

Claudette nodded. 'I can take care of everything.'

He looked at her with new admiration. 'I knew you would finally come around to my way of thinking – after all, we have the same blood.' He smirked.

As he got up to leave, he nodded at her. 'There may be a cut in it for you too, Claudette, if you do well.'

She forced a smile as she fought her rising anger. Everything was in place and Philippe had just walked into his own trap.

She stood, straightening her skirt. 'I'll arrange it,' she said.

As she turned to leave, his voice stopped her.

'Claudette.'

She looked back.

His expression had softened, just a little. 'You know, I do this for us. For people like us, who grew up with nothing.'

A part of her wanted to believe him. But then she thought of Marguerite and Jean-Luc and their daughters. Of every person who had begged Philippe for salvation and been sent to their death instead.

She smiled, but it was hollow. 'Goodbye, Philippe.'

And with that, she walked away.

Claudette had never stepped foot inside le Glaive Noir, renamed by the Nazis – until tonight.

She had passed by it many times, the swastika-emblazoned banners flanking its entrance an unmistakable mark of what lay beyond. The building itself had once been an upscale gentlemen's club, a place where Parisian aristocrats drank fine brandy and debated literature. Now it had been hollowed out and turned into something else entirely, a gathering place for the most powerful Nazi officers in the city.

From some information gathered by the Resistance, they knew Obersturmführer Neumann was a nightly visitor. She produced the fake documents Malina had given her for the doorman, and he waved her in.

As she entered, the sheer force of its atmosphere pressed down on her. The room was thick with cigar smoke and the cloying scent of expensive cologne. Ornate wall lights cast a dim glow over the polished mahogany bar, where men in tailored uniforms laughed too loudly and clinked beer glasses in celebration of their victories on the battlefield.

The walls were adorned with Nazi propaganda, portraits of Hitler in rigid frames, an iron eagle carved into a wooden statue. A large red banner with a black swastika was draped behind the bar, its presence an ever-watchful sentinel.

Other men in immaculate uniforms sat at round tables, drinking and laughing with an air of terrifying ease. SS officers smoked in elegant chairs, their leather gloves resting on the arms as they spoke in hushed tones. Waitresses in tight black dresses moved between them, their eyes lowered, their expressions carefully neutral.

Claudette suppressed a shudder.

From around the room eyes watched her, assessing, weighing her presence. She felt the weight of their gazes, cold and calculating, as she made her way deeper into the club. Among the sea of Nazi uniforms, she searched for the man she had come to find, Obersturmführer Neumann.

Finally, her eyes landed on him at a corner table, surrounded by a small entourage of officers. Neumann's posture was relaxed, his gaze sharp as it swept the room. He exuded an air of power that seemed to command obedience from those around him.

As Claudette approached, she could feel the tension crackling in the air like electricity. Every step felt like a step closer to the edge of a precipice. She had rehearsed this moment in her mind, but now that it was here doubt crept in.

Neumann watched her she neared his table, his eyes narrowing slightly in curiosity. Claudette could sense the scrutiny in his gaze, the unspoken question of why she was there in a place where she clearly did not belong. But she held her head high, her expression composed and unwavering. This was nothing worse than what she had faced as a child growing up in poverty.

'Obersturmführer Neumann,' she said, and nodded politely, her voice steady, despite the rapid beating of her heart. 'I hope I'm not intruding.'

Neumann's companions exchanged glances, some sporting sneers while others watched with guarded interest. Neumann himself leaned back in his chair, studying Claudette with a cool detachment that sent a shiver down her spine.

'Not at all, Mademoiselle,' he replied, his German accent crisp and precise. 'What brings you to le Glaive Noir this evening?'

Claudette took a deep breath, summoning all her courage for what she was about to do. She knew the risks involved, but if she was to right this wrong it would take courage.

'May I have a word with you in private?'

Neumann's lips curled into a faint smile, his gaze lingering on her face for a moment longer, before he gestured to an empty table close by. 'Of course, Mademoiselle.'

Claudette followed him to the secluded corner, her every sense on high alert. As they sat down, a waiter appeared as if summoned by an invisible hand, and asked for their orders with a subservient bow. Claudette shook her head but

Neumann ordered without looking up, his attention solely on her.

Once they were alone, he leaned back in his chair, lighting a cigarette and blowing it out in a slow, controlled stream. 'You have piqued my curiosity, Mademoiselle. What is it that you wish to discuss?'

Claudette was unflinching, her blue eyes holding his stare. 'I come bearing information that may be of interest to you,' she began, choosing her words with care. 'Information that concerns a certain individual who has been undermining your operations in the city.'

Neumann's eyebrows lifted imperceptibly, a faint frown marring his otherwise composed features. 'Go on.'

She fought to remember the words she had rehearsed with Malina. 'I was doing some work for my brother, listening to conversations as he asked me, and I overheard one person saying how a Jewish person gave all his money to a corrupt police officer for false papers to get out of the city. This man takes bribes from Jewish families, promising them safe passage and forged documents.'

Neumann's expression remained steady, but she saw the hint of interest in his eyes. 'And who is this corrupt officer?' he enquired, his tone harsh and controlled.

'They didn't say, but I thought you might want to know that such treachery is being carried out right under your nose,' Claudette continued, her voice steady. 'It reflects poorly on your operation here, I believe, sir, does it not?' She knew she was skating on thin ice, but she had to chip away at his pride in order to provoke him into doing something.

Neumann's jaw tightened and a flicker of annoyance crossed his features before he schooled his expression back into neutrality. 'I appreciate your candour, Mademoiselle. This is indeed a serious accusation. Why are you bringing this information to me and not your brother?'

Claudette held Neumann's gaze.

'I believe it's the governing forces who are legally entitled to receive any funds from these transactions.'

'And what do you want to gain from this?'

'I do have one request, if you're willing to listen and if you agree. I would be willing to help you trap this person.'

The Nazi shifted in his chair, the dim light of the club casting shadows across his face, accentuating the sharp angles of his features as his gaze lingered on Claudette, calculating and shrewd, as she outlined her petition.

31

PARIS, JUNE 1941

Gigi

Gigi was sitting on the floor by the window, her knees pulled against her chest, a blanket draped around her shoulders like a fragile kind of armour. The sky outside had turned the colour of ash, heavy with late-afternoon rain that hadn't yet fallen. She hadn't lit the lamps. The shadows suited her mood.

It had been days since Olivier had walked out with that maddening finality. '*No, this is the last time I'll see you like this.*' His words still echoed inside her like a slammed door, sharp and unfinished.

She had replayed the moment hundreds of times. The way his voice had caught. The way his eyes had lingered on hers just a beat too long before he turned away. She told herself she was done thinking about him. That it didn't matter. That it was better this way.

But her heart didn't seem to agree.

So, when the knock came – three measured raps against the wood – her breath caught sharply in her throat. For a moment she just stared at the door, unable to move. Her fingers tightened around the edge of the blanket.

It's him.

She rose slowly, brushing down her skirt with trembling hands. Her footsteps were hesitant across the floor, every part of her preparing to see him again, to demand an explanation, to beg him to stay... she didn't know which.

She pulled the door open.

But it wasn't Olivier.

It was her ballet master, Jacques, wearing his usual stoic expression, softened by something close to... urgency? But it was the two small girls beside him that truly stole her breath. Identical. Wide-eyed. One stood in front; the other stood a little behind her sister, watchful. She peered up at Gigi with curiosity, her dark curls wild around her face.

'I need a favour,' Jacques said simply.

Gigi blinked at him, the ache in her chest still fresh, still raw. 'What kind of favour?'

'These twins have been studying at the school,' Jacques replied. 'I need someone to watch them for a few hours.'

She blinked. 'Of course.'

'Just for the afternoon,' he added.

Gigi opened the door wider. 'Come in, then.'

The girls stepped inside quietly, their footsteps light on the old floorboards. They looked around with interest, twin shadows trailing one another's movements. One of them reached for a ballerina figurine on the bookshelf, pausing just before her fingers touched it, as if waiting for permission.

'What are their names?' Gigi asked.

'Rebecca and Rachel,' Jacques answered.

She turned to him, studying his face. 'And where's their family?'

Jacques didn't meet her gaze. 'They're... gone. I'm looking after them until somewhere else for them can be found.'

Gigi's heart went out to them, so beautiful and full of life, already facing so much tragedy.

Jacques placed a hand gently on each twin's shoulder. 'Stay here till I get back. Gigi is a friend.'

Then, just as quickly as he'd arrived, he was gone.

Gigi stood for a moment in the quiet that followed. The girls were now wandering toward the open balcony doors, drawn to the sliver of sunlight and the sound of the street below.

They looked to her for permission, and she nodded.

The afternoon light warmed the balcony, gilding the small table. Rebecca and Rachel stepped out into the sun, their feet padding softly against the warm tiles. The breeze lifted the curls from their foreheads as they leaned over the railing, eyes wide with wonder at the world four storeys below.

Gigi watched them with curiosity. Jacques was always so aloof and withdrawn, normally showing very little care for his students' personal lives outside of the dance studio.

From the corner of her eye, she saw movement on the next balcony over. Eloise had stepped out, a basket of freshly laundered linen tucked under one arm. She looked up at the sound of the girls' laughter, her expression soft at first.

And then, it changed.

Gigi saw the exact moment her friend went pale. The blood drained from her face, her eyes locked on the girls. The basket slipped slightly in her grip before she recovered and set it down mechanically on the chair beside her. Her gaze flicked to Gigi, and then quickly away.

'Eloise?' Gigi called gently across the joined balcony. 'Are you all right?'

But Eloise didn't answer. She gave a small nod, tight, polite, turned swiftly and disappeared through her open door.

Gigi blinked. It wasn't like Eloise to be cold. If anything, she was usually the one reminding Gigi not to take things so seriously, always the first to joke, to roll her eyes, to rescue a moment with dry humour. Her manner was unsettling.

Gigi's eyes returned to the twins, who now sat cross-legged beneath the tiny iron table, picking at the petals of a daisy one of them had found.

The memory of Eloise's expression settled over Gigi like a fine layer of dust.

Jacques returned later that afternoon, just as the sun dipped lower behind the rooftops, bathing the balcony in burnt gold. He carried himself with that same stiff, silent grace he always had, his mouth a thin line, his eyes filled with concern.

Rebecca and Rachel ran to the door before Gigi could even rise, clutching their satchels and ballet shoes, their chatter tumbling out in a mess of giggles.

'You were very good today,' Gigi said softly as she helped Rachel buckle her shoe.

'Can you be our dance teacher now?' Rebecca asked suddenly, peering up at her. '*Please!*' she begged.

'We want you,' Rachel added, with the unwavering earnestness only children can manage. 'Please, Uncle Jacques, *please.*'

Jacques raised an eyebrow, but said nothing. Gigi turned toward him, her smile easy. 'I have no objection. I guess it is up to your uncle Jacques.'

He didn't smile back. 'We'll see,' he said simply, then offered Gigi a quiet '*merci*' and ushered the girls out with a nod of farewell before the door clicked shut behind them.

Gigi stood there for a moment, staring at the spot where they had just been. Something still lingered, though. That look on Eloise's face.

She crossed the living room and slipped out onto the shared balcony. The pale laundry Eloise had folded earlier sat forgotten on the chair in a tidy stack. Gigi gently knocked on Eloise's open door.

'Eloise?' she called softly.

A pause.

Then a voice. 'Come in.'

Inside, the apartment was dim, the air cooler. Eloise sat on the edge of her couch, hands clasped tightly in her lap. Her expression was composed, but her eyes betrayed her.

'I wanted to check on you,' Gigi said. 'Earlier, you looked as if you'd seen a ghost.'

Eloise looked down at her hands. 'It caught me off guard, that's all.'

'Do you know the girls?' Gigi pressed gently.

'No, I have never met them before.'

A beat.

Gigi waited, letting the silence stretch.

Eloise finally sighed and leaned back into the cushions, as if the weight of the moment was pressing down on her. 'I used to dance, you know. Years ago. Before I worked backstage. Before everything changed. Something about the girls reminded me of myself at their age.'

'I didn't know you danced,' Gigi said, surprised. 'Were you at the school?'

'Yes,' she said bitterly. 'Jacques was my teacher.'

'He never mentioned—'

'He wouldn't,' Eloise cut in. Her voice had gone cool, edged. 'My time there ended... *badly*.'

The room seemed to hum with what Eloise left unsaid. But Eloise closed herself off with a slight shake of her head.

'You don't have to tell me,' Gigi said softly. 'But if ever you want to talk about it...'

Eloise nodded, her mouth a tight line. 'Thank you.'

Gigi stood to leave, but at the door she hesitated. 'You looked scared,' she said. 'Not just surprised.'

Eloise didn't respond right away. She stared out the window, her profile etched in shadow. 'Some ghosts,' she said finally, 'don't stay buried forever.'

Gigi paused just outside the door, glancing back one last time through the crack before it clicked shut behind her. The apartment was dim, the shadows swallowing Eloise whole as she sat unmoving, her hands still clenched in her lap.

The episode unsettled Gigi more than she wanted to admit.

She had spoken about Jacques many times before, about rehearsals at the studio just below them, about his critiques and habits and maddening precision. Eloise had never reacted. Never even flinched.

But today had been different. Was it the twins? The dark-eyed girls, so close in age to the dancer she had been, Gigi imagined, from all those years ago? Or was it something deeper?

Gigi stepped back into her own apartment, but the feeling trailed her like fog.

There was more to Eloise's past than she had shared, and Gigi was certain it touched Jacques Leclerc and the two little girls who had showed up at her door.

32

PARIS, SUMMER 2011

Lily

The pin slid into the corkboard, right beneath the faded photograph of Malina Laurent-Masson.

Lily stepped back, her eyes scanning the network of string, clippings and scribbled notes that had taken over the board in the back of the room. The newest card was written in her cleanest script, and the weight behind it made her stomach tighten.

Fontaine-Blanche. 1933. Stillbirth. Only one child.

The words didn't feel like closure; they felt like loss.

Given the world she was from, Malina, with her short hair and wild expression, had probably carried that heartbreak in silence.

Lily folded her arms across her chest, lips pressed tight.

She imagined the way Malina must have walked back into the world after that, perfectly dressed, carrying a secret that changed the shape of her life.

Lily blinked hard, grounding herself with the scratch of the pen as she updated a nearby tag with the words *Not my grand-mother* next to Malina's name.

One mystery narrowed, and one woman ruled out.

And yet, Lily's chest ached worse than before.

The scent of vanilla and something vaguely burnt drifted towards her. Effy balanced two mismatched mugs in one hand and a plate of lopsided shortbread in the other.

'Tea,' she declared, 'and biscuits I may have overcommitted to.'

Lily gave a soft smile as she accepted a mug and eyed the plate. 'You didn't burn them that badly.'

Effy peered at one with regret. 'This one looks like it resents being born.'

She dropped into the worn armchair by the window, pushing aside a pile of old theatre programmes. Her gaze drifted toward the corkboard. 'So... we're eliminating suspect number one?'

Lily sat across from her, the steam from her mug rising between them. 'Julien managed to pull up birth and death records confirming she never had any children apart from this one that hadn't been recorded. So, Malina only had one child. A stillborn girl.'

Effy's smile faded. She set her tea down with unusual care.

'God, that poor woman.'

She was silent for a long moment. Then she leaned back, eyes on the board.

'I suddenly remembered last night that I did meet her once – she was an artist and no longer a Laurent-Masson, she went by a different name, which is why I didn't click right away. I just thought Malina was cold, angry and distant,' Effy said, and exhaled slowly, the kind of breath that lets sorrow settle in, before adding, 'Everyone has a story,'

She took a thoughtful sip of tea, her gaze still resting on the corkboard. Lily watched her, smiling at today's ensemble. Her friend wore wide-legged trousers of deep indigo linen, paired with a cropped velvet jacket embroidered in scarlet and gold. A cascade of beaded necklaces clinked softly at her chest, and her feet were slipped into scarlet ballet flats that match the rest perfectly. It was quintessential Effy: bold, bohemian and delightfully unbothered by convention.

'So,' Effy said casually, 'what happened after you left the haunted spa of secrets? Presumably you needed a moment to... emotionally decompress. Preferably near bread and wine.'

Lily rolled her eyes, but her cheeks flushed a little. 'Of course, we went for lunch. There was a small café nearby.'

Effy's brows rose. 'And?'

'And we ate,' Lily replied, too quickly. 'Talked about what to do next.'

Effy leaned forward, narrowing her eyes. '*And?*'

'*Effy!*'

Lily tried to suppress a smile, but the truth flickered at the edge of her thoughts anyway. The moment in the café had been brief, quiet, but it had stayed with her longer than she liked to admit. Julien's hand had covered hers on the table, just for a moment, when she'd choked up talking about her mother.

She had received a call during their lunch, from Clare, who had told her the doctors were reassessing their mother's case and there were some concerns. Clare would call again when she knew more. Julien hadn't said anything as she had hung up and sobbed. He hadn't needed to. The warmth of his hand on hers had been enough.

When she finally looked up, his eyes had been on her, steady, unwavering. Their hands had lingered together longer than they should have, her pulse leaping at the quiet intensity in his gaze. He'd leaned in slightly, as if caught in the same pull, and for a suspended heartbeat she thought he might kiss her and with a shock she had thought she might let him. Her lips parted before she caught herself and pulled gently back, her breath trembling. He had cleared his throat and withdrawn, but the charged air between them had never quite settled.

But she didn't tell Effy that.

Instead, she shrugged and said, 'He's been kind. Patient.'

Effy smiled softly. 'I really like him.'

'You hardly know him.'

'I know how someone makes you look when you talk about them,' she said with a smirk. 'And you've been lit up all day.'

Lily opened her mouth to argue, but her phone buzzed sharply across the table, cutting through the moment.

The name on the screen made her stomach drop.

Clare

Lily stood to take the call, turning her back to the corkboard and stepping toward the window as she answered.

'Clare?'

Her sister's voice was hushed, the kind people used in hospital corridors. 'Hey, I didn't mean to scare you. I just thought you'd want to know... Mum's vitals dropped a little overnight. They've stabilised now, but the doctor says it's not... good.'

Lily pressed her free hand to her stomach. 'Is she still unconscious?'

'Yes, same as before. But now they're saying that if she doesn't improve by the weekend...' Clare didn't finish the sentence. She didn't have to.

Lily stared out at the sky, grey and unmoving above the rooftops. 'I'll come tomorrow. First thing.'

'I think she'd want you here,' Clare said gently. 'You were always her favourite.'

Lily let out a breath that felt like it had been trapped in her chest all day. 'That's not true.'

'She made your birthday cakes from scratch.'

'She made yours too.'

'She *burned* mine,' Clare said with a laugh.

That won a small smile from Lily, even if it faded fast. 'Text me if anything changes before tomorrow.'

'Will do.' A pause. Then, softer, 'You okay?'

'I will be,' Lily said. 'I just... need to finish this for Maman. So she has something good to focus on once she is awake.'

She hung up and stood there for a moment, phone still at her ear, her hand braced against the windowsill.

Behind her, Effy said nothing.

Lily stood and gathered herself. Her thoughts thick and jumbled, her body still. She picked up her phone again, thumb hovering over Marcus's name. Maybe, just maybe, he'd want to know her mother had taken a turn. That this wasn't about history or obsession, it was about family.

She dialled.

Straight to voicemail.

She tried again. Same result.

Her hand tightened around the phone. Something sharp flickered beneath her skin. *I shouldn't have to chase my own husband*, she thought. And she grabbed her coat and headed for his office.

The receptionist at the sleek, glass-fronted office was new, young, maybe mid-twenties, with a tidy chignon and red-rimmed glasses. She looked up from her screen with polite efficiency.

'Can I help you?'

'I'm here to see Marcus Deveraux.'

'Do you have an appointment?'

'No, I'm his wife.'

The woman blinked. 'I'm sorry, *who* are you?'

Lily felt a surge of frustration at the receptionist's confusion, but she kept her composure. She repeated slowly, 'I'm Lily Tremaine. His wife. Is he available?'

'Oh. I... I'm sorry, I didn't realise he was married.'

There was a pause. Just long enough.

'I mean, of course,' the woman stammered, cheeks flushing, 'I'm fairly new here.'

Before Lily could respond or think, Marcus appeared at the far end of the hallway. He spotted her and crossed the space with just enough urgency to feel off.

'Lily,' he said, offering a quick, closed-lipped smile. 'This is a surprise.'

'I called,' she said.

'Ah.' He glanced toward the receptionist. 'Well, I've been in meetings.'

He placed a hand lightly on her shoulder and ushered her into his office before she could say another word. The door clicked shut behind them.

But Lily couldn't shake the look on the receptionist's face: wide-eyed, hesitant and confused.

Why hadn't Marcus told her he was married?

33

PARIS, JULY 1941

Claudette

A sharp summer breeze bit at Claudette's exposed skin as she walked briskly through the streets of Paris, her breath unfurling in pale tendrils against the unusual morning chill.

The city had not yet fully woken, and for a moment she could almost believe in the illusion of stillness, of normality, until the sharp snap of a swastika overhead, its red and black stark against the pale morning, joined with the weight in her chest to shatter the illusion. It was a reminder that danger was never far, and before the day was over it might come for her.

But, today, everything would change.

She would play her part carefully, leading Philippe straight into the snare they had set for him. Now, all that remained was to watch him walk willingly into his own destruction. Her fingers curled into fists inside the pockets of her coat as she approached their usual meeting place.

She paused just outside the entrance, inhaling deeply. Behind her, across the street, Malina stood half-shrouded in the doorway of a bookshop, blending effortlessly into the morning bustle. Their eyes met, and Malina gave her the barest nod.

It was time.

Inside, the café was dimly lit, the scent of bitter coffee thick in the air. A handful of patrons lingered in the corners, reading newspapers, muttering over drinks, their faces obscured by curling cigarette smoke.

Philippe was already seated near the back, his long fingers drumming idly against the wooden table.

'Ah, *sœur*,' he greeted her, gesturing to the seat across from him. 'You look... terrible.'

Claudette forced a small, wary smile and slid into the chair. 'Busy night. I have something for you.'

Philippe's brows lifted slightly, interest flickering in his sharp gaze.

Their conversation was cut short abruptly as the waitress arrived and set down a mug of coffee in front of Philippe. The liquid inside was thick and black, swirling with bitterness Claudette could almost taste in the back of her throat.

'I have spoken to the Jewish family, they are willing to meet with you,' she continued, keeping her voice low.

Philippe took a slow sip of his coffee, watching her carefully over the rim of the cup. 'And?' he prompted.

'I can set up a meeting,' she said, boldly.

He smirked, the glint of greed unmistakable. 'I will decide the place.'

She shook her head. 'I have already arranged it.'

He regarded her for a long moment, the smirk fading into something harder. 'No, we will do it my way,' he said, his voice like ice.

Claudette's heart gave a sharp jolt. 'Not any more.'

Philippe leaned forward, his voice dropping into something far more dangerous, something only she would recognise. The tone he had used when they were children, when he had wanted something, when he had always got his way.

'You don't get to dictate terms to me,' he murmured, his fingers tightening around his cup. 'You're here because I *allow* it. You're still breathing because I *allow* it. And you'll give me the information I need, because I *allow* it.'

Claudette stiffened, but she did not drop her gaze. 'Not this time. I've done enough for you, Philippe,' she said, her voice unwavering. 'If you want this lead, we do it my way.'

Under the table her knees were shaking, but it felt good to stand up to him.

Philippe's eyes narrowed.

'How dare you set terms with me,' he said, his voice silk wrapped around steel.

She forced a smile. 'Then I guess I'll take my information elsewhere. I'm sure you're not the only corrupt gendarme I can find. Maybe there's someone else who'd be interested in getting a cut of their wealth.'

She made a move to stand. Philippe's hand shot out, gripping her wrist. For a moment, the noise of the café seemed to vanish. The strength of his grip was cutting off her circulation.

'*Sit,*' he commanded.

She stared him down. 'Let go of me, Philippe.'

Something flickered in his eyes. Surprise. She had never stood up to him before. Not like this. Slowly, his fingers uncurled. She lowered herself back into her seat, but she was still in control.

He studied her for a long moment, the tension stretching like a drawn bowstring. Then, with a sharp exhale, he leaned back, fingers drumming against the tabletop.

'Fine,' he said at last. 'Where and when?'

Claudette let herself breathe again. 'Tomorrow night. A warehouse near rue de la Roquette.'

Philippe nodded, clearly unsatisfied. 'I need their details, then I'll see them there.'

Claudette reached into her coat and slid him a folded note, the false details, the trap. Then she stood, letting her fingers brush lightly over the table's surface, just enough to leave him with the illusion of camaraderie.

She turned and walked away, her heart hammering against her ribs.

It was done.

The next evening, rue de la Roquette lay in shadows. The warehouse stood at the far end, a hulking structure of iron and wood, its windows darkened, its purpose unknowable to passers-by. At the back, a door was already open.

Philippe arrived just as expected, dressed in a long wool coat, wearing his usual self-assurance like a robe. He carried a satchel; inside, she guessed, were the forged papers.

A man provided by Neumann was already waiting for him. He played his part well. He was thin, anxious, his hands trembling slightly as he extended a bundle of notes.

Philippe smirked and took the money, his fingers running over the crisp bills, before slipping the false documents into the man's coat pocket. 'A pleasure,' he murmured, smug in his deception.

And then, a voice, like a blade slicing through the night.
'*Halt!*'

The doors burst open, the heavy wooden panels slamming against the warehouse walls. A flood of Nazi officers poured inside, their boots pounding against the stone floor, their pistols raised in cold precision.

Philippe's face went white.

From the darkness, Obersturmführer Neumann emerged, his expression impenetrable. He stepped forward with the slow, deliberate gait of a man who already knows the outcome.

'Trading in false papers, Mercier?' he said, his voice almost amused. 'Profiting off the Reich's generosity?'

Philippe straightened, his face snapping into a mask of icy detachment. 'This is a mistake.'

Neumann snapped back, 'The only mistake is that I trusted you.'

The Nazi gestured, and two officers seized Philippe by the arms, wrenching them behind his back.

'Take your hands off me!' Philippe snarled, struggling.

Neumann leaned in, voice like steel. 'Did you think you were untouchable? That the Reich would turn a blind eye to your corruption?'

Philippe opened his mouth to protest. Then he saw her. Claudette. Standing in the shadows just beyond Neumann, watching.

For the first time in a long time, she saw fear flicker in his eyes.

'*You*,' he whispered.

Claudette's breath caught, a lifetime of tangled memories pressing against her ribs. Brother. Blood. The boy who once pulled her by the hand through crowded markets to find a place to beg, the man who had since twisted that bond into a chain that wrapped so tightly it had suffocated her.

And now he was the one cornered.

Relief surged through her, sharp and shameful all at once. Relief that the weight he held over her was gone. Relief that, at last, she was safe. But threaded through it was something darker, grief, perhaps, or the faint ache of watching family destroyed by choices he had made himself.

Her fingers curled into her palms, nails biting skin. She didn't speak, couldn't. She only held his gaze, steady, as the officers dragged him away.

Philippe wrenched against the officers holding him, his breath ragged. '*Claudette!* But you're my sister!'

She held his gaze, seeing him now for what he truly was, not the untouchable man he had built himself to be but a coward who had believed himself invincible.

'You made your choices,' she whispered. 'Now live with them.'

The officers dragged him away, his shouts of protest swallowed by the night.

Claudette exhaled.

For the first time since this started, she felt free.

Claudette took a slow breath before stepping into Obersturmführer Gerhard Neumann's dimly lit office the next day. The heavy scent of cigars and leather filled the room, oppressive in its weight. Neumann sat behind a broad wooden desk, fingers steepled, watching her with calculating interest.

'Mademoiselle Mercier,' he greeted her, tilting his head slightly. 'You have come for your reward?'

She forced herself to hold his gaze. 'I wish to request the release of a prisoner.'

Neumann raised a brow, intrigued but not yet dismissive. 'And why would I do that?'

Claudette straightened her shoulders, her voice even. 'Because if my brother was corrupt enough to deceive you, how can you be certain he did not set up this person as well?'

Neumann leaned back, his gloved fingers tapping idly against the desk. 'It is not usual for us to release prisoners who have broken the law.'

She took a step closer, lowering her voice. 'Consider it a show of loyalty. I have proven useful to you. Perhaps you might find me useful again.' She knew she was walking a tightrope. But it was the only way she could think of to put this right.

Neumann studied her, assessing the layers beneath her words. Finally, he exhaled through his nose, nodding once. 'Very well, give me the details, I will look into it, but I can't promise you anything. But do not mistake this for kindness, Mademoiselle. Just gratitude for helping us.'

Claudette forced a small, empty smile. 'Of course, Obersturmführer.'

Her pulse hammered, but her hands stayed steady as she reached into her coat pocket. The folded slip of paper with two words on it burned against her palm.

She laid it carefully on his desk.

Neumann's eyes flicked down, then back to her, sharp with curiosity. His gloved hand closed over the note, slow and deliberate.

Claudette exhaled, the air trembling in her chest. The choice was made.

Whatever happened next, there was no undoing it.

The next evening, the theatre was unusually quiet. The weight of the war had settled heavily over them all, yet the work continued – props to fix, lights to test, costumes to mend. Claudette was helping the lighting crew when a sudden commotion caught her attention.

Voices, hurried footsteps.

Then she saw her.

A silhouette against the bright work lights.

Marguerite.

Jean-Luc remained frozen momentarily before he sprinted towards his wife to embrace her tightly as if he would never release her. There was a strangled cry from his daughters, who appeared from the wings, their small feet pounding against the stage as they raced to their mother. Their tiny arms flung around her waist, their faces pressed into her dress as sobs racked their small bodies.

The theatre exploded into a cacophony of cheers and laughter along with joyful weeping. The sound of homecoming.

Claudette swallowed hard, the sight nearly breaking her. When she stepped forward, Marguerite pulled her in, hugging her tightly, eyes brimming.

'They told me you did this,' she whispered. 'You are the one I have to thank.'

Claudette shook her head. 'I was just righting a wrong. That's all.'

And for the first time in what felt like forever, Claudette allowed herself to cry.

Tears of relief.

Tears of redemption.

Tears for the girl she used to be.

Tears for the woman she had become.

34

PARIS, OCTOBER 1941

Gigi

Gigi stood at the front of the dance studio, her posture straight, her arms crossed loosely as she watched Rebecca and Rachel try to mirror her movements. Since the ballet had closed it had been hard to find dance work, so she was glad of the teaching Jacques had given her.

'Again,' she said gently.

Rebecca straightened. Rachel's shoe ribbon was coming loose, and she paused to retie it. Gigi moved closer, knelt beside her and guided her small fingers into the loop. The twins' brown eyes watched her, wide and solemn, far too knowing for their young years, the light catching them with a quiet intensity that stood out against their pale complexions. As Rachel's head tilted in concentration, Rebecca's shifted the same way, the mirrored movement so instinctive it made Gigi's chest ache.

'You're holding tension in your shoulders,' Gigi said softly. 'Let your arms float.'

Rachel grinned. 'That's pretty.'

'It's also easier on the muscles,' Gigi said, straightening with a smile.

The October chill had seeped into the building despite the sputtering radiator, and the girls wore light cardigans over their practice dresses. Gigi kept a wool wrap over the cardigan at her waist, and her mended stockings were just warm enough to keep the bite off her legs.

At the window of his office, Jacques stood quietly, arms folded, observing like a ghost. He didn't speak, but Gigi felt his eyes on her. It wasn't approval, not quite, but something closer to recognition.

Suddenly, the outer studio door slammed open.

The sound snapped across the room like a gunshot.

Rachel jumped. Rebecca froze mid-step.

Gigi turned, her heart jolting, as a man stormed in, his coat soaked with drizzle, jaw clenched, eyes blazing. He didn't acknowledge her. Without a word, he crossed the studio floor and threw open Jacques's office door.

It slammed shut behind him.

'Again,' Gigi said, keeping her voice level, though her hands had started to tremble. 'From first position.'

The girls resumed, but their attention wavered.

Through the office window, the argument began low, then rose until it carried through the thin plaster.

'You had no right!' the man hissed.

'I had *every* right. It wasn't about you,' Jacques replied, calm but firm.

'Not about me? Do you think I don't see it? What you two are doing? She is my *wife!*'

'She chose *me*,' Jacques snapped, his voice rising.

The girls resumed their practice, but Gigi's attention fractured. There was a thud, fist or chair, Gigi couldn't tell.

'You seduced her!' the man spat.

'It wasn't seduction,' Jacques shot back. 'It was *love*. Something you clearly know nothing about.'

A pause, sharp, charged.

Then the vistor went on, his tone dry and brutal. 'Who do you think you are, some sort of gigolo like Olivier Moreau? Please. You're not nearly suave enough to pull it off.'

Silence.

Gigi's breath caught. Her heart kicked hard in her chest.

The visitor said something next, too low for her to catch, but his voice was laced with venom. Her stomach tightened. Gigolo? What kind of dangerous game was Olivier playing?

She looked at the girls, who were now watching her instead of dancing, uncertain.

Gigi crossed to the gramophone and lifted the needle, silencing the music.

'That's enough for today,' she said, with a weak smile.

The door to the office stayed shut. Neither man emerged.

As she helped the girls pack their things, Gigi worked hard to keep her hands steady, straightening Rachel's collar, brushing off Rebecca's sleeve with her fingers as the words Jacques had said vibrated in her mind.

Finally, the office door opened. The other man stormed out, barely sparing her a glance. He looked past her and walked straight out the studio doors. The silence he left behind thudded through the room like a heartbeat.

Gigi didn't hesitate. Once the girls were bundled into their coats, she strode toward Jacques's office and stepped inside.

He was shrugging into his own coat, movements slow and tight.

'What was that about?' she asked, her voice firm but controlled.

Jacques didn't look at her. 'Nothing you need to worry about.'

'He mentioned Olivier. What does he have to do with this?'

Jacques hesitated. Then, quietly, 'Olivier has his own secrets. I already told you not to become mixed up with him, didn't I?'

He stepped past her and opened the door to the corridor. 'I need to get the girls home,' he said with finality, implying that their exchange was over.

His coat flared behind him as he disappeared down the corridor, a child holding each hand.

Gigi stood alone outside the empty studio, her pulse thudding, the echo of a new danger settling like dust in the silence. What was Olivier really hiding? And why, even now, after everything, did her heart still twist toward him, like an addict reaching for a poison she knew she shouldn't touch? In the time they had been apart, instead of her feelings weakening they had only grown and seemed to hollow her from the inside out. Her desire for Olivier was a hunger that was never satisfied.

Later, with a plan, she knocked on Eloise's door; her voice was unsteady.

'I was going to stay in,' Eloise said, glancing at the cold windowpanes. 'It's freezing out there.'

'Please!' Gigi begged. 'I need to talk to Olivier. Even though we're not together, I need to know he's all right. Malina's gone off to some art exhibition, and Claudette's pulling another late night at the theatre. And I can't go alone!'

Her friend reluctantly agreed. They wrapped themselves in wool coats and gloves, scarves pulled high against the damp cold and the blackout-dark streets, and hurried out while the curfew was still a few hours off.

When they arrived, the club was already humming. A soft saxophone floated above the low clatter of glass and murmured conversation, and the dim light cast warm halos on the dancers pressed close beneath the chandeliers.

Onstage, Joséphine Duval shimmered in silver, her voice smooth as silk as she launched into a sultry rendition of 'J'ai Deux Amours'. Gigi let the music soak into her bones, the ache in her chest numbing slightly under the rhythm.

But then Eloise froze beside her.

Gigi followed her gaze.

Olivier.

He was seated at a table near the back. His sandy curls slightly tousled. A glass of whisky untouched on the table. And in front of him, a woman, elegant, blonde, laughing as she leaned in close. Her hand lingered on his arm.

Gigi stared, stunned. Somewhere in her deepest thoughts she had believed he had been pining for her as she had been for him.

Eloise exhaled sharply. 'Well, he didn't waste much time, did he?'

Gigi didn't answer. Her stomach cramped into a knot. No matter what she tried to do, she still loved him.

They sat in silence through the rest of the song. Gigi's eyes flicked back toward the table every few minutes. She watched as Olivier leaned in to say something low in the woman's ear. The woman laughed again, tossing her hair. When he stood to head to the bar, Gigi moved.

Eloise raised a brow. 'Where are you going?'

'I need to speak to him.'

He was talking to the barman and didn't see her coming. When he did, his lips parted slightly as if he might say something.

But Gigi didn't give him a chance.

'Well,' she said. 'You moved on quickly.'

Olivier let out a slow breath. 'Gigi—'

She folded her arms. 'Don't worry. I'm not here to make a scene. Or throw myself at your feet, or beg you to come back.'

His expression showed both loss and longing. 'Then why are you here?'

'Because I needed to say one thing. Just because I'm younger than you doesn't mean it would have been a mistake.'

His jaw tightened.

'You never gave us a chance,' she went on. 'And now? Now you've missed yours.'

Olivier reached for her hand but stopped short. 'You don't know everything.'

'Then tell me.'

'I can't,' he said, voice low. 'Because I care about you more than you realise. And involving you in my life... it's not safe.'

Gigi shook her head. 'That's a coward's excuse.'

Before he could answer, a soft, honeyed voice cut in.

'Oh dear,' the glamorous blonde said, gliding up beside them. 'Is my husband bothering you?'

Gigi froze. *Husband.*

The words hit her like a slap. Her breath caught in her throat, and she turned slowly to face the woman, who smiled with deliberate sweetness, her red lips a perfect bow.

Gigi's voice cracked slightly. 'Your what?'

The woman rested a possessive hand on Olivier's chest. 'My *husband*,' she repeated, her gaze never leaving Gigi's. 'He does have a way of attracting female attention. But I can assure you, he's quite taken.'

Olivier looked stricken, caught between protest and silence.

His eyes met Gigi's, full of guilt.

Gigi stepped back as if he'd physically struck her.

'Gigi...' Olivier began, but the words fell apart.

She turned on her heel and rushed away.

Eloise looked up as Gigi returned, her face hot, hands shaking slightly.

'We're leaving,' Gigi said, voice clipped, brittle.

Eloise didn't ask. She stood, cast one quiet look toward the bar, and followed her.

As Gigi pushed through the velvet curtain behind the stage, her breath tight in her chest, a hand caught her arm.

She turned sharply.

Joséphine.

Still radiant from her performance, she held a silk robe tight around her shoulders, and looked at Gigi with eyes that missed nothing.

'You think he doesn't care, *chérie*, but that man is drowning.'

Gigi pulled her arm away. 'He's a liar.'

Joséphine raised a brow, calm and unshaken. 'Perhaps, but not with you.'

Gigi blinked, the hurt rising again like bile.

'He's married,' she whispered. 'He let me fall for him while he...'

'There is always more to a story,' Joséphine said gently.

Gigi moved past her and vowed not to cry.

At home, she changed out of her dress, wiped lipstick from her lips and washed the scent of smoke and perfume from her hair. She braided her hair, poured herself a glass of wine and curled up in the chair by the window with her knees drawn in.

And then a knock at the door.

Three steady raps.

She froze.

Her heart beat once, twice, and she stood slowly, bare feet silent on the floorboards.

She opened the door.

Olivier.

His coat was wet from a light rain, his curls damp and unkempt, eyes shadowed and tired. She began to close the door on him.

'Please,' he said, voice rough. 'Let me explain.'

Gigi stared at him, stone still.

'What I have to do,' he said, 'is bigger than us. Bigger than this... than a relationship.'

'Oh, so now it's not even about *love*,' she said bitterly. 'It's about some noble mission? Or is it just about saving your neck?'

His jaw clenched. 'You don't understand.'

'Then make me understand,' she snapped. 'What possible excuse could you have for letting me fall for you when you're married?'

He stepped forward, urgent now. 'Annaliese and I... It's not what it looks like.'

She swallowed hard. 'Are you married?'

The silence was answer enough. Finally, he gave a single, almost imperceptible nod.

Her chest tightened. 'And were you married when you were with me?'

His face twisted, pain etched deep, but he didn't deny it.

Gigi's breath shattered in her throat. She stepped back, the floor tilting beneath her. Whatever he was hiding, whatever part he claimed to play, none of it erased this truth and pain, which were almost too hard for her to bear.

35

PROVINS, SUMMER 2011

Lily

Their journey to the hospital had been cloaked in an uneasy silence, broken only by the rhythmic hum of tyres on the motorway.

Lily cast a quick look at Marcus during the drive, but he remained absorbed in his laptop, fingers dancing over the keyboard, eyes fixed on the screen. The glow illuminated his face, highlighting the furrow in his brow, a look she had grown all too familiar with.

As they arrived, a comforting sense of security washed over her. Her childhood home of Provins always calmed her, with its charming half-timbered houses, wooden beams darkened and weathered by time. Lily carefully navigated the car through the Porte Saint-Jean, one of the few remaining fortified gates.

Lily parked near the Église Saint-Quiriace and turned to her husband. His profile was still illuminated by the cold glow of the screen, a stark contrast to the warm, timeworn stone, and the chasm between them felt as wide as the centuries-old charm surrounding her.

'We're here,' she announced, unable to keep the sharp tone from her voice.

She stepped out into the early morning air and tightened her coat to shield herself from the growing emotional distance between her and Marcus.

Lily's thoughts drifted to Julien. His attentive presence during their recent excursions was a stark contrast to this. She pushed her thoughts away and, taking a deep breath, prepared herself to face the stillness of her mother's room.

Inside, the hospital was plain and functional, a low stucco building with clean lines and no attempt of charm as the scent of antiseptic clung to the cool air. Lily walked swiftly through the corridor. Marcus trailed a few steps behind, and flipped open his laptop again the moment they passed the front desk.

She found the right room number, and he seated himself outside as she entered. Inside, her mother's room was dim, the blinds tilted to block the morning sun. The only sounds were the steady beep of machines and the occasional whisper of a nurse's footsteps in the hallway.

Her sister was holding her hand.

They exchanged a brief hug as Clare updated her in a whisper. 'The doctors said she is really fighting, and her prognosis is better this morning. She gave us quite a scare yesterday, but she picked up overnight. I need a break. I'll go and get us a coffee.'

Lily nodded as she approached the bed slowly, her pulse rising in that strange way it always did, as if part of her still expected her mother to turn and smile. But her face was still, her eyes closed, her hands folded loosely above the blanket.

She sat down in the chair by the bed and reached for her mother's hand, cool and limp, but familiar in shape. She laced their fingers gently and leaned forward.

'Hi, Maman.'

Her voice came out a little cracked, but she didn't clear her throat. She didn't want to sound composed.

'I wanted to tell you... I think I'm getting closer to finding Rachel.' Her eyes flicked to the window, where the golden roofs of Provins peeked between the trees. 'I hit a dead end, but I am having some success finding your birth mother, who I am hoping may have clues to Rachel's story. Your mother was one of four women and I ruled out the first two. One was called Malina. She only had one child that was stillborn, so it wasn't you. And another, Gigi, was too young.'

She paused, watching for any flicker, any breath that caught just slightly out of rhythm. But there was only the beep of the machines.

'That leaves just Claudette or Eloise.' She smiled faintly. 'I know, those names don't mean anything to you right now, but with more digging soon one of them might...'

A lump formed in her throat as she blinked down at their joined hands.

She closed her eyes. 'Please hold on. I want you to know the truth before... before it's too late.'

Her mother didn't stir. But Lily stayed there for a long time, fingers still wrapped around hers, hoping that somewhere behind those closed eyes her voice was getting through.

When the nurse arrived to check on her mother, Lily moved outside to give her space. Marcus had disappeared and the waiting area smelled faintly of vending-machine coffee and hand sanitiser. Her sister came back and Lily stirred the paper stick in her plastic cup even though she hadn't added sugar. Clare sat down in the stiff vinyl chair in the corridor next to her as the nurse finished her duties. Her sister's face was pale with tiredness.

'She looks the same,' Lily said quietly, eyes fixed on her cup. 'Like she's just sleeping.'

Clare nodded, then tilted her head to study her. 'You okay?'

Lily gave a weak shrug. 'I keep thinking I should be here

more. That I'm not doing enough. You're here every day. You see the doctors, talk to the nurses. I just—' Her voice broke.

Clare sat forward, resting her elbows on her knees. 'Lil, stop. You're doing exactly what she asked you to do. You think I don't know how proud she would be that you are doing all this research?'

Lily blinked, caught off guard by the softness in her sister's voice as Clare went on. 'I'm just here to hold her hand and keep things from falling apart. But you're giving her *answers*.'

Lily swallowed hard. 'Do you really think that's what she wants right now?'

'I think,' Clare said gently, 'if she woke up and you weren't here, but you'd found Rachel... she'd be absolutely thrilled.'

They sat in silence for a long moment. Outside, the familiar bells of Provins chimed, echoing through the ancient streets like a heartbeat.

Clare went to call her husband, and Lily lingered near the wide window at the end of the corridor, sipping the now-cold coffee and absently watching a pair of sparrows flit across the hospital courtyard below.

She headed back to her mother's room, her steps slow, her mind drifting. Then she saw Marcus.

He was standing by the far window, just around the corner of the corridor, partially hidden by a potted plant. He had his back to her, phone pressed to his ear, his voice low but clear as she approached him to update him on her mother.

'No, it's fine. I told her I'd be busy with calls,' he said, and chuckled softly before ending with, 'I miss you too...'

Lily stopped moving, her heart dropping into her stomach, her legs feeling weak. Her fingers curled around the coffee cup, but she couldn't feel it any more. Everything stilled. Her throat dried. Her heart thudded somewhere far behind her ribs.

She watched him end the call and turn casually, only to freeze when he saw her.

A flicker of panic crossed his face before he caught it, replacing it with a practised smile. 'Lily, hey. I was just finishing a call...'

She couldn't speak.

For one unbearable moment, she simply stared at him, like the world had slowed down around her and she'd fallen through the middle of it.

He shifted. 'It was just a—'

'Are you still seeing her?' Her voice was low and hoarse.

Marcus flinched. 'What?'

'Don't lie to me.' She took a step forward, her body trembling. 'You said it was over. Are you still seeing her, that woman I saw you with?'

He didn't answer.

The seconds stretched, brittle and unbearable.

'It's not what you think,' he finally said, his voice taut. 'It's... complicated.'

'No, it's simple.' Her words sliced the air. 'You *promised* me. You looked me in the eye and swore you'd ended it. And now I hear you telling her you miss her, while my mother is lying in a hospital bed.'

He rubbed his forehead. 'Can we not do this here?'

She marched down the corridor. All she could hear was the rush of blood in her ears and Marcus's voice echoing in her mind. '*I miss you too.*'

The car was silent, heavy with tension that pulsed beneath the skin. Lily sat rigid in the passenger seat, arms wrapped around herself, fingers digging into her elbows. The distance between them spread like mould.

She'd been stupid to trust him, had even played it down in her mind. But hearing it – feeling it – was something else entirely. Like being kicked in the chest.

Now they were two strangers in a car. Years of love, trust, ordinary days and rare extraordinary ones shattered into pieces too small to save.

Lily turned to the window, pressing her forehead to the glass as if the cold could steady her. Nothing felt real any more.

The silence stretched. Then...

She turned to him slowly, disbelief tightening her chest. 'After everything you promised me...'

'Lily.'

He said it like it hurt. No arrogance, no defence – just raw, stunned grief cracking through the man who had treated his marriage like something unshakeable.

He hesitated, long enough to tell her everything she didn't want to know.

'It's... not like that,' he said. 'She's a friend. Someone I—'

Lily laughed, dry and disbelieving. 'A friend?'

'Yes. Like you and Julien are friends.' Bitterness leaked into his tone.

The words landed like a slap. Rage rose fast behind the guilt.

'Oh my God, Marcus. You did not just say that.'

'You spend half your time with him,' Marcus snapped. 'Whispering in galleries, taking road trips, sharing secrets, what am I supposed to think?'

She turned toward him, eyes burning.

'What are you supposed to think? That while my mother is dying, someone actually showed up to help me with her final wish.' Her voice cracked. 'I've been trying to hold her life together, and mine, while you shut down and left me to carry it all.'

She let out a sharp breath. 'In return, you humiliated me, and I was a fool to believe you.'

He reached for her hand.

She flinched. 'No. Don't. You don't get to touch me.'

He sat back like he'd been slapped, dragging a hand through his hair.

'I just… I couldn't breathe at home,' he said, voice cracking. 'Everything was so heavy. Every day felt like walking into a storm. You were buried in your mother's illness, chasing shadows from the past. I felt like I didn't exist.'

Lily stared at him, stunned.

'At work, I had space. I could focus. I didn't feel like I was drowning there.'

'You didn't even try,' she said.

He didn't argue. Just looked away, jaw tight.

'Tell me her name,' Lily said. 'The woman who has destroyed my marriage. Say it.'

He didn't answer.

'Say it!' she yelled.

A car in front braked sharply. Pulling his attention back to the road, Marcus slammed his foot on the brake, barely missing the bumper. The tyres screeched; the car jolted.

'Jesus!' he yelled, yanking the wheel into a layby. Stones crunched beneath the tyres as they stopped.

They sat in the stillness of a tension louder than words.

He threw the gear into park, flung open the door, stepped out and paced at the roadside with his arms crossed.

Lily sat frozen for a minute or two, heart pounding, then opened the door and stepped out slowly.

Marcus turned. His face was pale, jaw tight.

'I didn't mean for it to happen,' he said.

The wind tugged at her coat, but she didn't feel it.

'Then why did you let it? You could've talked to me,' she said. 'You could've been honest. Instead, you lied. Every day.'

'I didn't know what to say.'

'You tell the truth, Marcus! You tell your wife when you're falling out of love with her. You don't wait until she finds out in a hospital hallway, two doors from her unconscious mother.'

She stared at him. 'Are you sleeping with her?'

He flinched. Said nothing.

'You know what?' she said quietly. 'Don't answer. It's not about that any more. It's that you gave up. You walked out without leaving. You checked out of our life.'

He exhaled, still avoiding her eyes. 'It wasn't just me.'

'No,' she said, tears unshed. 'It wasn't. But I stayed. I tried. You were already somewhere else.'

Silence swelled between them.

'Are you in love with her?' she asked.

'I don't know.'

The sting of his admission made her laugh, bitter and exhausted. 'That's not an answer.'

'It's the only one I have.'

The wind swept across the fields. Lily stepped back, arms dropping.

'Then here's mine,' she said. 'I'm done waiting. I'm going to figure out what's right for me. And right now? That's not you.'

Marcus looked at her. Something flickered in his eyes – guilt, loss, maybe both.

But she didn't soften. Not this time.

She walked to the car and opened the door. Her voice was steady now.

'Take me home.'

36

PARIS, OCTOBER 1941

Gigi

Olivier exhaled, running a hand through his damp hair. 'We are married. And I loved her once, years ago, before the war.'

Gigi's brows lifted in disbelief. 'So what? You're separated? Estranged? Conveniently married only when it suits your story?'

He flinched. 'She is still in love with me, Gigi. And she's powerful. Her family entertains the highest ranks of the Nazi command in Paris. Every whispered secret passed between men in uniform happens in our drawing room.'

'And you're just... sleeping with her to get the Resistance what it needs?' she spat, voice cracking. 'Is that your *noble* excuse?'

He didn't answer right away, which was worse than a yes.

Finally, he said, 'I've never lied to you, Gigi. I couldn't. But I didn't tell you about her because I knew what it would do to you.'

'What it's doing to me is not the point,' she said bitterly.

'You should've told me the truth. That's what people do when they love each other.'

She froze the moment she'd said it, her hand flying to her mouth like she could pull it back. She hadn't meant to say it out loud.

Olivier's eyes widened, his whole body going still.

'*Gigi...*' he breathed.

She took a step back, as if the force of what she'd admitted might knock her off her feet. 'I didn't mean, I mean, I didn't plan to...'

But he moved toward her slowly, carefully, his voice softer than she'd ever heard it.

'I know,' he said, taking her in his arms. 'I feel the same about you.' He held her like she was something he couldn't bear to damage. 'You have no idea how hard it is for me not to be with you every minute of every day. Do you think I haven't imagined it? Waking up beside you and existing in a world that isn't falling apart?'

Her eyes welled, the heat of his words breaking through the numb shell she'd been building around herself.

'I was going to tell you everything, why we were together, why I had stayed with her—'

'I guess it was more convenient to continue having a lover as well as a wife,' Gigi snapped. 'And by the way she was dressed, she obviously has money. I'm guessing she takes really good care of you.'

'Don't,' he said sharply, the pain in his voice silencing her. 'Don't think for one moment that any of this was easy. That is why I tried to end this. I left you because I had to, not because I wanted to.'

She blinked at him, trying to process the chaos in her chest. 'You let me fall in love with you, knowing you belonged to someone else.'

His hands came up to her face, cradling it gently. 'I haven't belonged to her in years. I belong to *you*, I have tried to fight it, but I love you, Gigi, with all of my being.'

Gigi stared up at him, her lips parted to speak, but instead of listening, he kissed her.

It wasn't soft.

It wasn't sweet.

It was urgent, desperate, like he'd been starving for her and had finally broken. His mouth claimed hers, and she matched it, pouring every ounce of confusion and longing into the kiss.

Her hands gripped the back of his head, tugging him closer. She didn't know what possessed her; she just knew she wanted him in any way she could have him.

Hurriedly, she began unfastening the buttons of his shirt, needing to feel something real, something solid.

He caught her hand, pressing it still. His forehead dropped to hers, breath uneven.

'Gigi,' he whispered. 'I want you. I want you so badly it hurts.'

Her throat tightened. 'Then why are you stopping?'

His jaw flexed, the words ragged. 'Because if I stay, I'll lose everything I've been doing during this war. And there is more at stake than just you and me. And I'll put you at risk. I can't let that happen. I'll never stop loving you. But tonight...' His lips brushed hers once, trembling, almost a goodbye. 'Tonight I have to disappear. Not from you, never from you. But from your world. Because if I stay, people will die, and you may be one of them.'

He turned and disappeared into the corridor, and his shadow vanished into the dark.

Gigi stood in the doorway, her body still burning from his touch, her hands shaking. She pressed her palm to her lips, tasting him, and knew one truth with agonising clarity.

This was not the end.

37

PARIS, SUMMER 2011

Lily

The light coming through the kitchen window was thin and colourless, the kind of early-morning glow that made everything look faded and brittle. Lily sat at the table, her hands wrapped around a mug of tea that had gone cold hours before.

They had talked all night. Argued. Whispered apologies that didn't quite land. Circled the same pain over and over like vultures over a carcass, hoping to find something worth salvaging.

At 2 a.m., she had shouted. At three, he had cried. By four, they were too tired to do anything but sit in silence, two ghosts in the shell of a marriage. After he left for work, she wandered numbly around the apartment. Tidying, cleaning.

She pulled down his best suit from the wardrobe to take to the cleaners, and as she shook out the lapels her fingers brushed something stiff in the inner pocket.

A small, thick envelope. A quick note scribbled on the front.

I will never forget this event celebrating you and the night we had afterwards. All my love Yvonne

Her stomach dropped.

Fingers numb, she opened the flap and pulled out a stack of glossy photos. Her breath caught. Marcus, seated at an intimate table with the same woman she had seen on the street. The woman's lipstick matched her wine. Her hand rested on Marcus's wrist. Her eyes sparkled in the way they do when a woman feels chosen.

Another image, Marcus laughing, leaning toward her. Another, his lips nearly brushing hers. Lily's pulse thundered in her ears. The timestamp on the receipt inside was just a week ago.

She sat on the edge of the couch, chest heaving, remembering his words.

It's not like that, she's a friend.

For a moment, she just stared at the photos, Marcus smiling across the table, his fingers entwined with Yvonne's.

Then something inside her snapped and a rage built in her that she hadn't known she was capable of. She stormed into the bedroom and flung open the closet as the anger took over.

She yanked down shirts, grabbed handfuls of suits, ties, socks, shoes, whatever she could find. It all went into boxes. Hangers clattered to the floor. She didn't care.

Her vision blurred, but she didn't stop. She moved from room to room, scooping up his belongings. His toothbrush. His laptop charger. His whisky from the top shelf. A book with his stupid notes in the margin.

You make me better. He had written that in the corner of a recipe card once.

Liar.

In the hallway cupboard, she found the cases he took on

business trips. She threw everything into one with a thud that rattled the lid.

She slid the top photo from the pack into a plain envelope. Pulled out a piece of stationery. The pen trembled in her grip, but she forced the words onto the page:

Don't worry about coming back. I'm changing the locks.

She folded it, sealed the envelope and placed it on top of the box.

Then she picked up her phone and called a courier.

'Rush delivery,' she said, her voice like broken glass. 'To an office on rue du Faubourg.'

The gallery was quiet when she arrived, sunlight slanting through the high windows. Marcus's boxes had already gone; the courier had wheeled his life away in silence.

Effy looked up from behind the counter, eyes narrowing.

'You look like death warmed up,' she said.

Lily dropped her bag and sank onto the stool. 'Rough night.'

Effy disappeared into the kitchenette and came back with two mugs of tea, tipping a splash of brandy into one.

'Drink this. Your circles are darker than your eyeliner.'

Lily took a burning sip that settled like courage.

The door burst open with a jangle of the bell.

'Lily!' Marcus stood there, rain-soaked and breathless.

Lily set her cup down. 'You got your things?'

'You sent all my stuff to the office? By courier?'

Seemed more dignified than throwing it out of the window,' she said.

'You changed the locks? Are you *kidding* me? Don't you think that's a little extreme?'

From the back, Effy called, 'Only if you think betrayal is a minor inconvenience.'

Marcus's jaw tightened. He turned back to Lily. 'Can we talk? Please. In private?'

She stepped round the counter. 'What is there to talk about, Marcus?'

'I've been trying to fix things.'

'Oh, thank you for your benevolence,' she said. 'I suppose loving me and Yvonne at the same time was exhausting.'

He flinched. 'It didn't mean anything. You're blowing this out of proportion.'

Effy appeared with a clipboard. 'Thank God it was meaningless. That always makes cheating easier to digest.'

Marcus ignored her. 'We were disconnected.'

'And instead of talking to me, you connected with Yvonne.'

'But Lily, I still love you.'

She stepped back. 'What good is love without trust?'

'So that's it?'

'You don't even seem sorry,' she whispered. 'You just seem sorry you got caught.'

He flinched.

Effy's tone dropped. 'You should go, Marcus. I don't think you're wanted here.'

He swung towards her. 'Where the hell am I supposed to live?'

'You could move in with Yvonne,' Effy added sweetly. 'Unless, of course, she is married too.'

His expression answered for him.

'Sounds like you've got complicated logistics ahead,' Lily said. 'I'll forward your letters.'

He stared at her a moment longer, regret finally creeping in, but it was far too late.

'Goodbye, Marcus,' she said, sternly.

'Yes, goodbye, Marcus,' Effy echoed. 'I hope you find what you're looking for. It certainly isn't here.'

He left without another word, the door swinging shut behind him.

Effy spoke gently. 'He never deserved you. But someone else does.'

Lily exhaled, grief and guilt knotting in her chest. 'I need space. From men. From everything.'

'That's fair,' Effy said, already turning away. 'Just don't take too long, darling. Some doors don't stay open for ever.'

38

PARIS, OCTOBER 1941

Gigi

The next morning came like a bruise.

Gigi hadn't slept. She moved through her apartment like a ghost, her body aching in places her mind couldn't name. She needed answers, answers she wasn't getting from Olivier.

By eight, she was walking through the quiet morning streets. Curfew notices and ration charts fluttered on the lampposts in the early breeze. She reached the grand door with the brass knocker at number 12 rue des Martyrs.

A well-dressed maid let her in. Joséphine Duval's flat was like stepping into a jewel box. Velvet drapes, deep green and gold. Silks and satin throws, record albums in neat stacks, a vase of wilting roses on the piano. A scent of jasmine perfume clung to the air, layered over something sharper – whisky. Somewhere behind it all, a phonograph played faintly, a Billie Holiday song, slow and aching.

The maid led her to Joséphine, who sat on the balcony with a black lacquered cigarette holder poised between her fingers, her silk robe a deep sapphire blue that caught the light like water, tied with perfect symmetry at the waist. A long ivory scarf, featherlight and effortless, was looped lazily around her neck. The air outside was laced with the warm, heady scent of amber and tuberose, her signature perfume that lingered in the fresh air. When Gigi stepped through the French doors, Joséphine didn't turn.

'I was wondering when you'd come,' she said lazily, as she tapped ash into a small jade ashtray. 'You know, heartbreak usually brings women to my door for knives or answers.'

'Right now, I want both,' Gigi said flatly.

Joséphine gave a small, tired laugh and finally looked at her as she spoke to the elegant woman in the grey uniform and crisp white apron.

'Beatrice, could you bring some coffee for my guest, please?' The woman nodded and, as soon as she had disappeared, Gigi spoke.

'What is going on with Olivier? I want to know the truth about his marriage and what he is involved in. Do you know?'

Joséphine didn't speak for a long moment and, as Billie Holiday crooned on about God blessing the child, she gazed out at her stunning view of Paris. She seemed to ponder the question as she raised her gold-tipped cigarette holder to her lips. The smoke from her Gauloise lingered in the air, sharp, and unapologetically Parisian.

'You know,' she finally said slowly, 'he was practically a boy when he met her.'

Gigi blinked. 'Annaliese?'

Joséphine nodded. 'This was years ago. Before the uniforms. Before the flags. Before Paris belonged to anyone but Parisians.'

She leaned against the balcony railing, her silk robe slipping slightly from one shoulder.

'Olivier had just finished conservatory. He had the kind of

face girls wrote poems about and the kind of talent that made them cry.' She paused. 'He didn't come from money. But music gave him access to salons, soirées, summer estates in Normandy where old families let their daughters fall in love with handsome pianists for a season.' She smiled faintly as she continued. 'Annaliese was one of those daughters. Only she wasn't simply French. She was also a golden-haired half-German, a whirlwind in silk gloves. Her father was already whispering things about Germany's strength. About "the coming order". But back then, she didn't care about politics. Only art. Only the way Olivier played Chopin like his heart might shatter.'

Gigi sat completely still, listening.

'They were *beautiful* together,' Joséphine said wistfully. 'God, I hated how beautiful they were. And when I began to perform, he used to bring her to my shows all the time.'

Her voice dropped. 'And for a while, they were happy. They married before the Anschluss. Before the Reich had teeth.'

'What changed?' Gigi asked.

Joséphine's eyes sharpened. 'War changes everything. And Annaliese, she knew how to stay above it all. She saw the way the world was turning and adjusted her posture accordingly. When Germany marched into Europe, she didn't hide. She welcomed it. Champagne toasts to victories that left bodies in the streets.'

Gigi's stomach turned.

'And Olivier?' she asked softly.

Joséphine stubbed out the cigarette. 'He watched the woman he once loved transform into something he couldn't recognise. He couldn't tolerate it, and they separated. She let him go. Quietly. No scandal. But she never stopped loving him, in her way.

'Then he was approached by someone high up in the Allied forces. They needed someone on the inside, someone with a front-row seat to the enemy. So, he went back to her, apparently willing to get in bed with her and the Germans, and she welcomed him back with open arms.' Joséphine's voice grew cold.

'And because maybe some part of him still remembered who she used to be. Or maybe he thought if he saved the country he could save her too. He embraced his mission and he listened while men in uniform boasted about the next town they'd burn. And it seemed to be working well... until recently.'

'What happened recently?' Gigi asked, the concern tightening her throat.

Joséphine turned back to her, her gaze sharp and level.

'*You* happened, *ma chérie*. And now he is walking a razor's edge. One wrong look. One out-of-place phrase, one photograph in the wrong hands, and it's over. That's why he lied. I have seen the way he looks at you, it's the way he used to look at her, that's why he so conflicted. Not because he doesn't love you. But because he does.'

Gigi gasped. Heat flooded her chest, pain, disbelief, a wild flicker of hope she despised herself for feeling.

She looked up, eyes burning now, not with sadness, but with clarity.

Beatrice returned, gracefully balancing a gleaming silver tray bearing a polished coffee pot, an Art Deco milk jug and sugar bowl and two delicate cups.

'Real coffee this morning,' she said with a sly smile. 'Another gift from your favourite admirer.' She set the tray down with practised ease.

Gigi watched in quiet awe. Even in wartime, nothing seemed beyond Joséphine's reach. Unlike so many other things, the war hadn't dimmed her sex appeal, only burnished it.

Beatrice poured from the coffee pot that glinted in the morning sun, its rich aroma mingling with the lingering scent of Joséphine's perfume.

As she stirred her cup, Gigi tried to untangle the shocking information she'd discovered about Olivier and the dangerous game he was playing. She sipped the coffee slowly, feeling its warmth spread through her veins, steeling her resolve as her host continued.

'But it's not just Annaliese who makes this dangerous,' Joséphine continued. 'It's everyone else.'

'What do you mean?'

Joséphine turned, her expression sharp now. 'Very few people know what Olivier is really doing. Outside of myself and one or two high-level Resistance contacts.'

Gigi swallowed hard as Joséphine continued.

'Some think he's a coward. Others think he's a collaborator. A traitor in a tailored coat. That's the price of deep cover. Even his allies would shoot him, if they didn't have the full picture.'

Joséphine's voice dropped and became brittle. 'I only found out because he needed someone to help find a courier. And because of our history... he knew I could keep a secret.' She took a long drag from her Gauloise, the tip glowing like an ember of something burning deep inside her. 'Unfortunately, that was a mistake.'

Gigi looked up sharply. 'A mistake?'

Joséphine took a long slow sip of her coffee and Gigi noticed her fingers stiffen around the handle as she continued.

'Camille was young. Brave. She wasn't Resistance, not really. A singer I knew, just a girl with sharp instincts and a pretty smile who knew how to walk through a room without leaving a shadow. That was her gift.'

She stared down at the table. 'I knew what I was sending her into. So did she. But he needed her.' Her voice thinned. 'And I was wrong.'

Gigi was almost frightened to ask. 'Why?'

'She vanished after a party three weeks ago. Gone. No one saw her leave. Two nights later, they pulled her from the canal.'

Joséphine finally looked at Gigi, eyes unflinching. 'Still wearing her uniform.'

'Do you know what happened to her?' Gigi asked softly.

'We don't, and we can't prove it was anything to do with the underground work she was doing for Olivier. Only something happened that resulted in her paying for it with her life.'

The silence that followed felt heavy.

Then Joséphine set down her cup and leaned back, suddenly more exhausted than elegant.

'And now,' she said, 'he has an even greater problem.'

Gigi's heart beat faster. 'What do you mean?'

Joséphine lit another cigarette. 'He stopped by yesterday to see if I could find him another courier.

'The end of next month, there are very important VIPs arriving from Berlin. High command. They are staying at Annaliese's estate, and they're not just coming for wine and flattery. They're bringing orders. Maps. Intelligence meant for distribution across the Western Front. Whatever they share over their time there, whatever Olivier hears, could shift the balance of the war. The Allies need it. And they'll need it fast. Or it will be too late.'

Gigi swallowed hard.

Joséphine's hand shook just slightly as she tapped ash from her cigarette.

'As a host, it would be difficult for him to get away without provoking suspicion. And I can't send another girl in,' she whispered. 'Not after Camille.'

She stared out for a long moment, then turned sharply, eyes flashing. 'I *won't*.'

She looked up at Gigi, her expression suddenly harder, sharp enough to cut.

But Gigi didn't flinch as she considered her words. Billie Holiday had long since faded into silence. The only sound left was the soft tick of a clock and the faint murmur of the street below.

'I can do it,' she said, steady and clear.

Joséphine blinked, as if she hadn't heard her right.

She looked at Gigi like she was seeing her for the first time.

'No,' she said softly, almost to herself. 'No, Gigi, I told you all this so you'd understand why he is the way he is, not so you'd throw yourself into this mess.'

'I do understand.'

'No,' Joséphine said again, more firmly now. She crushed out her cigarette and studied it before saying, more softly, like it hurt to say: 'Camille was my friend. She wasn't meant to die for this.'

Gigi sat still, but inside something flared hot and unmovable.

'I'm sorry you lost her,' she went on, quietly. 'I truly am.' Her voice hardened, just enough. 'But I'm not her. And I can't sit here and do nothing while he walks into that situation with no help, no way out.'

Joséphine didn't speak.

Gigi clenched her jaw. 'If you won't help me, I'll find another way. I'll find someone else. I've made up my mind.'

Joséphine turned, her eyes narrowing.

'I would rather do this with you,' Gigi continued, holding her gaze. 'I trust you. But either way, I'm going. I will find out where she lives, and find a way into that house.'

The air between them pulsed, charged.

Joséphine blinked slowly. 'You are infuriating.'

Gigi gave a faint smile. 'So I've been told. Let him know you have found him a courier, but don't tell him it is me.'

Joséphine nodded. 'If you insist on doing this. You will need training as a maid, and how to be discreet. Tomorrow. Avenue Montaigne. Ten sharp. The woman there will fit you for the uniform and walk you through your mission.'

Gigi nodded.

Joséphine grabbed Gigi's hand. 'If anything, *anything*, feels off, you leave. I don't care if the message burns in your pocket. You walk. You *live*.'

Gigi didn't blink. 'I will.'

Joséphine finally let go.

'You'd better,' she murmured. 'Because I don't think I could bury another one.'

The building on avenue Montaigne looked ordinary, tucked between a shuttered bakery and a tailor's shop. No sign, no number, just a door that opened to three short knocks, one more after a long pause.

A woman with grey-streaked hair and a severe bun peered out. 'You're late,' she whispered, and turned without waiting.

Inside, the air smelled of starch and tea. Racks of uniforms lined the walls. 'I'm Colette,' she went on briskly. 'You'll speak only when spoken to. Now, strip.'

Gigi obeyed, the weight of another woman's fate pressing against her skin. Camille's dress slid over her shoulders, too loose, too haunted.

'You are no one,' Colette murmured after fitting her with a black wig and drilling her through hours of preparation. Gigi learned to balance trays without spilling, to move silently, to keep her eyes down, to blend into the background. 'But only if you remember you are no one.'

By dusk, Gigi's arms shook from balancing trays, her spine aching from the false stoop. Still, she kept walking the narrow hall, again and again.

Finally, Colette pressed a folded napkin onto the tray. 'This is the message. You carry it, you vanish. If you falter, you die.'

Gigi pivoted, the glasses rattling, her heartbeat louder than her steps. At the far end of the hall, she caught her reflection in the cracked mirror.

Not the dancer. Not the girl Olivier loved.

A stranger stared back, hollow-eyed, forgettable. And in that instant, Gigi wondered: was this who she had to become to survive?

And to save Olivier?

39

PARIS, SUMMER 2011

Lily

After Marcus left, Lily desperately needed a distraction and so turned her attention back to the search for her grandmother. She knew her heart would take a while to recover, but until it did this mission would be the thread that kept her stitched together. She informed Effy of her decision as the older woman brought her a peppermint tea. And, sipping the hot warming liquid, Lily rose and crossed to the corkboard pinned to the back-room wall.

She stared at the photograph Madeline had given them: *Gigi, Eloise, Malina, Claudette.*

Her eyes fixed on Claudette's face. Something about her expression, proud but weary. Like someone who knew too much and smiled anyway.

A memory surfaced, Madeline's voice, casual but certain: *'Claudette worked behind the curtain at the theatre for years. She practically lived there.'*

Lily leaned in, uncapped a red pen and circled Claudette's name.

Palais Garnier. Stage manager. 1938–?

Lily was still standing there, arms folded, when the gallery bell chimed from out front.

She frowned. 'Aren't we closed for lunch?'

Effy didn't answer right away. A moment later, Julien appeared in the doorway, camera bag slung over his shoulder and a hesitant smile on his face.

Lily blinked, her breath catching before she could stop it. The sight of him, broad-shouldered, curls tumbling across his brow, that quiet steadiness in his eyes, sent a ripple through her she hadn't been ready for.

He lifted a hand in greeting. 'Hey, Effy said you might need backup today.'

Lily turned to Effy, who sipped her tea with the unbothered air of someone who'd just planted a bomb and was waiting for the smoke.

'I might have given him a call,' Effy admitted with a hint of guilt. 'I thought you could use some company, someone with a friendly smile and a bit of charm.'

Lily shot her a look, but it didn't stick. Effy just sipped again.

Julien took a cautious step forward and if he noticed the circles under her eyes he didn't mention it.

'Is that okay? I can help doing more research today, if you like?'

Lily exhaled slowly. She was feeling incredibly fragile, and gazing at Julien's handsome face wasn't helping at all.

'I was thinking of trying to find a reason to speak to the staff at the theatre,' she said.

Julien thought for a minute, then his face lit up with an idea. 'I brought my camera. We could pretend we're writing a piece on backstage women of the war. They'd probably give us access.'

Lily hesitated. Everything inside her felt like it was treading water, her marriage, her emotions, her life. But *this*, this was a current. Forward movement. Purpose.

'Okay,' she said at last. 'I'll call the stage manager now and see if he is willing to see us.'

The Palais Garnier rose out of the Paris morning like something half-dreamed, its golden statues gleaming against a pale sky, the marble steps washed clean from last night's rain. Lily stood at the edge of the plaza, notebook in hand, her breath misting in the cool air.

Julien stood beside her, camera strap wrapped loosely around his hand.

'The light is great here,' he murmured.

Lily gave a faint smile, but the nerves bubbling beneath her skin kept it from reaching her eyes. This was the first time she'd been alone with him since everything changed. Since she'd split up with Marcus. And it felt disconcerting.

The quiet between them was not awkward, exactly. But heavy with things unsaid.

They climbed the steps together and stepped into the theatre's front hall, where the hush of red velvet and burnished gold seemed to swallow their footsteps. An usher, clearly used to artist types, barely glanced at their cameras and notebooks before waving them through with a distracted smile.

Backstage was a different world, narrow corridors, worn wood, the faint scent of old make-up and paint. It felt lived in, layered.

Lily followed the corridor lined with photographs of productions past, her pace slowing with every step. Performers frozen mid-pose. Crew members adjusting lights. Seamstresses pinning last-minute hems.

And then, *there*.

A black-and-white photo: a woman in her thirties standing

in the wings, clipboard tucked under one arm, headset crooked over her ear.

Claudette.

She was older than in the photo from Madeline's archive. Still serious, still pulled together, but softer somehow. The curve of her smile, faint but unmistakably the same.

Lily leaned in close to read the tiny label below.

CLAUDETTE M., STAGE MANAGER, LA FILLE MAL GARDÉE, 1950.

Lily opened her notebook and scribbled down the detail.

'She's all over this hallway,' Julien said, scanning further down. 'Look!'

More photos. Claudette helping lift a set curtain. Claudette giving direction with one hand while adjusting an actor's costume with the other. Claudette standing beside what looked like a director, mid-conversation, her hand lifted in a gesture of quiet command.

'It's like she ran the place,' Lily whispered.

They turned a corner and stopped in front of a door marked STAGE MANAGER'S OFFICE.

Julien knocked twice.

A few seconds passed, then a man opened it, mid-forties, a bit rumpled, pencil behind his ear. 'You the journalists?'

'Something like that,' Julien said with a polite smile. 'We're working on a piece about women behind the scenes during the war.'

The man nodded. 'You're after information about Claudette, then. Everyone always is.'

The man waved them in and closed the office door behind them with a soft click. The room was exactly what Lily imagined a stage manager's space would be, organised chaos. Neatly labelled binders of past productions crammed onto shelves, a cracked coffee mug holding mismatched pencils, and a colour-coded wall calendar so dense with notes it resembled an art piece.

'I'm Michael Bernard,' he said, extending a hand. 'Been managing this place about ten years now.'

'Julien Renaud,' Julien replied, shaking his hand. 'And this is Lily Tremaine.'

Michael's gaze lingered on Lily for a moment, like he was trying to place her.

'We were hoping to learn more about Claudette,' she said. 'We came across some photos and heard she worked here for decades.'

Michael gave a fond huff, like someone recalling a battle-hardened general. 'Claudette started backstage when she was seventeen and didn't leave until she was seventy.'

He pointed toward the wall behind his desk. There, hanging in a simple silver frame, was a photograph. Claudette, much older than in the hallway photos, standing in the centre of the stage, flowers in her arms, a standing ovation behind her.

The caption read: CLAUDETTE MOREAU – OVER 50 YEARS OF SERVICE, PALAIS GARNIER.

Lily stepped closer, staring at the image. Claudette's face was lined, her posture proud. There was something unshake-able about her presence, even then.

'She looks...' Lily began.

'Like she ran a country?' Michael supplied, grinning. 'That's about right. Nothing slipped past her. She trained half of us.'

'When did she leave?' Julien asked gently.

Michael's smile faded a little. 'She started slipping a few years after that photo. Dementia, I think. Her daughter moved her out of the city.'

Lily's pulse ticked faster. 'Do you have an address?'

'No, but I've got her daughter's number in an old file,' he said. 'Hang on.'

He opened a metal drawer, thumbed through a folder and pulled out a creased business card.

'Here, Sylvie Brunet. That's her daughter, and the last I heard Claudette was still alive.'

As Lily took the card, a wave of something sharp and tender surged in her chest.

After they left the office, she read the faded print again and again as if the truth might rise from the paper itself.

She'd seen Claudette in photographs. Studied her face on the corkboard. Circled her name with red ink. But now, she wasn't just a name; she was *real*. A heartbeat. A face that might, just might, mirror her own.

Lily blinked hard, her throat tightening. She didn't speak.

Beside her, Julien watched quietly, giving her space.

'You okay?' he finally asked gently.

Lily nodded. 'Just tired, I didn't sleep well,' she lied. She still felt raw from the morning and really wasn't ready to share the news of her failed marriage just yet.

She looked once more at the framed photos on the walls. Claudette, proud, standing beneath the stage lights she'd once commanded.

She could be the answer to everything, Lily thought.

She placed the card inside her notebook. 'I have to see her,' she said, her voice low but certain. 'I need to know the truth. Before it's too late.' She slipped the notebook shut, fingers firm around it, and, for the first time all day, she felt the faintest glimmer of hope. Answers were no longer hidden in the past.

Two days later, they were on their way to the address on the card. The countryside blurred the car window in green and gold streaks as the city gave way to winding lanes and sleepy hamlets. Lily sat in the passenger seat, she had spent the past two days trying to come to terms with the end of her marriage, but the truth pressed heavily on her chest. She felt she owed Julien more than silence.

Taking a steadying breath, she turned slightly toward him. 'Julien, I have something to tell you.' Her voice wavered, but she pressed on. 'My marriage... it's over. I asked him to leave.' She gave a small, brittle smile. 'Seven years, just... *gone*.'

Julien's hands tightened briefly on the wheel. He glanced at her, his expression softening. 'I'm so sorry, Lily. I know that's not what you wanted.'

Then, almost hesitantly, he reached across and gave her hand a gentle squeeze. The warmth of his touch made her eyes prickle with tears.

'I know we haven't known each other long,' he said quietly, 'but I'm here, in whatever way I can help.'

Her throat felt constricted. Gratitude, guilt, longing, they pressed so tightly together she could barely breathe. She nodded and turned her face toward the blur of fields, but his hand lingered just long enough to steady her before returning to the wheel. His presence beside her was like an anchor she hadn't realised she needed.

As Julien shifted gears and took a sharp curve, Lily inhaled deeply and forced herself back to the present.

They passed through a village with moss-covered rooftops and lace-curtained windows. Children played; a woman swept the doorstop of a bakery.

Life. Ongoing. Ordinary.

Lily held her breath for a beat.

'Do you think I'll know?' she asked, forcing her mind to move on.

Julien raised an eyebrow. 'Know what?'

'If Claudette's the one. If she's... my grandmother.'

Julien was quiet for a moment, then said, 'I don't know. You may feel it. Somewhere deeper than logic.'

She nodded slowly, but a shadow still clung to her thoughts.

I just need one truth to land. Something solid. Something real.

They turned off the main road, tyres crunching gravel, as the sign for the house, *La Maison des Saules*, came into view.

Sylvie's home sat at the top of a small rise, its stone facade weathered to a soft grey by decades of wind and rain. Faded green shutters flanked tall windows, most of them open to the warm air. A crooked iron gate creaked as Julien pushed it open, and Lily followed him down the path lined with lavender and overgrown rosemary.

The place didn't hide its age; it wore it like a wool cardigan: frayed at the edges but warm and dependable. Birdsong filtered from the orchard behind the house and, somewhere nearby, windchimes clinked lazily.

'This is the kind of place I want to live when I'm older,' Lily murmured as they reached the front steps.

'I'll meet you here,' he said warmly. It was meant as a light comment, but the words settled over Lily like a weight. She wanted to believe in that future. She wanted it so badly it hurt.

Before they could knock, the heavy oak door opened and a woman stepped out, she had ash-grey wispy hair and reading glasses hanging on a chain around her neck. She was wearing a sensible cardigan and a long skirt. Her eyes moved between Lily and Julien with calm alertness.

'*Bonjour*,' she said. 'You must be Lily Tremaine?'

'Yes,' Lily replied, stepping forward. 'Are you Sylvie?'

'I am,' the woman said. 'Michael from the theatre said you might be looking for my mother.'

Lily's breath caught. *Could this woman be my aunt?* The thought flickered through her with a rush of hope and fear so sharp it nearly unsteadied her.

'She's had a slow day, but a gentle one,' Sylvie added, oblivious to Lily's inner conflict. 'Sometimes the quiet ones are the best for her memory.'

She looked at Lily more closely, eyes narrowing slightly in a way that wasn't unkind, just curious.

'She won't remember everything,' she said. 'But sometimes... *sometimes*, something slips through. A song. A name. A look.'

She opened the door wider. 'Come in.'

The inside of the house smelled of fresh flowers. The furniture was old but lovingly kept: velvet chairs with new slipcovers, lace doilies on side tables, faded rugs that once had been vibrant. Framed black-and-white photos lined the hallway, family portraits, childhood moments, a dog with oversized ears lounging in a garden. Lily's eyes flicked across them hungrily, searching for a trace of her mother's smile, her own jawline. Was it there, or was her hope inventing it?

Sylvie led them to a cosy sitting room with French doors that opened into the back garden. The room was filled with plants, sunlight and the faint sound of classical music.

Claudette sat in a high-backed chair by the window, her profile outlined in gold light. Her hair was pinned neatly, though wisps had escaped. A shawl embroidered with tiny birds rested across her shoulders. She seemed to be humming, something minor and wistful.

'Maman,' Sylvie said softly. 'You have visitors.'

Claudette turned her head slowly, her eyes distant but not vacant.

Lily stepped forward and knelt beside the chair. 'Hello, Claudette. My name is Lily.'

Claudette blinked. For a long moment, she said nothing.

Then, she reached out and gently touched Lily's cheek with a trembling hand.

'You're so beautiful,' Claudette whispered. 'Just like me when I was young.'

The words pierced Lily's chest. Her pulse fluttered wildly. Did Claudette really mean her? Or was it only the rambling of memory's haze? She wanted, needed, it to be true.

She didn't dare speak.

Behind her, Julien shifted, and Sylvie's eyes darkened ever so slightly with something – recognition? Pain?

Claudette's hand dropped softly into her lap, and her gaze wandered back to the window.

Lily didn't move from her place beside the chair. She watched Claudette's profile, unsure whether to speak or stay silent, afraid that either might break the spell.

She finally found words.

'You used to work at the theatre, didn't you?' she asked gently, her voice barely above a whisper.

Claudette's lips twitched into a smile just for a second.

'The wings were always cold,' she murmured. 'Velvet curtains... smelled like dust. Most people hated it. But to me, it was home.'

'I'm trying to learn more about someone from back then,' Lily said. 'A set of twins, Rachel and Rebecca.'

Claudette's fingers stilled. Her expression turned distant, lips parting.

'Yes, Rebecca and Rachel, I told her not to say anything, it was our secret,' she whispered as if remembering something from long ago. 'Not a word. Not if we wanted them to stay safe.'

Lily leaned forward, her heart pounding. 'Told who?'

But Claudette didn't answer. Instead her gaze drifted past them, unfocused as she continued. 'They were holding hands. Always holding hands.' She smiled faintly, then the smile faltered. 'Beautiful girls. Too beautiful for this world.'

Her fingers twitched in her lap, fumbling as though

searching for something. 'So small, so brave. I thought... I thought my heart would break.' Her voice dropped, the words breaking apart. 'Safe... safe... but trains don't always mean safe, do they?'

She began humming again, softly, and then mumbled, 'So much heartbreak, but decisions had to be made for the good of all.'

Julien took a step closer. 'Do you think she's talking about herself? Or someone else?' he murmured.

'I don't know,' Sylvie said. Her voice was soft, but her hands were clenched.

Claudette turned back toward Lily. Her eyes glistened with some emotion just beyond reach as she ran shaky fingers through her own hair.

'Curly... just like yours,' she murmured. 'We never spoke of it again. It was a secret.'

Lily tried again. 'Spoke of what?'

But Claudette's expression was already changing, her mouth folding into a distracted smile, her focus drifting.

They waited there for a long time hoping for more. But she only brightened again when her daughter said, 'It's time for your nap, Maman,' and bent to help her gently from the chair.

Claudette offered no resistance, only glanced once more at Lily before letting herself be led away.

'Just like you when I was young,' she repeated over and over, softly, as they disappeared down the hall.

Lily remained kneeling long after the door had closed.

When Sylvie came back she suggested they have something to drink. They stepped into the garden as the warm light shifted toward late afternoon. The air smelled fresh and a robin chattered from the wrought-iron fence while bees hovered lazily around the flowering rosemary.

Sylvie led them to a small bench beneath a pear tree, its branches heavy with fruit. Obviously sensing the intense emotions between the two women, Julien pulled out his camera and walked a respectful distance away to take pictures further down the garden.

Something about her face tugged at Lily's thoughts. Did she see her own mother's high cheekbones in Claudette? Or was it just wishful thinking? She wanted so badly for Claudette to be her grandmother.

'There's something still very... composed about her,' she continued.

Sylvie nodded. 'She was always like that. Even when I was a girl. She didn't raise her voice, but you knew not to cross her.' She paused, fingers lacing and unlacing in her lap. 'She didn't let people in easily. And I think... there were things she never let herself feel.'

Lily hesitated. 'Did she ever talk to you about her past? Before you were born?'

Sylvie's jaw shifted. 'Little things. In scraps. I know she had a very hard childhood. Once, when I was maybe fifteen, she said when she was my age she had hated mirrors.'

Lily looked at her. 'Why?'

'She said she'd once let go of a piece of herself. That she had never been able to get back and she missed it with all her heart.'

The silence between them tightened.

'She never said more than that,' Sylvie continued, her voice lowering. 'But I always wondered... if it had something to do with her stepfather. He was a brute of a man, so a woman who knew him told me.'

Lily leaned forward. 'Was there abuse?'

Sylvie's expression darkened. 'She never used that word. But yes, I understood it to be true. There were shadows in her eyes when she spoke of him. I was too young to ask what she meant. But now I wonder.'

Lily's chest ached with a complicated, rising hope.

'Do you know if she was... pregnant before she met your father?'

Sylvie exhaled. 'I don't know. But it wouldn't surprise me. She grew up under very difficult circumstances. There were a lot of secrets. Her brother was put in prison for crossing the Nazis during the war.'

Lily glanced toward the house, thinking, *That could be my grandmother.*

'I'll talk to her doctor,' Sylvie said. 'See if anything's in her file. Notes, records, anything.'

'Thank you,' Lily whispered. 'Even if it's nothing, I need to follow it through.'

Sylvie nodded and reached over to rest her hand briefly on Lily's.

'You deserve to know where you come from,' she said kindly. 'We all do.'

The gravel crunched softly beneath their feet as Lily and Julien walked slowly back toward the car. Neither of them spoke at first. The sky above the countryside was streaked with rose gold, the kind of evening light that made everything look softer than it truly was. Lily glanced back once, at the ivy-covered walls of La Maison des Saules, the curtain in Claudette's sitting room fluttering gently in the breeze.

'She touched my face,' Lily said, breaking the silence. 'And said I looked like her.'

Julien gazed at her but didn't interrupt.

'I know she might've been talking about someone else. Maybe even no one. But the way she said it...' Her voice cracked slightly. 'It felt *real.*'

Julien opened the passenger door for her, and she climbed in slowly.

As he rounded the front of the car, Lily stared at her reflection in the side mirror, looking for any resemblance to Sylvie.

Her fingers were trembling again.

Julien gave her a soft, steady look as they walked back to the car. 'I hope the same for you too.' He opened her door, then moved around to the driver's side. Once they were both settled inside, he continued, 'Maybe she will open up more another day, or Sylvie will find something so you can be sure.'

She nodded, turned toward the windscreen and whispered, more to herself than to him: 'Please, let this be the place the story ends.'

And as Julien started the car and pulled away from the old house, light slid off the rooftops behind them, leaving only the hum of the engine and the weight of something that felt very much like truth.

As they merged onto the main road, golden light flickering through the trees, Lily leaned her head against the window. The glass was cool against her temple. Her thoughts spun. Claudette's trembling hand, Sylvie's careful words, the feeling of standing on the edge of something enormous and unfinished. Without a word, Julien reached for the dashboard, adjusted the air conditioning toward her, then slid a CD into the stereo.

The first lilting notes of 'Mon Amant de Saint-Jean' floated through the speakers, melancholy, romantic, impossibly French.

Lily blinked. 'Is that... Lucienne Delyle?'

He nodded, eyes on the road. 'You mentioned her, on the train south.'

Lily's brow furrowed. Had she? The memory surfaced slowly. Yes, she'd been talking about music, about the songs she loved to play.

Lily was confused. 'But you said you had never heard of her.'

'I hadn't. But I thought this would cheer you up,' he said, a little coyly.

She looked at the CD case. The CD wasn't the original, the one he had bought. There was just a handwritten title in neat block letters that said FOR LILY.

He'd burned it himself.

For her.

She turned to face him, a quiet astonishment rising in her chest. He wasn't watching for a reaction, wasn't waiting for praise, just driving, calm and steady, the faintest smile softening his expression.

With Marcus, affection had come with timing and intent, planned, presented, performed. But with Julien, it came like this: in a quiet warmth of being known.

It was a few days later, just after midday, and the gallery was quiet. The last of the morning's foot traffic had vanished, and only the hum of the street outside remained.

Lily was standing at the back worktable getting ready to hang a new piece of art in a spot one had sold from that morning when her phone vibrated beside her.

She answered quickly, stepping into the storeroom for privacy. 'Hello?'

'Lily, hi. It's Sylvie. I hope it's not a bad time?'

'No, not at all,' she said, though her stomach twisted with a knot of anticipation.

Sylvie hesitated before saying, 'I... spoke with my mother's doctor this morning. I asked if there was anything in her history, anything that might suggest a pregnancy before she had me.'

'And?'

'He said... there was scarring. Internal. From what he described, an improperly handled abortion. Likely done when she was very young.'

Lily leaned against the wall, suddenly cold.

'He told me it was a miracle she had me at all. The damage was that severe.'

'I'm so sorry,' Lily said, barely able to find her voice. 'That must have been hard to hear.'

'It was,' Sylvie admitted. 'But I thought you deserved to

know. So, I think it is impossible that she ever gave birth to twins.'

Lily nodded, even though Sylvie couldn't see it. 'Thank you for letting me know.'

They said goodbye, and Lily stood, the phone still pressed to her ear long after the call had ended.

She had so wanted it to be Claudette, wanted to hug her grandmother, wanted her mother to meet her, meet the woman who had given birth to her.

But it was not to be.

40

PARIS, OCTOBER 1941

Eloise

Gigi's apartment was dim and quiet, save for the soft patter of the twins' feet on the worn floorboards. Rachel and Rebecca were twirling silk scarves through the air, laughing as they attempted clumsy pirouettes. Rebecca tipped sideways into a pile of cushions and let out a delighted shriek.

From the kitchen doorway, Eloise watched in silence.

The cup of tea in her hand had long gone cold. Her other arm folded tight across her stomach, as if trying to contain something that had been threatening to surface for a long time.

They were so *luminous*. The way they moved, effortlessly in sync with each other, their little bodies already understanding rhythm and shape, balance and grace. There was no reason they should remind her of anyone. But something about them, the way they laughed, a look on their faces when they were hiding something. It was all too familiar.

Gigi appeared beside her, drying her hands on a dishtowel. 'You've gone quiet.'

Eloise didn't answer at first. Then, softly, 'I met him when I was seventeen.'

Gigi blinked. 'Who?'

'Jacques.'

'My ballet teacher?'

Eloise set the teacup down, her fingers lingering on its rim as if afraid to let it go entirely. 'I was a dancer at the school. I used to stay after to ask questions I didn't really need answers to. He always had time for me. Said I had the kind of mind that didn't settle.'

Gigi said nothing, just stood beside her, silent and steady.

'It wasn't supposed to happen.' She gave a hollow laugh. 'But he would look at me a certain way and, even though he was older than me by ten years, I knew there was something between us. A spark.'

She swallowed. Her voice changed, no longer dreamy but bitter at the edges.

'When I turned eighteen, we kissed for the first time in the rehearsal room. I thought I was in love. And when I got pregnant, I didn't even know at first. I thought I was just exhausted from rehearsals, and when it was confirmed it was too late to do anything about it safely, I had to go through with it. My parents were heartbroken, but he took me to a clinic outside the city. Quiet. Discreet. He paid for everything.'

Gigi's eyes widened, the dishtowel twisting tighter in her hands. 'Eloise. I'm shocked, I have always thought of him as control, discipline, authority.' Her voice cracked with disbelief. 'Not a man who would take advantage of one of his students. Of you.'

Eloise felt the words settle between them like a weight, the truth of them undeniable. Eloise's hand moved unconsciously to her throat as she continued, aching in memory.

'I gave birth to twins. I remember blood. *Pain.* Jacques

holding my hand and saying everything would be all right. Then the darkness took me.'

She closed her eyes, as if trying to will away the next part.

'When I woke up, he told me they hadn't made it. That I had also nearly died. That it was better I didn't remember too much.'

She reached for Eloise's arm, her fingers curling gently around it. 'Oh, Eloise...' she whispered, her voice breaking. 'How terrible for you. I'm so sorry this happened to you.'

'For years I believed him. For years, I hated myself for surviving them. But now...' Her voice caught. 'Now I look at them, those girls...'

Her gaze locked on the twins as they toppled together onto the rug in a heap of giggles and limbs.

'...I know it's irrational, and maybe it's my grief still rearing its ugly head. But it is too coincidental. They are staying with him, they are the right age. Gigi, I think they're my daughters.'

The silence that followed was heavy and holy.

Gigi gently took the cup from her hand and set it on the table. 'Oh my God, Eloise. What are you going to do?'

Eloise looked back at her, jaw tight, eyes burning.

'I'm going to confront him,' she said. 'He owes me the truth.'

The rehearsal room at the ballet school was dark, save for the sliver of moonlight cutting across the floorboards. The scents of rosin and sweat clung to the air, familiar, sharp, grounding, and outside somewhere a German truck downshifted on the boulevard.

Jacques was sitting at his desk in his office, scribbling notes onto a sheet of music. He didn't hear the door open.

Eloise stepped inside, her fingers curled tightly around the strap of her handbag. Her breath was shallow.

She stood there for a long moment, her heart pounding like

it wanted to escape her chest. The ghosts of her former self lingered in every corner of the room – the girl who had stayed late after class, the one who had believed in love, the one who had been told her children had died.

The quiet thud of the door closing behind her seemed to echo off the walls.

Jacques looked up at the sound.

He seemed startled by her presence. 'Eloise?' His voice was wary. 'What are you doing here? Is something wrong?'

She stepped forward slowly, her heels clicking on the wooden floor.

'No, Jacques. Nothing's wrong,' she said, her tone deceptively calm. 'I just came to say, I know now why you've been avoiding me all these years.'

He straightened. 'I haven't—'

'*Don't,*' she cut in sharply. 'Don't insult me with lies. Every time I walk into a room, you walk out. You cross the street when you see me. You haven't looked me in the eye since...'

Jacques said nothing, his mouth tightening.

'I told myself it was because I'd failed. Because you hated me. That maybe you blamed me for losing your children. That you couldn't stand the sight of the girl who'd bled too much and brought nothing but sorrow into your life.'

She took a step closer, her voice rising. 'But it wasn't hate, was it? It was guilt. You knew what would happen.'

She took a stuttering breath. 'They didn't die, did they?'

Jacques's face drained of colour. He opened his mouth, then closed it again as she continued.

'Rachel and Rebecca. They're mine, aren't they?'

He didn't speak.

'I remembered, Jacques. The blood. The pain. The way you said everything would be all right. And then you told me they were dead.' Her voice cracked. 'But they're not, are they? You *lied* to me.'

Jacques rose to his feet, his face tight. 'Eloise, I—'

She didn't let him speak. 'You let me grieve them. For *years*. You let me think I lost them when all this time—' Her voice broke off into a strangled whisper. 'They were alive. And I never got to hold them.'

'I was trying to protect you—' he finally whispered.

'*Don't!*' she snapped. 'Don't make this about you being gallant. You stole them from me.'

'I saved you,' he said, too loudly. 'You were dying. You don't remember how bad it was. You had lost too much blood. The doctors didn't think you would survive. I... I didn't know what to do. I panicked.'

'You should have told me the truth.'

'You think I didn't want to?' His voice trembled with something close to shame. 'You were eighteen. I was a grown man. What we had... it was wrong. I should never have—'

'Don't you *dare* try to rewrite this with your guilt,' she snapped.

He stepped away from her, running a hand through his greying hair.

'I placed them somewhere safe. With someone who could protect them. Love them. And then as Hitler started to march upon Europe I couldn't give them back to you. I'd be putting all of us at risk.'

'Who gave you the right to decide my fate, or theirs?'

He met her eyes, and for the first time there was only fear.

She spun back to him, fury blazing. 'You had no right.' Her voice climbed, breaking on the words. 'You had no right to take them from me and never tell me. Years of grieving empty graves while my daughters were alive. You watched me fall apart and you let me.' Tears flooded and she did not wipe them away.

He stepped forward, hands lifted as if he could steady the air. 'I made the only choice I could.'

'*No!*' she shouted, the word echoing through the empty

office. 'You made the only choice that suited you. Your reputation, your tidy life, your *control*.' She jabbed a finger at his chest. 'You played God, and you stole what was mine. You kept them from me,' she cried. 'You kept them from their mother.' Her shoulders shook, anger and grief colliding. 'You lied. You lied to a girl who trusted you with her life.'

She swallowed hard, chest heaving. 'I carried them. I bled for them. I woke every night hearing them cry in a room that did not exist.'

He reached for her. 'Eloise...'

She stepped back, eyes blazing. 'Do not touch me.' The tears kept coming, hot and relentless. 'You do *not* get to comfort me.'

For a moment neither of them spoke. The office seemed to tilt, the mirrors throwing back two people who no longer recognised each other.

'I am going to tell them!' she shouted, each word carved from stone.

'You can't,' he said, matching her tone. 'We're both Jews, Eloise. If anyone ever finds out they're ours, if someone traces them back to you, to me... you know what that means. You'd be signing their death certificates. The lists, the raids, families are being dragged to Drancy.'

She had heard about this place. An internment camp outside Paris, the place where Jews were held before being deported east.

'They deserve to know who they are,' she fired back. 'They deserve a mother who did not abandon them, and the truth that you buried because it was easier for you.'

His voice tore. 'Even if it would seal their fate?'

She drew in a shuddering breath, realising the truth in his words. She wiped her face with the heel of her hand, lifted her chin. 'I will never, ever forgive you for this,' she growled.

He took one helpless step after her. 'Eloise, please.'

She turned on her heel and walked to the door. In the corridor she pressed her palm to the cold wall, bent for a single breath, then straightened and kept going, tears streaking down her cheeks.

Two faces rose in her mind as she stumbled forward, two small bodies she would never hug, tiny faces she would never cover in butterfly kisses, hands she would never hold. The daughters she had carried, bled for, and lost.

Her girls.

But they would never truly be hers, and she would never stop mourning that.

41

PARIS, SUMMER 2011

Lily

The soft chime of the gallery door snapped Lily from her thoughts as she hung up the phone after Sylvie's call.

She turned, brushing a stray lock of hair behind her ear, expecting another customer.

But it was Julien.

He stepped inside, wind-tousled and perfect. He hesitated when he saw her expression.

'You okay?'

She tried to smile but failed. 'I just got off the phone with Claudette's daughter.'

His brow creased as he stepped closer. 'And?'

'She's not the one.' She could hear the disappointment in her own tone and obviously he could too. 'There was a pregnancy when she was very young. But it ended in a botched abortion. Her doctor said it was a miracle she had Sylvie at all.'

Julien winced. 'I'm sorry.'

Lily nodded, her throat tight. 'It's strange. I didn't realise how much I'd started to hope.'

There was a pause, gentle and understanding.

'I might have something to cheer you up,' Julien said, voice low.

Lily looked up, surprised.

'I made a call this morning,' he continued, slinging his bag to the floor. 'To the Archives Départementales. They hold adoption records and wartime guardianship files. I asked about any references to a woman giving birth to twins in the year your mother was born, and then having them adopted. They found a file that might be of interest to us.'

'There is also something about a guardianship reassignment in 1943. He wouldn't say anything more over the phone. But he's holding the file for us. If we want to come and take a look.'

Effy's voice chimed in from behind the stacks. 'Take a look at what?' She emerged from the back room holding a mug in each hand, one for her, one clearly for Lily.

Julien gave her a sheepish smile and related what he had told Lily.

'Mm.' Effy handed Lily the mug. 'Sounds intriguing, you should go.'

Lily turned to her. 'Are you sure? I have been spending a lot of time away from the shop doing this.'

'Of course I'm sure. At my age, living vicariously through you is the only excitement I get,' she said with a wave of her hand.

Lily knew this to be untrue – even though Effy was in her eighties she had a fuller social calendar than many women half her age.

'If you're sure...'

'Go on,' she insisted, waving her hand with a jingle of the bracelets on her wrist. 'I have Monsieur Bellows here to keep me company,' she added, gesturing toward a bright painting by a promising young artist that needed to be hung.

Julien held the door. 'I made an appointment. I think we should go.'

The Archives Départementales was nestled on a quiet street just off the boulevard Saint-Germain, a stately stone building with ivy clinging to its edges and iron lanterns flanking the door. Inside, it smelled of time, aged paper, polished wood and lemon oil.

The reading room was hushed, its tall windows letting in pale afternoon light. A single archivist sat behind the reference desk: a thin man in wire-rimmed glasses and a navy blazer, who stood as they approached.

'Monsieur Renaud?'

'Yes,' Julien said, offering a polite smile. 'This is Lily Tremaine. We're here to view the Morel file?'

The archivist nodded and disappeared into a back room. Moments later, he returned with a worn folder. He laid it on the table between them and quietly returned to his desk.

Lily and Julien sat side by side, the folder a silent weight in front of them.

Julien reached for it first, flipping open the cover. Inside were several neatly typed forms, their edges brittle, their ink still sharp.

Lily leaned in.

```
Birth record — November 1932.
Children: Rebecca and Rachel — twin
females.
Mother: Eloise Morel.
Father: Jacques Leclerc.
```

Lily let out a breath and sat back in her chair... Jacques Leclerc... *Uncle Jacques.*

She pressed her lips together. Her heart thundered in her ears.

Next came a guardianship declaration, dated just after the birth. Signed by Jacques Leclerc.

```
Guardian designate, in the event of
incapacitation or hardship. To ensure
the girls are raised in a suitable
household.
```

Then another document, more formal.

```
Adoption placement, December 1932. Adop-
tive parents: André and Mireille Durand,
Normandy.
```

Julien read aloud softly, 'No compensation rendered. Terms agreed upon in private counsel. Girls to be raised as Durands.'

Lily stared at the page. 'So, they gave them away,' she said quietly.

Another file followed, this one dated October 1942.

Lily read aloud, 'Reinstated guardianship: Jacques Leclerc. Upon death of André Durand in active combat, June 1940, and subsequent death of Mireille Durand from pneumonia, July 1942.'

'What about Eloise?' Lily asked. Julien's expression darkened.

'According to the records, she disappeared in 1947. No death certificate, no trace. She could be anywhere - or nowhere.'

'Oh how sad, they lost *two* mothers,' she whispered.

Julien didn't respond right away. He was watching her with quiet intensity.

Lily glanced up at him. 'I wonder if Eloise even knew about this. Why would she not be on the guardianship papers too?'

The silence that followed stretched, filled with unsaid things.

Then Julien reached out, hesitantly at first, and laid his hand over hers. 'Are you okay?'

The warmth of his skin against hers, the steadiness of his touch, it nearly undid her as she nodded.

And in that moment, everything came into focus. Her grandparents. Her marriage. The pull toward something real, something that felt like truth.

Julien flipped to the last page of the file.

Clipped behind the guardianship reassignment, there was a thin, yellowed note, handwritten in faded ink.

Temporary care of minors assumed by Madame Edel Marchand (sister of deceased adoptive mother). Residing at 14 rue des Tilleuls, Caen, Normandy. Children later collected by Jacques Leclerc, birth father, on 3 November 1942.

Lily leaned forward, her pulse quickening.

'Edel Marchand,' she murmured. 'She took them in, even if only briefly. She was the last person who saw them before Jacques brought them back to Paris.'

She looked up at Julien. 'If Rachel ever tried to return to that family, if she reached out to someone, it may have been her...'

Julien nodded. 'Then that's where we go next.'

Lily stared at the name again. A place. A person. A chance.

A whisper of hope stirred inside her.

'I'm going to try and contact her,' she said decisively.

Outside, the air was crisp and golden. The two of them walked side by side in silence, their footsteps echoing down the narrow cobblestones.

Julien stopped at the edge of a small square. A fountain trickled lazily in the centre, its basin surrounded by stone benches and flowering trees.

Lily sat without a word.

He sat beside her, the copy of the file the archivist had made for them still in his hands.

She was staring straight ahead, her eyes fixed on nothing and everything, the ripple of water, the soft light on the buildings, the ache in her chest.

They had fallen into silence. Lily's gaze lingered on the water, but her thoughts had already drifted. Claudette's words rose in her mind again, insistent, and she spoke them out loud. 'There was so much heartbreak, but decisions had to be made for the good of all.'

Her voice caught on the edge of something fragile. 'That's what I can't stop thinking about. How they surrendered everything for one another during the war, safety, future, life itself. One of them gave up their right to their daughters.' She paused, one hand rising to her throat. 'Then I look at what Marcus and I became. Seven years, and I can't name one thing he ever gave up for me. He only... he only took. Piece by piece. Until I disappeared.' She drew in a shaky breath and whispered, 'That's not what love is.'

'No, it's not,' he responded, his voice husky with emotion.

She looked at him then, and the weight of the last few weeks swelled inside her. Every shared moment, every glance that lingered too long, every conversation that had gone too deep pressed against her heart.

'Julien...' Her voice was barely more than a breath.

His fingers brushed hers, tentative at first, then curling slowly until he held her hand as though afraid she might slip away.

'I wasn't going to say this,' he murmured. 'I told myself I'd keep it simple. Help you find answers, then disappear when you didn't need me any more. But I've already failed at that. Even though I tried not to.' His thumb traced a line across her knuckles. His gaze flickered to her mouth and back again, raw with restraint.

'I've fallen in love with you, Lily. I didn't mean to. I know it's messy, complicated, unfair. But it's true. I hate seeing you unhappy. And I know I could love you better than what you have known.'

Her heart swelled with gratitude, fear, longing.

Before she could speak again, he leaned in.

The kiss began soft, tentative, like a question. His lips brushed hers, reverent, and she thought she might break from the tenderness of it. Then something inside her gave way and she kissed him back, everything deepening. His hand slid to the small of her back, pulling her closer, while her fingers curled into his shirt, clinging.

For a few glorious moments, she drowned in him, alive in a way she hadn't felt in years.

But then her bare left hand where a ring should have been was stark against the fabric of his jacket. The place she was in tore through the haze like a blade.

She froze. Trembling, she pulled back, her breath breaking against his lips.

'Don't,' she whispered, pressing her forehead to his. 'Please... don't kiss me.'

His hand cupped her cheek, thumb catching a tear. 'Lily...'

'You don't understand,' she said, voice shaking. 'I want this. You. More than I've wanted anything in years.'

'Then what's wrong?'

'I can't. Not yet.' Her breath shuddered. 'I'm too fragile. My marriage, my mother, everything. I'd only screw this up if I rushed into it now.'

Julien's jaw tightened, but he didn't let go. His forehead

rested against hers. 'Then tell me when. Because every time I touch you, it feels *right*.'

Her tears spilled, warm against his hand. 'You make it sound so easy.'

'No,' he murmured. 'I know it won't be. But I promise you, I'll fight for you. Every day. If you'll let me.'

She closed her eyes, torn apart by the truth she couldn't bring herself to speak. Her body still hummed with the memory of his kiss, the warmth of his hand, the safety of his presence. She wanted to step forward, to let herself fall into everything he offered, but another part of her recoiled, still bruised, still afraid.

With an effort that felt like tearing herself in two, she stepped back, her breath shaking. 'I need us just to be friends. For now, until I can feel less raw...'

Julien's gaze burned into hers, wounded but steady. His voice was quiet. 'If that's what you need, then I'll wait. But I can't unlove you, Lily. My heart belongs to you.'

She nodded, hating the way her chest clenched at his words, then turned before she shattered completely. Every step away from him tugged against something she wasn't ready to name.

By the time she reached the street, her hands trembled. She pressed her bare ring finger against her palm, as though she could still feel the echo of his touch there. The taste of his kiss lingered, a reminder of how close she had come to surrendering.

She told herself she was doing the right thing, protecting herself, keeping space until she could breathe again. And yet, with every step the ache only deepened, leaving her caught between yearning and fear, uncertain which way her heart would ultimately take her.

42

———

PARIS, OCTOBER 1941

Gigi

The rain was still falling when Gigi heard the familiar rattle of a key struggling in the lock down the hall. She stepped out just in time to see Eloise pushing against the swollen wood of her door, her shoulders tight with strain.

'Eloise,' Gigi said gently, moving toward her. 'Are you all right?'

Her friend did not answer. Gigi hesitated only a moment before following.

Eloise's apartment was neat as ever, everything in its place, but Gigi could see it in her friend's expression: Eloise was unravelling. She crossed quickly to her bedroom and flung open the wardrobe doors, then began pulling things out: coats, scarves and dresses, until they littered the floor in a disordered heap.

'Eloise, please...' Gigi said softly, stepping closer. 'Talk to me.'

'I have to find them,' Eloise whispered, almost to herself. Her hands shook as she dropped to her knees and tugged an old trunk from the back of the closet. The latch resisted, then gave with a groan. She dug through layers of costumes and faded programmes until her fingers closed around something small, fragile.

She drew it out slowly. Faded pink satin, dulled nearly white with age. Ribbons trailing like ghosts. 'My first pair,' Eloise whispered, cradling them in both hands as tears spilled down her cheeks.

Eloise went into Gigi's apartment, not even acknowledging her other friends, who had gathered there after Gigi had told them what had happened. Instead, she went straight to the bedroom where the twins slept, the slippers cradled against her chest. The room was hushed, lit only by the faint glow of the streetlamp seeping through the corner of the blackout curtains. She sank to her knees beside the narrow bed.

Rebecca and Rachel lay curled together, mirror images in sleep, their breaths rising and falling in soft, uneven rhythm. Rachel murmured something unintelligible and reached for her sister; Rebecca's hand twitched as though answering. The sight brought tears to Gigi's eyes as she watched.

Eloise leaned close, brushed a stray curl from Rebecca's brow and pulled the blanket higher around their shoulders. Her tears fell silently as she bent over them, whispering.

'I should have been the one to kiss your foreheads each night before you went to bed. To tend to you when you were ill, to clap at your ballet recital. My arms should have been your safe place. My voice, singing your first lullaby...'

Her sob caught, as she pressed the slippers between them, satin ribbons splaying across the blanket.

'My little dancers,' she whispered. 'These are the pieces of me I was never allowed to keep. If I cannot be your mother, let these be my gift. Let them carry you further than I ever could...'

Behind her, the other women stood in the doorway, silent witnesses. Gigi's hand pressed against her lips, Malina's stern face was softened by tears, and Claudette's eyes glinted in the dim light. Not one of them could look away.

'I never stopped loving you. Not for a breath, not for a *second*. Even when I thought you were gone, my heart remembered you.'

When she could bear no more, she rose, her body heavy as stone, and followed the others back to the sitting room.

She told them everything. Jacques's betrayal, the hidden adoption, her helplessness. Her voice was raw, but resolute.

'They are Jewish, as I am,' she said quietly.'

The silence deepened until Malina's voice trembled through it. 'But what about after the war, when they are older?'

Eloise's answer came like a prayer torn from her chest. 'One day at a time. One secret at a time.'

Claudette's jaw tightened, but she inclined her head, her voice steady though her eyes betrayed her sorrow. 'Then this is for the good of all.'

The words settled over them like a stone, sealing something vast and irrevocable. One by one, they gave their agreement. A pact forged in love and silence.

From the street below came the sudden crack of boots striking cobblestones, urgent, uneven. Shouts in German followed, sharp and commanding, echoing between the narrow buildings. Then a cry, a man's voice, cut short by the thunder of a single gunshot.

The sound split the night. The women drew in a collective breath.

They heard the stirring, before the girls appeared in the doorway. Rachel clutched Rebecca's arm, eyes wide with fear, while Rebecca held the satin slippers tight to her chest, as if they could keep her safe.

'Gigi,' she whispered, her voice thin and trembling, 'are these yours?'

The room froze.

Gigi crouched before them, her throat tight. She glanced toward Eloise, who stood motionless in the shadows, tears streaming down her cheeks.

'They belonged to your mother,' Gigi said gently.

Rachel's eyes widened, her voice breaking. 'You know her?'

'Yes,' Gigi whispered, her voice thick. 'She was a dancer, too. Kind and beautiful. She loved you very much.'

Rebecca hugged the slippers to her chest, tears slipping silently down her cheeks. 'Where is she?'

Eloise's breath caught audibly, though she stayed rooted in place.

'She is no longer with us. But she will always be with *you*,' Gigi said at last. Her voice was soft, careful. 'She is watching over you.'

Rachel spoke up, her voice trembling. 'I miss her. Even if I never knew her, I miss her.'

Rebecca met Gigi's gaze, searching. 'But why did she have to leave us?'

The question pierced the air like broken glass. Gigi's voice trembled as she gathered them closer. 'Sometimes life takes people from us. Your mother didn't leave because she stopped loving you. She left because the world was cruel. But her love has never left you. It is here.' She pressed a hand to Rachel's chest. 'And here.' She brushed Rebecca's damp cheek. 'And in these ballet shoes too.'

Rebecca clung to the shoes, sobbing. Rachel bit her lip hard, trying not to cry, but her body shook.

From the shadows, Eloise sank into a chair. The other women bore the weight in their own ways as the girls moved back into the bedroom. Claudette stood still as stone, her whisper raw – 'This is for the good of all' – though her voice cracked on the final word. Malina muttered under her breath, eyes hard with fury, 'Children should never have to ask such things.'

Eloise was pale and wordless. Her girls were close enough to touch, and yet still, impossibly, heartbreakingly out of reach.

43

PARIS, AUTUMN 2011

Lily

The phone rang just as Lily was adding up their takings for the day. She almost didn't answer; the day had been long, and her thoughts felt brittle, but when she saw Julien's name flash across the screen her heart stuttered. After their last parting, she had wondered if she would ever see him again.

'Lily?' His voice was bright, almost breathless. 'A package just arrived from my aunt in Lyon. She found some of my grandfather's things in her attic and thought I should have them. I... well, I thought maybe I would open it with a friend.'

Her stomach relaxed. He was telling her he was okay with where they were at, willing to accept her need to go slowly.

'At your apartment?'

'Yes. Above the shop.' A light laugh followed, nervous, as if he could already feel her hesitation. 'It just didn't seem right to open it alone.'

After she hung up, she sat for a long while, staring at the phone in her hand. The thought of going to Julien's apartment sent a nervous flutter through her chest.

Effy breezed in from the back, trailing the scent of lily and lavender. She wore a robe the colour of ripe plums, and her hair was piled high and pinned with jewelled combs. 'Darling,' she said, taking one look at Lily's face, 'whatever it is, say yes.'

Lily blinked. 'I haven't even told you.'

'You don't need to. I know how your face lights up when he calls.' Effy's bangles clinked as she waved a dismissive hand. 'You're separated, *free*, Lily, whether you've admitted it to yourself or not. Go and enjoy yourself.'

Effy's certainty pressed against the last of Lily's doubts. By the time she stood before the narrow door beside Julien's shop, her palms were damp, her pulse racing.

Julien met her and showed her up the stairs. 'Come in.'

His apartment surprised her. She had imagined clutter like the shop below, stacks of prints and negatives spilling across every surface, but the space was ordered and calm. A tall lamp glowed amber in the corner. Books lined a low shelf, spines worn but tidy. A framed photograph of the Seine at dawn hung above a neat desk. Everything seemed deliberate, cared for.

The air smelled faintly of garlic and herbs. On the small counter, two plates waited, and steam was rising from sauce in a pan on the stove.

'You cooked?' she asked, startled.

His smile was boyish, almost shy. 'It's nothing fancy. Just pasta with my mother's recipe. But I thought, if we're going to open a box from the past, we should fortify ourselves first.'

They sat cross-legged around the low coffee table, knees brushing its edge. Wine glasses gleamed in the lamplight. Lily twirled her fork, tasted, and found herself smiling despite everything. 'Julien, this is wonderful.'

He grinned.

The moment felt warm in its simplicity. No tablecloth, no careful performance, none of the brittle politeness of Friday dinners with Marcus. Here, conversation flowed easily: photography, Effy's outrageous fashion, the changing season. She realised with a pang that she was happy, truly happy, in a way she hadn't been in months.

When the plates were empty and the wine had left a soft warmth in her chest, Julien set his glass aside and gestured to the parcel waiting on the table.

'Well,' he said gently. 'Shall we?'

Lily nodded, her heart beating faster.

The string snapped, the paper fell away and Julien opened the box. Inside lay a jumble of relics: a Rolleiflex camera, a cracked-spine journal, programmes from long-forgotten plays and photographs tied with faded ribbon.

Together they sifted through the items. Their shoulders brushed as they leaned closer, warmth sparking in the quiet.

Then the journal slipped, hitting the floor with a dull thud. Lily stooped quickly to retrieve it. As she lifted it, a folded piece of paper slid free from the binding.

'What's this?' she murmured, unfolding the fragile sheet. 'Maybe it's a love letter?' she said, raising her eyebrows in expectation.

The ink was rushed, uneven.

Make sure Leclerc is at his dance studio this evening.
We will arrest him there and you will be rewarded.

The name blazed up at her, searing...*Jacques.*

She looked at Julien, her face draining of colour. It took a minute for the truth to surface, to become real to her. 'This is about my grandfather,' she whispered, the words barely escaping her lips.

He took the paper from her trembling hands. His own expression collapsed, his mouth parting in horror. 'No. Lily, no. This can't be true...'

But it was. The silence between them thickened, heavy with grief and guilt.

Lily pressed her fists to her mouth, her body shaking. 'My grandfather died at the hands of the Nazis. Because of this. Because of *him*.'

Julien's voice broke. 'I didn't know, I swear to you, I didn't know.'

She shook her head, tears stinging. 'I'm not blaming you. Of course I'm not. But Julien...' Her throat closed, and the words scraped out raw. 'This will break my mother's heart to know he was betrayed by a friend. She has felt so alone all of her life.'

The words shattered her even as she said them.

Julien bowed his head, shame carving deep lines into his face. 'I don't have an answer,' he whispered. 'Only that I would give anything for it not to be true.'

The paper lay between them, fragile and poisonous, while the lamplight flickered in the silence. For the first time since she had met him, Lily wasn't sure if she wanted him near.

Julien reached for the journal again, his hands unsteady. 'There must be more,' he muttered, almost to himself. 'Maybe he never delivered it. Maybe they didn't—'

Lily clung to the hope in his words, her heart pounding. 'Yes. Maybe Jacques escaped. Maybe he wasn't taken.'

Her voice faltered, but Julien had already begun flipping through the brittle pages.

His eyes scanned the cramped handwriting, his breath coming unevenly. His fingers trembled as he turned another page and scanned the jagged scrawl. His throat tightened. 'There's something here.'

Lily leaned closer, her breath shallow.

He read aloud:

'A man I hated got away from his comeuppance tonight. I tried to get him arrested. He must have been warned, or perhaps he

was simply clever enough to smell trouble coming. Either way, he slipped through their hands. For a moment, I thought he would go on untouched.'

Lily's chest constricted, hope sparking in her veins. Julien's voice caught, but he forced himself onward.

'Fortunately, it did not last. I found him. When the time came, I pointed the way, and they took him. I was glad to hear he died in a cell, broken and alone. Justice, at last.'

The words hit like blows. Lily's relief shattered, her pulse roaring in her ears. 'No,' she whispered. 'No, no...'

Julien's hand tightened around the page, but he continued, his face ashen.

'They say he left behind twin girls. I tell myself it is better this way. Better they grow up without a father like that, without his pride and foolishness to curse them. They are better off free of him.'

Lily sat back, her hands flying to her mouth. Tears burned hot in her eyes, spilling before she could stop them. 'He's talking about my mother and her sister.'

Julien closed the journal with shaking hands, unable to look at her.

Lily pressed her palms flat against her knees, trying to steady her breath. The journal sat between them on the table, its pages still vibrating in her memory: *Better they grow up without a father like that...*

'Your grandfather, it's too much, Julien...' Her voice cracked, tears spilling unchecked.

He leaned toward her, eyes raw. 'Lily, don't let this come between us. I am not him.'

'I know.' She shook her head fiercely. 'I know you're not. But my mother...' Her throat closed, and she pressed a trembling hand to her chest. 'Her health is fragile. She's already slipping away. And she has spent her whole life mourning the parents she never knew. To learn this, to hear that betrayal came from the man whose grandson I—' She broke off, her voice trembling. 'It could shatter her.'

Julien's hand tightened over the journal. His voice was quiet, tentative. 'Does she need to know?'

Lily looked at him sharply, tears burning in her eyes. 'Yes. There will be no more secrets. That's how we got here, years of silence, of half-truths. I won't be one more person who lies to her, who keeps something this important hidden. If she found out another way, if she learned I'd been with you this whole time and never told her...' Her breath caught. 'It would make me no better than everyone else who failed her. Who hurt her with their lies and secrets.'

Julien flinched at her words, though she hadn't meant them as a blow.

Her voice softened, but it was steady. 'I wouldn't be comfortable introducing you to her, without her knowing the weight of our history. Not knowing this would hang between us.'

The words seemed to drain the air from the room. Julien's eyes were full of guilt, his shoulders heavy with shame he hadn't earned.

She stood, brushing at her skirt though her hands shook. 'This feels like a sign. A sign to stop before I go any further. I don't have the strength for this, Julien. Not with my marriage ending, not with my mother so near the edge, not with you and I becoming...' She didn't finish.

His lips parted, as if to argue, but no words came.

'I told you I could be your friend,' she whispered. 'But even that isn't fair to you or me right now. I need space. To breathe. To gather myself. Away from men, from you.'

For a heartbeat, she thought he would pull her into his arms, but instead his hands dropped to his sides. The restraint made it worse; it felt final.

She stepped away, pressing her palm to her mouth to hold in the sob. 'Goodbye, Julien.'

The words fractured in the air.

He didn't follow her to the door. Didn't call her back. Just stood in the lamplight, grief etched into every line of his face as she slipped away.

On the stairwell, her vision blurred with tears. She told herself this was right, that she couldn't risk any more pieces of herself breaking, or her mother's fragile heart shattering under one more cruel truth. That was the noble reason, the selfless one.

But as she gripped the rail and forced herself down each step, another truth pressed hard against her chest, sharper, more terrifying: it wasn't only about her mother. It was about her. About the way she had already started leaning into Julien, already ached when he wasn't near, already imagined what it might mean if she let herself fall. And she had fallen. That was the truth she couldn't outrun. Somewhere between the first photograph and the last glass of wine, between his steady hand on her arm and his quiet loyalty, she had fallen in love with him.

The realisation hollowed her out. Because loving Julien felt as impossible as it was undeniable; to risk her heart again, after Marcus, after betrayal, after everything, felt like stepping off a cliff with no promise of ground below.

So she would push him away, telling herself it was to protect her mother. But deep down, in the quietest part of her soul, she knew the greater fear was her own: that if she stayed, if she let herself love him fully, she would never find the strength to let him go.

And risking her heart again terrified her.

44

PARIS, NOVEMBER 1941

Gigi

One evening the following month, just before dusk, Gigi arrived at the grand mansion on avenue Montaigne. Ivy crawled over stone walls, tall shutters framed dark windows, and the wrought-iron gate opened with a groan. Her breath misted in the evening air as she paced up the drive, her uniform clinging like borrowed skin.

None of her friends knew what she was doing; she was sure they would have tried to talk her out of it if they knew how dangerous this was. She had been given last-minute instructions from Colette and Joséphine about where to make the drop, once Olivier handed her the coded message, and fear clawed at her ribs. He still didn't know his new Resistance contact would be her, and she had no idea if her presence could expose them both.

Inside, the house was warm and gilded. Light spilled from chandeliers and the air was thick with perfume and cigar smoke.

When she knocked at the back door, the head housekeeper

waved her in with a flick of her fingers. No welcome, no names. Just an efficient wave and murmured commands.

Gigi crossed to the drinks table and took her tray, six crystal flutes balanced with shaking hands she forced to stillness. She adjusted her apron. Lowered her gaze. As she stepped into the main room, laughter ricocheted off marble walls as German officers in polished boots clustered with cigars and cognac.

Annaliese moved among them like a swan in white silk, her red lips curved, her hand brushing a general's sleeve.

At the far end, seated at the piano, was Olivier. Broad shoulders, sandy curls tousled just so. Her stomach flipped as his fingers drifted over the keys with effortless grace.

Gigi crossed the room, chin down, tray steady. Simone from Marseille. Indifferent. Invisible. She kept her focus forward as laughter swelled around her. A general clapped Olivier too hard on the back, and still his playing did not falter.

The last note faded. That was when he looked up, and saw her.

His hands froze on the keys. For an instant, his social mask crumbled, disbelief flashing through his eyes; his lips parted, and she gave the smallest shake of her head, a plea as much as a warning. The air between them burned with unspoken recognition, ready to ignite all they meant to each other if either dared to move.

Gigi kept walking, her eyes lowered, the tray balanced perfectly on one hand.

Annaliese glided to the piano, silk trailing. 'My love,' she purred, kissing Olivier's cheek. 'You always play better when we entertain powerful men.' She turned to the officers, flashing a smile. 'Wouldn't you say, gentlemen?'

They laughed. She snapped her fingers. 'You, champagne.' She didn't look at Gigi, just pointed.

Gigi stepped forward, tray steady though her pulse was not. She kept her head down, the wig and dim lighting her only protection. Would Annaliese recognise her from the jazz bar? The officers' eyes slid over her, appraising, one lingering with a smirk that made her skin crawl.

When she reached Olivier, she saw it, the hardening of his jaw, the flicker of something fierce in his eyes as he caught the officer's gaze straying toward her. His hand closed around the stem of the glass, fingers brushing hers, deliberately, a second too long. His eyes locked on hers, searing, and in that heartbeat, she read it all: the jealousy, the warning, the fear. The last thing he had wanted was for her to be in danger, and yet here she was, in a room where he could not shield her.

'To winning this war!' Annaliese toasted.

'To France's finest composer!' another jeered.

Glasses clinked. Champagne fizzed. Olivier lifted his glass, but his eyes hadn't left hers.

She turned away and was swallowed back into the current of servants, her breath unsteady. Behind her, his music began again, darker, sharper, every note struck with a violence that felt like it was meant to protect her, even if it never could.

Later, in the butler's pantry, he cornered her. His hand slammed against the doorframe, caging her in. 'What are you doing here?' he hissed, his voice low, furious. 'Are you out of your mind?'

She slipped past his grip with deliberate calm as she gathered more glasses. She saw the flash of frustration in his eyes, the way her composure seemed to infuriate him. 'Good to see you too,' she said, her smile small, defiant.

'You need to leave. This isn't a game, Gigi.' His eyes blazed. 'Do you have any idea what they would do if—' He broke off, breath sharp, as though saying it aloud would make it real.

Instead of shrinking, she stepped closer, the heat of her body brushing his. 'I'm here to help you. I'm your way out,' she whispered, her words steady but her pulse racing.

For a heartbeat, his face went rigid. Then it broke, shock,

disbelief and anger all at once. His voice was hoarse. '*You're* my contact?' He shook his head, almost laughing at the madness of it. 'Good God, Gigi... do you know what happened to the last one? They pulled her body out of the canal.'

The words hung between them, heavy and merciless. But she didn't flinch.

His eyes searched hers, furious, terrified, and yet, apparently drawn. His breath faltered, and his gaze dropped to her mouth. He leaned in, as if he might kiss her just to silence the recklessness of what she had done.

'*Gigi.*' The name escaped him, ragged.

Then Annaliese's voice sliced through the corridor.

They tore apart, masks snapping back into place as the door opened. Olivier reached for a bottle with perfect composure, though his knuckles were white.

'Is everything all right, darling?' Annaliese asked, her gaze sweeping the cramped pantry.

Gigi kept her head slightly bowed, pulse racing. Would Annaliese recognise her? They were so close in this small space.

'Yes,' he said easily, his smile flawless. 'I was just getting another bottle of port.'

Her eyes lingered on Gigi, calculating. Gigi forced herself to remain still, to breathe evenly. 'She can do that, you should get back to our guests. Simone, isn't it? I need more napkins. Commander Von Richter has managed to spill his drink again.'

'Certainly, Madame,' Gigi replied in the subservient manner she had been taught.

The dining room shimmered as gold chandeliers flickered light across the polished mahogany table, and wine glasses captured the warm glow of candlelight, meticulously set for an extravagant dinner party.

The scent of roast duck mingled with floral perfume, earthy cigar smoke and a faint trace of starched linen.

Gigi moved between the chairs, quiet, efficient, invisible, as a uniformed butler carved the meat tableside with the solemnity of a priest and other maids tended to silver domes of vegetables.

At the long, elegant table, officers chatted over one another in sharp, clipped German. Deep in conversation with one of her guests, at the head of the table sat Annaliese.

Next to her was Olivier. She rested her gloved hand on his forearm as though to say, *Mine.*

Gigi passed behind him once.

She didn't look at him. He didn't turn.

But something passed between them anyway.

A spark. A warning. A memory.

Gone before it could catch fire.

The officers were in high spirits, drunk on power and good wine.

'To the Atlantic Wall!' bellowed a colonel.

'To the Luftwaffe and their gift to the British navy!' another laughed.

'To Paris!' a third added. 'Finally learning how to behave!'

Their laughter rang too loud, too forced.

A ruddy-faced general leaned back, cheeks flushed with drink. 'Berlin expects a swift Allied retreat by summer. The Americans are soft.'

'My wife just sold our home in Munich,' said another with a thin smile. 'She's already choosing her Paris address for after the war.'

The table erupted again, but it was brittle, defensive. Gigi felt the falseness of it. They were drinking against fear.

Annaliese lifted her glass, her smile sharp as a blade. 'To having you all as my neighbours,' she purred.

Olivier followed without hesitation, adding to her toast. His words in German drew murmurs of approval, but sounded shocking to Gigi. Different to the beauty of their own French language. As he sipped his wine, his eyes stayed on Gigi as she moved around the table, serving with steady hands. His gaze weighted, fierce and watchful.

At the end of dinner, the tall doors opened with a groan. The men stood, buttoning jackets, laughter still booming as they reached for cigars. Candlelight flashed against mirrors and gilt frames; the heavy scents of meat and claret lingered on the air. Annaliese kissed a general's cheek and motioned toward the eastern wing.

'You'll find your usual cigars waiting, gentlemen. The ladies and I will retire to the sitting room for dessert and coffee. And I do hope someone asks Olivier to play again. He's particularly inspired this evening.'

In the smoking room, the mask shifted. Oak-panelled walls closed around them, leather chairs creaked under-weight and cigar smoke thickened the air. Without the ladies to impress, the charm dropped away.

'They've shifted supply south—'

'It's a feint. They'll come through Calais—'

'Rommel says the coast is sealed—'

'Rommel is a politician now—'

The voices were dulled, edged with unease. Gigi moved through them quietly, tray balanced, head bowed. Each time she passed Olivier she felt his eyes on her, hot with anger, heavy with fear, as though willing her to understand. She did. Alone with these men, she could feel the danger bleeding through their laughter, the stakes hidden in every word.

And now she knew what it cost him to shield her from it.

She moved to refill Olivier's glass, but he waved it off with a slight shake of the head. Instead, he rose slowly from his seat and gave a tight, courteous nod.

'Excuse me a moment,' he said in clipped German. 'The wine is catching up with me.'

A few of the men laughed and made jokes about French fragility. Olivier exited the room, his footfalls even, his posture relaxed. Gigi finished pouring the last glass and slipped back toward the corridor. Outside, he was waiting.

He moved towards her casually and lifted a brandy glass. And in the same motion, he slid a folded square of paper beneath the edge of a linen napkin on her tray.

Their eyes caught. For an instant his mask fell away. There was no fury now, no fear, only sadness and love, unguarded, aching. His lips shaped the words soundlessly. *I love you.* It was raw, desperate, as if he believed this might be the last time he'd ever say it.

Gigi's heart slammed against her ribs, but she did not blink. She turned without hesitation and walked toward the exit, the tray balanced on her open palm. She didn't look back.

The tray felt heavier now. The folded sheet music beneath the napkin barely weighed an ounce, but to Gigi it might as well have been lead. Her pace was steady, her face composed, though inside a small, private grief uncoiled. For a single impossible second, she wished for a life that had dealt them a different hand, something ordinary. The wish dissolved the moment it rose. She could feel the heat of it and the cruelty of its impossibility.

Cigar smoke clung to her dress as she passed through the wide doorway and into the corridor. When she turned the corner, she shifted her weight and, in one practised motion, slid the folded paper into the pocket sewn into her apron's inner lining. It disappeared in less than a second. She kept walking.

A voice called out somewhere behind her, sharp barking in German. Her breath caught. But it wasn't for her. The voice softened into laughter, and a door closed. Still, her heart didn't slow.

In the pantry, she set her tray down. The message pressed flat against her hip, burning through the fabric like a brand.

The night dragged on in slow, deliberate beats.

Gigi returned to work as if nothing had changed. She cleared glasses, refilled carafes and gathered ashtrays still warm with cigar ends. All while the message pressed against her skin. She didn't touch it and didn't even glance toward Olivier. She didn't have to. She felt him the way a dancer feels music before it begins.

The mood had shifted in the grand salon, softer now, sleepier. The sharp edge of power had dulled beneath layers of brandy and fatigue. Chairs had been drawn closer. Cravats loosened.

And then, Olivier sat at the piano.

Gigi paused in the shadow of the corridor archway.

He rested his fingers on the keys for a long moment, appearing unsure which world he wanted to call forth. And then he played it.

'Dancer in the Shadows'.

Her song. A slow, aching piece, graceful and haunting.

To the guests, it was just a pretty melody. But to her, it was a message. He was still hers.

She stood there for just a second and let it wash over her. Then she turned away.

Once the last guest left, Annaliese came to the kitchen. '*Merci à tous,*' she said to the staff with a smile that didn't reach her eyes. 'You've made our guests feel quite at home. You should be very proud.'

Behind Annaliese, Olivier appeared. He held a crystal glass in one hand, his drink untouched. His face was serious. Gigi didn't move.

'Yes, thank you,' he added. But his eyes found hers. Just for a moment. It was the smallest of looks, yet it carried everything, fear, gratitude and something just shy of goodbye.

She gave a nod. Barely visible. Then turned away, slipped through the service door and into the night.

The air hit her like water, cool, sharp, real. She didn't run. She didn't glance back at the house that had nearly swallowed her whole. The message was still tucked against her hip. And the echo of 'Dancer in the Shadows' was still playing in her mind, long after the last note had faded.

The streets were nearly silent as Gigi walked down the dark alley. Her heels echoed too loudly against the stone, even though she tried to walk lightly. The message, still folded inside her apron pocket, felt heavier than it had all night.

She turned the corner toward the café. Almost there. Almost—

'*Halte!*'

The shout snapped through the night like a gunshot.

Two men stepped from the shadows, German patrol, rifles slung over their shoulders, the glint of black boots catching the weak light from a shuttered window.

Gigi froze.

One of them raised a flashlight and shone it directly in her face. 'You're out past curfew.'

She swallowed, remembering what she had been taught to say, keeping her voice low, breathless but not panicked.

'I was working at the party for Madame Annaliese Laurent,' she said quickly. 'Serving drinks. It ran late. I'm on my way home now.'

As soon as she mentioned Annaliese's name, one of the other soldiers quickly said something to his companion in German.

The flashlight hovered. The soldiers exchanged a look.

'You have identification?'

She reached slowly into her pocket and retrieved the forged papers Colette had given her.

The man studied it. Then looked at her again, not with suspicion, but with a flicker of amusement.

'I imagine it was a good party,' he muttered.

'Madame Annaliese is very demanding,' Gigi replied.

The second soldier lowered his rifle. 'Go,' he said. 'Straight home.'

She nodded quickly, ducked her head and kept walking. Not too fast. Not too slow. Just a maid going home from a long night of rich people and roast duck.

She reached the alley behind the café. Lifted the lid of the rusted bin. Beneath, exactly where Colette had said, it was waiting: a hollow, cloth-lined compartment, just big enough for a message.

Gigi slipped the folded sheet inside. Closed the lid.

She stepped back into the shadows, her heart still hammering in her chest.

45

NORMANDY, AUTUMN 2011

Lily

The cottage sat at the end of a gravel lane near the beach in Normandy, its stone walls thick with ivy, shutters faded to a soft sea-foam green. A cat dozed on the low windowsill, and barely lifted its head as Lily stepped through the garden gate.

She paused at the door. The air was damp with salt and seaweed, and gulls cried faintly overhead, but her thoughts were elsewhere, on Julien. How instinctively she wished he were beside her now, steadying her with that quiet presence. He should have been here for this, sharing the weight of it, the history she might be about to touch.

Because this cottage could be the last missing piece. The woman inside had once taken in Rachel and Rebecca, even if only for a short time, during the war. Her name had been mentioned on the adoption papers. She was the sister of their adoptive mother, the one thread Lily had yet to pull. If the past was ever to give up its secrets, it might be here.

Her chest tightened. She told herself it was what she needed, space to breathe, space to let her heart mend. She wasn't ready to leap into something as serious as Julien seemed to want, and yet... and yet, she missed him.

Drawing in a deep breath, she knocked gently at the door.

A moment passed.

Then another.

At last it creaked open, and a small, silver-haired woman stood there, wrapped in a cardigan too big for her frame. Her eyes were sharp despite her age, eyes that had may have once memorised the faces of two frightened girls clinging to one another.

'Madame Marchand?' Lily asked softly.

The woman blinked, then nodded slowly. 'Yes. And you must be the daughter of one of them, you look alike.'

Lily's breath caught. 'I'm Rebecca's daughter. My name is Lily.'

Mrs Marchand opened the door wider. 'Come in, *ma chère*. Please, call me Edel. I've waited a long time for this.'

The living room smelled of lavender. Sun streamed through the windows, casting the lace curtains in a golden glow. Photographs lined the mantel, some wartime black-and-whites, others faded Polaroids. One, near the centre, showed two little girls in ballet slippers.

'I didn't know if I'd ever meet someone who knew about that time again,' Edel said, settling into her chair with effort. 'So many have passed.'

Lily sat across from her, heart hammering. 'I found your name in the adoption records. You cared for the girls, for my mother and her twin, after your sister died?'

Edel nodded. 'Only for a few weeks. I was nineteen, newly married, and had a newborn of my own. I wanted to keep them, but it wasn't possible. Jacques... he came and took them. Said he would raise them himself.' Her eyes misted over. 'I never stopped wondering what became of Rebecca.'

Lily swallowed. 'Rebecca, my mother, survived. She became a dancer. She... she's very ill now.'

Edel's lips trembled. 'And Rachel?'

Lily's voice dropped to a whisper. 'She disappeared during the war. I have reason to believe she is still alive. And I was hoping—'

'I heard from her,' Edel interrupted gently. 'Years ago. It was a letter. She found me somehow.'

Lily's breath caught. 'She did?'

'She remembered me.' Edel smiled faintly. 'Called me Tante Edel. Said she survived... but she thought Rebecca hadn't. She didn't say much, only that she had been taken to Australia. That she had a new name. A quiet life. But she remembered the dance. Always the dance.'

Lily blinked back sudden tears. 'Do you still have it, the letter?'

Edel shook her head. 'No, not the letter. But... I called her once. I kept the number. I don't know if it would still work, but you can try.'

She reached for a small address book on the table beside her and turned pages worn at the edges till she found the page she was looking for.

Lily dialled the number, her fingers trembling so violently she almost dropped her phone.

One ring.

Two.

Three.

A click, then a woman's voice, gentle, warm, touched with the music of an Australian lilt.

'Hello?'

Lily's throat constricted. 'Rachel Durand?'

The pause was so long it felt as if the line itself might shatter.

The voice was cautious, almost fragile. 'I was once, who is this?'

'My name is Lily Tremaine.' She pressed a palm hard to her chest, willing her heart to steady. Pausing before finally saying words she had never believed she would say. 'I'm your niece. Rebecca's daughter.'

The silence that followed was heavy, thick with years and distance. Lily pulled the phone from her ear to check the screen, half-afraid the call had dropped, then replaced it. She caught the faintest sound of breathing, ragged, unsteady.

'I...' Rachel began, but her voice cracked and fell away. When she spoke again, it was a bare whisper. 'I'm sorry. What did you say?'

'I'm Rebecca's daughter,' Lily repeated, more softly this time. 'Your twin sister's daughter.'

A rustle. A sleeve brushing the receiver. A sharp, uneven inhale.

'*No.*' The word was small, broken, as though it had travelled a thousand miles through disbelief. 'That... that can't be possible.' Her voice thinned to a thread. 'She died, during the war—'

'No,' Lily said gently, firmly. 'She didn't. She survived, but now she's very ill. She recently slipped into a coma. Finding you was the last thing she asked of me. She's alive, Rachel.'

On the other end came the quiet collapse of someone's world and the rebuilding of it in the same breath, first a gasp, then a shudder, then the sound of a soul breaking open. The sobs were soft at first, then helpless.

'All this time,' Rachel wept, her words torn and uneven. 'All these years... I can't believe it.'

'She never stopped looking for you,' Lily whispered, her own vision blurring, her voice breaking.

Beside her, Edel was openly weeping.

A muffled exhale, the sound of a hand pressed over the mouthpiece, and then, through tears, through disbelief turning into fierce, unshakeable resolve, Rachel's voice came, trembling but certain.

'I have missed her so much. As soon as she wakes up... I want to speak to her.' The words came splintered, then gathered strength. 'Tell her I'm here. Tell her I love her. Tell her I never stopped loving her, not for a heartbeat. And tell her...' Her voice wavered, thick with years she could never get back. 'Tell her she's the part of me I've been yearning to find again for my whole life.'

46

PARIS, 1941

Gigi

Her Resistance work had been going well all week, quiet, invisible work. Each night, she served drinks. Each night, a slip of paper passed beneath a napkin. Each night, her pulse stayed steady. No one noticed the maid.

It was a far cry from ballet and the lead role she'd danced what felt like a hundred years ago, but it felt just as precise. Just as vital.

Now, in the hush before the final dinner, Gigi stood by the window polishing silverware, her false name stitched over her like a second skin.

Behind her, the doors creaked open.

'Mademoiselle Valette?'

A voice warm, cheerful, wrong.

'*Gigi!* Gigi Valette, what are you doing here?'

Her heart slammed once. The name hung in the air like a blade. She didn't turn. Training said: *Don't. Breathe. Think.*

Slowly, she pivoted, the cloth still in her hand. Pierre the florist stood in the doorway, beaming, arms full of cream roses.

'Gigi, it's me, Pierre! The man who proposes to you from the street every day!'

She reached for Simone's voice. 'I think you're mistaken, sir. My name is Simone.'

Her voice came steady, but her fingers trembled on the silver. A glance sideways. Footmen nearby. The head butler. And there, slipping away like smoke, the quiet maid. Had she heard?

Pierre stepped toward her. 'Why are you in that terrible wig? And why aren't you dancing?'

The scent of roses turned sickly sweet, like chloroform. She forced her chin down.

'I'm just a maid,' she said, sharper now. 'You're mistaken.'

She set the fork down with a soft ring and walked, calmly, carefully, toward the service door.

She heard Colette's stern voice in her head: *'Don't run. Remain calm.'*

But the thought seared her: *He said my name.*

She slipped out of the salon, heart pounding, down the corridor, into the butler's pantry.

It had all been going so well. Until now.

A door creaked behind her.

'The mistress would like to see you,' the butler said. 'In the small salon.'

Her breath caught.

'You are to come *now.*'

Gigi tugged at her apron with trembling fingers and followed. The salon doors closed behind her with a soft click.

The room smelled of jasmine, Annaliese's scent. A tray of untouched tea sat on the low table like a prop in a play. Olivier stood by the fireplace, arms folded tightly across his chest. He turned when she entered, brow creased, not with anger, but with something worse.

Fear.

Annaliese sat by the window, swathed in dove-grey silk, one gloved hand trailing the rim of her teacup. She didn't look up, as though Gigi were simply another servant called to account for a misplaced spoon.

Finally, she spoke as she peered at her.

'Simone, isn't it?'

Gigi kept her face blank. 'Yes, Madame.'

Her heart thundered, remembering the time they had met before, and she prayed the dim light in the jazz bar and her altered appearance would be enough.

A faint smile curved Annaliese's lip. 'Is that your real name?'

Gigi's pulse spiked. 'Yes, Madame.'

Olivier broke in. 'Anna, is this really necessary? The florist was clearly confused.'

Annaliese turned slowly and stared at her husband.

'Methinks the gentleman doth protest too much,' she purred. 'So you know this... Simone?'

A beat of silence. No one moved. Gigi's throat tightened.

Annaliese turned, her gaze sharper now. 'Tell me, what is this the other maid heard? Are you a dancer?'

The air went razor-thin.

'No, Madame.'

Annaliese narrowed her eyes. 'Somehow, I don't believe you.' She peered at Gigi as if seeing her for the first time.

'There's something familiar about you. Have we met before?' Her gaze sharpened with recollection. 'Yes... Now I remember. You were speaking to my husband in that jazz bar once. I didn't recognise you, you look so dowdy now. And your hair is darker. Did you let yourself go?'

Gigi's blood ran cold. She forced herself to remain still, to keep her expression neutral.

Annaliese's eyes narrowed, calculating. Then she reached for the bell-pull.

Within moments, the household staff had filed in, stiff, uncertain.

Annaliese rose from her chair, voice clear. 'I value this house. Its order. Its loyalty. If anyone here has seen something out of the ordinary, now is the time to speak.'

Silence.

Then, a small voice: 'I did notice something, Madame...'

All eyes turned. It was the quiet maid. Hands clasped, voice steady despite her wide eyes.

'It was after the dinner for the officers. I was clearing a champagne tray. I lifted a napkin and thought I saw something, faint marks. Just a few. It looked... odd.'

Annaliese smiled gently. 'And who brought in that tray, dear?'

The girl hesitated. 'I-I think it was... her, Madame.'

She pointed directly at Gigi.

A hush. Even the butler's mouth parted slightly.

Annaliese turned to Gigi. 'A girl in disguise. A false name. Markings on a napkin.' She sighed. 'What we're doing here is too important to take risks.'

She laid a hand on the black telephone. 'I think my friends in the Gestapo may wish to speak with you.'

The moment snapped like a string.

Gigi's breath caught. The staff gasped.

'*No!*' Olivier said sharply.

Annaliese turned, one hand still on the receiver.

'I have something to say,' Olivier said, his voice calm, but his eyes burning.

Annaliese gave a small nod. I thought you might,' she purred. She dismissed the staff, then lit a cigarette with slow precision.

'Who is she, Olivier? Another lover? You're bedding them young these days.'

He took a subtle step in front of Gigi as if to protect her from the harsh words.

Before he could speak, Gigi stepped forward. 'I was hired to do a job. I did it. I am not his lover, or your pawn. I'm a dancer who needed work, and yes, I changed my name.'

'Because you were ashamed?'

'Because I wanted to be discreet. There's a difference.'

Annaliese's eyes sparkled. 'Not discreet enough to avoid suspicion.'

'I didn't write messages,' Gigi said. 'I served drinks. Folded napkins. Whatever your maid saw, it was a mistake.'

'Is that so?' Annaliese asked. 'Then what if I let the Gestapo decide? They have very persuasive tactics.'

She reached for the phone again.

'Don't do this,' Olivier said. 'This isn't about her, and you know it.'

'Then what is it about?'

'This is about your need to control everything and everybody, including me. You have capitulated to an enemy to hold on to that power. You've forgotten what it means to belong – you were born to a French mother. Doesn't that mean anything?'

She snapped back, 'Yes, I feel loyalty to power. To survive. You always loved Paris more than it loved you.'

'And your loyalty to me?' Olivier asked.

She laughed bitterly. 'Don't insult me. You answer that every time you look at her.'

Gigi looked away.

Olivier stepped forward, his voice steel. 'You think you hold all the cards. But you don't.'

Annaliese raised an eyebrow.

His gaze flicked briefly to Gigi before returning to his wife. 'There's something I want to show you.'

Without waiting for a reply, he strode from the room.

The silence he left behind was heavy. Gigi's breath trembled in her chest.

Annaliese turned toward her slowly, studying her with contempt. 'Do you honestly believe you matter?' she asked softly, almost sweetly. 'You're no different than all the others. Pretty little things, always thinking you're special, the love of his life. But you're not. You're just another nobody in a long, embarrassing line.'

She rose and began pacing slowly. 'There was the shop girl in Vienna, the violinist in Prague, that absurdly dramatic painter's muse in Marseille... He tires of you all in the end. Do you know what you are?' Her smile was knife-thin as she continued. 'A distraction. A pleasant waste of time.'

Gigi stood perfectly still, the cruelty slicing into her like glass. But she said nothing.

Annaliese's tone sharpened. 'I have built a life, a name, in this city. I have protection and privilege. You have... what, exactly?'

She stopped pacing. Her voice dropped to a hiss. 'He will eventually discard you, just as he has all the others.'

Footsteps returned. Olivier entered, something pale clutched in his hand.

The air shifted.

'Remember when your father gave us that china cabinet?' he said lightly. 'And how enraged your mother was that he had given it away?'

Annaliese flicked ash into a silver ashtray. 'What is all this about, Olivier?'

He continued, 'You had it sent out to be refinished. Well, when it came back, the foreman asked me to sign, and handed me this.'

He set the letter and a photograph on the tea tray with slow, deliberate care.

'They were hidden. I kept them. Waiting to see if I ever needed them.'

Gigi moved closer; over his shoulder, she could see the faded ink. The letter was dated 1924. Signed by Aaron Weill.

Ma chère Hélène...

If she is a girl, promise me we will call her Annaliese, after my grandmother Chana-Liese. Rabbi Kahn will bless her the first Shabbat. Do not be afraid. You can leave your husband. I will take care of you and our daughter.

Tucked with the letter was a photograph. She could see a woman who looked remarkably like Annaliese, Hélène, with a dark-haired man and a baby between them.

He turned it over. On the back, written in ink: *Pour notre Annaliese* – Shabbat, 1914 – A.W.

Annaliese went pale.

'No. This is a lie. My mother would never...'

'Wouldn't she? Can you take that chance?' Olivier murmured. 'Just imagine the shock, the utter humiliation when Colonel Gerhardt realises he entrusted his most sensitive meeting to a Jewess. And brought his esteemed friends here to drink from her glasses and eat from her plates.'

She lunged for the letter. Olivier stepped back quickly, lifting it just out of reach.

'Of course,' he added, 'I have made copies.'

Silence, thick and final.

'What do you want?' she whispered, her voice a growl. 'Now the servants have heard this she will have to take the fall, otherwise tongues will wag and who knows where that will take us.'

'You want someone to take the fall?' Olivier said. 'Fine, let it be me.'

'*Olivier*—' Gigi began.

He held up a hand. 'She's not who you're looking for. I am.'

He turned back to Annaliese. 'I've been pursuing her. She thinks I love her. But you know me. It was just... fun for a while.'

Annaliese studied him. Then looked at Gigi with a smug expression of satisfaction.

Before Gigi could respond, Olivier continued, 'She's young, was soft-hearted. Easy to charm. It's over.'

Gigi stared at him, the finality of his voice sinking in like stone.

She couldn't speak. Couldn't move.

Annaliese crushed her cigarette into the ashtray. 'As I suspected. You always did have a taste for things you couldn't keep. I am finished with your betrayals, Olivier. You have embarrassed me enough.'

She turned to Gigi one last time. 'Get out and don't come back. I never want to see you again, either.'

Gigi left the room, her feet moving on instinct, eyes burning. Olivier's words were cutting, and hard to swallow. Had it all been a sham? Behind her, the door clicked shut.

And then she heard it. Annaliese's voice, low and measured.

'Colonel Gerhardt? Yes, I believe you'll want to question my husband. I'm afraid he's been working against us.'

47

PARIS, AUTUMN 2011

Lily

Even though pieces of her mother's life were finally coming together, the reality of the devastation of her own hit her as she left Edel's, and Lily had cried all the way home.

But now as she entered Paris, she was dry-eyed.

Her phone rang just as Effy disappeared into the back room of the gallery late that afternoon. She stared at it for a second, still feeling the echo of her own voice, the sting of what had transpired; without Julien it had seemed empty somehow. Her hands trembled faintly as she reached for it without even looking at the name of the caller.

'Hello?' she said absently.

'Lil?'

It was Clare.

Lily straightened. Her heart beat hard in her chest.

'She's awake.'

For a moment, Lily couldn't breathe.

She blinked hard, as if the world around her had gone momentarily out of focus. '*Maman?*'

'She's awake,' Clare repeated. 'She opened her eyes an hour ago,' she added, her voice thick with emotion. 'She's weak, but she's asking for you.'

Lily pressed a hand to her mouth, a sob escaping before she could stop it. Her knees gave slightly, and she sank onto the nearest chair.

'Is she... okay?'

'She's tired. Disoriented. But she knew who I was. And she said your name, Lil. She asked if you'd found the deposit box.'

Lily let out a shaky laugh. 'Of course she did. I'm coming, I'll be there in an hour.'

She hung up the phone, but still gripped it tightly as if afraid the moment might vanish.

Effy appeared in the doorway, her arms full of bubble wrap and packaging tape. 'That didn't sound like a bill collector.'

Lily stood slowly, her voice trembling. 'She's awake.'

Effy froze, her expression softening instantly. 'Your mother?'

Lily nodded. Her lips parted, but no words came, just a wave of emotion so big it tightened her throat.

Effy set the bubble wrap down without a word and crossed the room.

'Oh, darling.' She pulled Lily into a tight hug. Lily collapsed into it, her forehead resting against Effy's shoulder. 'That's wonderful.'

'I'm going now,' Lily said, pulling back. 'I need to be there.' She pulled the photos off the corkboard and stuffed them in her bag as she gathered her things.

Effy nodded briskly. 'Of course. Go.'

'I can't wait to tell her that not only have I located her sister, I've found out who her birth mother was.'

Effy called after her, 'Give her a hug from me!'

Lily turned back, tears in her eyes. 'I will.'

· · ·

The motorway stretched ahead, silver and still in the evening light, but Lily barely saw it. Her hands gripped the wheel tighter than necessary, knuckles pale, heart pounding like a drum. She hadn't dared to imagine this moment. Not truly. Not after so much silence.

But now... now everything had changed.

Her mother was awake.

And Lily, after weeks of searching, had the answers.

She had found her mother's twin. The lost half of a story buried by war, hidden behind closed doors and sealed records.

She glanced at the worn envelope on the passenger seat. Inside was the original photograph of the four women in front of the Montmartre building, arms slung over shoulders, eyes full of life. Eloise stood slightly apart. The woman who had given birth to Rebecca and Rachel. Her grandmother.

She blinked hard as her eyes blurred with tears. She cried for the girls who had survived the unthinkable, and still found a way to live.

48

PARIS, DECEMBER 1942

Gigi

Night pressed close to the windows, the blackout curtains leaking a thin rim of street light. The kettle breathed on the stove.

The knock came, just three short raps. Then one. Her heart stuttered. Was it Olivier? She still hoped even after all this time.

It had been over a year since she had last seen him. She had been told he had been taken by the Gestapo, but no one had heard anything from him since then, not even Joséphine. So much she wanted to tell him – about the new ballet, humbler than the old spectacles before the war, yet exquisite all the same. About the afternoon she turned a corner in Montmartre and, hearing one of his favourite melodies spill from a restaurant, ran inside only to find not him but a friend, a fellow musician, playing his line softly in a smoky bistro; and the morning she had heard again the faint, stuttering strains of the carousel's calliope, where a stranger in oily overalls whispered, almost reverently, that he was keeping it alive, his quiet way of giving Paris back a better time.

She crossed the small apartment quickly, wiping her hands on her skirt, and opened the door just enough to peek through the crack.

A young girl stood there, no more than sixteen, with panic in her eyes. One of Jacques's students, Gigi realised. The girl stepped back to reveal two smaller figures beside her, standing silently in the dim hallway.

Rebecca and Rachel.

They wore their matching black-and-white checked dresses beneath thick coats, and their hats were slightly askew. Thin from rationing, their slight frames seemed almost swallowed by the heavy wool. Dark, thick hair curled stubbornly beneath their brims, and identical pairs of wide brown eyes stared up at Gigi, solemn and unblinking. There was a fragility about them, yes, but also a quiet intensity, as though even at ten years old they had already learned what it meant to carry the weight of the world without breaking.

She prepared herself for the worst. Raids had become harsher since the summer roundups, and worse still after the Germans crossed into the so-called Free Zone in November.

The student spoke first. 'Right at the end of my class, there was a raid. Jacques got away. But the soldiers destroyed every-thing.' Her voice trembled. 'He said... he said to bring them to you.'

Gigi's hand flew to her mouth. 'Come in, quickly,' she whis-pered, pulling the door wide.

The girls stepped inside, silent as ghosts, and the student gave one final nod before disappearing back into the snow.

Gigi bolted the door and knelt before the twins, gently brushing windblown hair from their cheeks.

Rachel's lip trembled. Her knuckles were bone-white.

Gigi rose, schooling her face into calm. 'Let's get those coats off. You must be frozen.'

She led them into the warmth of the kitchen, coaxing them

to sit while she added more water to the kettle and lit the stove. The silence behind her felt too heavy, like grief too big for words.

When she turned, the girls were sitting side by side at the table, eyes still wide, not speaking.

'I've got cocoa, I got some with my rations this week,' Gigi said gently.

That earned her the smallest smile from Rachel.

When the kettle whistled, Gigi busied herself preparing their drinks, pretending the room wasn't filled with the ache of everything unspoken. Outside the window, snow had started to fall again, dusting the balcony in silence.

She carried two mugs to the table and set them down.

Rebecca stared at her mug but didn't touch it. Rachel did the same, both girls frozen.

Rebecca looked up. 'Will Uncle Jacques come here later?'

Gigi sat. 'Not tonight, sweetheart.'

The girls exchanged a look, one of those twin glances Gigi had come to recognise. Wordless. Bonded. Frightened.

'You're staying with me for a little while,' she said, summoning a warm smile.

Rebecca's face crumpled. Rachel reached for her sister's hand under the table.

'He told us to be brave,' Rachel whispered. 'To come to you if anything happened.'

Gigi's throat tightened. 'You're safe now.'

Rebecca looked up. 'Do you know? About Uncle Jacques?'

'Know what, sweetheart?'

The twins exchanged a glance, wordless, bonded. Rebecca spoke barely above a breath.

'He's our father. Our real father. We have to call him Uncle so no one finds out we're...' She faltered.

'Jewish,' Rachel finished.

Gigi felt the air leave her lungs. They had known all along.

All this time, she'd thought she was protecting them, when they'd been protecting themselves.

'He made us promise,' Rebecca continued. 'To keep us safe. But now he's gone.'

Gigi gathered them into her arms. They trembled against her.

'Your father is clever. He knows how to stay hidden. Do not worry.'

The girls clung to her as she stared at the falling snow, wondering how many more secrets this war would force her to keep.

Later, after they'd fallen asleep curled together on the small bed in the corner of her bedroom, Gigi stood in the doorway and watched them. The ballet shoes Eloise had given them were tucked under Rebecca's pillow.

A lump rose in her throat, as she wondered where their journey would take them.

She quietly left the apartment and knocked next door.

When Eloise opened, Gigi kept her voice to a whisper as she explained what had happened to Jacques, finishing with, 'Your girls are here.'

Eloise came immediately. No words. She sat beside the bed, hands folded, and watched the twins breathe. Tears ran soundlessly down her cheeks and she did not touch them. She only kept watch.

After a long, still minute, she lifted her eyes to Gigi and whispered, 'What will become of them?'

Gigi whispered back, 'We will find a way to keep them safe, I promise you.'

.   .   .

It was the day after Christmas when the door burst open just before noon, letting in a swirl of cold air and the sound of laughter. Malina was bringing the twins back from her family's estate.

Rachel came in first, cheeks red from the cold, followed closely by Rebecca and Malina. The girls' eyes sparkled, their voices tumbling over one another.

'There were *horses*!' Rachel said breathlessly.

Rebecca clutched her sister's arm, nodding fiercely. 'And sleigh bells. Real ones!'

'And a piano in the drawing room!' Rachel added.

Gigi smiled at their joy, but something in her chest tightened. Just two days before, on Christmas Eve, she had stepped into her apartment, snow clinging to her coat, her arms still tingling from the warmth of her parents' hugs. She had set a bundle of leftovers on the kitchen table, slid the bolt into place and whispered to herself: 'It's done. The plan is in motion.'

The memory pressed in now as the twins chattered on. She had spread her mother's hand-me-down clothes across the table that night, ready to pack.

Malina smiled indulgently, unwinding her scarf. 'They've been spoiled, but it was good for them.'

Gigi stepped forward, gathering the girls into a hug. 'I missed you both,' she said, brushing a kiss onto each of their heads.

'You should've come,' Rachel said.

'I had some things to take care of,' Gigi replied with a soft smile.

Malina gave Gigi a long look, picking up on the undercurrent. 'I'll leave you to get them settled.'

When the door closed behind her, the warmth of the apartment returned. Gigi ushered the girls out of their coats and helped them out of their boots.

'Come sit,' she said, patting the edge of the small table. 'I have something important to tell you.'

They obeyed quietly, sensing the shift in her tone. Rebecca pulled the ballet shoes from her coat pocket and set them on her lap, fingers automatically stroking the worn ribbons.

Gigi took a breath, then knelt beside them so they were at eye level.

'I need you both to be very brave,' she said gently. 'Do you think you can do that for me?'

The girls nodded, solemn now.

'In a few days,' Gigi continued, 'you're going to go on a journey. A special one. With my sister Charlotte. She's going to take you somewhere safe, far away from all this.'

Rachel's eyes widened. 'Far away from Paris?'

'Yes,' Gigi said. 'To the south. It's warmer there. Quieter. And there will be other children, too. Other children that are also Jewish.'

Rebecca looked unsure. 'But what about you?'

Gigi's smile faltered just slightly. 'I can't come with you. But my sister Charlotte will take good care of you. And I'll be thinking about you every day.'

'Will Uncle Jacques come?' Rachel asked.

Gigi reached out and tucked a curl behind the girl's ear. 'Maybe later. But this is what he would want, for you to be safe.'

There was a heavy silence.

Rachel leaned into Gigi's shoulder. 'Will you write to us?'

'I will,' she promised, though they all knew letters might never reach them. 'I'll find a way.'

She held them there for a moment, arms wrapped around their thin shoulders, anchoring them to her chest.

'I'm so proud of you,' she whispered.

And though they didn't understand everything that was happening, the girls nodded, accepting the weight of her words.

Gigi kissed each of them again and stood, blinking quickly.

'I'll help you pack tomorrow.'

The girls went off to the bedroom, their voices low, their

footsteps padding softly. Gigi stood alone in the kitchen, hands trembling as she picked up a tea towel, and stared out the frosted window.

Soon they'd be gone.

And everything for them would change.

It was early January and the fog clung to the city like a blanket, muffling the sounds of Paris in its embrace.

At the edge of the platform, Gigi stood with her hands gripping the girls' shoulders, her breath blooming in the cold air. But she didn't feel it; her thoughts were with her friend. Thirty minutes before they had left for the station, Eloise had slipped in as the girls buttoned their coats. She'd knelt without a word, straightened Rachel's scarf, fixed Rebecca's hat, and let her fingertips hover, one breath from their cheeks. Tears had slid down her own and she turned away before they could see.

Gigi's thoughts were brought back to the present as the steam from the waiting train hissed and swirled around them like ghostly ribbons, wrapping their goodbye in a quiet kind of magic.

Charlotte was already gathering the rest of the children ready to board.

Rebecca and Rachel stood on either side of Gigi, bundled in their coats, hats slightly crooked, Eloise's ballet shoes in Rachel's hand.

'You remember what I told you?' Gigi asked, forcing her voice to stay even.

Rachel nodded. Rebecca slipped her hand into her sister's, squeezing tight. 'We'll stay together no matter what happens,' she whispered fiercely. 'We'll protect each other. *Always*.'

Gigi gave them a tight smile. 'That's right. And don't forget, you're going to a village where the sun is warmer, and you can dance every day, if you want to.'

The train gave a soft groan, like a reminder that time was running out.

She knelt down and brushed a gloved hand across Rachel's cheek, then Rebecca's. 'You are so brave. So strong, my beautiful ballerinas.'

Rachel threw her arms around Gigi's neck suddenly. 'Will we see you again?'

Gigi held her tightly. Her throat burned. 'Yes,' she said, with hope. 'One day.'

Rebecca leaned in too, wrapping her arms around Gigi's waist. The three of them clung to each other in the fog.

Charlotte appeared in front of her. 'It's time.'

Gigi stood, adjusting the girls' collars, tucking the stray strands of hair beneath their hats. She placed a kiss on each forehead, her lips lingering as if they could press memory into skin.

They stepped toward the train.

Rebecca climbed first, then turned to help Rachel onto the train. They both looked back one last time. Rebecca waved first, then Rachel raised her hand, fingers splayed.

Gigi waved, her heart swelling and splintering all at once.

Then the train lurched and began to pull away.

She didn't move. She stayed where she was, the icy wind stinging her eyes, watching as the girls' small faces became two soft blurs behind the glass.

When the train disappeared into the mist, she finally exhaled.

Not a sigh.

A sob.

She pressed a hand over her mouth, her shoulders trembling. They were gone. She was alone. But they were safe. And that had to be enough.

49

PROVINS, AUTUMN 2011

Lily

The hospital loomed ahead like a beacon in the dusk, its windows glowing gold. Lily pulled into the car park and rushed through the lobby.

Clare met her outside the room, her face pale but alight with something Lily hadn't seen in weeks.

Hope.

Clare whispered, 'She asked for you, again.' Then added quietly, 'Rachel's been up since before dawn. She wanted to be awake for this.'

Lily nodded, her heart squeezing. Rachel had set her alarm in the middle of the Australian night just to be on this call. Barely trusting her legs, she moved toward the door.

Inside, the room was dim and quiet. Machines beeped their steady rhythm. Her mother lay small in the bed, eyes closed, but her breath was even. Her face peaceful.

'Maman?' Lily stepped closer, her voice shaking. 'It's me. Lily.'

Rebecca's eyelids fluttered. Slowly, she opened her eyes.

A moment passed. Then, so faint it was barely a whisper, 'Lily?'

Lily's breath caught. She bent over the rails and folded herself into her mother as gently as she could, mindful of tubes and tape. Cheek to her mother's hair. Rebecca's hand found Lily's shoulder and patted once, then stayed there, the way she used to when Lily was little.

'I'm here, Maman,' Lily said into the hollow of her mother's neck with a sob. 'I got here as fast as I could.'

Lily slid into the chair and took Rebecca's hand in both of hers. The skin was warm and paper-thin, familiar. Rebecca's gaze drifted over Lily's face, forehead, cheekbone, mouth, as if relearning her.

Lily tried to smile; her chin quivered. 'I have something to tell you.'

Rebecca didn't speak, but her hand twitched in Lily's.

'I found out information about your birth mother,' Lily said gently. 'Your mother, my grandmother. Unfortunately, she disappeared after the war. Her name was Eloise Morel. She was young, just a girl herself when she had you and your sister.'

Rebecca's lips parted. '*Eloise...*' She mouthed the name with reverence.

Lily squeezed her hand. She took out the photograph of the four young women and showed it to her mother.

Rebecca blinked up at her daughter, tears shining. 'Thank you,' she breathed. 'For finding her. For giving me back my mother.'

Lily nodded, swallowing hard. 'There's more.'

Rebecca's fingers tightened in hers.

'Eloise led me to someone else,' Lily whispered. 'Someone who's been searching for you, too.'

She fumbled for her phone, her hands shaking, and pressed the call button. It rang twice.

'Hello?' a voice said, steady, and already breaking.

Lily's voice cracked. 'She's awake. Mum's awake.'

Lily set the phone to speaker and guided it into Rebecca's hand.

A breath, a heartbeat, then:

'Rebecca,' the voice said, thick with years and love. 'It's me. Rachel. I never stopped looking. I never stopped loving you.'

Rebecca made a sound that was part laugh, part sob.

'Rachel,' she whimpered. The years of separation melted away in that single word, bridging the chasm of absence that had obviously haunted her soul.

Lily watched, a tender ache in her chest, as the reunion she'd arranged unfolded.

Beside her, Clare let out an uncontrollable sob.

Rachel's words echoed on the speaker. 'Get well, I'm coming home.'

They stayed like that, two voices stitched across an ocean, until Rebecca became fatigued.

When the call finally ended, Lily tucked the slippers beneath her mother's pillow.

'For when she gets here,' she whispered.

Rebecca nodded. 'For when we start again.'

Night pressed its ear to the window; the ward lights dimmed.

As Rebecca's eyes closed in rest, Lily laid her head beside her mother's cheek, Clare on the other side, as they listened to the steady metronome of breath.

Across the world, under a different sky, a sister with the same features as the woman sleeping in a hospital bed closed a suitcase and traced a map with her fingertip.

Preparing to make a trip she had only ever dreamed about.

50

PARIS, SUMMER 1944

Gigi

The sky was dipped in honey and ash, streaks of gold smudged by smoke and distant haze. Paris was holding its breath.

And so were they.

On the narrow balcony that bridged their apartments of shared memory, Gigi, Claudette and Eloise sat in a semicircle of mismatched chairs and upturned crates. A bottle filled with cheap wine rested between them, sweating in the heat.

The city below was quieter than usual. Curfew approached. Boots no longer thundered on the cobblestones quite as often, but they hadn't disappeared either.

Malina arrived last, folding a newspaper in her hand as she ducked out through her balcony door.

'Well?' Claudette asked, already leaning forward, as if her whole body might inhale the news.

Malina didn't bother sitting. She unfolded *Libération* and tapped the top corner. 'The Allies crossed the Seine. The front is pushing east. And the Resistance has already begun their push from within. It's happening.'

The others blinked at her, wine forgotten, breath suspended.

'You're certain?' Eloise asked softly.

Malina nodded. 'We had word even before the paper. There's movement everywhere. They say it could be weeks, but maybe just days, before the Germans fall back.'

Claudette exhaled. '*Mon Dieu*,' she whispered. 'Maybe this time it's real.'

Gigi remained silent, eyes scanning the rooftops as though expecting the news to arrive on the breeze. Her hands stayed wrapped around her glass, though she hadn't yet taken a sip.

Malina, ever attuned to the unspoken, glanced over. 'Still nothing about Olivier?'

Gigi shook her head. 'No word.'

The silence that followed was full of things none of them dared say.

Claudette grinned wickedly and changed the subject. 'You'll never guess who finally got married.'

Malina raised a brow. 'Who?'

Gigi blinked. 'Pierre?'

Claudette nodded. 'To the baker's assistant. The one with the limp and the very large—'

'—*heart*,' Eloise interjected, amused.

'Right, heart,' Claudette said, smirking. 'Apparently she's loved him since the year he got himself stuck in the bakery door.'

Gigi managed a smile. 'And is she...?'

'Already pregnant,' Claudette confirmed with a mock gasp. 'He moved fast once he stopped proposing to Gigi.'

'I sort of miss it,' Gigi admitted, surprising even herself.

Claudette clinked her glass gently against hers. 'He'll always be your first almost-husband. That's worth something.'

The group laughed then, the sound rising into the still-warm air, defiant and full of life.

For a moment, just a moment, the war was something happening beyond the railings. Not between them. And Paris, battered, bruised, and blinking awake, felt a heartbeat closer to breathing free.

Later that evening, after the laughter had faded and the others had drifted back to their own apartments, Gigi remained on the balcony alone. The last light of day had melted into the city's bones, and the glow of lamplight flickered behind drawn curtains across the road.

She sat with her back to the wall, legs curled beneath her, a worn shawl wrapped around her shoulders. The wine bottle was nearly empty.

Behind her, inside her apartment, the record player spun a slow, melancholic waltz. One of his favourites. One she hadn't been able to put away.

It was the music that made him feel real.

The others didn't ask any more, not really. Malina hadn't needed to say it; her look had said enough – grieving a ghost was a fool's errand.

But Gigi couldn't stop listening for the sound of his footsteps in the hall. Couldn't stop wondering if he was still alive, couldn't accept that somewhere under the smoke and rubble of this city he'd simply... *vanished.*

She had given herself to the Resistance even more fiercely in the months after his arrest. When she wasn't dancing, she was surviving, working with Malina. Once even stealing money from a German soldier and being chased across town and forced to hide out at her parents' house overnight.

Her last contact had said nothing. Just that the name Olivier Moreau had disappeared from every ledger. She pulled her knees tighter to her chest, resting her chin there, and stared out into the blue-black dark.

She had made peace with never knowing. Almost.

But that didn't stop her from dreaming of him, of music in his hands, a pencil behind his ear, of laughter across a room, of the way he'd whispered her name.

The wind picked up, rustling a newspaper on the empty chair beside her.

Her eyes drifted to the window opposite. Claudette's curtain fluttered with movement, then stilled.

Everyone had returned to their routines, to their tiny hopes. The theatre still limped along with half-filled seats and half-paid actors. Gigi took the jobs she could, background roles, understudy spots, even a hand in costuming. Whatever let her keep one toe in the world she used to belong to.

But her heart no longer lived on stage. It lived in music she couldn't bear to finish. In silence she refused to break.

She closed her eyes. She didn't know if he was out there. But with rumours of armoured columns on the roads to Paris, in the hush before liberation, she let herself believe that maybe, just maybe, he was, and that he hadn't let go either.

51

PARIS, AUTUMN 2011

Lily

A month later, Rebecca sat in her small front garden, a faded wool blanket the colour of heather tucked over her knees, silver-streaked hair softly pinned at the nape of her neck, the faded ballet shoes trembling between her paper-thin fingers.

The October breeze carried the scent of fallen leaves and distant woodsmoke.

'Won't be long now,' Lily murmured, tucking the blanket's frayed edges around her as Effy stood close, pressing her knuckles to her mouth until they whitened.

The soft whisper of tyres on rain-dampened gravel broke the quiet. Clare's midnight-blue sedan rolled to a stop at the rusted wrought-iron gate.

The door opened with a creak that seemed to echo across decades, and out stepped an older woman, her mother's mirror image, but touched by another life entirely. Her skin was bronzed by the unforgiving Australian sun, creased at the eyes and mouth with laugh lines, her silver-streaked hair loose and wind-tossed down her back like a girl's. She wore a simple linen dress the colour of sand, well-worn leather shoes polished for the occasion, and the unmistakable air of someone who had travelled across oceans and continents to be there.

There wasn't a dry eye among the small gathering as Rachel made her way along the garden path, one hand light on a walnut cane, the other resting on Clare's arm, her knuckles prominent against pale skin.

Rebecca pushed herself to her feet with trembling determination, the blanket slipping from her knees and pooling in a heap at the chair's edge.

They moved toward each other, slow at first like figures in a dream, then faster, until the stick clattered to the stones and the blanket lay forgotten.

When they finally met in the dappled shade of the ancient apple tree, they fell into each other's arms, holding on as if the intervening decades might try to tear them apart again.

The only sound was their sobbing, raw, grateful, unstoppable, punctuated by half-formed words, as if a great weight of unspoken memories had been lifted from them both.

'You're home,' Rebecca breathed through her tears as she cupped Rachel's weathered face between palms mapped with blue veins. 'I always knew you'd come back to me.'

52

PARIS, JULY 1944

Gigi

One morning just before dawn, she heard a knock.

Not the fearful pounding of Gestapo boots. But a gentle, deliberate knock.

Her heart stumbled.

She opened the door. And there he was. *Olivier*.

His face was thinner, his cheekbones sharper, a faint bruise fading under one eye. His coat hung looser, as if the time had carved him down to bone and resolve. But he was alive.

Her heart lurched so hard it hurt. She didn't hesitate. With a sob she hurled herself into his arms, clinging to him as if the world might rip him away again.

He caught her, crushing her against him, lifting her clear off the ground. She wrapped her legs around his waist, fingers tangling in his hair, her tears soaking his neck.

'*Olivier!*' Her voice cracked against his mouth. She kissed him through the word, desperate, sobbing.

'Gigi, my love,' he gasped, kissing her back, kissing her

cheeks, her lips, her throat. 'I promised... I promised myself I'd come back.'

'I thought' – she could barely get the words out between kisses – 'I thought you were dead.'

'They kept me... all this time...' His voice broke. His lips found hers again, trembling. 'But I held on. I thought of you every day.'

She pulled back just enough to see his face, wet with her tears. She kissed him again, softer this time, grounding herself in the weight of him, in the miracle that he was here.

They clung to each other, gasping, their sobs tangled with laughter, their words spilling out in fragments between kisses.

He lifted her and carried her into the bedroom, and they made love, their bodies a tangle of limbs in a dance of reunion and rediscovery.

When at last their first wild storm of kisses gave way to something gentler, they found themselves together in each other's arms in the narrow bed. The shutters rattled softly with the early wind, the room dim with the morning light.

Olivier traced her face with the back of his hand as though committing her to memory all over again. 'You are real,' he whispered, voice rough with wonder. 'You are here.'

She kissed his palm, smiling through fresh tears. 'And so are you.'

For a long while they lay there, listening to each other breathe, their bodies curled close, as if afraid the other might vanish should they let go.

Later, she rose, pulling an old quilt around her shoulders, and returned with bread, a wedge of cheese and half a bottle of wine she had been saving. They sat side by side against the headboard, bare skin warmed by the blanket, the food spread between them on a chipped plate. She fed him a crust, laughing when it crumbled against his chin. He caught her wrist and kissed the inside of it, lingering as if he never meant to stop.

They ate little, spoke much. He told her fragments of his captivity, how he had survived the days by humming symphonies in his head. She told him of nights when she thought she heard his footsteps on the stairs, only to wake to silence. Each word was broken by kisses, as if language alone could never hold all that pressed between them.

'You took the fall for me, with Annaliese,' she said softly, brushing her thumb across his bruised cheek. 'I should be furious with you.'

'I would do it again,' he murmured with a grin. 'A thousand times.'

She leaned her forehead to his. 'Fool.' But her smile was tender, and her kiss was full of gratitude and love.

They stayed like that, wrapped in each other, the bread growing stale on the plate, the wine forgotten in its glass. Time bent around them, giving back for a while, what war had stolen.

And then came the knock.

Sharp. Sudden. Ordinary, and yet it split the fragile world they had rebuilt in those few precious hours.

They froze. She pulled the quilt tighter as Olivier slid from the bed, already reaching for his coat.

Gigi opened the door. A young man, too young to fight, stood there, dusty and breathless, holding out a telegram.

Her fingers shook as she signed. She scanned the message once. Then again.

'What is it?' Olivier asked, standing close, his hand brushing hers.

Gigi swallowed. 'Bad news. One of my sisters is ill. Very ill.'

He did not hesitate. 'Then you must go to her. And I will go with you. I never want to be apart from you again.'

Tears blurred her vision. She nodded, clutching the telegram in her fist. 'Thank you.'

He gathered her hand into his, threading their fingers together.

Gigi sensed the war was not yet over for her, the city not yet free. But in that moment, wrapped still in love and in loss, they knew they would face what came next side by side.

EPILOGUE

FRANCE, NOVEMBER 2011

Lily

The train pulled into Saint-Antoine-sur-Mer just as the golden light of the late afternoon spilled over the rooftops, bathing the quiet streets in warmth.

Lily stepped onto the platform, the scent of salt and lavender wrapping around her, the sounds of the small coastal town humming in the background, the rhythmic clang of the church bell, the distant crash of waves against the rocky shore.

It was exactly as she remembered it.

Yet, everything was different.

She adjusted the strap of her bag over her shoulder and took a steadying breath. This was her second time arriving here, but, unlike before, she wasn't chasing ghosts. She had no agenda, no investigation to piece together, no unanswered questions gnawing at her.

Only a single painful truth: she was no longer married.

It had been months since she had thrown Marcus out, months since the discovery of his affair had shattered whatever illusion of love she had been clinging to. The divorce wasn't finalised yet, but the hardest part, the decision to leave, was behind her.

Relief and grief coiled together in her chest as she stepped forward, her suitcase rolling lightly over the uneven stone path.

She had needed to get away.

Somewhere familiar, somewhere quiet. Somewhere that had once made her feel alive.

Saint-Antoine-sur-Mer had been the obvious choice.

She had told no one she was coming, had barely even planned it. She booked the train ticket on impulse, told Effy she'd be away for a few weeks, and packed a small bag.

There was something freeing in that. No expectations. No responsibilities. Just her, the sea and time to think.

As she walked through the village, the pastel shutters of the old stone houses glowing in the evening light, she found herself gravitating toward the familiar.

The same narrow streets where she and Julien had walked, following the threads of her family's past. The same seaside restaurant where they had once shared a bottle of wine, talking about things that had mattered.

She tried not to think about him.

She always did.

Even after everything that had happened, after the pain of discovering his grandfather's betrayal, after the way she had walked away from him in anger and hurt, Julien Renaud still lingered in the spaces between her thoughts. After she settled into her little hotel, she sauntered down to the café to eat alone. The weight of all the meals she'd be eating alone hit her, and she pushed the thought away.

She wasn't ready to face that yet. Not tonight.

Tonight, she just wanted to sit by the water, sip wine and let herself exist.

She found a small restaurant, tucked away on the quieter side of the port, where the waves lapped gently against the rocks just beyond the terrace. The scent of grilled fish and lemon filled the air, and a few scattered patrons lingered over their meals, speaking in low, easy murmurs.

Lily slipped into a seat near the railing, where she could watch the sun sink into the horizon.

She exhaled slowly.

For the first time in a long time, she felt like she could breathe.

She signalled to the waiter and ordered a glass of crisp white wine and whatever fresh seafood they recommended. There was something freeing about being alone like this, about knowing she didn't have to answer to anyone. As she waited for her drink, she pulled out the letter she had received the day before she left.

Dear Lily,

I hope you don't mind me writing to you like this. My name is Esther Walker, and I believe your family is part of my mother's story.

My mother's name is Sophie, and she is elderly, but her memory is fading. In the past couple of years, I have begun searching for the children she once knew, children who were with her on a train out of Paris in January 1943. Among them were two sisters, twins.

Not long ago, my partner, Édouard, came across an article in a French newspaper about two women, Rebecca and Rachel, twin sisters who had been reunited after many years apart. When I showed my mother the photograph in the article, she knew instantly. She said it was them, the same twins from that train.

Your mother and aunt are the last two war children I have been trying to find and I cannot tell you what it would mean for her to see them again. We are planning a gathering of the

surviving children from that journey in the coming year. My
hope is that you, your mother and her sister might consider
joining us. It would be a chance for them to see each other
again after all these decades, and for me to give my mother this
wish.

I write this with the deepest respect, and with hope that you
might say yes.

With warmest regards,

Esther

Lily swirled the golden liquid in her glass, watching the way
the last slivers of sunlight caught the rim, casting a soft glow
onto the table. The warmth of the wine spread through her
chest as she took a sip, easing the tightness that had lingered
there for too long.

Another reunion. First her mother and Rachel. And now
this gathering of strangers who had once been children together
in the most dangerous of times. It felt like the past was determined to keep drawing her in, weaving her deeper into its web.

She let out a slow breath, closing her eyes for a moment,
allowing the sound of the ocean to steady her.

And then, a shift in the air. A whisper of movement.

Something, someone who felt familiar, maybe someone she
had met here on her last visit, was walking toward the
restaurant.

She dismissed it. Just another stranger in a town that had
already begun to feel like home.

But then, something pulled at her, an unshakeable feeling, a
presence. And she looked up. Her breath stopped.

There, walking toward the restaurant, toward her, was
Julien.

For a heartbeat, she thought she had imagined him. The

way the twilight softened his features, the wind ruffling his dark curls, the unguarded expression on his face as he scanned the terrace, like a memory she had conjured into being.

But he was real. He was here.

And then, as if he had felt her stare, his eyes met hers.

They both stilled. For a long moment, neither of them moved, neither of them spoke. Then, at the exact same time, they both said it.

'Effy.'

Lily let out a soft, startled laugh, the tension in her chest breaking for just a second.

Julien, too, exhaled, a quiet chuckle, his lips pulling into that same crooked, hesitant smile she remembered so well.

'Of course it was Effy,' she murmured, shaking her head.

Julien took a step closer, sliding his hands into his pockets. 'She didn't tell you?'

'I never even told her I was coming here. Just that I was taking a break.'

Julien lifted an eyebrow. 'That's interesting.'

Lily tilted her head. 'And you?'

He let out a breath, rubbing a hand over the back of his neck. 'She came by the shop yesterday.'

'And?'

'She said I looked tired. That I needed some time away.' He met her gaze then, something unspoken passing between them. 'And there was only one place I wanted to be.'

Lily's heart stuttered.

For the first time in months, she allowed herself to really look at him.

The same warm, chestnut eyes. The same unruly curls. The same easy, grounded presence that had drawn her to him in the first place. But something had changed. There was a weight to him now, something heavier behind his gaze, as if the time apart had carved its own scars.

And maybe, she realised, she wasn't the only one who had been hurting. The space between them felt fragile, full of all the things left unsaid. Lily glanced down at her half-finished glass of wine, then back up at him.

'Sit with me?' she suggested, her voice quieter now.

Julien hesitated only for a moment before pulling out the chair across from her and ordering a drink.

And as he settled in, their eyes met once more.

And for the first time since everything had fallen apart, Lily felt like maybe, just maybe, this wasn't the end of their friendship after all.

The scent of salt and citrus lingered in the air, mingling with the gentle murmur of conversations around them. Lily studied him over the rim of her glass, still adjusting to the fact that he was here, that fate, or Effy, had somehow nudged them back into each other's paths.

Julien reached for his wine glass, tilting it slightly. He took a sip, and studied her for a moment before setting the glass down. 'You look good.'

She blinked, caught off guard by the quiet sincerity in his voice. 'So do you,' she said, softly.

There was too much to say. Where did they start?

Julien finally broke the silence. 'You and Marcus?'

She exhaled, swirling the stem of her glass between her fingers before answering. 'Getting a divorce,' she said softly. The word was getting easier to say now; it wasn't so jarring to her heart.

Julien didn't say anything at first. He only watched her. Then he nodded slowly. 'I'm sorry, Lily.'

She gave a small, tight smile.

The moment stretched between them, the terrace lights flickering in the sea breeze.

Lily exhaled. 'And how are you?'

He leaned back slightly, running a hand through his curls,

hesitating for only a second before continuing. 'I've spent the last few months telling myself I was fine, that what happened between us, between our families, was just history. But it wasn't just history to us.'

Lily swallowed, her heart hammering against her ribs.

'I needed time,' he admitted. 'To sit with what I had learned about my grandfather. He was my hero, and then to find out he had turned in Jacques was hard to come to terms with. I think about that night a lot.'

Lily was surprised. 'Which night?'

He exhaled. 'When you found out the truth about my grandfather.'

Lily nodded slowly. She had spent months trying to forget that night, but now it came rushing back, sharp, painful.

'I owe you an apology. I was harsh with you when I was just really angry at Marcus.'

Julien exhaled. 'I hated hurting you.'

Lily looked at him then, really looked at him.

For the first time, she saw it, the weight he had been carrying.

And the love.

It had never gone away.

She wasn't sure what it meant. Or what she was ready for. But she knew she didn't hate the situation any more, and, now her mother was happy and growing stronger, maybe she could bear the truth of her father's death.

Lily reached for his hand and threaded her fingers through his. Julien stilled, his breath catching.

She squeezed, just once. A simple acknowledgement. A beginning.

His fingers tightened around hers.

And for now, that was enough.

A LETTER FROM SUZANNE

Dear Reader,

I sincerely hope you enjoyed reading *The Secret Twins of Paris*. If you did enjoy it and want to keep up to date with my latest releases, just sign up at the following link. Your email address will never be shared, and you can unsubscribe at any time.

www.bookouture.com/suzanne-kelman

When I first began writing *The Secret Twins of Paris*, I knew I wanted to capture not only the courage of those who resisted tyranny but also the heartbeat of a city that never stopped creating beauty, even in its darkest hour.

Paris during the Occupation was a city of contrasts. Beneath the curfews and the fear, music still played in smoky jazz clubs, and dancers still took to the stage under the watchful eyes of the German command. The theatre and ballet communities became unlikely havens, fragile sanctuaries where art, love and defiance intertwined.

At the Paris Opéra, the legendary choreographer Serge Lifar, once a protégé of Sergei Diaghilev, continued to direct and perform throughout the war. His presence in Occupied Paris remains one of history's great contradictions. Though criticised for his association with the regime, Lifar also protected many of his dancers from deportation and kept the theatre alive when it could easily have gone dark. The dancers under his direction lived double lives: performing by day and, in some cases, passing messages or hiding fugitives by night. Their courage and contradictions inspired much of the world you have just stepped into.

Equally extraordinary was Josephine Baker, the American-born performer who rose from poverty to become one of the most dazzling stars of her time. She used her fame as a weapon, carrying coded messages written in invisible ink on her sheet music and smuggling intelligence across borders for the French Resistance. Baker's home in the South of France became a refuge for those fleeing persecution, and after the war she was awarded the Croix de Guerre and the Resistance Medal for her bravery.

The fictional character Joséphine Duval in this novel was inspired by Baker's remarkable story. Because Josephine Baker was often travelling during the years when my story takes place, I created Joséphine Duval as a way to honour her spirit, a performer whose grace, courage and wit mirrored Baker's own, and who could exist within the theatre world of my characters. Through Joséphine Duval, I wanted to pay tribute to all the artists who used their art and their courage as quiet acts of rebellion.

Many people risked their lives not on the battlefield but in rehearsal halls and music cafés and behind stage curtains. Their stories, echoing through time, remind us that resistance takes many forms. Sometimes it is a dancer refusing to stop moving, a musician refusing to stop playing, or a woman refusing to stop believing in love and freedom.

Each book in the series has told the story of a different woman connected by sisterhood, courage and art. Gigi's journey brings us one step closer to completing their tapestry, but there is still one last sister's story to tell, Charlotte's. Her story begins where this one leaves off and continues the thread first woven in the free prequel, *The Paris Orphans*.

Thank you for journeying with me through this world of courage, art and endurance. I hope *The Secret Twins of Paris* leaves you with a sense of admiration for those who kept the lights of the theatre burning when the rest of the world was dark.

With all my gratitude and love,

Suzanne

www.suzannekelmanauthor.com

 facebook.com/suzkelman

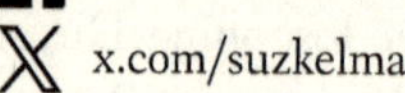 x.com/suzkelman

ACKNOWLEDGMENTS

As I look back on the journey of writing *The Secret Twins of Paris*, my heart is full of gratitude for all those who have walked beside me in bringing this story to life. Every book is its own adventure, but it's the extraordinary people around me who make the process such a joy.

To my wonderful editor, Jess Whitlum-Cooper, thank you for your vision, insight and endless encouragement. Your thoughtful guidance and sharp editorial eye always elevate my work to places I couldn't have reached alone. Collaborating with you continues to be one of the great privileges of my career, and I'm deeply thankful for the care you give to every page.

To my brilliant publisher, Bookouture, your passion, professionalism and creative spirit form the heart of everything you do. You turn stories into experiences, and dreams into books held in readers' hands. My deepest thanks to each member of the team for your expertise and enthusiasm.

To the exceptional individuals who keep these worlds spinning: Jenny Geras, Peta Nightingale, Imogen Allport, Lizzie Brien, Mandy Kullar, Hannah Snetsinger, Occy Carr, Melanie Price, Alex Crow, Alba Proko, Ria Clare, Jacqui Lewis, Becca Allen, Charlotte Hegley, Richard King, and everyone at Bookouture whose hard work makes all the difference. Thank you for your talent, kindness and dedication.

My heartfelt appreciation to Kim Nash, Noelle Holten, Jess Readett and Sarah Hardy; your continued support and commitment to connecting books with readers is nothing short of magic. I'm so grateful for your belief in me and the stories I tell.

To my husband, Matthew Wilson, thank you for walking beside me through every chapter of this journey. Your support, patience and love give me the courage to keep going.

To my son, Christopher, you are my constant source of pride and joy. Your thoughtful perspective and encouragement remind me why stories matter.

To my dear friends, Melinda Mack, Eric Mulholland, Shauna Buchet and K.J. Waters, your friendship and laughter brighten even the longest writing days. Thank you for standing by me with so much love and cheer.

And finally, to you, my readers, thank you for opening your hearts to these stories and for journeying with me through history, loss and love. Your letters, messages and unwavering enthusiasm remind me daily why I write. I'm endlessly grateful for every one of you.

Here's to more stories shared, more discoveries made, and to the enduring power of hope that binds us all.

With love and gratitude,

Suzanne

PUBLISHING TEAM

Turning a manuscript into a book requires the efforts of many people. The publishing team at Bookouture would like to acknowledge everyone who contributed to this publication.

Audio
Alba Proko

Commercial
Lauren Morrissette
Hannah Richmond
Imogen Allport

Cover design
Debbie Clement

Data and analysis
Mark Alder
Mohamed Bussuri

Editorial
Jess Whitlum-Cooper
Imogen Allport

Copyeditor
Jacqui Lewis

Proofreader
Becca Allen

Marketing
Alex Crow
Melanie Price
Occy Carr
Cíara Rosney
Martyna Młynarska

Operations and distribution
Marina Valles
Joe Morris

Production
Hannah Snetsinger
Mandy Kullar
Nadia Michael
Charlotte Hegley

Publicity
Kim Nash
Noelle Holten
Jess Readett
Sarah Hardy

Rights and contracts
Peta Nightingale
Richard King
Saidah Graham

Dear Reader,

We'd love your attention for one more page to tell you about the crisis in children's reading, and what we can all do.

Studies have shown that reading for fun is the **single biggest predictor of a child's future life chances** – more than family circumstance, parents' educational background or income. It improves academic results, mental health, wealth, communication skills, ambition and happiness.

The number of children reading for fun is in rapid decline. Young people have a lot of competition for their time, and a worryingly high number do not have a single book at home.

Hachette works extensively with schools, libraries and literacy charities, but here are some ways we can all raise more readers:

- Reading to children for just 10 minutes a day makes a difference
- Don't give up if children aren't regular readers – there will be books for them!

- Visit bookshops and libraries to get recommendations
- Encourage them to listen to audiobooks
- Support school libraries
- Give books as gifts

There's a lot more information about how to encourage children to read on our websites: **www.RaisingReaders.co.uk** and **www.JoinRaisingReaders.com**.

Thank you for reading.